SAUL'S FALL

SAUL'S FALL

A Critical Fiction

HERBERT

LINDENBERGER

The Johns Hopkins University Press

Baltimore and London

To provide a local habitation for a text that ranges far in time and space, the author has placed the scene of its editorial labors at his own university. The editor and other personages who people the book and the incidents described at Stanford are all figments of the author's fiction-making fancy. Resemblances to anybody living or dead are wholly coincidental.

The Johns Hopkins University Press, Baltimore, Maryland 21218
The Johns Hopkins Press Ltd., London

Library of Congress Catalog Card Number 78–22003
ISBN 0–8018–2176–2
Library of Congress Cataloging in Publication data will be found on the last printed page of this book.

ORLANDO HENNESSY-GARCIA

SAUL'S FALL

An Authoritative Text with
Relevant Background Materials
and Essays in Criticism

EDITED BY

MILTON J. WOLFSON

Associate Professor of English
Stanford University

FOREWORD BY

HERBERT LINDENBERGER

Professor of Comparative Literature and English
Stanford University

To my wife, Luella,
who endured

Contents

BACKGROUND MATERIALS, PART TWO
Analogues to *Saul's Fall* from the Author's Earlier Writings

ESSAYS IN CRITICISM, PART ONE
Contributions by Fellow Writers

ESSAYS IN CRITICISM, PART TWO
Contributions by Literary Critics

Illustrations

Foreword

I feel both honored and delighted that my talented young colleague
Milton Wolfson has asked me to write a few words to introduce this
volume on which I have observed him working with considerable energy
and dedication over the past couple of years. From the moment he first
described it to me I gave him all the encouragement I could, for I was
aware that, however the book turned out, the notion of preparing an
elaborate edition of an unpublished work (complete with what he calls
"analogues" from the author's other unpublished writings as well as essays
in criticism representing a variety of methods and ideologies) was a most
original, indeed audacious, undertaking.

Professor Wolfson assures me I actually saw the author of these
materials during his one visit to Stanford, that in fact I passed the two of
them while they were walking across campus in search of a coffee lounge.
I do not remember this incident at all, and am frankly relieved I was not
introduced to Mr. Hennessy-García, for a meeting might well have forced
me to fix an attitude toward him that would have colored my reading of
both his play and his various autobiographical writings. Never having met
him, I find myself alternately moved and repelled by this figure, who, like
his character Saul, keeps his reader wondering precisely what stance, be it
identification, compassion, pity, impatience, disapproval, or disdain (or
some shading between any of these) he should take toward him. Moreover,
since I have not had to observe Mr. Hennessy-García's excessive shyness
in person, I have been able to read him as the performer who comes
through unabashedly in every word he writes, even at those moments in
which he advertises his withdrawal from the world. He has kept me so
aware of his performing role I was never quite certain whether to take him

in earnest or in jest, and as often as not I have elected to read him both ways at once.

Although it is Mr. Hennessy-García who has obviously made this volume possible in the first place, I ask the reader not to minimize the role that the editor has played both in rescuing these writings from an almost certain oblivion, and in ordering his selection into a coherent and uncommonly intricate whole. Every new venture in any field of endeavor involves risks, and I commend Professor Wolfson, who is still at that relatively early stage of his career where people like to play it safe, for his willingness to wander outside the common paths that young academics customarily tread. At the time he first explained to me in detail what he was doing, I told him (perhaps in a more jocular manner than he was prepared for) that he seemed to be putting together a strange brew concocted out of *Tristram Shandy*, *Sartor Resartus*, *Memórias Póstumas de Braz Cubas*, *Doktor Faustus*, *Anatomy of Criticism*, *Pale Fire*, *The Pooh Perplex*, *S/Z*, and *Glas*, not to speak of the various Norton Critical Editions that have supplied him with his basic editorial model.

By the time I saw the final manuscript I felt convinced that, however tenaciously it was rooted in earlier works (and I still believe in the correctness of my initial intuitions as to what these are), this edition is a new thing in its own right. Like everything new it asks that readers be willing to overcome whatever earlier prejudices they have acquired as to how to go about reading a book, especially one that demands some effort and accommodation on their part. Since Professor Wolfson is particularly eager for his readers to try out some of the new and unconventional modes of reading that he suggests in his introduction, I take this opportunity to ask them not to set the book aside until they have been able to make their own pact with both the editor and the author, even if this means accepting some clauses that they are not accustomed to including in their reading contracts.

Although I have always jealously guarded my prerogative to vote secretly on personnel matters, I hope that Professor Wolfson will view these words endorsing his book as some indication of the regard I expect to continue holding toward him when, as he explains in his disarming way in the introduction, he comes up for promotion to full professor in my department.

HERBERT LINDENBERGER
Professor of Comparative Literature and English
Stanford University

Acknowledgments

To the John Simon Guggenheim Memorial Foundation and the American Council of Learned Societies, whose refusal to support this project serves as a useful reminder that one had best stick to the straight and narrow path (whatever one's actual intentions) in preparing grant applications.

To the American Philosophical Society, for their generosity in giving me a travel grant to undertake a study of certain problems in the history and theory of rhetoric at the Newberry Library, Chicago, the unexpected results of which are the rhetorical analysis described in the section of this book entitled "The Margo Experience."

To Betsy Jablow, for allowing me to reproduce her photographs of the Stanford workshop production of *Saul's Fall*; to Mary Davison, Ann Mueller, John Wang, Karen Ward and (cited last only because she married a man with a name at the tailend of the alphabet) Luella McGillicuddy Wolfson, for their help in the artwork and illustrative material; to the Fine Arts Museums of San Francisco for permission to reproduce William Wetmore Story's statue of Saul.

To those colleagues and friends—Fernando and Carmen Alegría, Maclin Bocock, Edward J. Brown, W. B. Carnochan, William Chace, Joaquim-Francisco Coelho, Martin Esslin, J. Martin Evans, Marjorie Flaherty, Ellen Frank, Albert and Barbara Charlesworth Gelpi, Albert Guerard, JoAn Johnstone, Naomi Lebowitz, Herbert and Claire Lindenberger, Charles R. Lyons, Marjorie Perloff, Egon Schwarz, Mihai Spariosu, Gloria Spitzer, and William M. Todd III—who were willing to share their reactions to the project and, whatever private thoughts they may have entertained, refused to discourage me from carrying it out.

xvii

To my students who, even though they did not participate in the project itself, served as a constant and living reminder that one's scholarship, no matter how absorbing, must regularly be interrupted by teaching.

To the three little W's, Mark, Susan, and Matthew, whose unceasing demands to be taken to Disneyland were totally ignored during my long period of absorption.

To the dedicatee, who was willing to believe in this project simply because she knew I believed in it and who quietly remained a good sport about deprivations that only she and I will ever know.

And to the onlie begetter, that true procreator Orlando Hennessy-García, to whom (if I may play upon the immortal words of his character Saul) I call, "You out there, wherever you are, surely you had no idea that manuscript you sent would draw me into your world to the point of self-extinction."

MJW

Orlando Hennessy-García:
A Chronology

1936	25 August. Born in London, the only son of Beatrice Hennessy and Pedro García; the latter had been killed shortly before in the Spanish Civil War.
1937(?)–1939	Travels with mother to various Mediterranean cities.
1940	Sent to Canada to escape German air raids over Britain.
1940–1949	Lives with a succession of foster families in various places in Canada. Known to have attended Fort Edmunds School, Fort Edmunds, Ontario, during the academic year 1948/1949. In that year publishes "A Hero's Death in the Spanish Civil War" in the school magazine, *The Scroll*.
1949–1954	Attends various private schools in the United States and spends short periods with his mother in New York after her arrival there from London about 1949. Known to have attended the Morris School, Bridgetown, Connecticut, in 1954.
1954	8 September. Gains U.S. citizenship. Late September: Enters Bard College, Annandale-on-Hudson, New York.
1955	Suicide of mother during first half of this year. June–July: Visits relatives and former nanny in England. July–August: Visits relatives in Spain.
1956	Brief romance of sorts with a fellow student Margo (pseud.). Leaves Bard College at end of academic year 1955/56. By June is half-way through manuscript of an autobiographical novel, *A Prelude to Nothing*.

1956 to 1964–1968	Whereabouts and activities uncertain, except that he is known to have visited a New York City specialist in internal medicine on 9 October 1960.
1964–1968	Moves to Mendocino, California, at some time during this period.
1964–1968 to 1978	Remains in Mendocino working on literary projects. Somewhere between 1956 and the Mendocino period abandons *A Prelude to Nothing*, which, presumably during the Mendocino period, he recasts into another uncompleted novel, *Cold Clay*. Writes "Mendocino Diary" during one week in May in the early 1970s. Writes *Saul's Fall* probably between 1974 and early 1978.
1978	2 March. Mails manuscript of *Saul's Fall* to the editor of this volume.
	20 April. Visits editor at Stanford University.
	26 May. Suitcase containing his literary manuscripts and selected memorabilia arrives in editor's office. Whereabouts and activities since that date uncertain.

INTRODUCTION

The Editor to the Reader

An introduction is ordinarily a routine matter, something you toss off just as a book is being sent to the publisher in order to reassure him you're the sort who's willing to go through all the motions he expects of you, as well as to assure your readers (even if they never bother looking at introductions) that there's a purpose behind what you've just put together. That's the way it works with pretty nearly all books, at least those that fit into the usual categories, and I'm the first to confess I wrote the usual quick and routine introduction to my first book, *Metaphors of Moral Ambiguity in Modern Drama*, which, though originally my Yale doctoral dissertation, was in its much revised and published form largely responsible for the tenured position I am proud to hold at Stanford University today.

But the volume before you is no ordinary book. At first glance it looks like the usual sort of edition that goes by such names as casebook, critical edition, or whatever else a publisher might choose to call a book centered around some famous literary work, which is generally published together with such relevant background materials as letters by the author or passages from his other works that have some obvious (and sometimes not so obvious) bearing on the main work. This type of volume normally concludes with a selection from the early reviews of this work plus some critical essays about the work written by famous (and sometimes not so famous) scholars who ideally represent the most diverse points of view that prevail at any given time.

This is very much that kind of a book, though with one crucial difference: the play around which it is centered has never been published before and has, in fact, been staged only in a student-directed workshop production that I helped arrange at Stanford for an invitational audience. Except for the review of this production that appeared in the local newspaper (the reviewer, I might add, found his way into the theater without an invitation), nothing about the play has ever appeared in print. Indeed, although the author, who is now in early middle age, has written copiously over the years, the only piece of his that has appeared in print is an extravagant tale he wrote at thirteen for his school literary magazine in a small Canadian city. Unlike the other critical editions after which it is modeled, this one had to draw its background materials (which make up about half the book and take up considerably more space than the play itself) not from an established canon of the author's work, but from those of his unpublished writings that have direct bearing on the play. The final section of the book, which as in all such critical editions consists of diverse essays in criticism, could not (except for the review from the *Palo Alto Times*) be drawn from an existing body of writing; instead, I commissioned essays from critics representing what I took to be the major contemporary approaches to the study of literature.

The uniqueness of the volume before you may become evident if I say I am aware of only a single earlier book that, printing a hitherto unpublished major work, labeled itself a critical edition. This was Georg Büchner's *Woyzeck*, first published in 1879, long after the author's death and in what we now recognize to be a thoroughly corrupt text. Although the quality of this edition can be blamed partly on the fact that the *Woyzeck* manuscript was discovered in extremely poor condition, I might add that the editor, one Karl Emil Franzos, who was essentially a journalist and literary enthusiast, not only helped corrupt the text through the chemicals he used in hopes of deciphering it more easily but also lacked those fundamental editorial skills that I hope and trust you will discover in the present edition (the fact that Alban Berg's opera, which was based on Franzos's text, is called *Wozzeck* instead of *Woyzeck*, is ample testimony to how sloppy editing can immortalize a misspelling of a work's very title!).

But perhaps I should digress no further without at least saying a word or two about how I came into possession of *Saul's Fall* and its various background materials. In early March, 1978, I received in the mail a typewritten manuscript of the play accompanied by a brief letter from the author, whom I had never met or even heard of. Orlando Hennessy-García, who is half British and half Spanish but has spent most of his life in Canada and the United States, had been living as a recluse of sorts for some years in the small and remote northern California coastal town of Mendocino. I shall not go into detail about him at this point, for you will have ample opportunity in the course of this volume to make his acquaintance. Through my well-known interest in modern drama I ordinarily get a number of new plays in the mail—most frequently the products of aging and aspiring lady authors who cultivate styles that were antiquated even during their youth and whose labors I am accustomed to drop into a large and rusty garbage bin directly outside my office in the Stanford Inner Quad. Fortunately, I did not relegate *Saul's Fall* to this fate, and the only reason I can give for this is the infelicity of the title (the old ladies would have chosen titles such as *The Tragedy of Saul*, *A Psalm for Saul*, or just plain *Saul*). So I left the manuscript on my desk and glanced through it a day or two later during a lull between classes. Almost immediately I recognized that I had come across something thoroughly original in style and overwhelmingly powerful in the effects of those scenes I first looked at (the first, I believe, was the one called "Prayer," and from there I went to "Endings" and then back to "Battle 1" near the beginning of the play—I might add that people who wade their way through new manuscripts know better than to start on the first page).

My initial reaction was fully confirmed by a later reading of the scenes in their intended order, and I quickly and spontaneously sent the author a congratulatory note. (I shall explain no more here about what subsequently happened between him and me, for you will find a detailed description of my brief and not altogether satisfactory relationship with him in a later section of the book.) Suffice it to say that although my initial intention was simply to bring his play to the attention of our drama department and the few publishing houses and journals that print new plays, I did not conceive the idea for this edition until, soon after my single meeting with him, I received a suitcase full of manuscripts of his early writings as well as a number of documents that will be described (and in appropriate instances printed) later in the book.

As I read through his two early and uncompleted autobiographical novels, as well as the essays and poems that he himself had labeled "*Saul's Fall* Overflow," I recognized not only the extraordinarily high quality of his writing in a large number of literary forms but also that each of the play's scenes (or episodes, as he prefers to call them) is linked stylistically or thematically, or both, to at least one, and sometimes several, of his other writings. At the same time I recognized that each episode is also related to at least one and, more often than not, several passages from famous plays (above all Shakespeare's) and also to certain operas with which the author, doubtless on the basis of recordings that he must have listened to in his self-inflicted isolation, was obviously quite familiar. My classifying bent being what it is, I soon found myself charting what I called a "Table of Analogues" that every reader will have to consult regularly to get the full benefit of this book (to give it the prominence it deserves I have risked alienating potential readers and placed it here at the start of the volume).

Soon I realized that, through my editing of Hennessy-García's writings, as well as the essays in criticism that I began to envision as a necessary part of the book, I could present the world with what (if I may resort to the terminology of the social sciences) is essentially a communications model that details the complex process by which literary works are designed, produced, distributed, and consumed. Through a study of the materials within this volume, you will note how a text draws on a multitude of other texts by the same author and earlier authors, how it seeks to communicate with potential audiences, and, finally, how it is received in profoundly different ways by those who record their reactions to reading it. Moreover, since the author's writings have not yet achieved the status customary to

TABLE OF ANALOGUES

EPISODE	PARALIPOMENA	PUBLIC ANALOGUES	PRIVATE ANALOGUES
"Preface"	"Envoi" "The Three Disquisitions: On Fashion"	Prefaces to: Milton, *Samson Agonistes*; Shelley, *Prometheus Unbound*; Hardy, *The Dynasts*	"Mendocino Diary"
"Prologue"	"Envoi" "The Three Disquisitions: On Relationship"	Shakespeare, *Henry* V, "Prologue" Monteverdi, *Orfeo*, "Prologue"	"Growth Paper" "Mendocino Diary"
"March 1"	"Lyric Suite 1": 2, 6	Mussorgsky, *Boris Godunov*, "Prologue," i Wagner, *Parsifal*, I	"Three Projects" "Four Poses"
"Healing 1"	"Lyric Suite 1": 4 "Lyric Suite 2": 2, 6 "King David's Memoir"	*Coriolanus*, V, iii, 94–182 *Parsifal*, III, ii Ibsen, *Rosmersholm*, opening pages	"Sunday Dinner at the C's" "Three Projects" "Scoldings of the Week" (Monday, Tuesday)
"Battle 1"	"The Three Disquisitions: On Fashion" "King David's Memoir"	*Antony and Cleopatra*, I, ii; II, v; III, vii; III, xiii	"Growth Paper" "A Night Out with Cousin Paco"
"Healing 2"	"Lyric Suite 1": 1, 3, 4, 5, 6, 7 "Lyric Suite 2": 2, 6 "King David's Memoir"	*Othello*, III, iii, 353–360 *Samson Agonistes*, 46, 1168–69, 124, 126–127, 1381–82 Beckett, *Waiting for Godot*, Lucky-Pozzo scenes *Endgame*, passages near end	"Three Projects" "Four Poses"
"Prayer"	"Envoi" "Lyric Suite 1": 1, 2, 6, 7 "Lyric Suite 2": 1, 7 "The Three Disquisitions" (endings of all three) "King David's Memoir"	*Boris Godunov*, II *Parsifal*, I, ii	"Growth Paper" "The Margo Experience" "Four Poses"

EPISODE	PARALIPOMENA	PUBLIC ANALOGUES	PRIVATE ANALOGUES
"Intermezzo"	"King David's Memoir"	*King Lear*, IV, vi	"Scoldings of the Week" (Monday) "Her Three Attempts"
"Council"	"Lyric Suite 1": 2	*Julius Caesar*, III, ii Verdi, *Simon Boccanegra*, I, ii	"Sunday Dinner at the C's"
"Healing 3"	"Lyric Suite 1:" 1, 3, 4 "Lyric Suite 2": 2, 6 "King David's Memoir"	*Henry IV, Second Part*, IV, v	"Calling on Nanny"
"Conspiracy"		*Richard III*, IV, ii *Richard II*, V, iv	"Fairy Tale" "Four Poses"
"Inquiry		*Macbeth*, IV, ii, 79–84 Goethe, *Faust*, 11338– 11377 *Prometheus Unbound*, II, iv Büchner, *Dantons Tod*, I, ii; III, iv; IV, ix	"A Hero's Death in the Spanish Civil War" "Four Poses"
"Prophecy 1"	"Lyric Suite 1": 6, 7 "The Three Disquisitions: On Relationship"	*Hamlet*, III, iv, 103– 136 *Macbeth*, I, i; I, iii; IV, i	"Scoldings of the Week" (Wednesday, Saturday)
"Battle 2"	"Lyric Suite 1": all sections "King David's Memoir"	*Richard III*, V, iii Also diverse battle scenes from various other plays by Shakespeare	"Three Projects" "Scoldings of the Week" (Saturday) "An Epistolary Exchange"
"Prophecy 2"		*Macbeth*, II, ii; IV, i; V, v, 38–46; V, viii, 9–22	"Scoldings of the Week" (Tuesday, Friday, Saturday)
"Proclamation"	"King David's Memoir"	*Henry V*, II, ii, 166– 181	"An Epistolary Exchange"
"Execration"	"Envoi": end of 5 "King David's Memoir"	*Richard III*, I, iii; IV, iv Racine, *Britannicus*, IV, ii; V, vi	"An Epistolary Exchange" "Scoldings of the Week" (Saturday)
"Endings"	"Envoi": 5 "Lyric Suite 1": 3, 6 "The Three Disquisitions: On Relationship, On Masturbating"	*Henry VI, Third Part*, V, vi *Richard III*, V, iv *Richard II*, V, v *Dantons Tod*, IV, iii; IV, v	"Growth Paper" "The Margo Experience" "Her Three Attempts" "Four Poses" "Mendocino Diary"

EPISODE	PARALIPOMENA	PUBLIC ANALOGUES	PRIVATE ANALOGUES
"March 2"	"Envoi": end of 1–4 "Lyric Suite 1": 2, 4, 5 "Lyric Suite 2": all sections "King David's Memoir"	*Richard II*, V, vi *Julius Caesar*, III, ii *Coriolanus*, I, i Shaw, *Caesar and Cleopatra*, Caesar's various speeches on ruling	"Growth Paper" "Mendocino Diary
"Epilogue" ·		Aristotle, *Poetics* Horace, *Ars Poetica* *Coriolanus*, V, vi, 148 *Samson Agonistes*, 1758 Above all, diverse epi- logues to plays of the restoration and eighteenth century	"Scoldings of the Week" (Saturday, Sunday)

NOTE: I have not included earlier versions of the Saul story within this table. As Pro-fessor Smith indicates in his article in this volume, there is no evidence that H-G drew from any earlier version outside the Bible, except for the *Dead March* from Handel's *Saul*, though he may not have been familiar with other parts of this oratorio.

works published in critical editions, here is a rare opportunity for readers to approach a text with that freshness they can experience only through an author and a text for whom the world has not yet created a halo effect.

I make no secret of the fact that the idea for this project came at a most propitious moment in my career. It is well known that those who have recently completed their first books and been honored with promotion to tenured rank ordinarily undergo a professional crisis that, by the very nature of things, turns out to be a personal crisis at the same time. (My wife, Luella, to whom this volume is dedicated, can testify to all the details.) Here you've reached the rank of associate professor, you stand at the threshold of what all around you hope will be a distinguished career, and you wonder what in God's name you're going to write next to justify the faith that everybody has in your promise. (Promise, they call it, not achievement—the latter word is saved for your old age, long after you've actually done the things they designate by that word!) Even though my tenure assures me a job here for life, the thought of not making it to full professor at the appointed time (normally six years after reaching the associate professor rank) is more than somebody like myself—a Jewish boy from Brooklyn who has made it into this, the most WASPish of America's prestige universities—is quite prepared to contemplate.

If this book were simply an ordinary critical edition of some famous, established work such as *Samson Agonistes* or *Huckleberry Finn*, I should make no special claims for it. It would be considered little more than a textbook, and textbooks, though they sometimes make you a good bit of money, do not count as genuine achievements in the academic world (if I were interested primarily in money, I should never have chosen this profession anyway). But I am convinced that in its originality and in its potential impact upon future literary study, the volume before you goes considerably beyond my earlier *Metaphors of Moral Ambiguity in Modern Drama* (which, incidentally, got quite decent reviews, though I know I have already outgrown that book).

Finally a word or two on how to use this communications model. Because of the variety of styles, both within the play itself and in its various analogues to Hennessy-García's other writings, it could be called a veritable anatomy of generic forms and rhetorical situations (my later "Note: On the Generic Inclusiveness of This Book" supplies a comprehensive list of these forms and situations). All readers will have to accustom themselves to shift gears, as it were, as they move from one passage to another. I can imagine some people starting not with the play itself, but with a passage from one of Hennessy-García's autobiographical fictions and then, with the aid of my "Table of Analogues," moving back to those scenes of the play that are analogous to the earlier passage. Or you might start by reading the Shakespearean (or other) passages that stand behind a scene, then read the analogous scene within the play, and finally move to the analogues of the scene in the author's other writings. Or you might even begin with one or more of the critical essays, for these, contradictory though some of them may seem to be, will help you to shape the particular mental perspectives through which you can then look at the play. (Since you will find yourself leafing back and forth considerably more than you do with ordinary books, I have instructed the publisher to use the most durable paper he could locate.) What I offer you, then, is a quite original reading experience (my senior colleagues in English to whom I have described this experience assure me this goes beyond the kind of originality they generally look for when they make recommendations for promotion).

But you may also choose, if you wish, to read the book in the order of its pagination (and as far as I'm concerned, you may stop at any point and quietly put the book away). Although I can assure you (as well as my senior colleagues) that nothing the likes of this has been done before, I also recognize that the originality of the project may put off some prospective readers. People often claim they want something that's new, but they usually mean they want what is *just a little* new—nothing that will violate their notion of what constitutes a book, but simply something to add a bit of unaccustomed seasoning here and there to a dish they're already quite familiar with. As with sex these days, let every reader do what feels most comfortable and pleasurable. No questions asked.

This is surely the point where I should stop and simply print the text of *Saul's Fall*, but I have one more thing to say (I promise only one). As you will note by now, I am parenthetical and digressive to an extreme, which, given the nature of this project, makes me a most appropriate editor. You will find a number of notes (with the formal heading "Notes") strewn throughout—sometimes, I warn you, at the most unexpected, even inconvenient places—and you will also find a multitude of parenthetical remarks (as you have already done in this introduction) within my own commentaries, as links between Hennessy-García's writings, and between the contributions of the various critics. As you can see, I'm expansive by nature, an oral rather than an anal type, Protean rather than Procrustean. Expect an interruption, relevant or not (though ultimately you will find it quite relevant) at any time. But except for some photos of the workshop production, which I can't resist including, I promise never to interrupt the play itself, which I present in the precise text that Hennessy-García (whom, given my natural informality, I shall henceforth refer to simply as H-G, just as I shall call myself MJW) sent to me without the slightest expectation, I'm sure, of the astonishing monument I should end up erecting for him.

SAUL'S FALL

SEVENTEEN EPISODES

Orlando Hennessy-García

Old King Saul had a hideous fall
What a hideous fall had he!
(Ancient Rime)

PREFACE

The Author of these episodes must inform the reader that he has been unable to work within the more recent dramatic modes, all of which, in his opinion, have pretty much worn themselves out. Take, for instance, the mode of the Absurd: who need be told again that people cannot measure up to traditional ideals or that human communication is difficult? Or take the mode of Cruelty: it wasn't very long before audiences became so thoroughly irritated by the masochism expected of them that, but for the fact that they were subject to legal constraints, they would gladly have torn the actors to pieces before returning home from the theater. Or take the Epic mode: instead of breaking the illusion to make us think more about the author's ideas, the songs and the projections called attention to themselves as just one more mannerism among many. Or that offshoot of Epic, the Documentary: while pretending to make us experience historical events as they really were, it was actually a way an author could bully his audience into some ideology or other. Moreover, the spontaneity between actors and audiences that some of these modes have cultivated now appears as unspontaneous as any earlier dramatic convention, for instance the relation of hero and confidant in French classical plays.

Tired though he is of the prevailing modes, the Author makes no pretension of suggesting a new school or method of dramatic writing. A pretension of this sort would violate his natural distrust toward groups and the fashions they generate, publicize, and compel others to follow. And if he refers to the reader rather than the audience within this preface, it is because, recognizing the unlikelihood of performance within our contemporary theater, he has decided for now to offer these episodes to the reading public alone. Who, after all, can expect to have serious work performed in an institution run by rebels without purpose, dogmatists without intellect, decadents without style?

Yet since what he has written may seem strange at first reading, he wishes to call attention to the fact that he conceived these episodes after the model of musical composition. Not, certainly, in any strict or literal sense: anyone who would identify the Witch's persistently negative tone in "Prophecy 1" as an ostinato could be reminded that a similar effect is to be found throughout the history of comedy. Rather, music has provided a

13

series of analogies used principally for their suggestive power. Among these analogies one might cite, first, the dramatic method peculiar to opera— not the Wagnerian music-drama or the styles that derive from it, but the older opera in which each segment maintains its distinctiveness in relation to every other. Certain passages strive to create the effect of arias, duets, or ensembles—to the point that a set speech may, like certain famous arias, assume and explore a single-minded attitude, such as pleading, praying, raging, or admonishing. Although the chorus has been assigned a major role, it functions chiefly as part of the total ensemble, for the Author, cognizant of the countless failed attempts to revive choral declamation in post-Classical drama, has not allowed the chorus to speak as a group except for an occasional word or phrase—and this usually the repetition of something that has already been spoken by an individual character.

As a second musical analogy, one might cite the twelve-tone system, not in any precise or technical sense, but in the way it provides a critique of tonal music. Just as the twelve-tone system seeks to suppress whatever might remind the listener of the tonal system, so these episodes attempt to frustrate our traditional expectations (even those fostered by the experimental theater of recent decades) regarding plot, characterization, and the relation of the parts of a play to the whole. And as with much post-tonal music, our perceptions, as we move from one episode to another, are meant to be jarred so that we must never feel quite sure about where we stand.

The third analogy lies simply in the idea of a composition, whereby a theme, or a group of related themes, is subjected to rigorous and changing treatment. The formal rigor for which the Author has striven is quite frankly a response to that sloppiness of form which contemporary theatrical writing, in its attempts to force therapeutic benefits on its audiences or to raise their political consciousness, has all too assiduously cultivated. And as with any musical composition the proper performance of these scenes would demand a precision of ensemble that is not often achieved in the non-musical theater. No strict analogy, however, should be sought to any particular species of musical composition. Some readers may take these episodes to be a musical suite in which a diversity of rhythmical forms are juxtaposed to one another. Others may take them to be a theme with variations, in which the rime cited in the epigraph above is translated and developed into a variety of dramatic styles.

Whatever particular analogy the reader may discern, the idea of a musical composition should help clarify what might otherwise strike him as a fragmentary mode of organization holding these episodes together. The reader will note that the classification given in the subtitle is neither *comedy* nor *tragedy* nor *history* nor that amorphous designation *play* which most modern writers, despairing of finding a proper fit for their work among the traditional rubrics, have used to endow their titles with some generic identity. Rather, the Author refers simply to "episodes" to prevent those who demand unity in its more superficial sense from barking before they properly sniff the booty they have gone after. As in a baroque suite or romantic symphony or song cycle, each episode was conceived as a discrete entity, with a distinct beginning, middle, and end—and each was at the same time designed to play an integral role in the development of a larger whole that has its own beginning, middle, and end. For those readers who may feel uncomfortable with analogies that draw together works from diverse media, the Author can happily cite a literary analogy: each episode may be viewed as one of those highly charged images—independent, yet related closely, though without overt explanation, to the other images around it—out of which many of the best poems in our century have been composed.

Finally, the Author asks that no special emphasis be attached to the religious or historical significances that have accumulated over the years around the subject that dominates these episodes. Although he sometimes plays upon the reader's memory of these significances to achieve specific effects, the spirit in which he wrote dictates that a subject have only those meanings we choose to inject into it and shape it with at any given moment. One could justify using the story of Saul simply by virtue of the fact that the hero's name rhymes with the word *fall*. The Author offers neither revelation nor history nor any easily discernible ideology; the primary fact about these scenes remains the fact of fall.

CHARACTERS

SAUL

DAVID

SAUL'S DAUGHTER

CHORUS of 12 to 15 who serve varying functions from episode to episode
—as a group they play roles such as soldiers, messengers, attendants, and
the crowd on the street; as individuals, roles such as the Witch of Endor,
Samuel, and David's Father.

PROLOGUE

Woman's face spotlighted and surrounded by darkness. She looks upward, as though to indicate she is not willing to be intimate with the audience she is addressing. Her voice has a somewhat unearthly quality that can be attained through imitation of the Sprechstimme *cultivated by Schoenberg and his circle. Each section is separated by a short ritornello that can be borrowed from Monteverdi.*

Ritornello, to be completed before face becomes visible.
VOICE (*in a formal tone*): I speak to you as the spirit of . . . (*stops herself abruptly, then takes up a less formal tone*) or perhaps I should put it another way and tell you I am not the author speaking, nor a particular character from this play, nor the kind of person whom some authors pull off the street to reassure their spectators that there's somebody just like them up here.
(*Ritornello*)
At an earlier time I should have been able to say I am here to please you, but that is not possible now. Or I might have aimed to pour terror into your breasts, but that is not possible now. Yet rest assured I shall not scold you in hopes of reaching contact through whatever anger I am able to awaken in you.
(*Ritornello*)
It's only fair to say at the start that I'm not a tragedy, or a comedy, or a history—or even one of those pieces to which they attached the word "absurd" when none of the older terms seemed to apply. The shape in which I come to you may jar you at times, for instead of moving steadfastly toward some clearly foreseen end, I keep saying the same things over and over again, though in an astonishing variety of ways.
(*Ritornello*)
To help you tune your expectations, I shall let you give me any of these labels: a narrative without plot . . . a history without reliability . . . an opera without music . . . a ceremonial without joy . . . a riddle without solution . . . a game without fun . . . a logic without reason . . . a revelation without authority. If this is not enough enlightenment, I can only add: attend me!

17

Transition: Quick darkness, followed by ritornello, which, before it can be completed, collides with the fanfare that opens the next scene.

MARCH 1

Gabrieli-like fanfares sporadically during the scene. Long fanfare before scene lights up, then fanfare ends. Chorus gathered together with Saul's Daughter in front of them, all looking to offstage right.

SAUL'S DAUGHTER: Praise him!
CHORUS: Praise him!
(*Short fanfare*)
DAUGHTER: Praise Saul!
CHORUS: Praise Saul!
(*Short fanfare*)
DAUGHTER: Praise our king!
CHORUS: Praise our king!
(*Larger fanfare. Saul enters carried on a platform by four attendants. He holds his head slumped to the side, pays no attention to anything around him, does not move until later, as indicated.*)
DAUGHTER: Stop a moment to hear our praise. (*Attendants stop. Short fanfare.*) Praise Saul, king of Israel.
CHORUS: Israel's king!
DAUGHTER (*more passionately*): Conqueror of the Philistines!
CHORUS: Great conqueror!
DAUGHTER (*even more passionately*): Savior of his people!
CHORUS: People's savior!
DAUGHTER: We send you our gratitude, our love, our praise! (*Fanfare starts as entourage begins to move off. Daughter, interrupting, stops fanfare and entourage.*) Stop, we have much more praise to give! (*Short fanfare. Saul moves his head to look upward, but does not look directly at Daughter or Chorus.*)
CHORUS: Hail!
DAUGHTER: We owe you our lives and our honor.
CHORUS: Honor and lives!
DAUGHTER: If you could see your way to battle for us once more (*Saul's head abruptly falls into its earlier slump, in which it remains until his exit*), your name will be honored forever.
CHORUS: Forever if!
(*Fanfare, entourage begins to move again.*)
DAUGHTER (*interrupting, stops fanfare and entourage*): Stop, our praise is still not finished! (*Short pause, as she moves a few feet in the direc-*

tion of Saul, but stops well before reaching his platform.) We praise you for all your fine intentions toward us, even though you have not felt able to do battle for us lately.

CHORUS: Intentions be praised!

(*Fanfare, but not until entourage starts.*)

DAUGHTER (*interrupting fanfare*): Stop, give us one more chance to voice our praise! (*Fanfare which had started earlier is completed.*) Praise to you, Saul, despite this miserable slump that has kept you out of the field.

CHORUS: Praise despite!

(*No fanfare, but entourage starts, crosses most of stage before it is finally halted, as indicated later.*)

DAUGHTER: Stop, stop, we beg you one more time. (*Entourage continues, she rushes to one of the attendants in front of platform, grabs him by the arm until attendants are forced to stop. She tries to look Saul in the eye, is unable to get his attention*). Come out of your slump, father, give us cause for praise.

CHORUS: Cause for praise!

DAUGHTER: Saul, king, father, come out of that slump, pull yourself together, think of the rest of us, stop sinking into yourself! (*Fanfare suddenly starts, attendants quickly move platform off left, Daughter shouts over fanfare toward offstage left.*) Stop, we beg you, you've betrayed us, yes, you've betrayed us and you're sure to be our downfall yet! (*Worn out, she is held up by several members of chorus. Fanfare is heard ever more distantly offstage left. Daughter rallies to speak up again, but fanfare can hardly be heard by this time.*) Curse the slump that has robbed us of our king!

CHORUS: Curse the slump!

(*Transition: Fanfare is heard going off into the distance, then collides with some harp arpeggios intermixed with low human moans; arpeggios and moans end well before lights go on; some moments of total silence before lights go on.*)

HEALING 1

Stairway to upper level, with a door on upper level opening to a room from which sounds emanate sporadically during the scene. As lights go on, Saul's Daughter is supervising two servants who are arranging flowers in vases. Flowers and vases are uncommonly profuse.

SAUL'S DAUGHTER: There's never enough time to do what needs doing.

SERVANT 1 (*to Daughter*): Is this the length you want them?

DAUGHTER: You might want to vary the length a bit more to make them look the way they grow in nature. Like this, I mean. (*She demonstrates on some flowers, as both servants watch.*)

SERVANT 2: Like this?

(*During this demonstration, the first sound is heard from the upstairs room. It is so low that it can only be heard during the time that Daughter is demonstrating and when no conversation is going on. Both servants look at one another suspiciously as they become aware of the sound.*)

DAUGHTER (*continuing to demonstrate as though nothing had been heard from above*): Now you don't want a whole bunch of spindly stems showing. Instead, you want to cut each flower a different (*a louder sound, this one unmistakably a moan, is heard from upstairs. Servant 1 almost drops the flowers in her hand, exchanges an even more suspicious glance with Servant 2 as Daughter goes on speaking.*), a different size, and then it's important to fill in each of the open spaces with greenery, something fluffy above all. (*A louder moan is heard, servants exchange glances, look upstairs to trace source of sound. Daughter speaks up firmly to them.*) You needn't concern yourself with anything but the floral arrangements. (*Servants try to continue working, but take side glances at each other and upstairs even though no sound comes from above at this point.*) You'll have to move more efficiently if you expect . . .

(*Another sound is heard, Servant 2 stops, looks at Servant 1, who stops and speaks up.*)

SERVANT 1 (*very politely*): Perhaps I might ask what sort of noise this is we're . . .

DAUGHTER (*interrupting brusquely*): You've been hired to get this room looking friendly enough to welcome the young man coming over here to (*she hesitates a moment*), to work with the king. (*Daughter hands Servant 1 some more flowers, just as the same sound, this time lower in volume, is heard.*)

SERVANT 1 (*flinching*): It's not someone who might be needing our help, I hope? (*Daughter maintains a cold silence.*) Someone out in the street, I mean.

DAUGHTER (*handing a huge number of flowers to Servant 2*): Whatever happens out on the street has nothing to do with us.

(*Louder moan, this time too loud to be ignored. Servant 2 drops her flowers, stoops desperately to pick them up.*)

SERVANT 1 (*to Daughter, while trying to continue arranging her flowers*): I'm afraid that wasn't out on the street.

DAUGHTER (*heaping more flowers on Servant 1, and speaking with an angry edge*): All right, it's obviously no secret to anybody that my father's not been well. (*She slows down, unable to hide a certain sadness.*) No, he's not been at all well, my father's not been well at all.

SERVANT 1: I was only trying to be helpful.

DAUGHTER (*snapping at her*): We have lots of people assigned to meet my father's needs. You needn't concern yourselves, either of you. (*Loud sound from upstairs as though a piece of furniture were hitting the floor. Servants obviously show a hard time working.*) I must recommend equanimity to you. There's nothing like a little equanimity to help people weather these things. (*Another thud from upstairs, this one distinctly lighter than the previous one. Servants glance sideways at each other.*) Equanimity, please. (*Knock on door from the outside, Daughter speaks patronizingly to Servant 1.*) I shall ask you to let the young man in, and I know I can trust you to keep your equanimity. (*She gestures for servant to answer door. Servant 1 walks nervously, casting quick glances upstairs. She opens door and an old man walks in. Servant 1 quickly retreats, goes back to her flowers. Daughter speaks to old man, as though rehearsed, and from a distance.*) How do you do? I'm the king's daughter and we bid you welcome. (*Suddenly she looks at him closely, looks confused.*) You are not, I assume, the young man we were expecting—David, I mean. Perhaps I've got my signals crossed.

OLD MAN (*laconically, after a pause*): I'm his father.

DAUGHTER: And your son—David's his name? He's on his way, I assume? (*Same thud as before is heard from upstairs. Daughter looks around nervously as do the servants, who glance knowingly at one another. Daughter speaks to David's Father.*) Pay no attention. Somebody's obviously moving furniture around.

DAVID'S FATHER: I didn't notice anything.

DAUGHTER (*relieved*): Fine, then. I won't burden you with our problems. We'll get down to business. Your son is complying with our request, I presume?

DAVID'S FATHER (*sternly, after a pause*): If I choose to give my permission. (*Soft howl from upstairs.*)

DAUGHTER (*before howl has subsided*): Pay no attention. It's nothing to get excited about. Now, to get back to your son ...

DAVID'S FATHER: It wasn't furniture moving this time.

DAUGHTER: To get back to your David ...

DAVID'S FATHER: I said it wasn't furniture moving up there (*He points*) this time.

DAUGHTER: I never said it was, sir. Now, to resume what we were saying about David ....

(*Louder howl from above. This time all four on stage stop in their tracks. With subsequent noises from upstairs, the servants, who try to go on with the flower arranging, quake conspicuously whereas the other two show a higher measure of control.*)

DAVID'S FATHER: I'm afraid that's the crux of the matter. (*Same howl, but shorter, and they all stop again.*) You pretend we are talking about different things, but in actuality they're part of the (*still shorter howl*) . . . same thing, yes, that's what I mean, that thing up there. (*Stunned silence, but no sound from above.*)

DAUGHTER: All right, I may as well come out with it openly. I speak to you as a concerned daughter.

DAVID'S FATHER: I speak to you as a concerned father.

DAUGHTER: My father is suffering unspeakably.

(*Short, desperate gasp from above.*)

DAVID'S FATHER: My son has to consider his safety in these matters.

DAUGHTER: I am asking him simply to exercise his healing powers.

DAVID'S FATHER: And I ask you to acknowledge the risk to his young life.

DAUGHTER (*quietly but cuttingly*): You'd do well to subordinate personal to national concerns.

DAVID'S FATHER (*gradually raising his voice*): You'd do well to be more respectful of those whose services . . .

DAUGHTER (*interrupting haughtily*): Quiet. Your talk serves no purpose except to make my father's condition worse. (*She holds her hand up to signal him not to speak, looks upstairs as though to listen for a sound from there. Long pause, no sound. She speaks sternly, but in a very quiet voice.*) I'm afraid we are at loggerheads, sir.

DAVID'S FATHER (*in a normal tone of voice*): That's my impression, lady. (*He turns abruptly to leave.*) My son's been waiting for me outside. I'll let him know he's not needed after all.

DAUGHTER (*raising voice a bit*): Not needed? You've misconstrued what I had to say.

DAVID'S FATHER: Not at all. We've both come to recognize that whatever help you need will have to be from someone other than my son. (*He starts to walk out.*)

DAUGHTER (*rushing after him, tugging him by the arm*): One moment, please. (*He stops, though with a tentative look.*) You've put enough time and effort into this visit, both you and your son, that it's worth your while to stay a minute longer. You'll listen to what little I have to say, I can see you will, and I promise it'll only be a moment. (*David's Father seems to assent grudgingly. Daughter moves away, as though preparing for a speech.*) I fear I never made myself clear. Those things are hard when you consider the pressures under which we live here— interruptions of the most dire sort (*she looks briefly upstairs*)—as you've heard with your own ears. No, I can scarcely blame you for the anxieties you voice. If I were in your position I should also think twice before I entrusted a son to the whims of a patient such as our king. In fact, I can only admire you for the protectiveness you show—it's only natural, after all. Not that there's any real danger to your son if he undertakes the task we've honored him with. (*Shriek from upstairs, though a bit muffled. Daughter goes on as if nothing happened.*) The various sounds you've heard are doubtless a bit misleading in the impression they leave. One would think that anyone who'd enter the king's chamber is exposing himself to all manner of violent acts. But I can assure you that's not the case at all. I've been in there any number of times and I've never had a moment's worry about my safety. His bark, to put it in the common parlance, is a good bit mightier than his bite. No doubt you or David have heard of one or two incidents, and I won't hide these from you. Yes, it's quite true he threw some objects (*louder shriek than the last, Daughter shows some nervousness but quickly goes on*), but the rooms, I can promise you, have since been cleared of anything that's remotely throwable. Yes, and you've probably felt deterred by the talk that was circulating for a time about my father's attempt to choke one of the servants. Those rumors always get blown up out of all proportion. I fully understand how anybody can get panicky if he thinks someone's about to lunge at him. What actually happened we'll probably never know, since the hysteria that this particular incident set off in the servant as well as his friends ruined any chance of ever getting at the truth. Suffice it to say that a person such as your son has all the delicacy necessary to prevent anything from getting out of hand in the first place. In fact, from all the reports we've received about him, his skill in handling those who have temporarily lost their reason is little short of what one could call phenomenal. But I won't waste my energy, or your time, in flattery, no, I don't want you to feel I'm putting pressure on you in any way. The choice is solely yours and David's, and if one or both of you choose not to fulfill this task, I shall honor your decision, no matter what the consequences to the king, to his family, and, for that matter, to the nation. It would be easy enough to use tricks of persuasion to help you bend your will, but that's not my way, that isn't my way at all. I could cite the innumerable reports—fully verified, I assure you—of the magic David can exercise with his harp, how he could melt even the sternest of gods through the power of his music. Or I could take another tack and cite the glory that would (*Shriek from upstairs, louder and longer than anything before—something one might imagine from Oedipus in the ancient Athenian theater at his moment of recognition. At first, Daughter tries to keep talking as though nothing had happened, then realizes she cannot go on and freezes till it subsides, then somewhat nervously picks up where she had left off*) the glory that will be David's if he can bring our king back to life, back to what he was at an earlier, happier time when the enemies who are now virtually at our doorsteps were beaten down without mercy the moment they threatened to violate our borders. (*She pauses, looks upstairs nervously as though expect-*

ing another outburst, then goes on.) But I'll say nothing that might make you think I'm trying to anticipate or manipulate your reply, no, nor do I expect you to tell me on the spot, for this is surely the sort of decision one must take under advisement, in consultation with David, of course, and I am confident I shall know your answer soon enough, nor does it need to be made in any formal way. Go then (*she points to the door*), our door will remain open to you if you choose to use it, and if I see you returning with your son I shall know that my pleadings and his sufferings have not been in vain.

(*David's Father, who has listened intently throughout, walks out. Daughter and servants occupy themselves with the flower arranging during a long silence punctuated by sporadic soft moans from upstairs. Daughter glances alternately upstairs and in the direction that David's Father went off. David enters alone, looks around shyly at first, Daughter gasps for joy, gets on her knees. Members of the chorus slowly enter behind him, obviously curious to witness what they can of what follows. David, embarrassed at the Daughter's kneeling before him, quickly assumes an earnest and efficient pose. Throughout this period there are sporadic low sighs and moans from upstairs.*)

DAVID (*curtly to Daughter*): You can cut down on the ceremony and show me where to go.

DAUGHTER (*standing up and pointing upstairs*): It's up there. I . . . I won't hide the fact it's where . . . those sounds . . . his sufferings (*Her voice grows faint, David brushes her aside, walks up the stairs resolutely. As he reaches the top, his father rushes in carrying a harp.*)

DAVID'S FATHER (*frantic*): He forgot his harp.

(*He hands it to a member of the chorus, who relays it to another, until somebody else gets it up to David. David opens the door to the upstairs room, looks in, but we hear no sound from inside now. He walks in resolutely with his harp, shuts the door. Tenseness among the crowd, Daughter goes to base of stairs, throws herself across the stairs. Chorus and David's Father move behind Daughter. Suddenly the silence is broken by several harp arpeggios, but the last arpeggio is cut off in the middle, after which there is a short silence, then a violent sound one might imagine as that of a harp crashing against the wall. Daughter gasps directly after the crash. Then a long silence in which everyone remains motionless. The silence is broken by a succession of deep, low sounds that seem at first to express grief. All figures on the stage listen intently and with shows of fear. Gradually the sounds show themselves to be not weeping, but laughter, at first a deep, raucous laughter close to what earlier seemed weeping, then a lighter, more serene laughter. Soon it becomes evident that Saul and David are laughing together. Members of the chorus look at one another, make statements such as "The king is laughing," "He's healed." Door opens, Saul comes out followed by David, both look thoroughly worn out. They come to the railing, smile serenely, though showing fatigue. Daughter quickly picks several flowers from a vase, throws them up, throws more at Chorus, who start pelting Saul and David with flowers. Gradually what starts as an incomprehensible set of sounds from the chorus begins to cohere in a shout, "Praise Saul! Praise our king!")*

Transition: A moment or two of silence after the lights go off; then the sound of swinging doors opening and closing two or three times before the lights go on.

BATTLE 1

Saul on throne, which is placed in center facing forward. Three attendants sit on floor before him. Behind are two swinging doors, one at left, the other at right. Throughout the scene one messenger after another enters through the swinging door at right, comes before Saul, gives a message, and leaves through the door at left.

MESSENGER 1 *(racing into room)*: The Philistines are up in arms again. Your men are asking for you.

ATTENDANTS *(moaning)*: Woe, woe.

SAUL: Tell them to calm down.

(Messenger leaves as new one comes in.)

MESSENGER 2: There's a giant out there shouting curses at you.

(Chorus gasp in dread.)

SAUL: I'm immovable.

(Messenger leaves, new one enters.)

MESSENGER 3: Your men say they'll be forced back to Ziklag if you don't come right away.

(Attendants gasp in horror.)

SAUL: You're bothering me.

(Messenger leaves, new one enters.)

MESSENGER 4: He's nine feet high.

(Attendants make a long moan. Saul doesn't answer or move in any way.)

MESSENGER 4: I said that giant's nine feet high. *(Saul stamps his foot, messenger rushes out.)*

SAUL *(before new messenger can enter)*: Bar the door!

(Attendants rush to hold back the door, which has started to swing open as they approach it. All three push to hold door closed, while loud knocks are heard from other side of door. Saul remains motionless on throne. Attendants make noises to indicate effort in holding door back, but it is finally forced open, with attendants thrown backwards and falling to floor,

*from which they slowly get up. Three messengers enter at once and at first
try to speak at the same time. Finally one is able to articulate his message
alone.)*

MESSENGER 5 (*to Saul*): Your forces are starting to rally.

(*Attendants, gradually recovering, clap hands in joy.*)

MESSENGER 6: That was earlier. The giant has frightened them back half a
  mile.

(*Attendants moan.*)

MESSENGER 7: That was earlier. They're dispersing towards Gilgal. The
  nation's fate is in your hands.

(*Messengers rush out together, each struggling with the others to get out
first. Meanwhile, attendants gesture toward Saul pleadingly. Suddenly Saul
perks up, jumps to his feet as a new messenger comes in.*)

SAUL (*to attendants and interrupting messenger before he can speak*):
  Bring me my gear!

(*Attendants cheer wildly, clamor around Saul. During succeeding speeches,
attendants remove his robe, outfit him in battle gear. One goes to a set of
scabbards in the wall, brings out several swords for Saul to inspect.*)

MESSENGER 8: The giant has chased your men out of Michmash.

SAUL (*while being outfitted*): In what direction? (*Messenger moves toward
  exit without answering. Saul speaks up anxiously.*) Toward what position?
  (*Messenger rushes out as new one comes in.*)

MESSENGER 9: The food supply is running out at Ophrah.

SAUL (*trying to get messenger's attention as latter runs out*): Where's the
  giant? I've got to know.

MESSENGER 9: Ask the next messenger. (*Runs out, new messenger runs in.*)

SAUL (*holding a sword in the air, interrupts new messenger as the latter
  starts to speak*): I don't care what you were planning to say, but you've
  got to tell me in what direction I'm to find the giant.

MESSENGER 10 (*as though not listening to Saul*): They've run out of
  boulders at Eshlemoa.

(*Attendants sit down near throne when they have finished outfitting Saul.*)

SAUL (*shouting after Messenger 10 as he runs out*): Where's the giant? I
  ask you, where's the giant?

(*Saul runs out the door after the messenger. Meanwhile a new messenger
has come in.*)

MESSENGER 11 (*oblivious of the fact that Saul is not in the room*): Your
  men waiting for you in Borashan are demoralized.

(*Saul comes in through the door he had earlier run out of, looks hopelessly
confused, doesn't notice Messenger 11 going past him until messenger is
virtually out the door. They almost collide, but Messenger 11 continues to
door without acknowledging Saul.*)

SAUL (*shouting after Messenger 11, who continues out*): Where's the giant? I can't fight him till you give me some sign.

(*Meanwhile he drops his sword, attendants moan, and a new messenger has come in.*)

SAUL (*to new messenger before he can speak up*): Don't say anything. You all have me hopelessly confused.

(*Messenger 12 exits without having spoken. New messenger enters. During this period, Saul, as though reconsidering, has stooped over to pick up sword, but quickly drops it before raising it up, doesn't listen as messenger speaks.*)

MESSENGER 13: They're desperate in Zeborim as well as Gibeah, not to speak of Arabah . . .

SAUL (*suddenly perking up, interrupting him and pointing at him*): I've made up my mind—send David out to fight that giant.

(*Attendants gasp in fear.*)

MESSENGER 13 (*trying to continue while Saul tries to interrupt*): But if you consider Jeshamon together with Siphnoth . . .

SAUL (*interrupting, this time shouting*): I said, go send David to fight that giant.

(*Messenger looks confused, Saul gives him a push and a kick towards door, then returns to sit on throne.*)

MESSENGER 13 (*continuing as he is pushed out the door and heard from afar*): Aijalon might have proved the right spot, but nobody's going to argue about Ramah.

(*Meanwhile a new messenger has entered.*)

MESSENGER 14: The giant's taunting what's left of your men.

SAUL: Don't get excitable. I've seen to everything.

(*Messenger exits, new one comes in.*)

MESSENGER 15: David's only six feet tall.

(*Attendants hold hands in prayer.*)

SAUL: He can fend for himself well enough.

(*Messenger leaves, new one comes in.*)

MESSENGER 16: David's marched out, your men have left their positions to back him up.

(*Attendants cheer.*)

SAUL (*menacingly to attendants*): Stop! It's too early to know what's going to happen.

(*Messenger goes out, new one comes in.*)

MESSENGER 17: David's taunting the giant.

(*Attendants look to Saul for a signal to allow them to cheer.*)

SAUL (*to attendants*): Quiet or I'll knock you all down.

(*Attendants freeze. Messenger leaves, new one comes in.*)

MESSENGER 18: The giant is taunting David for bringing nothing but a slingshot.

(*Attendants look to Saul for a signal, but he remains impassive. Messenger leaves, new one comes in.*)

MESSENGER 19: The giant is stalking David. Your men are dispersing.

(*Attendants look up to Saul, wait for him to speak before showing a reaction*).

SAUL: I knew we never had a chance. Let David be a martyr to the nation.

(*Attendants moan. Messenger leaves, new one comes in.*)

MESSENGER 20: He's knocked his head off!

SAUL (*solemnly, though hiding a certain satisfaction*): Have David buried with highest honors! (*Saul raises his arms in a histrionic gesture of mourning. Attendants moan. Messenger leaves, and this time four messengers enter flanking David, who carries a huge giant's head at the end of a pike. Victory bells are heard from offstage. Saul maintains his mourning stance a moment, then takes a double-take as he realizes his error, suddenly falls into a slump as in first scene. Attendants cheer David, Saul remains immobile in his slump.*)

Transition: Victory bells continue, then collide with low sounds of growls as lights slowly go on.

HEALING 2

Throne at front of stage facing forward, sheet covering it, nobody in it. Saul on the floor crouched like an animal, David leaning against a pillar quite a few feet away. Low growls from Saul.

DAVID (*arms folded, not moving, speaks coolly*): Keep going on, if that's what suits you. (*Somewhat louder growl.*) You'll wear yourself out. (*Long pause, no sound.*) I'm prepared to wait till you're ready to act like a human being again. (*Low growl, softer than the last.*) No, I say. (*Louder growl, David moves slowly, cautiously toward Saul, speaks to him in a scathingly cold manner.*) I said No. (*David continues moving cautiously toward Saul, who comes out with low growls. David stops a few feet away, freezes, growls gradually stop. David looks benignly at Saul, moves forward till he is next to him, prepares to pat him on the head. Saul suddenly snaps at David's hand, growls fiercely. David hits him across the face, Saul cringes.*) That was bad. (*Saul gives out with some low growls. David moves backward a big distance, then speaks up in a matter-of-fact tone.*) We'll start again. (*David gets down to Saul's height, approaches him slowly walking in a stooped position, holds his hand out low, stops. He moves a few more inches until he is next to*

Saul, holds hand out again, pats Saul on shoulder and under the chin. No growl. He moves hand gradually upward to pat him on the head. Saul gradually turns around, reclines head on David's shoulder. David speaks, calmly stroking his head.): It's all right. You'll be fine.

SAUL (*articulating words as though he hadn't spoken for a long time*): My . . .

(*Pause.*)

DAVID: Don't strain yourself.

SAUL: My life . . .

DAVID: Don't rush it. There's lots of time.

(*Pause, as David continues patting Saul's head.*)

SAUL: My . . . life . . . my life . . . (*suddenly lets it out in a plangent tone*) my life is over!

DAVID (*stroking his head*): You'll think better when you've calmed down a bit. (*Saul gets a bit restless, sits up by himself, David gets up, raises him up slowly, though he continues helping to support him during the following interchange.*)

SAUL: You . . .

DAVID: Yes?

SAUL: You don't . . .

DAVID: Don't be afraid to say it.

SAUL: You don't know (*Points to his heart, almost falls, but quickly recovers.*) . . . You don't . . .

DAVID (*filling in*): know what.

SAUL: Yes . . . what goes on . . .

DAVID (*filling in*): inside there.

SAUL: Yes, inside here. (*He points to heart, nods in assent.*)

DAVID: But I can well imagine.

(*Saul slowly moves away, as though not having walked for some time. David helps him a bit, then moves back to the pillar. Saul walks back and forth as though gradually gaining confidence. He tries out a few gestures with his hands, then with his arms, then starts speaking, at first hesitantly, but gradually takes up the manner of an old-time actor. From his tone, the audience should be aware that he is quoting and re-doing lines from well-known plays.*)

SAUL: "It's the end, we've come to the end. I don't need you anymore." (*Saul looks over to David, as though awaiting a response. David pays no attention.*) "If I can hold my peace, and stand quiet, it will be all over with, sound and motion, all over and done with." (*He again awaits a response, does not get one, speaks up more resolutely.*) "We're on earth, there's no cure for that."

DAVID (*somewhat nonchalantly*): Talking like that is no way to get you going again.

SAUL (*after pondering a moment*):
> "Whom have I to complain of but my self?
> All these indignities, these evils
> I deserve and more."

DAVID (*interrupting*): That's not the right tack either.

SAUL (*as though seeking a way to start again*):
> "Can this be he, whom unarm'd
> No strength of man, or fiercest wild beast could withstand?"

DAVID: That's a start at least.

SAUL (*picking up momentum*): "I begin to feel
> Some rouzing motions in me which dispose . . ."

DAVID (*beginning to show some enthusiasm*): This is the sort of thing I've been waiting for!

(*Saul slumps back for a moment. David rushes to prop him up.*)

SAUL (*gaining confidence again*): "O now for once
> Welcome the clear mind, welcome content." (*He starts to weaken a bit.*) I'm not exactly sure I can go on.

DAVID (*patiently, as he helps get Saul's body back into position*):
> "Welcome the clear mind, welcome content," you said.

SAUL (*pulling himself together*): "Welcome content," yes,
> "And welcome the glittering spears, the rising swords . . ."

DAVID (*interrupting*): Superb!

(*During Saul's succeeding lines David removes sheet from the throne, picks up the crown that had lain under the sheet, beckons Saul, who gradually moves to throne as he recites.*)

SAUL: "Welcome the bold and spirit-jarring clarion,
> Saul's royal banner, tumult, riot, din,
> And all that gorgeous panoply of . . ."

(*Out of breath, Saul sits down on throne, speaks softly*): It's been a while since I've been able to express myself adequately.

DAVID (*quietly*): You don't want to overdo it.

(*David strokes his head gently, then places crown on his head. During this time, unbeknownst to Saul, David has gestured to the back as though summoning Chorus by prearrangement. They come out quickly, David gestures for them to remain silent, then he quickly turns the throne around on its swivel and lets Saul face the crowd. Fanfare as in first scene is heard from backstage.*)

DAVID (*pointing to Saul*): Behold your king!

CHORUS: Hail Saul!

(*Saul remains motionless at first, then David pats him on the head briefly, Saul gradually raises arms to welcome the cheer.*)

CHORUS: Hail Saul!

(*Saul lifts arms more fervently.*)

MEMBER OF CHORUS: Hail David, who has restored our king to us.

CHORUS: Hail David!

DAVID (*sternly*): This is Saul's day, not David's. Hail Saul, warrior, leader, king, who killed our enemies by the thousands.

CHORUS: Saul killed his thousands, Saul killed his thousands.

HALF OF CHORUS: (*those standing near member who just spoke*): David killed his *tens* of thousands.

DAVID: *Saul* killed his tens of tens of thousands.

MEMBER OF CHORUS: *David* killed his tens of tens of tens of thousands.

(*Chorus now divides in half, first half starting "Saul killed his tens of tens of tens . . .", the other half, like the second voice of a fugue, starting several words later with "David killed his tens of tens of tens of . . ."*
The scheme below indicates how the passage should be phrased to make each half of the chorus distinct.)

CHORUS 1: Saul   killed   his tens of   tens of   tens of   tens of
CHORUS 2:   David   killed
CHORUS 1:   tens of   tens of   tens of   tens of   tens of   tens of . . .
CHORUS 2:   his tens   of tens   of tens   of tens   of tens   of tens . . .

(*David throughout this passage acts as leader of that half of chorus hailing Saul. After a short time, almost imperceptibly, Saul's outstretched arms move down, he suddenly jerks chair around on its swivel so that he is facing audience and lets his head fall in a slump. David rushes to comfort him. Sound of chorus suddenly cut off as lights go out.*)

Transition: *Silence for a few moments after the lights go off; then a few short clarinet squibbles that continue as the lights go on, but end before Saul speaks.*

PRAYER

Stage empty except for a boulder or two that have been placed to indicate a natural landscape.

SAUL (*after a long silence, during which time he seems to be working up the courage to speak up*): You up there, wherever you are, I'm not asking you to speak to me. That would be asking too much. Give me a sign, like the thunder you used to send me just as we'd pull out our arms for battle. It's not that I always heard it all that distinctly—there were times, in fact, I hardly heard it at all. For all I know I might have heard you with my inner ear alone, but that didn't matter. When I knew you were giving me a sign, that in itself was enough, more than enough to rush in against a thousand enemies, tens of thousands for all I know, and not even think whether all those bodies were going to crush me.

I defy you.
(Photo by Betsy Jablow)

We had one victory after another in those days, and all my men were able to bear down on them in just the way I was. What I did, they did. It was as simple as that, with nobody waiting around and begging you for signs. No, we just felt and knew without stopping to ask. (*Long pause, with a clarinet squibble.*) Then it ended, and I'll never quite figure out when and why. The first thing I knew, something came over me when I rushed into the enemy. It was as though you weren't quite with me, but of course I don't mean to give you the blame. I didn't pay much attention and I managed to leave litters of bodies strewn all over the battleground, just as always. But the next time as I was calling my men together it came over me again and I began to wonder would I want to run when the enemy was rushing at me, and though I never said a word, my men must have felt there was something wrong, for once we got into battle, it was never the same again for any of us. I tried again, you know I tried, and each time we started I asked you for a sign. I didn't know when it would be, I didn't care how it came, it could be anything, thunder from up there, a light on the horizon, your hand brushing against my heart. (*Pause, with a short clarinet squibble.*) In fact, if a sign came my way right now I can assure you I'd get it, yes, I'd respond immediately—and I'd even fail to respond if that was the way I thought you wanted it. You shouldn't feel I'm giving you a hint, since if you don't think you can give me a sign I'd surely understand. You mustn't get the idea I'm pestering you unnecessarily. That's not my way and I trust you enough to know you're aware of that. But if you were ready to give me a sign regardless of anything I've said you mustn't hesitate to do so and you can be sure I wouldn't disappoint you. (*Pause, then speaks up suddenly.*) If I'm silent right now it's not that I'm waiting around for that sign. It's just that there's only so much anybody can say in these circumstances. And in all honesty I'm also getting a bit worn out from all this. Being without a sign for this long a spell finally takes its toll on a person, and I'm no exception. I'm sure it'd try most anybody's patience, and I may well have reached the point where I'm at the end of my rope. (*Pause.*) In fact, I suspect my silence right now is my way of telling you something that it's much too hard to put into words. You might even say that I'm the one who's giving *you* the sign, and I assume you'll understand without any explanation on my part. There's nothing wrong if *I* take the initiative for once. I wouldn't have had to, after all, if we hadn't lost contact all this while, but if you keep me waiting this long a time you'll have to realize you're taking your chances. Other people wouldn't have let you off this easily. I'm beginning to think it's those who refuse to be patient with you who manage to get your signs. You thought you could count on me not to pressure you, but perhaps it's time you learned that you can't go by past assumptions.

You've always thought you knew me, but I may as well say it directly,
you don't really know me at all. And even if you're trying to make contact with me right now, it's only fair to warn you I'm not ready to
acknowledge you, not yet, certainly, maybe never. You see where your
negligence lands you. You can't expect to discard me without even a
whimper from me. But it's not just a whimper you'll get, that's for sure.
My kind goes down shouting. You're not used to being talked to like
this. I know your ways—you raise up your heroes from the depths, you
lead them to think they're your special favorites, and then you drop them
without reason or warning. You've gotten away with this behavior for
much too long and even if the others you've dropped haven't the courage
to tell you, I for one will. That's right, I defy you. (*Long pause, no
clarinet squibble, then he speaks quietly.*) I suppose it wasn't much use
after all. Your silence has told me so and it's no use either of us pretending things can ever be what they once were when, full of your spirit,
I crushed your enemies by the thousands. I've had my day. That's the
sign you were giving me all along and I should have known. There's
precious little room for stars in your sky. It's only a small sky, after all,
and what few places there are, are taken. I'll go my way.
(*Slips off quietly.*)

*Transition: Clarinet squibbles after he finishes speaking, to continue after
lights go off, then colliding with harp solo.*

INTERMEZZO

*The three actors remain stationary throughout the episode. David is on the
lower level playing his harp, Saul on the upper level seated at a small table,
Saul's Daughter perched somewhere in between so that she has a good
view of David and Saul, neither of whom can see the other. Throughout
the scene she acts as a musical conductor, giving signals to David about
when to slow down or accelerate his tempo, or to start or stop playing altogether. Saul has a stone-studded and gleaming dagger that he tends to set
down into its holder on the table whenever the music starts playing and
to lift up when the music slows down or stops. The music throughout
the scene is the harp solo (though without its orchestral accompaniment)
from* Lucia di Lammermoor, *Act I. Only Saul's Daughter speaks during
the episode. She enunciates boldly and clearly and must always make herself understood above the music. Between episodes the music has started
at normal tempo, then slowed down conspicuously, and finally goes back
to normal tempo just before the lights go on. Saul is staring at the dagger
and as the music continues he seems to relax, gradually turning away from*

the dagger. His Daughter stares at him with eagle eyes, does not speak up until he turns away.

SAUL'S DAUGHTER: That's right, take your eyes off that thing, keep them away as long as you possibly can. The trick, and I've said this time and again, is to get yourself to make do without the music altogether and that's what we're going to put our minds to. Right? (*She signals David to slow down.*) We'll try once more. (*Saul's face clouds up, he looks at the dagger again, extends his hand to it.*) No, I don't want you touching the thing, you have no reason to just because the music has slowed down a bit. (*Saul holds his hand on the dagger uncertain whether to pick it up or leave it in the holder.*) All right, as long as you can resist picking the thing up, I'm perfectly content to see you look at it and even touch it now and then. That's fine with me, I don't want you to get the idea I'm scolding, I'm merely waiting for you to recognize on your own this can't go on forever. At some point the music is going to have to stop (*She signals David to slow it down further, until the notes become so widely spaced no melody is discernible*), that's right, there comes a point where David'll need another catnap and you'll have to be on your own for a while. See, the music's slowed down to next to nothing and you've managed to keep the thing in its holder all this time. It's a matter of simple weaning, anybody can do it. (*She signals David to stop altogether. At first Saul does not move.*) Nobody should have to be tied to a habit that way, a person can't function in this world, it makes him little better than an automaton. (*Saul starts to pull the dagger out of its holder.*) No, there's absolutely no reason you have to—simply tell yourself you have all the strength you need to hold back. (*He pulls the dagger out all the way, stares at it, gradually points it towards himself, but not in such a way that a thrust seems imminent. Saul's Daughter quickly signals David to start playing again, though in the slow tempo.*) Think hard what you're doing, you surely don't want to, you never really wanted to in the first place. (*Saul slowly returns the dagger to the holder, his Daughter signals David to stop.*) See, that's where you wanted it, safe in its holder, all along. We'll pretend you never slipped this time. Whenever the urge comes over you—and it's no use denying that urges like this are very real things indeed—you must remind yourself how beautifully you did for two whole hours last night without even a single note of music. I tell you this not for my sake or David's, though God knows he needs every wink of sleep you're willing to grant him— no, it's not for the rest of us, we'll surely manage to keep things going on our own, but it's for *your* own good you'll have to think of breaking this habit once and for all. (*During the preceding lines, Saul has gradually extended his hand toward the dagger.*) I won't say a thing. You're perfectly capable of holding back, *I* know it, David knows it, and now it's up to you to recognize the enormous potential you have for controlling yourself. (*During the last few words Saul has pulled the dagger out of its holder and pointed it toward his heart. He deliberates motionlessly during her following lines.*) No . . . no . . . you haven't the slightest intention, it isn't what you want: think of the pain, that wound gaping so raw you'll want to scream till your voice gives out, though that's nothing to the nausea that'll tear you inside out as you retch begging in vain for relief, though even that seems nothing to the blood that'll pour out in such volume you'll be relieved if you could only faint from the sight. No, that isn't what you want at all. (*She pauses, as though hoping her words have had a deterrent effect. Suddenly his facial expression and his way of aiming the dagger make her realize she has no time to lose. She shouts at David with a conspicuous loss of control.*) Start the music, you fool, he's going to *kill* himself! (*David starts playing at a frantic tempo. Saul, jarred out of completing his act, slowly puts the dagger back in its holder, gradually gains a serene expression, which he maintains until the end of the scene. His Daughter, thoroughly shaken, holds her hand over her face and no longer notices either Saul or David. David slows down to normal tempo as the lights go out.*)

Transition: Harp solo goes on after lights go off, is cut short by banging of gavel.

COUNCIL

Just before lights go on we hear a gavel pounding amid considerable talk and laughter. Saul, holding gavel, is seated at back center of an oval table, with six to eight councillors distributed at equal distances around the table. Councillors, ignoring Saul, are loudly chatting and joking with one another.

SAUL (*still pounding gavel*): Your attention, please! (*Gradually they quiet down, some but not all of them looking at Saul, who speaks solemnly.*) I have convened you here today on a matter of grave importance, one which, given . . . (*In the course of the sentence they have started speaking to one another again, and Saul, flustered, starts pounding gavel once more.*) I must ask your indulgence, this is a matter of . . . (*Councillors' chatter has become louder than ever, Saul tries to speak through it, pounding gavel once or twice while speaking.*) Your attention, please —we can be through this thing in three minutes if you . . . (*Noise has become so great he gives up, closes his eyes briefly, steps back, then with a sudden burst of resolution pounds gavel more fiercely than before. Noise*

*and joking start to calm down, councillors begin to look at Saul, who,
unaware of them, keeps pounding in desperation without trying to
speak up. They begin to ignore him again and become at least as noisy as
before. Saul goes on pounding automatically as lights go out.*)

Transition: *One knock of gavel, though without sound of talk, is heard
after lights go out; long pause, then David's line "I am not a paranoiac"
spoken in the dark and repeated by David after the lights go on and the
next episode starts.*

HEALING 3

*Saul on his throne, which faces sideways. David sits in a chair facing him
at close range.*

DAVID (*quietly, didactically*): I am not a paranoiac.
SAUL: I am not . . . a . . .
DAVID (*in same tone as before*): I am not a paranoiac.
SAUL: I . . .
DAVID: Say the whole thing, please.
SAUL: I am . . .
DAVID: Not . . .
SAUL: Not . . .
DAVID: I want the whole sentence.
(*Long pause.*)
SAUL (*quietly*): I am not a paranoiac.
DAVID (*clapping hands together*): That was lovely.
SAUL: I am not a paranoiac. I know I'm not.
DAVID: Of course not.
SAUL: I never was. I'm not now. I never will be.
DAVID: I know you won't.
SAUL (*resolutely*): I will never be a paranoiac.
DAVID: Well spoken.
SAUL: I will never . . .
DAVID (*interrupting him, as though to put a stop to the sentence*): That's
    fine for now.
SAUL (*standing up*): I believe I can face it now.
DAVID: Of course you can. I always knew you would. (*Gets up to help
    Saul straighten his robe.*) It doesn't do to have one's robes mussed up.
    You want to feel like a king, after all.
SAUL (*moving away suspiciously as David straightens his robe*): I *am* the
    king.
DAVID: Nobody's ever had the slightest doubt. (*Looks at Saul admiringly,*

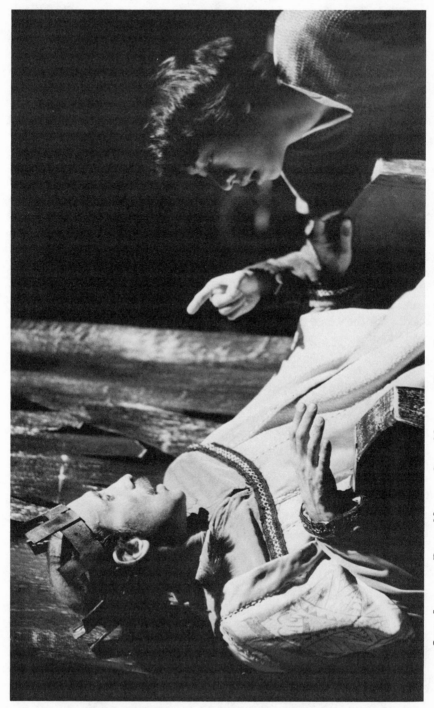

SAUL: I am . . .   DAVID: Not . . .   SAUL: Not . . .   DAVID: I want the whole sentence.   SAUL: I am not a paranoiac.
(Photo by Betsy Jablow)

notices that his crown is not straight, goes to straighten it.) Your crown's askew.

(*Saul moves away with a jerk and David is left holding the crown.*)

SAUL (*suddenly realizing that David has the crown*): Traitor!

DAVID (*rushing to place crown on Saul's head*): I was trying to help you straighten it.

SAUL: Traitor!

DAVID (*still trying to adjust it correctly*): You want it sitting straight to feel like the king you really are.

SAUL: And I know what *you* want. You want it sitting on *your* head. I know you for the traitor you are. You heard what I said? Or do I say it again? (*Sits down imperiously on throne, glowers at David.*)

DAVID: I heard it, but I want to hear you say something else again. (*David sits down again, smoothes Saul's robe gently, Saul gives him a fiery glance, then David speaks up as at beginning of scene.*) I am not a paranoiac.

(*Long pause as David stares at Saul in a friendly though firm way.*)

SAUL: I am not . . . a . . .

DAVID: I am not a paranoiac.

SAUL: I . . .

DAVID: Say the whole thing, please.

SAUL: I am . . .

DAVID: Not . . .

SAUL: Not . . .

DAVID: I want the whole sentence.

(*Long pause.*)

SAUL (*quietly*): I am not a paranoiac.

Transition: Saul's last line spoken in dark even more quietly than with the lights on; silence, then several short high violin squibbles.

CONSPIRACY

Saul on throne fondling a cat. Throne faces sideways, though in the opposite direction from preceding scene. Throughout the scene he maintains hold of the cat, which he pulls back with a short leash whenever it tries to escape. His fondling becomes intense at moments of tension or uncertainty.

SAUL (*to himself, but as though he wishes to be heard outside the room*): Is there no one here to rid me of this pain? (*Pets cat with almost desperate affection.*) No one? . . . I didn't expect so. (*Pets slowly with resignation.*) I must ignore the pain, even when it consumes all my

Is there no one here to rid me of this pain?
(Photo by Betsy Jablow)

thoughts. (*During the last line an attendant has come in slowly, his ear inclined so as to catch what Saul has to say. Throughout the scene his movements lightly suggest those of a ballet dancer. Saul speaks to himself, serenely ignores presence of attendant.*) One accepts the pain, whether relief is in the offing or not.

ATTENDANT: Did somebody call?

SAUL: I was mumbling to myself.

ATTENDANT: If there's anything I can do, that's what I'm here for—to help.

SAUL: No cause for alarm.

ATTENDANT (*starting to leave*): Everything under control then?

SAUL (*petting cat with some fervor*): As well as can be expected. Relief sometimes comes in unanticipated ways.

ATTENDANT (*coming back*): You mean there *is* something I can do?

SAUL: Please don't get me wrong. I've not asked you to do a thing.

ATTENDANT: But if there's any relief I can bring . . .

SAUL: It's always better when things go their own way, I mean take care of themselves without outside aid.

ATTENDANT: But if somebody can give just a little nudge here or there, things usually take care of themselves even better.

SAUL: Talking to you makes the pain feel more bearable already. I'm sure things will take care of themselves.

ATTENDANT: If you let me probe around a bit the pain might even go away altogether. (*Reaches his arm toward Saul.*) Now let's figure out in what particular spot it is.

SAUL (*retreating, lets himself get absorbed in cat*): It's almost too embarrassing when it gets that personal.

ATTENDANT (*lightly touching different parts of Saul's body, with Saul cringing*): Is it here? . . . Here? . . . Here? . . . Am I guessing right?

SAUL (*replying while Attendant is probing*): A bit, yes . . . here . . . a little more here than there.

ATTENDANT (*still probing*): You've got to give me more solid information. Here?

SAUL: Yes, somewhat.

ATTENDANT: And here?

SAUL (*hesitant*): Yes.

ATTENDANT: In other words, it hurts all over.

SAUL: You might say so. (*Pause, while getting absorbed in cat, after which he speaks up suddenly.*) It's absolutely terrifying.

ATTENDANT: Then there's nothing to do but root out the source of the pain. (*Touches another place.*) Now you must tell me, does it seem to radiate out from here?

SAUL (*gently pushing him away*): It's no use looking. The source isn't anywhere near the place of the pain.

ATTENDANT (*moving back*): An odd phenomenon indeed. (*Looks around himself suspiciously.*) It couldn't be anything elsewhere in the room, could it?

SAUL (*frustrated*): I don't think so. I hope not.

ATTENDANT: Then it must be outside somewhere. (*Starts toward door, speaks up suddenly.*) Is it a thing, a force, or a person?

SAUL: When you're feeling this way, you don't make distinctions.

ATTENDANT: Think. Concentrate.

SAUL: You have me stumped.

ATTENDANT (*impatiently*): How can you expect my help if you won't cooperate? (*Walks· out of room. Saul looks forlorn, hugs cat, looks longingly in direction Attendant went out. Attendant sticks his head back in, catches Saul's glance.*)

SAUL (*coyly*): I didn't mean to upset you. It's this pain, you see. It does strange, one might even say *distasteful* things to a person.

ATTENDANT (*moving close to Saul again*): Then we'll try a new way. I'll get to the point. Did you say his name begins with H?

SAUL: I never named anybody.

ATTENDANT: Then it begins with W.

SAUL: Absurd! I haven't the slightest idea who, but even if it is . . .

ATTENDANT: That leaves only an earnest young man whose name starts with D.

SAUL (*hugging cat*): I'm shocked to the quick!

ATTENDANT: I got you.

SAUL (*solemnly*): You got me wrong.

ATTENDANT: You'll be free of your pain in no time at all.

SAUL (*holding his ears*): Don't say it! Don't say it!

ATTENDANT (*pulling out a knife, which he brandishes in the air as he runs out*): Thy will be done.

SAUL (*quietly, to himself*): I never said a word! (*Suddenly gets up, in confusion releases his hold on cat's leash, runs in direction Attendant went out, shouts loudly after him.*) You heard that? I never said a word! (*Blackout.*)

Transition: High short violin squibbles, which collide with the sound of knocks on a door.

INQUIRY

Fronts of three simple dwellings on the stage, each with a large window through which the dweller will look out and speak in the course of the scene. Everything remains in darkness throughout. Henchman 1 carries a sack and Henchmen 2 and 3 carry lanterns. At opening the three Henchmen go to house on right, knock sharply.

CITIZEN 1 (*from inside with sleepy voice*): Who's there? What could anybody want at this hour when even the cows are asking not to be disturbed? (*More knocks.*) All right, all right, I'm willing to give up a little sleep if it means that much to you. (*More knocks.*) Coming, coming, you don't need to rush me after I've told you I'm coming. (*Citizen sticks head out of window.*) You ought to be more trusting and take a man at his word.

HENCHMAN 1 (*solemnly*): We've come to ask you to identify the name of our king.

CITIZEN 1: What's the matter? Did he get lost somewhere?

HENCHMAN 2: Our king has instituted a poll to ascertain how many citizens are familiar with his name.

CITIZEN 1: That's a big question. There've been so many. They come and go pretty fast. That's politics.

HENCHMAN 3: We order you to name your king.

CITIZEN 1: You're talking to somebody who's much too busy tending his crops and animals to think about those things you've got on your mind.

HENCHMAN 1: In the name of our king, we order you to cooperate in this inquiry.

CITIZEN 1: Come now, you can see I don't remember kings. It's likely I never heard his name and anyway it's late at night.

HENCHMAN 1 (*to other Henchmen*): Do we clobber, knife, or incinerate?

CITIZEN 1 (*realizing what they have in mind*): What? (*He tries to draw back, but Henchman 3 reaches into window and seizes him by the neck.*)

HENCHMAN 2 (*to other Henchmen*): Clobbering's all he's worth.

(*Henchman 1 pulls bat out of sack and clobbers Citizen 1 on head. The three Henchmen quickly move to next house.*)

CITIZEN 1 (*groaning*): They expect a poor citizen to know so much these days. (*Disappears into house as Henchmen knock at second house.*)

CITIZEN 2 (*from inside, in a feisty tone*): Who's trying to wake me up at this outrageous hour? Better think twice before you tear me from my sleep. (*Appears at window.*) Who *are* you? Speak up!

HENCHMAN 1: We're on orders from the king to ask you to identify his name.

CITIZEN 2: You can tell him he has some gall putting a question like that in the middle of the night—or, for that matter, at any time at all.

HENCHMAN 2 (*haughtily*): We are asking you to identify the name of your king.

CITIZEN 2 (*laughing*): That's some question! With a king like that, who needs enemies?

HENCHMAN 2: Are you or are you not going to tell us the name of your king?

CITIZEN 2: If it's the name *Saul* you want to hear, I can also assure you that I—as well as ten thousand others—will breathe a sigh of relief when David replaces him.

HENCHMAN 3: You must tell us at the risk of your life which one of these reigns as king.

CITIZEN 2: And if I do not care to acknowledge him?

HENCHMAN 1: We don't want your opinions, only his name.

CITIZEN 2 (*pausing a moment, then speaking up loudly*): He's a tyrant, you're his henchmen, and I defy you in the name of honor, justice, and truth.

HENCHMAN 1 (*to other Henchmen*): Which do we use?

HENCHMAN 3: This is a chance for a colorful example.

CITIZEN 2: I defy you!

(*Henchman 1 pulls gun out of sack, points it at Citizen 2 and spouts a cloud of fire into his face. When cloud dissipates, his face has disappeared and henchmen have moved to the third house and knocked at the door.*)

CITIZEN 3 (*from inside, in an anxious voice*): Who's there? Is anything the matter? (*Appears at window, looks at Henchmen.*) Can I help you in any way?

HENCHMAN 1 (*quietly, coldly*): You are asked to identify the name of your king.

CITIZEN 3 (*hesitantly*): That's a complicated question which needs some thinking to answer adequately.

HENCHMAN 2: You are under orders to identify your king.

CITIZEN 3: If you check my record you'll see I've always kept myself clean no matter who's been in power.

HENCHMAN 3: Then who's the king?

CITIZEN 3: Isn't it enough for you if I swear loyalty to our king, no matter what his name is?

HENCHMAN 1: Your king demands an answer.

CITIZEN 3: There's been a king named . . . Saul . . . who did rather well, don't you agree? (*No sign from Henchmen, who don't budge.*) You don't agree? Yes, I know he's had his troubles, which meant they had to bring in that young fellow whose name is David and who shows every sign of being able to take over as king if Saul should ever step down for any reason . . . don't you agree? (*No sign from Henchmen.*) Actually, Saul hasn't done badly at all. If you discount what some people say and judge him on the quality of his fighting alone, you've got an example of leadership of the highest order, don't you agree? (*No sign from Henchmen.*) But then David's a pretty scrappy fighter himself, like nothing anybody's seen since ancient days . . . don't you agree? (*No sign from*

Henchmen, long pause, after which Citizen 3 suddenly speaks up in a desperate tone.) Saul's been a glorious king!

HENCHMAN 2: Is he or is he not your king?

CITIZEN 3 *(tearing at his hair)*: I'll name anyone you tell me to, just take me out of this agony.

HENCHMAN 3: Name him.

CITIZEN 3 *(frantic)*: All right, I'll take a chance on . . . *(Whispers name.)* . . . Saul.

HENCHMAN 1: You must commit yourself in full voice.

CITIZEN 3 *(pulls himself together, then blasts out)*: Saul! *(Pause, then quietly.)* Was I right? *(Members don't answer, but move offstage left, are heard knocking at another house offstage. Citizen 3 sticks his head out of window as far as he can, shouts after them.)* Thank you, thank you, thank you!

Transition: Offstage knocks on door continue, collide with the sound of the chorus humming to simulate wind—this punctured here and there by electronic musical sounds.

PROPHECY 1

A gate stands at right, on lower level, with Saul at opening knocking frantically to get in. A ramp connects upper and lower levels. Part way up is a sinkhole. As lights go on, the Witch of Endor is sitting with a huge pile of apples on upper level, paying no attention to Saul or his knocking. She munches apples throughout the scene, often having to speak between bites. Near her perch is a pedal, which, when she steps on it, lights up a bolt of lightning and sets off the sound of thunder a few moments later. Chorus remains behind the scene humming throughout to simulate eerie sounds of wind. Throughout the scene neither the Witch nor Samuel ever speaks directly to Saul or looks at him.

SAUL *(between knocks)*: So what's this great Witch of Endor for, if not to tell people what's in store for them?

WITCH: They're always wanting me to give them things I don't have to give, tell them things I don't know to tell.

SAUL *(between knocks)*: Did you hear what I said? I've come to know what's in store for me.

WITCH: Nobody's ever accused me of being overfriendly with them. I can't figure why they don't go elsewhere for their prophecies.

SAUL *(stops knocking, speaks more calmly than before)*: All right, I'm asking you pure and simple. Is it or is it not inevitable you're going to have me fall?

WITCH: They're always asking for magic formulas.

SAUL (*getting wrought up again, knocks some more*): Will you or will you not let me in?

WITCH: They're never willing to listen, they're only wanting to be soothed or coddled. I've always said, if you come here for reassurance I can tell you one thing from the start: forget it! (*Takes a big munch.*) Much good it does my saying anything, they have skulls as thick as fortresses.

SAUL (*starting to knock again*): Is that all you ever do—talk and eat? (*Pause, no reaction from her.*) Have you no consideration . . . ? (*He lets the question peter out as he thinks for a moment, then pulls himself together and speaks up more assertively.*) You are ugly beyond all imagining.

WITCH: They have *their* rituals and I have *mine.*

SAUL (*after pausing, pulling himself together once more and assuming a different tone from any of the previous ones*): You might as well know you have a desperate man in front of you.

WITCH: They'll demean themselves mercilessly to subject you to their whims.

(*She takes a big munch, then goes nonchalantly to the pedal. With Saul watching her every movement, she steps on pedal, lightning lights up, Chorus increases the volume of its humming, and thunder quickly follows. Suddenly Saul finds himself able to open the door, he cowers a moment, walks through sheepishly. After stepping on pedal, Witch has sat down, continued her munching.*)

SAUL (*after things have quieted down and finding that the Witch has continued to ignore him*): Are . . . are you ready to give me the news? (*No reply, after which he speaks up a bit more assertively.*) If you're not prepared to do the job yourself, you can at least call up some being who will give me the information I need.

WITCH: You'd think they'd be happy just to have you let them in.

SAUL: I won't mince words, since it's clear to me it does no good with you. I'm merely asking you to perform your traditional obligations, whether or not you're inwardly prepared to go through with them. (*She alternates her munches with yawns.*) I know these things can be difficult when everybody's demanding your services, but that's no excuse in itself to . . . . (*During his speech she has nonchalantly returned to pedal, pressed it and set off the same sights and sounds as before. Saul, taken aback, cowers. As the noise calms down one becomes aware of a whistling noise under the sinkhole.*)

WITCH (*projecting her voice toward the sinkhole*): Yes, I'm coming, but you've got to remember I'm not as young as I was the last time. (*She descends the ramp with some difficulty; precariously, though still munching, she lifts the lid from the sinkhole and gradually returns to her perch.*

Samuel, dressed in a long priestly robe, slowly comes up, stretching his limbs as though they had been confined for a long while in a small space.)

SAUL (*cowering, showing awe as he recognizes Samuel*): Samuel! Yes, I was hoping all along she'd call you up. You're the one I most wanted to see.

SAMUEL (*to Witch, paying no attention to Saul*): What does this one want?

SAUL: Take a look at who's waiting for you here. It's Saul, the one you chose.

(*Saul steps forward to try for Samuel's attention.*)

SAMUEL (*to Witch*): I said, what does this one want?

SAUL (*getting on his knees*): Samuel, I'm the one you crowned king.

WITCH (*to Saul*): They all want the same thing. They want us to tell them everything is going to be all right.

SAUL (*to Samuel*): I never meant it that way. I came here to see if there's any hope left, that's all. Tell her I didn't ask for special favors.

SAMUEL (*to Witch*): It was one of those mistakes made long ago and hard to correct after a point. When I selected him he was minding his father's sheep, sent out to look for the lost ones. That's all he was good for, and he wasn't even much at that.

SAUL (*to Samuel*): You were the one who chose me, Samuel. If you had such doubts you should have left well enough alone.

SAMUEL (*to Witch*): He had every opportunity to show himself the stern and upright leader we were looking for. He ruined his chances.

SAUL (*protesting vehemently*): It was something that came over me. I had no control over it.

SAMUEL (*to Witch*): We had an incredible amount invested in him.

WITCH (*laughing cynically*): You never know when they'll start to bungle.

SAUL (*to Samuel, this time in a compliant voice*): If I've disappointed you, Samuel, let me say I'm terribly sorry for whatever embarrassment I've caused you.

SAMUEL (*to Witch*): I devoted the better part of my life to building him up. I gave him what power he had. He bumbled.

SAUL (*to Samuel, this time in a quiet, cutting tone*): I know what you're doing, Samuel. It's the old gratitude racket. I can see through it.

WITCH: They'll stab you no matter what you say to them.

SAUL: It was *you* who chose me, Samuel. It's time *you* owned up to some of the blame.

WITCH (*to Samuel*): How much are we prepared to put up with?

SAUL (*defiantly, before Samuel can answer her*): I don't know about *you*, but I've had enough. I came here to find out what my prospects are, not to have my nose rubbed into the past. Do I make myself clear?

(*Witch and Samuel look at each other during this speech impatiently, give each other signals. Witch presses pedal again, with the same results as before. Saul cowers again.*)

SAMUEL (*pointing to the sinkhole*): Have him come up here.

SAUL (*moving toward sinkhole*): You're willing to talk to me then?

SAMUEL: Have him come up so we can show him something. He'll have to stoop down.

SAUL (*kneeling, looking up to Samuel for a signal, but getting none*): I've got to know what I'm supposed to do.

SAMUEL: I said for him to stoop down and look in there.

SAUL (*sticking head into sinkhole*): It's dark.

SAMUEL: He never had much courage.

SAUL: I'm in as far as I can go and I don't see anything down there.

SAMUEL (*to Witch*): We'll have to hold him. He can't bend down by himself.

(*Witch grabs his legs, with one hand still trying to manage munching an apple as she holds legs. Samuel holds his hands behind his back and together they let him descend until he's fully half in the sinkhole.*)

WITCH: We seem to be getting heavier ones every year. (*A strange sound from inside the sinkhole. It could be taken either as a sign of horror or jubilation.*) They lose all self-control the moment you stick them in there. (*Same sound from sinkhole, but louder and longer.*) They get to be a bore after this point. (*Another sound, this time one of unmistakable glee.*) When people ask if I like this job, I laugh them in the face.

(*New sound from before, this one calmer, more satisfied.*)

SAMUEL: We can fish him up now.

(*Both pull him up, quickly let go, Witch returns to her perch, Samuel moves to the side and Saul gradually reestablishes his equilibrium.*)

WITCH: It's at this point they get carried away with themselves.

SAUL (*still reestablishing equilibrium*): I've not quite caught my breath, but I should say right off this is a most happy surprise. (*He looks at them for signs of recognition, but they are as uncommunicative as before.*) I don't mind all the reluctance you've shown, since I can see you were simply preparing me for the surprise. (*Looks again for recognition, but gets none.*) All right, it's not necessary for you to show any emotion directly, I can do without that. It was enough for you to let me see what I saw down there. And even if the rules of your job keep you from acknowledging me, I want to use this opportunity to express my gratitude. You'll understand if the proper words fail me. I was a warrior after all, and still am, and from what you've shown me down there, I know that I'm only at the beginning of bigger things. Let me say simply I got your message, and I'm thankful. In short, you've made me feel whole again.

WITCH: They're at their most expressive at this point.

SAUL: Say what you want, old hag. I accept these things as part of the game, and I assure you it's been worth all the uncertainty and what I mistakenly took to be abuse. I accept them with gratitude.

WITCH: They get to be pretty good speechmakers.

SAUL: I've never had any illusions about the way I make speeches, but from what you showed me down there I haven't the least inhibition to speak out and say with confidence that once I have fully trounced my enemies, both within and without my realm, I shall lay the most meticulous plans for my succession and seek a retreat in which I may, to the best of my abilities, compose an epic history of my people. (*He nods to the Witch and to Samuel.*) Again I thank you with all my heart and only hope that you will find my bearing worthy of the future you have mapped out for me.

WITCH: They always manage to move you at this point.

SAUL (*starting to the gate, speaks more softly as though himself moved*): I leave you in peace.

(*Pause.*)

SAMUEL (*sternly*): Not so.

SAUL (*stopping suddenly*): Is there something I missed?

(*The Witch giggles.*)

SAMUEL (*more sternly than ever*): He took what *might* have been for what *will* be.

WITCH (*quietly*): It takes a while for the main point to get through to them.

SAUL (*thoroughly confused*): I don't understand.

SAMUEL (*impatiently*): What he saw was what *might* have been—what might have been if he hadn't botched things up.

(*Witch giggles louder.*)

SAUL (*still confused*): Then what of my future?

SAMUEL (*resolutely stepping back into sinkhole*): He *has* no future.

(*Samuel quickly disappears into hole. Witch laughs loudly, moves down ramp to put cover over sinkhole. Saul moves about the stage like a confused and frightened animal, at one point finds himself on ramp above the Witch as she is limping slowly and about to put cover over hole. He stares at her a moment, then a malicious look comes over his face, he pulls himself together, moves quietly up to her from behind, gives her a fast and sure kick that lands her inside the hole. He steps on her head to hold it down, quickly places lid on sinkhole. Muffled screams of outrage are heard from below. He moves up the ramp, gradually assuming a pose of heroic dignity, stands at the top a moment listening to screams as they become more distant and gradually disappear. He picks up an apple, gorges it down. As he eats, his eyes light on the pedal, which he approaches with*)

*trepidation, but then presses resolutely. All the elements of the storm come
on louder than ever before. He starts to cower a moment, then pulls himself together, walks resolutely out toward the open gate as the lights go
out.)*

*Transition: Chorus simulating wind, but sound suddenly broken by the
sound of the anvil that starts the next episode.*

BATTLE 2

*Two groups—Saul and his men on one side, and David and his men on
the other—with lights alternately pinpointing one and leaving the other in
darkness. Each shift of focus is preceded by the sounding of an anvil, at
which time all sound and light on one side are suddenly blotted out and
after which the light goes on gradually to reveal the other side. Anvil
sounds at opening of first tableau, which shows Saul and his men, who are
confined to left side of stage.*

SAUL (*addressing his men in a sarcastic tone*): And whom do you *think*
   we're fighting? The Philistines, those age-old enemies always vigilant for
   weaknesses in our ranks? Tell me, is it these Philistines we are fighting
   today?

SOLDIERS: No!

SAUL: Of course not. And *why* not? Was it your king who set off this
   bloody civil war which daily threatens the very existence of our state?

SOLDIERS: No!

SAUL: And who is this traitor who crept slyly into my confidence with the
   sole purpose of destroying us all?

SOLDIERS: David!

(*Anvil and darkness. Lights reveal David and his men on right.*)

DAVID (*addressing his men*): Don't despair, friends. Whatever they
   choose to call us, we are not the rebels, the curs, the ingrates they make
   us out to be. I shall not remind you again of the many attempts that
   tyrant-king, whom I no longer deign to call by name, has made upon
   my life, attempts I have always had the good fortune to elude. No, I
   don't need to remind you of these things, you know them well enough,
   but I want you to remember that ours is a defensive action, that we ask
   only the restoration of those rights that he whom I do not care to name
   has wrested from us with that capriciousness to which we have too
   long . . .

(*Anvil and darkness. Both sides light up to show Saul held back by his
men on left, David held back by his men on right.*)

SAUL (*shouting across stage at David*): You're so tricky your men have to
   sleep on their spears to keep you from filching them!

DAVID (*shouting across stage at Saul*): You're so dumb you pick up your sword by the blade!

SAUL (*almost getting out of his men's grip*): You're so mean you're willing to slit your father's throat open if you think it can help you grab the crown!

DAVID (*almost getting out of his men's grip*): You're so lazy you let the mildew grow on your rear till your men all run away from the stink!

SAUL (*shouting louder*): You're so slimy you'll crawl through . . .

(*Anvil and darkness. Lights go on to reveal Saul addressing his men at left, though standing in positions different from those of the first tableau.*)

SAUL (*in a subdued voice*): And if I told you this my fondest wish, for the fulfillment of which I am prepared to reward the bearers with gifts far beyond the ordinary, for who cannot guess this insatiable desire, to have him brought before me, this hypocrite who professed to heal me once . . .

(*Alarum sounds.*)

SAUL (*shouting after his men as they take off for battle*): Go get him, get him, get him . . .

(*Anvil and darkness. Lights go on to show David and his men crouching on right. Alarum sounds.*)

DAVID (*starting to move offstage to right with his men*): We won't panic, friends. No harm in an orderly retreat.

(*They begin to move off quickly and quietly, crouching so as not to be seen. Alarum sounds again. Soon after, Saul's men cross stage from left, follow David's men off to right. One of David's men has fallen screaming. Two of Saul's men notice body, stay behind.*)

SOLDIER 1: What I see . . .

SOLDIER 2: What two of us see at this point . . .

SOLDIER 1: Hopefully no more . . .

SOLDIER 2 (*looking around*): No more.

(*Both move toward body as though competing to claim it.*)

SOLDIER 1: First one to see it . . .

SOLDIER 2: Can't be proved . . .

SOLDIER 1 (*turning body's face around with his spear, speaks with disappointment*): Not the one he wants, no chance of that.

SOLDIER 2 (*trying body with his own spear*): Just another ordinary soldier.

(*Both move away from body to follow their men.*)

SOLDIER 1 (*suddenly conceiving an idea, returns to corpse, points toward body's face*): If nobody could recognize him . . .

SOLDIER 2 (*shocked*): Desecration!

SOLDIER 1 (*poking spear relentlessly into face*): A lot of trouble for the reward one gets.

SOLDIER 2 (*deliberating a moment, then poking his spear into other parts of the body*): Anything to make the king happy.

(*Both put spears into their holder. Each lifts a leg of the corpse and they drag it off left.*)

SOLDIER 1: Heavier than I'd ever have thought.

SOLDIER 2: Worth its weight in reward.

(*Anvil and darkness. Light goes on to reveal David and his men slowly, cautiously returning from offstage right. They crouch as David begins.*)

DAVID: Courage, friends, one setback doesn't mean a thing in itself—unless we choose to make it mean something. (*He signals them to get up, lifts his sword up, they lift their spears.*) There isn't a better place to go than back to where they chased us from. (*They follow him toward left.*) Move with caution. Slowness pays off.

(*Anvil and darkness. Light goes on to reveal Saul at left on a raised area with a ramp leading down toward right. Corpse lies on ramp, face down. Saul throws money bags at the two soldiers who had brought the corpse, they rush offstage left hugging bags. Once he is alone, Saul turns slowly toward corpse, moves in an almost ritualistic way, approaching it hesitantly. He tests his foot lightly against the torso, hesitates a moment, then gives it a sharp kick, stands back again, hesitates, returns, bends over and pounds the top of corpse's head frantically with his fists, during which time we— though not Saul—become aware of shouts from his soldiers at offstage left.*)

SOLDIERS (*individual voices from offstage*): They're attacking! Come back here! Leave it! Flee for your life!

(*Meanwhile we notice David and his men moving slowly in gradually increasing light on right half of stage. Saul remains oblivious to everything except corpse, steps back again while contemplating it, returns, this time steps on torso and stamps on it violently. Alarum sounds, Saul's soldiers' voices are heard again from offstage left, Saul remains oblivious, steps back, stares down at corpse a moment, gives it a violent kick that sends it down the ramp. As he watches it roll down, his eyes meet David, who, holding a sword, leads his troops up ramp. In a sudden moment of recognition he screams "No!", dashes offstage left as David and his men run in pursuit of him. Alarum sounds, followed immediately by anvil and darkness.*)

Transition: Anvil, followed immediately by Chorus speaking "Saul must fall" with gradually increasing volume.

PROPHECY 2

Chorus, wearing large black masks, form a semicircle at rear of stage. Throughout the scene they move together a few feet backward and forward and repeat the words Saul must fall *with varying emphases as indicated. Before lights go on we hear them start in an indiscernible whisper until gradually we understand the words. Saul and his Daughter are kneeling side by side facing audience at front of stage. The words they speak must not be appreciably louder than those of the Chorus and their conversational tone should contrast with the solemnity of the Chorus. During first part of scene each of the three words spoken by the Chorus is given equal emphasis.*

SAUL (*listening intently, speaking up as soon as words become easily discernible*): I knew it, I knew it.

DAUGHTER: It isn't true, don't listen, they're trying to break your will.

SAUL: How would anybody hope to withstand them? (*He makes a move to stand up, but she reaches out an arm to hold him back.*)

DAUGHTER: Don't move. You must hold your position at all costs.

SAUL: How can I hope to avoid them?

DAUGHTER: You can avoid anything if you're willing to set your mind to it. (*As she speaks, the word emphasis gradually changes so that the final word is stressed—Saul must* FALL.) You're just using this as an excuse to retreat from battle, to forget about all the things you should have been doing all along.

SAUL (*interrupting*): Listen! (*They pause a moment as they discern the change to* "Saul must FALL.") It's more dire than before.

DAUGHTER: Not in the least! The main thing I hear is *fall*. So—somebody's going to fall. That's all they care about. It doesn't necessarily have to be *you*.

SAUL: You're not listening. It's *my* name they're calling. Won't you even try to listen?

DAUGHTER: Of course I'm listening. They're saying "Saul must FALL." What they care about is an action of some sort. Next thing you know they'll say "Saul must REIGN," "Saul must CONQUER." You can't predict from moment to moment.

(*During her speech the chorus has gradually changed its emphasis to* "Saul MUST fall.")

SAUL: You're still not listening. This is even more forbidding now.

DAUGHTER: Nonsense, they're simply warning you to be resolute, take matters into your own hand, pull yourself together. Once you've accepted the idea that you *must* do something, anything's at your command. It's up to *you* to choose what comes after "must" and not let others choose for you.

(*During her speech the chorus has gradually changed emphasis to* "SAUL must fall.")

SAUL (*enraptured*): Listen to them. I can believe *them* in a way that I can never believe *you*.

(*He gets up and turns to chorus.*)

DAUGHTER (*getting up to hold him back*): You're letting them drug you
with their words!

SAUL (*eluding her grasp*): I refuse to deny my *fate!*

(*Daughter pulls him back violently by his robes, holds him back from
chorus during her following speech.*)

DAUGHTER: Nothing's fated in the least. They're simply calling your name,
which means you can take it in any direction you want—yes, *Saul* can
do whatever he sets about to, *Saul* can control his destiny, *Saul* can
refuse defeat, he can exterminate his enemies, rule the world, anything
he earnestly chooses to will.

(*As she speaks the emphasis has gradually changed back to what it was at
the start, with each word given equal stress—"SAUL MUST FALL."*)

SAUL (*noticing the change of emphasis, makes a sudden lunge out of her
grip and runs toward chorus*): *Take* me!

(*Chorus, still speaking the same words, envelop him in a circle and then
form a semicircle as before but in the meantime Saul has disappeared
behind them. They speak their words more quietly, until they speak in a
whisper, as at the beginning. Daughter stares at them helplessly.*)

DAUGHTER (*shouting as though trying to be heard by Saul after he has
disappeared and chorus has quieted down to a whisper*): Coward!

*Transition: "Saul must fall" decreases in volume until the words are
indiscernible; before the sounds have died out we hear a light, even
drum-beat until first speech of next scene starts.*

PROCLAMATION

*David pacing back and forth with light drum-beat in background. A scribe
sits at a table taking down what David dictates. Several messengers stand
in line next to the desk waiting to pick up the order that David is dictating.
Drum-beat ends as soon as David speaks.*

DAVID: They must each be isolated—no, start over again. Let Saul and
every member of his family be isolated each from the other . . . (*He
pauses.*)

SCRIBE (*about to hand paper to Messenger 1*): Is this ready for promul-
gation?

DAVID (*firmly*): I have not yet said promulgate.

SCRIBE: Yes, sir.

DAVID: . . . be isolated each from the other, and let their places of isolation
remain secret and isolated from the general public. (*Scribe looks up
waiting for more. David pauses, paces, then speaks up abruptly.*) This
may now be promulgated.

SCRIBE: Yes, sir.

(*Light drum-beat resumes until dictation starts again. Scribe hands order to Messenger 1, who rushes out with it.*)

DAVID (*starting to dictate again*): We shall consider them not as enemies, only as . . . (*he pauses a moment*) . . . only as potential threats to the orderly reestablishment of . . . (*pauses*) . . . of, cancel the last three words, (*dictates again*) . . . threats to the proper reestablishment of order. This proclamation may be promulgated. (*Light drum-beat until dictation starts again. Scribe hands sheet to Messenger 2, who rushes out.*) We propose to treat them humanely, cancel the last word, (*pauses a moment*) . . . to treat them with the maximum of humanity allowable according to the purposes we have set forth. This may now be promulgated. (*Light drum-beat until David starts speaking again. While David paces, Scribe hands sheet to Messenger 3, who rushes out with it. David suddenly stops pacing, resolutely faces scribe and the remaining messengers.*) We have finished with all proclamations and promulgations for the day. (*Blackout.*)

Transition: Light drum-beat for a moment after blackout, then a long silence until lights of next scene slowly go on.

EXECRATION

Lights go on slowly revealing Saul's Daughter surrounded by an oval-shaped barrier large enough to give her some room to pace. Two Mutes remain outside the barrier throughout the scene. Their function is to respond with various gestures to the Daughter's pronouncements. Although the Mutes often glance at her, she remains conspicuously oblivious to their presence. As lights go on, the Daughter stands at right extreme of oval staring upward, walks toward the center of oval, stops, fixes her eyes at one spot on high as she begins to speak. During this period, the Mutes have looked mournfully at her, gradually take on a more hopeful look as she moves to center. A scenario for the Mutes is indicated in the column to the right of her speech.

Scenario for Mutes

DAUGHTER: Powers that be, hear me as I vent my rage. I do not ask you to free me from this miserable compound they've penned me into. Nor do I ask you to respond with pity or commiseration. Any response which would in any way soften the fury I feel inside seems intolable. If you care to thunder back at me, or swallow me into some gaping hole, I assure

Mutes look at her solemnly, arms spread out; they take brief glances at each other to confirm the awe they feel, move back in fear from thunder, fall down as though into a hole, you I won't object. This would simply fan my rage, and, in all frankness, I can think of nothing more comforting. *(She paces impatiently a moment, then speaks up.)* But I wouldn't want you to think I'm standing here waiting to hear from you. My only real concern is holding on to my rage, and if you have no stimulant to offer me, I can easily look elsewhere. *(She pauses a moment, then speaks up quietly but firmly.)* At my father, for instance. Not that I can see him anywhere nearby *(she looks around)*, nor would I want to. Who'd want to face a parent when he's reached the depths that this one has? But I haven't the slightest hesitation about speaking from this distance they've imposed between us, for I know there's no better way to keep my rage up. Yes, I'm addressing myself to you, father, wherever it is they've put you. *(Pause as she looks out to far left, points her finger menacingly.)* Now who do you think's to blame for the fact I'm penned up in here just as though I were an animal? Who was it, father, missed every chance that ever came his way to build up the dynasty he was supposedly destined for? Great House of Saul! A hovel you've made of it with the stupidity and incompetence that come so naturally to you. And don't think I wasn't aware of this all along. You thought I was there to comfort you in your distress, buck up your courage, overwhelm you with filial adoration. But that wasn't the case, I can assure you. I knew all along what I could expect of you—namely nothing. I naturally did what I could to slow down the damage you were systematically inflicting on us. Why shouldn't I want to save my own skin? That's my right, even if you were fool enough not to want to save your own, let alone mine. But then what's the good of raging this way at anybody as foolish as you? It's hardly worth the effort. You're so low in my eyes you can't possibly help me keep my

get up, blow with their mouths as though to fan her rage, lean upon one another, look indifferent,

look in different directions, search for him, then suddenly give up search at words "nor would I want to," point to ground to indicate his lowliness. Mute I gets ready to play Saul to Mute II's Daughter. I stays to left of II.

II points accusingly at I, who nods helplessly in assent to the accusations.

I begins to weep, watches as II gets on all fours. I looks mournfully around him, II gets up, points accusing finger at I several times, each time causing I to start weeping anew.

II strokes I lovingly,

suddenly pushes him away. I falls prostrate, II gives him contemptuous looks while mimicking Daughter's gestures for several lines.

anger up much longer. *(Pause, then she speaks up almost tenderly.)* There was a time when you loomed quite large to me. That was long ago when you would still come home with victories and I, not caring in the least if I acted the proper little girl they expected me to be, would wait for you at the city gate and tease you into tossing me in the air as you strutted in triumphantly with your troops of conquering men. Those were fine days, so fine the very thought of what's become of you sends loathing through my veins, loathing mixed with scorn. *(Pause, then quietly with an acid tone.)* You have fallen so low in my esteem I do not deem you worthy of my rage. *(Pause, as she moves nervously, indecisively, stares at barrier from several angles, strokes her hand along it, clutches it, strains against it.)* There's nothing like an immovable force to bring one's anger back. *(She beats her fists against it, speaks to it directly.)* At least you're made of real iron. You have no pretenses. *(She beats her body against it until she is out of breath, then speaks up quietly.)* But where do I move from here? I can try this place *(moves to another part)* or this one *(moves to still another part)*, but they're all the same and nowhere anything new to nourish my anger. *(She taps her knuckles lightly against the barrier.)* You're lifeless, dull, indifferent, not in the least worthy of the slightest exertion on my part. You've allowed me to deflect my rage from its real source, but don't think I'm not aware who's to blame for why I'm here. *(She moves to right end of oval, points offstage menacingly.)* I'm quite prepared to take you on, David, whether or not you choose to hear me. In fact, I wouldn't be in the least surprised if you had someone out there monitoring every move or sound I made. That would be thoroughly in keeping with all I know of you, and believe me I had ample opportunity to observe your ways. Not that we were ever enemies, at

II kicks I, moves away from him, assumes a tender look, looks offstage left.

I gets up, goes off left, reenters marching, picks II up, throws II in the air.

They hug each other, then I suddenly collapses on floor, grovels while II points accusingly.

I gets up, plays role of barrier while II mimics Daughter's gestures as she attacks barrier. I remains stiff, unbending to II's attacks.

I collapses, then gets up, moves to offstage right while II continues to mimic Daughter.

I reenters from right, now plays David. I stays distant from II, who acts as though he cannot see him.

I puts hand to ear as though listening from afar, then pretends to write down what he hears. I and II move toward each other, begin to cast least not overtly. In fact, we were inextricably tied to one another as allies, collaborating as best we could, each in our own interest, to prop up my father's tottering throne. But don't think I wasn't sure for even a moment what this strange alliance amounted to. I knew from the start what your real intentions were, and though you loved to flatter me for my co-operativeness, you can be sure all the while I kept my mistrust of you well concealed in full anticipation that once you had the chance, this (*she points around the oval*) is how you'd ultimately dispose of me. It's your style to make people delay the rage they feel toward you, to keep them charmed so they'll wait to let it out once you no longer have to face them. But I suspect you miscalculated a bit when you thought my rage would go unheard. Let whoever is listening in for you assure you that my rage toward you has barely begun, that once it reaches full force it will send such storms out over the sea, such quakes to test the earth's thin crust that you will have a multi-tude of woes to contend with in that new and untried regime of yours. And you needn't think yourself safe from me just because there were times I muttered a good feeling or two into your ear. Remember, what brought us together was the fact we each had a political aim of our own, and I want you to know that whatever crass intentions you nurtured toward me were returned in kind, even if neither of us dared let the other know what daggers we mentally plunged into one another. If I pros-trated myself before you after your fight with the giant, I did so knowing I had to feed your self-esteem to seal our alliance. And if I let you pin me to the floor and whisper the usual blandishments, don't think I had anything outside my own interests in mind. I never meant any of those supposedly loving things I sometimes said to you in return (*she clutches up*) and if there was a moment or two I fooled

friendly glances, then walk chumlike arm in arm. Both strain to hold up a mock-throne which gradually col-lapses. II looks suspiciously at

I, who smiles back flatteringly, they walk arm in arm, II casts suspicious glances at I, antici-pates a rebuff from I, who still looks flatteringly at II as he suddenly pushes him away. II collapses, I hides, II gets up, looks angrily at I, puts hands at each side of mouth as though shouting angrily.

I returns, puts hand to ear, listens smugly, indifferently to II's anger. At word "storms" I shows fear, at word "quakes" I's body jolts. I looks fright-ened as II continues shouting.

I returns to II, who mutters tenderly in his ear, then each independently pulls out a mock-dagger, and II prostrates himself before I, who looks proudly victorious.

I pins II to floor, whispers in II's ear.

II strokes I's head in a mechan-ical way which gradually becomes tender. II becomes myself into thinking I did, when everything inside me told me I should have known better, yes for a moment I let myself dream . . . that things could always be good between us *(during the last few words she has tried visibly to hold herself together, now breaks into tears, at first seemingly uncontrollable, after which the sobs become sporadic and suddenly stop as she comes to a realization).* My rage is flagging. If I'd had my wits about me, I should never have let this happen. *(She pulls herself together, points to right, raises her voice.)* I have nothing more to say to you, David *(she points left)*, nor to you, father. You are neither of you, believe me, proper objects of my rage. *(She moves to the front center of the oval and looks directly at the audience.)* It is myself I blame, myself I rage against! *(She beats her breasts with her fists, then extends her arms to the audience as though awaiting its approval.)* See, there's no place for self-pity when one's anger's at a peak. *(She gyrates back and forth with her body, virtually dancing, then extends her arms again to the audience, speaks quietly, though with a nervousness that shows signs of her imminent collapse.)* There's no more need for me to shout my rage now that I'm inwardly aglow. I ask only for a quiet sign of your approval—no clapping, please—only a silent show of admiration to keep this fire within me fanned. *(She points briefly at her breasts with both hands, then extends her arms again.)* When have any of you witnessed such power? *(She nods her head toward audience acknowledging what she takes to be their approval.)* Where have you seen such motions of the spirit? *(She nods her head again, but is fast losing the confidence she had displayed during the preceding lines.)* No? *(She tries to pull herself together again.)* Who would begrudge me this . . . this triumph? *(She starts to extend her arms to the audience, shows signs of strain, lets her arms fall, speaks up

hesitant, vacillates between tenderness and fear, tries to push I away, is unable to. When Daughter breaks down, both Mutes jump up, step out of their preceding roles, look at Daughter compassionately, wipe tears from their own eyes.

They act worn out, pant, try to pull themselves together. They look right, point disdainfully, look left, point disdainfully. They point disdainfully in both directions. They move to front of oval, between Daughter and audience, get on their knees, look worshippingly at her. They maintain worshipping pose for the rest of the scene, nod approvingly at the end of each of her sentences.

Mutes continue to nod approvingly even when Daughter asks, "No?"

weakly.) No? . . . No? (*She makes a final attempt to pull herself together, raises her arms in a gesture we have not seen before, looks directly at audience, slowly speaks up in a firm, loud voice.*) A fiery curse on each and every one of you! (*She gasps as soon as she has pronounced the words, begins to totter, tries to hold on to barrier as she falls, but in vain. She plops to the floor, remains motionless.*)	Mutes look alarmed, glance at each other. Mutes, still on knees, gesture at each other in fear, watch in horror as she falls.

Transition: When Daughter has collapsed, Mutes jump up, nuzzle up to the barrier, stare curiously at her for a moment, then come to front of stage, look back at her, and clap loudly—the first sounds that have come from them. During this period lights have slowly dimmed. Mutes remain clapping during darkness, are still clapping as lights slowly go up on next scene showing Saul on his bed. Mutes quickly realize they don't belong here, one nudges the other and they both quickly dash offstage before the scene opens.

ENDINGS

Saul on a large bed in center, several feet behind him a large easel on which a series of drawings will be displayed one after another in the course of the scene. Drawings to be changed by rope from above so that no other character is physically present during the scene. Each drawing has a particular number that Saul will call out at various intervals to effect a change. The drawings show Saul in the following situations:
> *no. 1: wearing a toga and taking a characteristically stoic pose;*
> *no. 2: wearing rags and in a contorted catatonic pose;*
> *no. 3: dressed for battle and holding his sword triumphantly;*
> *no. 4: same outfit but lying on the ground with an unidentifiable figure holding a triumphant sword over him;*
> *no. 5: wearing a black gown and looking earnestly upward.*
No drawing is on easel as Saul begins.

SAUL: I have considered how my death . . . No! I must consider how . . . No! I have considered how my *life*, through no fault of my own . . . No! I have considered how my life, through inherent flaws, compounded as they are by these my most outrageous and willful actions . . . No! (*He pauses longer than before, then starts as at beginning.*) I have considered how my death . . . . (*Raises voice to call number out.*) Number one! (*Saul turns around to watch drawing fall into place on the easel, stares at it a moment, then turns around with back to easel.*) Yes, I can withstand them all, be they buffets or insults or simply those daily irritations that, small in themselves, pile up until they turn into an intolerable burden. I have withstood them all, eyes and ears closed to everything that would dare to threaten my imperturbability. Steeled as I am, tempered beyond a point where even the strongest bend, I face my end as though I were another, impassible, immovable, regardless whether I have brought this end upon myself . . . (*Voice starts to break*) . . . yes, regardless of what is boiling inside me, eating away at my defenses . . . (*Voice weakens, he speaks up quietly*) . . . till there is nothing left to say. (*He speaks up loudly again.*) Number two! (*He turns around to watch the catatonic drawing appear, shudders, quickly turns away, speaks up quietly.*) Won't speak . . . won't move . . . won't even contemplate. Couldn't possibly even be aware what brought this on. (*Raises voice.*) I want number three! (*Turns around, watches himself with sword triumphant throughout his commentary, engages in gestures to simulate the action.*) Down with them, knock their heads open, cut them into shreds! (*Lowers voice.*) It's better at least than talking alone to myself. (*Raises voice.*) Slit them, yes, slit, kill, mangle, disembowel! (*Lowers voice, looks around bed.*) But what good's anger with nobody left to anger against? (*Resignedly, almost with dread.*) Number four! (*He does not look back at this drawing, which depicts him under a sword, but lets himself fall flat on his back, retaining this position for most of the following speech. He speaks softly at first and with an obviously willed patience.*) I must ask you to hold back a moment before you finish me off. There are certain matters we might as well get straight. For one thing, I don't want you to think I'm taking it out on you personally. You needn't even tell me who you are. That hardly matters. And if you're somebody who once swore eternal loyalty to me, that hardly matters either. There are no bonds, I've discovered. I'm even willing to call what you're doing a loyalty of sorts, for you're here to help me finish something that two can do better than one. And I'll be just as loyal to you in return. Yes, I'm here to be fully cooperative, to make it as easy for you as possible, since I recognize you're just a functionary, one who's here to do his job without passion, conviction, or even predilection. So you see, I understand you and I offer you whatever help you need. You mustn't fear I'll resent you, quite the contrary, I'm grateful for your services. And I consider myself fortunate you're willing to help me get through this quietly, without any fuss. We're in this together, tied firmly to one another. There are some bonds after all. We're both of us functionaries, thrown into roles that have nothing to do with what we really are. It hardly matters to them what goes on inside you or me. As far as they're concerned, I belong to the category "fallen king," and fallen kings are objects that have to be disposed of somehow. It's not enough to close me off from the world in this little room, for the category I belong to remains a source of fear to those who have taken away my power. I inhibit them, keep them nervous about whether they really have the power they think they have. All this by lying still on this bed. I'm coming to think I exercise more power from here than I ever managed to from my throne. Strange predicament, they think they have me at knife point, but all the while I keep them from wielding what they think is rightly theirs. They've come to fear me, it took them a while, but they've finally learned. They blamed me for one crime after another, but that was simply out of fear; they knew better than anyone it was their own crimes they blamed me for. (*During preceding few lines he has gradually raised both his head and his voice and continues to do so until end of speech.*) Yes, I know you all for what you are, and you're their henchman and a lowly one at that! I deny you all, I break whatever bonds you thought you may have had with me. Better keep back from me, stand back, I'm the one who's calling the stops these days, and I'm the one who'll have to grant permission if and how and when you complete the task you're here for. It's my fall, not yours. So I say out with you, out, before I lose patience and swat you one myself. Number five! (*He turns resolutely to watch the shift to the drawing of himself in the black robe, stares at it a long while before he turns forward and starts to speak.*) No, I've not known such freedom as I know now—I have accepted myself and have accepted all those I was once surrounded with, friends and enemies alike. I have accepted my crimes, the big ones and the petty foolish ones. I claim all responsibility, for that is my choice, and I am free. (*During his last few words he has shown signs of stuttering. He stops, turns to look at the drawing, quickly turns away, starts in a less pompous tone.*) What good is this outrageous freedom except to glorify one's end all the time that you know you're left with nothing to say and nothing to feel and nothing to be? (*He laughs.*) Except for the change of costume, I didn't find this one all that different from number one. (*As soon as he pronounces* Number One, *the first drawing comes down. Saul shouts when he notices it.*) No, I don't want that one at all. Off with it. Give me number three. (*Number three starts down, but Saul quickly shouts again.*) Off with it, off with them all! (*Drawing remains suspended a moment, Saul picks up a pillow from the bed, throws it at drawing, which quickly disappears. He throws other pillows at the easel, which he knocks down. He turns to the spot on the bed where the pillows had been, looks for the sword that the pillows had covered, quietly and with dignity removes it from scabbard as he speaks.*) That's right, no words, no gesticulations, no attitudes, no illusions. Let's face it, Saul, you're about to die and none of those notions you've stuffed your head with is going to alter that fact except maybe delay it a few minutes. (*Looks around himself briefly.*) Now, if a big rock would come this way and knock me down with one fell blow as it did that giant once. (*Stops himself, resumes more quietly.*) But let's not quibble over method. (*Looks around, as though seeking a new distraction.*) Don't think, sulk, talk—just do it. (*He injects sword into his heart precisely at the word* do, *at which time the lights go out and we hear the Dead March from Handel's* Saul *played on a hand organ.*)

Transition: Dead March from distance, gradually becoming closer as the lights go on.

MARCH 2

Music that had started at end of preceding scene comes closer. Chorus enter slowly from right. Staging should stress parallels to the opening scene. Saul's coffin enters carried by two attendants.

DAVID (*offstage*): Mourn him!

CHORUS: Mourn him!

(*David enters on same platform that had carried Saul in first scene. He wears crown, looks solemn and alert.*)

DAVID: Mourn Saul!

CHORUS: Mourn Saul!

DAVID: Mourn our dead king!

CHORUS: Mourn our dead king!

DAVID (*as coffin passes center of stage*): Stop a moment so we may give voice to our sadness.

(*Procession, including music, comes to a halt.*)

CHORUS MEMBER 1: He lived his life and now he's gone.

CHORUS MEMBER 2: He outlasted his best days.

CHORUS MEMBER 3: It's a relief he's finally dead.

DAVID (*sternly*): Mourn him!

CHORUS (*lackadaisically and without conviction*): Mourn him!

DAVID (*patiently*): We'll start again. (*He points to organist, who starts playing. Attendants start to raise coffin. Carriers lift up David's platform. David speaks up solemnly.*) Mourn him!

CHORUS (*again lackadaisically*): Mourn him!

CHORUS MEMBER 2: I can't.

OTHER VOICES (*at the same time*): I can't. Why should I? Who says to? Who's telling us what we're supposed to feel?

(*David signals organist to stop, carriers set down his platform, attendants set down coffin. Disgruntled whispers continue among chorus.*)

DAVID (*trying to speak over these whispers*): As your new king I ask you to accord him the respects we routinely pay our dead, whether they be royalty or commoners. He was human after all. His weaknesses were those he shared with all the race . . .

CHORUS MEMBER 3 (*interrupting, in a sneering voice*): He was a lousy king.

DAVID (*signaling organist to start*): Every human being has a right to flaws.

CHORUS MEMBER 4: Not when he treats you like animals. (*He knocks down organist to get him to stop, after which other voices quickly join in.*)

CHORUS MEMBER 1: Remove his name from the royal genealogy.

OTHER VOICES (*at the same time*): We've had enough! You're a hypocrite, David! He was a bastard and you know it!

DAVID (*quickly jumping off his platform to try to restore order*): Silence. I must ask that we all show the minimal reverence that's due the dead, be they heroes or criminals. (*Starts back to platform, signals organist to start.*) Mourn him!

CHORUS MEMBER 2 (*before David has got on platform or chorus can reply*): You're king now. What have *you* got to lose?

DAVID (*looking chorus member in eye*): You're my subject now and *you've* got a lot to lose.

INDIVIDUAL VOICES (*as several chorus members try to surround David*): Tyrant! Tyrant! Down with all kings! (*Other chorus members have surrounded coffin, one kicking at it wildly, another stomping on it, another starting to urinate on it. Those surrounding David find their attention drawn to the action around the coffin, and one moves toward coffin to pound it with his fists. Meanwhile David lithely jumps away from those surrounding him onto higher ground behind. He has quietly pulled a large whip out of his robe, and he cracks it loudly in an open space. Chorus, stunned, quiets down, David does not move. Only sound is from the urinating chorus member, who continues what he started. David cracks whip again.*)

URINATING CHORUS MEMBER (*quietly*): Can't stop once I've started.

(*Chorus Member next to him pushes him aside, forces him to finish urinating on ground. A murmur or two is heard from chorus as David slowly returns to platform.*)

DAVID (*starting to speak as he returns to platform*): It's time we cooled things down a bit, otherwise we'll start saying things we never even wanted to say in the first place. Maybe I should begin by getting rid of this thing. (*He throws whip out over heads of crowd so that it falls at stage front.*) I hate that noise as much as any of you do, but I think we need a moment to talk things over and get a few matters between us straight. (*Steps down from platform, moves closer to crowd.*) I don't much like talking from up there. It tempts a fellow to get tricky in the way he uses words on people. Just because some of you may be taken in by those who twist words around doesn't mean I'm going to practice those arts on you. It brings out the worst in people, not just in you but in me. I won't have it. If I wanted to talk that way I could tell you I feel overwhelmed by the burden that's been thrust on me, but frankly I don't feel overwhelmed at all and I even welcome the burden with a certain relish. (*Pauses a moment as though listening for murmurs from the crowd.*) I could also tell you I hope you'll find me worthy of your trust, and in a sense I actually do, but to tell it to you that way would be playing with your feelings, and that's not my style at all.

CHORUS MEMBER 3 (*interrupting*): Hypocrite!

DAVID (*continuing, as though not hearing interruption*): So, you can see . . .

CHORUS MEMBER 3 (*louder this time*): Hypocrite!

DAVID (*to person interrupting him*): I heard you the first time, sir, but I chose to ignore it. (*He turns to crowd again.*) Now. I won't insult you by trying to flatter you, and I won't try to run down your ex-king— though that would be easy enough—just to build myself up in your eyes. And I also won't hide the fact that I like being your new king. Everybody, in some corner of his self, has the idea of being king some place, somehow, some time, and by the same token everybody's going to be just a little jealous of the person who's managed to make it. This is something we might as well all accept as natural and not waste our time stewing about . . .

CHORUS MEMBER 4 (*interrupting*): Hey, David, what do you need a whip for?

DAVID (*pointing to front of stage and addressing questioner*): That whip's out there now and you're free to do what you want with it. (*He turns to crowd again.*) I won't pretend that things are going to be equal between us. When a battle needs fighting, I'll do it in my own good time, as I did with that giant once, and you can decide for yourselves if it pleases you. I am quite aware that I got to this place by a default of sorts . . .

CHORUS MEMBER 3: Then go back where you came from, David.

(*While Chorus Member 3 speaks, those around him pounce on him and beat him down; those further away shout phrases at him such as "Quiet" "Let David speak" "You go back."*)

DAVID (*to person beating heckler down*): Let's not be too hard on him. He really should have given me a chance to finish my sentence, since I was going to say that even if I got to this place by default, I haven't the slightest intention of letting anyone hamstring my actions on that account. And you can also be sure I know that the power I wield over you, no matter how efficiently I am able to enforce it, is ultimately subject to your will, and I fully intend to keep a keen eye on how well you put up with the things I do. You see, (*He points to the coffin.*) I don't care to fall the way that fellow in the wooden box did. There will be no grand confrontations between us, depend on that, no histrionics, no mysteries, none of that stuff great dramas are made of. Now, nobody's going to ask you what you're actually thinking inside, whether about Saul or about me, but we're going to have to get this ritual we started over and done with so that ordinary things can go on once more in their ordinary way. All right, we'll start again.

(*He signals organist, coffin-bearers, steps onto platform, signals carriers, speaks up more quietly than at opening, procession starts to march off left.*)

DAVID: Mourn him!

CHORUS (*compliantly*): Mourn him!

DAVID: Mourn Saul!

CHORUS: Mourn Saul!

DAVID: Mourn our dead king!

CHORUS (*by this time mostly off the stage*): Mourn our dead king!

(*Music is still heard in distance as lights go out on empty stage.*)

Transition: After a moment of darkness, lights quickly go on to reveal Saul's Daughter alone on the stage.

EPILOGUE

Spoken by Saul's Daughter:

> My rage is gone and all my passion's spent,
> I've reconciled myself to dull assent.
> David's assumed his long and crafty reign,
> Placidity's become the rule again.
> Saul's but a memory—though one that I
> Have not the faintest wish to glorify.
> Now that we've reached a state where all agree,
> What is there here to do for likes of me?
> (Force me to share your good, fine, common sense,
> I'll pay you back with cold indifference!)

(*During the succeeding lines the various musical instruments and noises that had been employed in the various episodes come in one by one, and in order of increasing loudness: first the violin and clarinet squibbles ["Conspiracy" and "Prayer"], then the chorus of winds ["Prophecy 1"], the harp ["Intermezzo"], the handorgan ["March 2"], the drum-beat ["Proclamation"], the gavel ["Council"], the anvil ["Battle 2"], the fanfares ["March 1"], until, all finally joined together, they come close to drowning out the Daughter's voice.*)

Oh for a life that gives me room to stage
My energies, my ecstasies and rage,
To plead, to flatter, mortify, berate,
To pluck your nerves, in short, manipulate!
Where can I find that shrill and seething place
Which leaves my soul sufficient breathing space?
Play on, discordances with conflict rife,
Your stridency has brought me back to life!
(*By the last line or two, Daughter has had to shout.*)
Enough's enough, now stop!
(*She raises her hands and the noise suddenly stops.*)
We've had our fun
And may as well admit our play is done.
We haven't aimed primarily to please,
To titillate, or terrify, or tease,
To move, disturb, vituperate, confuse,
To ridicule, to teach, or to amuse—
But all of these at once together stirred,
Like that cacophony which you just heard,
And styles from many times and places culled—
What unity you seek you'll find annulled.
Go home then, be ye satisfied or not,
And don't delude yourselves our tortuous plot
Can comfort with enough aesthetic balm
To lull you into post-cathartic calm.
Oh may sweet chaos dominate the day
To crown your memory of this our play!

BACKGROUND
MATERIALS

PART ONE

Paralipomena to
Saul's Fall

BIOGRAPHICAL NOTE

The author describes himself as the product of one of those international marriages that should have given him the best of two fine old worlds, but unfortunately left him with little more than an indiscriminate scattering of impressions. Given his lack of any clearcut identity, he does not feel prepared to go into those personal facts that readers customarily demand.

Note: In reply to H-G's biographical note

This is what I call a tease, Orlando—a few hints of something that might be interesting (though, I suspect, not very lurid) and then you leave us hanging. . . . Also, I've always been suspicious of people who complain of having little or no identity—they may well have so much of it they don't know how in God's name to handle all the excess. Finally, it's some chutz-pah, Orlando, to say you're withholding what "readers customarily demand" when you know good and well you have no readers except those I have found for you.

ENVOI

1. *To a prospective reader:*

I could start with some conventional greeting, but that might put you on your guard against possible designs I may have on you, and that's surely not the way I'd want our relationship to get started. Like it or not, you and I will need to establish a relationship of some sort, else you'll never get through my play, and all my efforts will have been in vain. You can see I'm being quite frank with you. I recognized from the beginning that I needed you, but I put off worrying about how you'd accept my work until I was done. If I'd been too concerned about our relationship, I can assure you I'd never have finished, perhaps not got beyond the first sketches. This is not to say I did not take you into consideration while I was writing. I most certainly did, for I was always quite aware what sort of response I wanted from you in any particular spot. As the play took shape, in fact, I realized that the responses I was asking of you from moment to moment were gathering their own momentum and creating what, hopefully, would absorb your heart and your mind for the hour or two of your engagement with me —perhaps even afterwards. There were times, as I wrote, that I even responded to what I was writing as though I were you and, for a short and, I admit, rather enjoyable space, found myself quite oblivious of the author's presence. There weren't many such times, but when they happened your enjoyment and general approbation did more than anything I myself could have done to keep me writing. So you see we did manage to set up a successful relationship well before you could have known of me or my play's existence.

2. *To a prospective member of the audience:*

I could start with some conventional greeting, but that might put you on your guard against possible designs I may have on you, and that's surely not the way I'd want our relationship to get started. Like it or not, you and I will need to establish a relationship of some sort, else you'll never be able to sit through my play, and all my efforts will have been in vain. You can see I'm being quite frank with you. I recognized from the beginning that I needed you, but I put off worrying about how you'd accept my work until I was done. If I'd been too concerned about our relationship, I can assure you I'd never have finished, perhaps not got beyond the first sketches. This is not to say I did not take you into consideration while I was writing. I most certainly did, for I was always quite aware what sort of response I wanted from you in any particular spot. As the play took shape, in fact, I realized that the responses I was asking of you from moment to moment were gathering their own momentum and creating what, hopefully, would absorb your heart and your mind for the two to three hours of your engagement with me—perhaps even afterwards. There were times, as I wrote, that I even responded to what I was writing as though I were you and, for a short and, I admit, rather enjoyable space, found myself quite oblivious of the author's presence. There weren't many such times, but when they happened your enjoyment and general approbation did more than anything I myself could have done to keep me writing. So you see we did manage to set up a successful relationship well before you could have known of me or my play's existence.

. To a prospective publisher:

could start with some conven-
onal greeting, but that might put
ou on your guard against what-
ver requests I shall make to you,
nd that's surely not the way I'd
ant our relationship to get
arted. Like it or not, you and I
ill need to establish a relation-
iip of some sort, else you'll never
ven read through my play, and all
iy efforts will have been in vain.
ou can see I'm being quite frank
ith you. I recognized from the
eginning that I needed you, but I
it off worrying about how you'd
ccept my work until I was done.
f I'd been too concerned about
ur relationship, I can assure you
d never have finished, perhaps
ot got beyond the first sketches.

4. To a prospective producer:

*I could start with some conven-
tional greeting, but that might put
you on your guard against whatever requests I shall make to you,
and that's surely not the way I'd
want our relationship to get
started. Like it or not, you and I
will need to establish a relationship of some sort, else you'll never
even read through my play, and
all my efforts will have been in
vain. You can see I'm being quite
frank with you. I recognized from
the beginning that I needed you,
but I put off worrying about how
you'd accept my work until I was
done. If I'd been too concerned
about our relationship, I can
assure you I'd never have finished,
perhaps not got beyond the first
sketches.*

5. To a prospective critic:

I could start with some conventional greeting, but that might put
you on your guard against possible
designs I may have on you, and
that's surely not the way I'd want
our relationship to get started.
Like it or not, you and I will need
to establish a relationship of some
sort, else you'll never finish sitting
through my play, and all my
efforts will have been in vain. You
can see I'm being quite frank with
you. I recognized from the beginning that I needed you, but I put
off worrying about how you'd
accept my work until I was done.
If I'd been too concerned about
our relationship, I can assure you
I'd never have finished, perhaps
not got beyond the first sketches.
This is not to say I did not take
you into consideration while I was
writing. I most certainly did, for I
was always quite aware what sort
of response I wanted from you in
any particular spot. As the play
took shape, in fact, I realized that
the responses I was asking of you
from moment to moment were
gathering their own momentum
and creating what, hopefully,
would excite your admiration for
the two to three hours of your
engagement with me—perhaps
even afterwards. There were
times, as I wrote, that I even
responded to what I was writing
as though I were you and, for a
short and, I admit, rather enjoyable space, found myself quite
oblivious of the author's presence.
There weren't many such times,
but when they happened your
enjoyment and general approbation did more than anything I
myself could have done to keep
me writing. So you see we did
manage to set up a successful
relationship well before you could
have known of me or my play's
existence.

1. *To a prospective reader:*

But now that I'm done writing, the time has come for me to change the relationship from the reader I worked up in my imagination to the real person on whom I must depend to give my play the attention and respect it needs to be adequately experienced. (Your affection, let us hope, will come later; in fact, if I can start merely with your attention, I'll also be willing to put off with your respect until you're convinced it's been properly earned.) It takes patience on both sides to get this relationship going, and I recognize it's up to me to make most of the adjustments, for we both know, even without having to say it, that I need you more than you need me. I might remind you that this is not the way things always were. There was a time when setting things up was easier than it is now. The world was small then, and once the writer was finished he had merely to say, "Go, litttle book," and he could then go on to write something else in full confidence that the fortunes of his book were in the secure hands of the patron who had cast his favor upon him before he had even started writing. And once you knew that somebody had placed his money and his pride on you, you felt he was committed to you and you didn't have to fret about any prospective reader except for the one you might have fancied to yourself while you were writing.

These days, however, I know I can't count on anything or anybody in advance. Yet I must also ask for a commitment from you in order to be read at all, and the very fact that I must solicit you in this way could well mar, or even prevent, any relationship we might establish. It may ease things a bit if I assure you it's not a huge or overwhelming commitment I'm asking, but only the amount of attention you need to see me through this play (mine isn't even

2. *To a prospective member of the audience:*

But now that I'm done writing, the time has come for me to change the relationship from the member of the audience I worked up in my imagination to the real person on whom I must depend to give my play the attention and respect it needs to be adequately experienced. (Your affection, let us hope, will come later; in fact, if I can start merely with your attention, I'll also be willing to put off with your respect until you're convinced it's been properly earned.) It takes patience on both sides to get this relationship going, and I recognize it's up to me to make most of the adjustments, for we both know, even without having to say it, that I need you more than you need me. I might remind you that this is not the way things always were. There was a time when setting things up was easier than it is now. The world was small then, and once the writer was finished he had merely to say, "Go, little book," and he could then go on to write something else in full confidence that the fortunes of his book were in the secure hands of some patron or players company who had cast their favors upon him before he had even started writing. And once you knew that people had placed their money and their pride on you, you felt they were committed to you and you didn't have to fret about any prospective audience except for the one you might have fancied to yourself while you were writing.

These days, however, I know I can't count on anything or anybody in advance. Yet I must also ask for a commitment from you in order to be heard at all, and the very fact that I must solicit you in this way could well mar, or even prevent, any relationship we might establish. It may ease things a bit if I assure you it's not a huge or overwhelming commitment I'm asking, but only the amount of attention you need to see me through this play (mine isn't

To a prospective publisher:

w that I'm done writing, I have
ne to you to ask you to help
ke it possible for others to read,
, and hopefully enjoy my play.
am not asking that you your-
‡ enjoy it, only that you be will-
to use the power that you
ınmand to give others the
ıortunity to do so.)

-akes patience on both sides to
ke the sort of arrangement I
 requesting, and I recognize it's
 to me to make most of the
ıstments, for we both know,
n without having to say it, that
eed you more than you need
. I might remind you that this
ıot the way things always
re. There was a time when set-
g things up was easier than it is
v. The world was small then,
l once the writer was finished
 had merely to say, "Go, little
ok," and he could then go on to
ıte something else in full
ıfidence that the fortunes of his
ok were in the secure hands of
 patron who had cast his favor
ın him before he had even
rted writing. And once you
ew that somebody had placed
 money and his pride on you,
ı felt he was committed to you
d would see to it that all the
ırs that needed opening were
ened to you.

ıese days, however, I know I
ı't count on anything or any-
ly in advance. Yet I must also
 for an arrangement with you if
 work is to be read or played
all, and the very fact that I
ıst solicit you in this way could
ll mar, or even prevent, any
ationship we might establish. It
ıy ease things a bit if I assure
u there is no large or long-term

4. To a prospective producer:

*Now that I'm done writing, I
have come to you to ask you to
help make it possible for others to
see and hopefully enjoy my play.
(I am not asking that you yourself enjoy it, only that you be willing to use the power that you
command to give others the
opportunity to do so.)*

*It takes patience on both sides to
make the sort of arrangement I
am requesting, and I recognize it's
up to me to make most of the
adjustments, for we both know,
even without having to say it, that
I need you more than you need
me. I might remind you that this
is not the way things always were.
There was a time when setting
things up was easier than it is now.
The world was small then, and
once the writer was finished he
had merely to place his drama in
the hands of the players company
for whom he customarily wrote,
and he could go on to write something else in full confidence that
the fortunes of his play were in
the secure hands of a group that
had cast its favors upon him
before he had even started writing
and that would automatically find
an appropriate audience for his
work.*

*These days, however, I know I
can't count on anything or anybody in advance. Yet I must also
ask for an arrangement with you
if my work is to be played at all,
and the very fact that I must
solicit you in this way could well
mar, or even prevent, any relationship we might establish. It may
ease things a bit if I assure you
there is no large or long-term*

5. To a prospective critic:

But now that I'm done writing,
the time has come for me to
change the relationship from the
critic I worked up in my imagination to the real person on whom I
must depend to give my play the
attention and respect necessary for
prospective readers and audiences
to approach it sympathetically.

Since ours can so easily become an
antagonistic relationship, it takes
patience on both sides to get the
relationship going, and I recognize.
it's up to me to make most of the
adjustments, for we both know,
even without having to say it, that
I need you more at this point than
you need me. I might remind you
that this is not the way things
always were. There was a time
when getting one's work known
and appreciated was easier than it
is now. The world was small then,
and once the writer was finished
he had merely to say, "Go, little
book," and he could then go on to
write something else in full confidence that the fortunes of his
book were in the secure hands of
the educated community that
assumed the worthiness of one's
work from the start without constantly putting an author to the
test.

These days, however, I know I
can't count on anything or anybody in advance. Yet I must also
ask for a sympathetic response
from you in order that others will
be willing to hear me, and the
very fact that I must solicit you in
this way could well mar, or even
prevent, any relationship we might
establish. It may ease things a bit
if I assure you it's not unqualified

1. To a prospective reader:

long as plays go). I recognize that any commitment, no matter how temporary, may arouse your skepticism or at least your reluctance. That's only natural given the fact we're strangers in an atomized and anarchic society in which nobody knows, let alone trusts, anyone else. I can't blame you if you feel the need to keep your distance, especially when there is a multitude of writers throughout the world shrilly shouting for your attention at the same time that I have come to ask your help. Whatever claims any of them may make, I for one am honest enough to admit I can offer you no absolute assurance you will ultimately feel that reading my work has been worth your while.

Yet I do not despair of a commitment (however tenuous) from you. You may not feel ready to make it by the time you've got through the first scene or even the second. (I am very patient.) And you may well feel this is not similar to anything you remember liking before. (You too must be patient.) But before too long you may suddenly feel something happening to you, a recognition that will make you exclaim, "This is it, this is the real thing!" Once this happens, it'll be smooth sailing for the two of us. You may even return to the opening scenes and read them with a new, more sympathetic eye. There's no telling in advance how or when or why this moment will come to you. (If I could plan for it in my writing, I'd surely do so.) Perhaps some incident or speech I've presented sets off something you've always felt strongly about; perhaps some physical discomfort you had when you began

2. To a prospective member of the audience:

even long as plays go). I recognize that any commitment, no matter how temporary, may arouse your skepticism or at least your reluctance. That's only natural given the fact we're strangers in an atomized and anarchic society in which nobody knows, let alone trusts, anyone else. I can't blame you if you feel the need to keep your distance, especially when there is a multitude of writers throughout the world shrilly shouting for your attention at the same time that I have come to ask your help. Whatever claims any of them may make, I for one am honest enough to admit I can offer you no absolute assurance you will ultimately feel that attending my play has been worth your while.

Yet I do not despair of a commitment (however tenuous) from you. You may not feel ready to make it by the time you've seen the first scene or even the second. (I am very patient.) And you may well feel this is not similar to anything you remember liking before. (You too must be patient.) But before too long you may suddenly feel something happening to you, a recognition that will make you exclaim, "This is it, this is the real thing!" Once this happens, it'll be smooth sailing for the two of us. You may even think back to the opening scenes and view them with a new, more sympathetic eye. There's no telling in advance how or when or why this moment will come to you. (If I could plan for it in my writing, I'd surely do so.) Perhaps some incident or speech I've presented sets off something you've always felt strongly about; perhaps some nearby noise that distracted you during the early scenes

3. *To a prospective publisher:*

investment involved, but only the financing necessary to publish this play (mine isn't even long as plays go). I recognize that any such request, no matter how modest, may arouse a certain defensiveness on your part. That's only natural given the fact we're strangers in an atomized and anarchic society in which nobody knows, let alone trusts, anyone else. I can't blame you if you feel the need to keep your distance, especially when there is a multitude of writers throughout the world shrilly shouting for your attention at the same time that I have come to ask your help. Whatever claims any of them may make, I for one am honest enough to admit I can offer you no absolute assurance that publishing my play will bring you greater rewards than will the work of someone else.

Yet I do not despair of reaching an arrangement (however tenuous) with you. You may not feel ready for it by the time you've got through the first scene or even the second. (I am very patient.) And you may feel this is not similar to anything you remember liking before. (You too, I hope, will be patient.) But before too long you may suddenly feel something happening to you, a recognition that will make you exclaim, "This is exciting, people will go wild over it!" Once this happens, it'll be smooth sailing for the two of us. You may even return to the opening scenes and read them with a new, more sympathetic eye. There's no telling in advance how or when or why this moment will come to you. (If I could plan for

4. *To a prospective producer:*

investment involved, but only the financing necessary to arrange a few performances of this play (mine isn't even long as plays go). I recognize that any such request, no matter how modest, may arouse a certain defensiveness on your part. That's only natural given the fact we're strangers in an atomized and anarchic society in which nobody knows, let alone trusts, anyone else. I can't blame you if you feel the need to keep your distance, especially when there is a multitude of writers throughout the world shrilly shouting for your attention at the same time that I have come to ask your help.

Whatever claims any of them may make, I for one am honest enough to admit I can offer you no absolute assurance that performing my play will bring you greater rewards than will the work of someone else.

Yet I do not despair of reaching an arrangement (however tenuous) with you. You may not feel ready for it by the time you've got through the first scene or even the second. (I am very patient.) And you may well feel this is not similar to anything you remember liking before. (You too, I hope, will be patient.) But before too long you may suddenly feel something happening to you, a recognition that will make you exclaim, "This is exciting, people will go wild over it!" Once this happens, it'll be smooth sailing for the two of us. You may even return to the opening scenes and read them with a new, more sympathetic eye. There's no telling in advance how or when or why this moment will come to you. (If I could plan for

5. *To a prospective critic:*

or overwhelming approval I'm asking, but only the amount of praise I need for others to approach my play with sympathy. I recognize that any request for approval, no matter how modest, may arouse a certain defensiveness on your part. That's only natural given the fact we're strangers in an atomized and anarchic society in which nobody knows, let alone trusts, anyone else. I can't blame you if you feel the need to keep your distance, especially when there is a multitude of writers throughout the world shrilly shouting for your attention at the same time that I have come to demand your praise. Whatever claims any of them may make, I for one am honest enough to admit I can offer you no absolute assurance you will ultimately feel that praising my work will enhance or even help maintain your reputation.

Yet I do not despair of approval (however tenuous) from you. You may not feel committed to my play by the time you've got through the first scene or even the second. (I am very patient.) And you may well feel this is not similar to anything you remember liking before. (You too must be patient.) But before too long you may suddenly feel something happening to you, a recognition that will make you exclaim, "This is it, this is the real thing!" Once this happens, it'll be smooth sailing for the two of us. You may even reconsider the opening scenes and view them with a new, more sympathetic eye. There's no telling in advance how or when or why this moment will come to you. (If I could plan for it in my writing,

1. To a prospective reader:

reading has disappeared; perhaps your fancy has simply been struck by the configuration of print on some page. It may be you also will need a little outside incentive to make that recognition take place—a recommendation from some well-known reviewer whose assurance of the worth of my enterprise will seem more convincing to you than mine; just a word from some respected friend whose tastes you like to share.

I shall not look too closely into your motives, for my concern is to get our relationship going in the first place. I have always known my work is at the mercy of accidents over which I have no control or even influence, and if your vanity needs priming before you will commit yourself, I have no choice but to go along with this.

2. To a prospective member of the audience:

has quieted down; perhaps your fancy has simply been struck by the physical movements of one of the actors. It may be you also will need a little outside incentive to make that recognition take place—a recommendation from some well-known reviewer whose assurance of the worth of my enterprise will seem more convincing to you than mine; just a word from some respected friend whose tastes you like to share, or a sudden discovery, through a certain tenseness in the air, that other members of the audience are enjoying what they see.

I shall not look too closely into your motives, for my concern is to get our relationship going in the first place. I have always known my work is at the mercy of accidents over which I have no control or even influence, and if your vanity needs priming before you will commit yourself, I have no choice but to go along with this. It may well be that the production you are witnessing does not do justice to the text I wrote.

To a prospective publisher:

ın my writing, I'd surely do so.)
rhaps some incident or speech
e presented reminds you of a
ırk whose success you envy;
rhaps some physical discomfort
ıu had when you began reading
s disappeared; perhaps your
ıcy has simply been struck by
e configuration of type on some
ge. It may be you also will need
ıttle outside incentive to make
at recognition take place—a
:ommendation from some well-
own critic whose assurance of
: worth of my enterprise will
m more convincing to you than
ne; just a word from some
ısted adviser whose tastes you
e to share.

:now you are not the sort for
ıom commercial considerations
: uppermost, but that you seek
estige above all—in full knowl-
ge of course that prestige in the
ıg run will likely result in finan-
l return for you. I shall not look
) closely into your motives, for
' concern is to get our relation-
ıp going in the first place. I have
vays known my work is at the
ercy of accidents over which I
ve no control or even influence,
d if your vanity needs priming
fore you will commit yourself, I
ve no choice but to go along
th this.

4. To a prospective producer:

it in my writing, I'd surely do so.)
Perhaps some incident or speech
I've presented reminds you of a
work whose success you envy; per-
haps some physical discomfort you
had when you began reading has
disappeared; perhaps your fancy
has simply been struck by the con-
figuration of type on some page. It
may be you also will need a little
outside incentive to make that
recognition take place—a recom-
mendation from some well-known
critic whose assurance of the
worth of my enterprise will seem
more convincing to you than
mine; just a word from some
trusted adviser whose tastes you
like to share; perhaps the enthusi-
asm that some actor you admire
expresses to take on the leading
role.

I know you are not the sort for
whom commercial considerations
are uppermost, but that you
seek prestige above all—in full
knowledge of course that prestige
in the long run will likely result in
financial return for you. I shall
not look too closely into your
motives, for my concern is to get
our relationship going in the first
place. I have always known my
work is at the mercy of accidents
over which I have no control or
even influence, and if your vanity
needs priming before you will
commit yourself, I have no choice
but to go along with this.

5. To a prospective critic:

I'd surely do so.) Perhaps some
incident or speech I've presented
reminds you of something you
liked in another play; perhaps
some nearby noise that distracted
you during the early scenes has
quieted down; perhaps your fancy
has simply been struck by the
physical movements of one of the
actors. It may be you also will
need a little outside incentive to
make that recognition take place
—just a word from some respected
friend in the lobby whose tastes
you like to share; a sudden discovery, through the tenseness you
feel in the air, that the audience is
enjoying what it sees; an inkling
that praising my play will make
you honored for your prescience
and your fine judgment.

I shall not look too closely into
your motives, for my concern is to
gain your approval in the first
place. I have always known my
work is at the mercy of accidents
over which I have no control or
even influence, and if your vanity
needs priming before you will
commit yourself, I have no choice
but to go along with this. It may
well be that the production you
are witnessing does not do justice
to the text I wrote. Moreover,
since much, perhaps even most
that you see is of poor quality, you
are all too accustomed to
approach any new work in a negative frame of mind. I can't blame
you for this; it's built into the role
in which you've been cast. But

1. *To a prospective reader:*

My options are limited, while you can exercise a free choice over whether you wish to engage with me or some other writer. (You may as easily elect not to engage with anybody at all.) Whereas I have poured my life's blood into this piece, you play a strictly passive role, insisting that I work some magic so that you may feel amused, or enlightened, or even disturbed—anything to lift you out of the boredom or the indifference in which you habitually live.

As I think of it, there's no reason
I should have to put this much effort
into you, approach you anxiously
with my pleas, excuses, hedgings, self-
deprecations. As you can see, I no longer
care to throw myself abjectly at your
mercy. I withdraw my work from whatever
scrutiny you fancied giving it.

That was easily said. If I had my choice in the matter, rather than subject myself to your will I should let my play languish on my shelf and gather what dust it will over the years. But I know that the words I have written, no matter how much force I believe they may possess, can exercise no more effect than the unheard crash of trees in a distant forest. I am enough of a pragmatist to know that if peace is still possible between us, I must be willing to negotiate, even on terms set by you. It seems just as well to erase what's been said between us. We'll start again.

2. *To a prospective member of the audience:*

My options are limited, while you can exercise a free choice over whether you wish to engage with me or some other writer. (You may as easily elect not to engage with anybody at all.) Whereas I have poured my life's blood into this piece, you play a strictly passive role, insisting that I work some magic so that you may feel amused, or enlightened, or even disturbed—anything to lift you out of the boredom or the indifference in which you habitually live.

*As I think of it, there's no reason
I should have to put this much effort
into you, approach you anxiously
with my pleas, excuses, hedgings, self-
deprecations. As you can see, I no longer
care to throw myself abjectly at your
mercy. I withdraw my work from whatever attention you fancied giving it.*

That was easily said. If I had my choice in the matter, rather than subject myself to your will I should let my play languish on my shelf and gather what dust it will over the years. But I know that the words I have written, no matter how much force I believe they may possess, can exercise no more effect than the unheard crash of trees in a distant forest. I am enough of a pragmatist to know that if peace is still possible between us, I must be willing to negotiate, even on terms set by you. It seems just as well to erase what's been said between us. We'll start again.

To a prospective publisher:

y options are limited, while you
n exercise a free choice over
hether you wish to engage with
e or some other writer. (You
ay as easily elect not to engage
ith anybody at all at this point.)
Vhereas I have poured my life's
ood into this piece, you play a
rictly secondary role, arranging
atters of a purely administrative
ature, such as the printing, the
ablicity, and the distribution.

s I think of it, there's no reason
should have to put this much
fort into you, approach you
ixiously with my pleas, excuses,
edgings, self-deprecations. As you
in see, I no longer care to throw
yself abjectly at your mercy. I
ithdraw my work from whatever
tention you considered giving it.

hat was easily said. If I had my
hoice in the matter, rather than
abject myself to your will I
hould let my play languish on my
helf and gather what dust it will
ver the years. But I know that
e words I have written, no
aatter how much force I believe
hey may possess, can exercise no
iore effect than the unheard
crash of trees in a distant forest. I
m enough of a pragmatist to
now that if peace is still possible
etween us, I must be willing to
egotiate, even on terms set by
ou. It seems just as well to erase
vhat's been said between us. We'll
tart again.

4. To a prospective producer:

*My options are limited, while you
can exercise a free choice over
whether you wish to engage with
me or some other writer. (You
may as easily elect not to engage
with anybody at all at this point.)
Whereas I have poured my life's
blood into this piece, you play a
strictly secondary role, arranging
matters of a purely administrative
nature, such as the casting, the
staffing, and the publicity.*

*As I think of it, there's no reason
I should have to put this much
effort into you, approach you
anxiously with my pleas, excuses,
hedgings, self-deprecations. As you
can see, I no longer care to throw
myself abjectly at your mercy. I
withdraw my work from whatever
attention you considered giving it.*

*That was easily said. If I had my
choice in the matter, rather than
subject myself to your will I
should let my play languish on my
shelf and gather what dust it will
over the years. But I know that
the words I have written, no
matter how much force I believe
they may possess, can exercise no
more effect than the unheard
crash of trees in a distant forest. I
am enough of a pragmatist to
know that if peace is still possible
between us, I must be willing to
negotiate, even on terms set by
you. It seems just as well to erase
what's been said between us. We'll
start again.*

5. To a prospective critic:

remember my options are limited,
while you can exercise a free
choice over whether you wish to
praise me or some other writer.
(You may as easily elect not to
praise anybody at all.) Whereas I
have poured my life's blood into
this piece, you play a strictly
passive role, insisting that I work
some magic so that you may feel
amused, or enlightened, or even
disturbed—anything to lift you
out of the boredom or the indifference that your job imposes on
you.

As I think of it, there's no
reason I should have to put this
much effort into you, approach
you anxiously with my pleas,
excuses, hedgings, self-deprecations. Although the praise you
mete out to me could help gain
recognition for my work at an
early stage, I am confident that I
shall ultimately establish myself
with audiences and readers despite
any condemnation or abuse you
may subject me to. Who or what
would you be, after all, without
the writer who gives you the
opportunity to react and respond
in the first place? I provide the
primary matter, while you are
merely the parasite that survives at
my behest. Your very presence in
my midst appalls me. Why should
I pay the slightest heed to one
who feeds jubilantly on the
entrails of those who gave him
life? I curse you and all your
band.

Note: On the distinction between journalistic critics and scholar-critics

As one who sometimes terms himself a critic, I should comment on H-G's apparent rejection of the species in the last of these envois. (H-G's strong feelings are particularly evident from the fact that he does not take back his words at the end as he does in the four earlier envois.) It is important to note, however, that H-G refers to a specific type of critic, namely, the one who reviews plays for newspapers—usually writing his piece between the play's end at eleven and a midnight deadline for the next morning's edition. Needless to say, one cannot expect a high degree of intellectual reflection in writing that is done under these conditions. Moreover, the persons who go into this line of work are essentially journalists—professional newspapermen who, as often as not, are those who could not succeed in the more glamorous sorts of reporting, such as crime and politics. (I have occasionally seen dropouts from Ph.D. programs in English end up at this type of job.) It is customary nowadays to use the term "journalistic critic" to distinguish these persons from academic literary critics, and it is unfortunate that H-G failed to supply the proper distinguishing epithet. (I carefully refer to myself as a "scholar-critic" to prevent unnecessary confusion.) It is also regrettable that H-G did not write a sixth version of his envoi addressed to the academic critic. But then whatever he might have addressed to the likes of me finds its appropriate answer in the very existence of an idea behind the present volume.

Note: On the discontinuity of this book

Nobody would contend you could read straight through this volume from beginning to end. Nor should you, for it's a critical edition, after all, which means that the work around which the edition is built needs to be surrounded by an unending array of materials, none of which are continuous with one another, but all of which feed into, and out of, the play. As the diagram below implies, there is no ideal order in which the surrounding materials need be read. Treat them as you would the hors d'oeuvres at a cocktail party. Go back and forth and sample what you will in whatever order pleases you. Does it matter if you take shrimp-in-rémoulade before the pickled mushroom? Or if you go back for another shrimp after the mushroom? (Or if you quietly skip the vegetable-in-sour-cream dip?) The only important thing is that at some point you read the play itself, which, to develop the metaphor I have unexpectedly lapsed into, is the cocktail that gives the party whatever excuse it has for taking place. But don't neglect the hors d'oeuvres: They are a necessary sop to keep you on even keel while you are drinking and they are also very good in themselves.

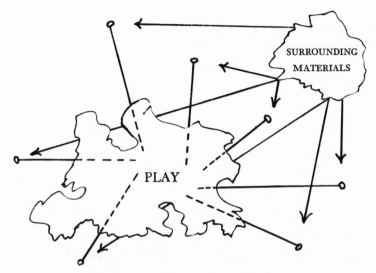

A visual explication of the preceding note.
(Diagram by Luella McGillicuddy Wolfson)

FIRST LETTER FROM H-G TO MJW

The following letter from H-G was attached to the manuscript of Saul's Fall, which arrived in a half-torn envelope without prior notice.

P.O. Box 3667
Mendocino, California
2 March 1978

Dear Professor Wolfson,

Since I am aware of your interest in modern drama, I take the liberty of sending you some seventeen episodes I have put together during the past few years. I have frankly felt like a criminal sitting here in Mendocino writing what I know in my bones will never be performed, or read, or known by anybody but myself. Do not feel the need to reply. I should not object, however, if you return some routinely pious expression of gratitude and encouragement, with a few cavils about an inconsistency or infelicity here or there—enough, that is, to sustain the credibility of your praise without unduly ruffling my sensibilities.

Sincerely,
Orlando Hennessy-García

SECOND LETTER FROM H-G TO MJW

The following letter from H-G arrived a few days after I had sent him a letter expressing my enthusiasm for his play.

P.O. Box 3667
Mendocino, California
22 March 1978

Dear Professor Wolfson,

It was kind of you to send such complimentary words to me about my writing. The code that prevails among civilized persons today does not necessitate anybody's replying to an unsolicited manuscript, and you can be sure I appreciate your effort in going beyond the call of social duty. As I read through your letter, however, I was forced to recognize that your praise amounted to little more than politeness. I thank you for your considerateness toward my feelings, even though I also realize that whatever hopes I may have entertained about your helping me publish my work (or even getting it performed) must be laid to rest.

Sincerely,
Orlando Hennessy-García

I shall not comment on my reaction to this letter, nor shall I elaborate on the parallels that I immediately saw between the attitude H-G was taking to me and the one that his Saul displays at certain moments in the play. Suffice it to say I was faced with the choice of letting the whole thing drop—Saul's Fall, Orlando Hennessy-García, and whatever mutually beneficial results could come his and my way if his play reached the right people—or deciding to put up with his peculiarities and pursue him some more. After a day or two of wavering, I decided on the latter course and sent him a letter more enthusiastic than the preceding one (though not too much more enthusiastic, else I should again have aroused his suspiciousness.) I also suggested we get together personally either in Mendocino or at Stanford, whichever he preferred. I got no reply this time and after a week or two pretty much gave up hope of continuing the relationship (if it ever amounted to that), though I had every intention of trying to interest what contacts I had in his play. Then suddenly, almost a month to the day after his letter, he appeared in my office without the slightest warning. Our meeting is described in the following section.

AN INTERVIEW WITH ORLANDO HENNESSY-GARCIA

I must confess I put off describing my meeting with H-G until a relatively late stage in the compilation of this volume. The actual writing should have been easy: after all, I have a tape of our conversation and except for a few words and phrases that my none-too-reliable recorder was unable to pick up, it was largely a matter of transcribing and adding a few explanatory comments here and there. But this was my one and only meeting with the man to whom this volume is dedicated and unless I reestablish contact with him before it goes to press, it will be the only eye-witness account to confirm or qualify the impressions left by the personal papers included in the volume. Not only that, but as I transcribed the tape, I recognized that H-G is simply not at his best in a personal encounter. I was disappointed in our meeting: or at least I was for a short period, and painfully so, as I shall explain in full candor at the end of this account. Yet in retrospect I have come to see this meeting as among the high points of my life, professional or otherwise. But the particular significance the meeting had for me is not likely to communicate with a reader (as it did not even for me at first) who has not yet become attuned to this strange and courageous man.

In a way that I have since found fully characteristic of him, H-G took the initiative and set the style for our meeting. In fact, he caught me by surprise. Given his morbid shyness and my own outgoingness, one would expect it to be the other way around, but then shy people manage to find their own way of asserting their will—nor would one want them any different: H-G has doubtless been able to survive only because he early recognized that people would walk all over him if he did not work out techniques to keep them at a distance or, if forced to deal with them, to not let them set the tone of the relationship.

About the worst time to catch an academic by surprise (apart from certain domestic situations) is when he has a flock of students waiting to move in on him one by one during his office hour. And that is precisely when H-G came to see me. Since he did not want me preparing for him in advance, he must have phoned the Stanford English Department, got one of the secretaries to tell him my office hours (they add up to three hours per week over two separate days—this is normal at a major university), and then simply appeared. So there I was in my office with a girl in tears because she had blocked on an examination, and besides her at least six students waiting on the floor in the hallway to see me (I'm by no means the least popular teacher around here—and I've never felt a conflict between my dual roles of scholar and teacher) in full knowledge that my office hours that day had scarcely half an hour to go, after which I had to

Since no photographs of Orlando Hennessy-García are known to exist, I commissioned this drawing of him captured the day after his visit to my office by three students who happened to be waiting to see me and were fortunate enough to catch sufficient glimpses of him so that they could put together what I considered a plausible portrait. My thanks go to Kathy Thurlow, who executed the actual drawing, and to Jim Browning and Sue Pleasants, who guided her with reminders along the way.

rush off to class. While trying to calm down the blocked student by offering her a hand-tissue (there's no better technique I've found for breaking the weeping ritual) I suddenly noticed an older person, obviously not a student, pacing back and forth among the students in the hallway. He had on a well-worn greyish turtleneck sweater, an equally well-worn pair of jeans (not the newer modish type, but old-fashioned Levis that could have been bought in a workmen's clothing store twenty years ago)—but I shouldn't describe him at this point, since in all frankness I didn't observe his dress or anything specific about him until later, when I learned who he was. At the time I first noticed him, I badly needed an excuse to interrupt the girl in tears (the tissue trick, though it obviously was working, had not been able to end the deep gulps still heaving up from her chest as she talked), so I got up, went to the hallway, and asked him if he was looking for anybody in particular.

"Do you know where I'd find Professor Wolfson?" he replied with what I took to be a deliberate indirectness, as though he were too shy to ask me directly if I was Professor Wolfson.

"I happen to be Professor Wolfson, but as you can see," I said as I gestured toward the horde of students waiting to see me, "I'm pretty much booked up the rest of this office hour."

"Your next office hour, they told me, isn't till . . ."

His speech was so slow and hesitant I found I had to interrupt to keep him from taking up the rest of my office hour with these technical details. "Tuesday," I filled in, "so could you come see me Tuesday? If you get here promptly at one, I'll see you at the start of my office hour and you'll be sure to get in." By this time I assumed that despite the informality of his dress, he could only be a textbook salesman, for why else would someone his age—and a total stranger at that—be waiting to see me? And I obviously had to keep my distance, just as physicians do from the pharmaceutical salesmen whom my brother (a nephrologist in New York) tells me are always after them.

So here I was seeking ways to ward him off, when he said in a voice so soft I didn't even react to the name, "I'm Orlando Hennessy-García. I'm passing through town, so I wasn't planning to be here Tuesday."

"Say that again, your name, I mean." (I wanted to be sure I hadn't substituted a familiar name in my mind for an unfamiliar one.)

"Orlando Hennessy-García," this time even softer than before, and in a distinctly apologetic tone, as though trying to excuse his very existence.

I did a double take after his name sank in. "You're here!" I exclaimed, clasping his hand heartily, then turned to the students who were watching avidly and wondering what was coming next (students have an uncommon curiosity about what they take to be authority figures). "This is Mr.

Hennessy-García, a terrific writer I've just discovered, discovered for myself, I mean, since he was kind enough to let me read his work. You'll be hearing lots about him, I can assure you you will, so I'm asking you please give me a chance to talk to him a bit the few moments I have left before class. I know you won't mind coming back Tuesday under the circumstances, though if anybody has something urgent you can catch me as I come out of class—Room 206, that is."

I quickly realized I'd come on too strong, not for the students, of course, who adjust themselves to anything, but for my visitor Hennessy-García, who had shrunk away to the entrance and would certainly have disappeared for good if I had not strode after him (tripping, alas, over two students still sitting in the hallway), grabbed him by the arm and marched him straight into my office, where my conferee was watching the hallway spectacle so eagerly nobody would have guessed how recently she had been wallowing in tears.

She demanded the blocked examination paper back before I could get her out of the office. I was so distracted by now that I forgot where I had put it and looked desperately through my desk and briefcase, all the while keeping an eye on my shy visitor, who looked as though he might escape from me any minute. As I went through the briefcase I noticed my cassette recorder and quickly realized I should have to try getting it turned on and into my pocket without H-G's noticing it. (In view of the difficulty of talking to him under even the most ordinary conditions, he would surely have evaporated into air if I'd announced I was taping our conversation.)[1]

To hide my transfer of the recorder I made a loud fuss shuffling papers

---

1. Among those I have shown the materials gathered for this book are some who have reproved me for taping my meeting with H-G without his prior permission. These people I consider my friends, and I take their criticism seriously despite my disagreement with them. I have tried to make clear to them my awareness of the ethical controversies that go on in the sciences and social sciences on the use of human subjects for research. The issues being debated in these controversies are very complex indeed, and I do not pretend to mediate in this area. With regard to my taping the author around whom this volume is built, I ask simply, What is better, an inaccurate transcript of our meeting made from memory and full of unconscious errors intended to place the transcriber in the best possible light, or a fully accurate record that portrays both participants as they really are? Though I had thought this question would settle the matter, I must confess feeling rankled by one reader (someone close to me whose criticism I have always valued and often acted upon) who reacted to the transcript by calling me an "awful human being." Although I am not precisely sure what constitutes an awful human being, I can reply that being a conscientious and enterprising editor sometimes means—at least according to her definition—having to be an awful human being. The best orchestral conductors, opera impressarios, film directors, editors, magazine publishers, college presidents, corporate managers, heads of state are all probably quite awful human beings. These are the people who seek and get results in what they do. Those who enjoy the benefit of these results should be willing to share in whatever guilt they insist on ascribing to the editor. Anybody who feels unable to share in this guilt might do well to turn a few pages and skip this section altogether.

back and forth between briefcase and desk and pretended to take considerably longer to locate the teary girl's paper (she was of course fully
recovered by now) than I needed. Although I pushed the red "record"
lever down while slipping the recorder into my pocket I worried throughout
my interview with H-G whether it was actually managing to get a decent
account of what went on between us. Was it turned on loud enough to
catch our words clearly, and hopefully also the particular way his voice
faded off at the end of sentences? Was it possible I had never properly
turned it on at all? The agonizing thing was I couldn't check without
giving the whole thing away.

During all this confusion I kept up a conversation both with the student,
who disappeared as soon as she was able to grab her paper, and with H-G,
or rather, I talked at him for a while until we could settle down somewhere.
I begged him to let me call my wife Luella to ask her to set an extra place
for dinner that night (I could even have her feed the children early so
we'd not be bothered), but he shied away, as I fully expected. He insisted
he was only passing through, so I asked him at least to see me after my
class, which was hard for me to skip since I had a couple of hundred
students on my hands all enthralled by modern drama, but he said—well,
this is where the tape began to pick us up.

HENNESSY-GARCIA (*the tape picks up in the middle of a sentence*):
... half an hour of your time.

WOLFSON: Don't mind my time, for God's sake. I've got all the time in
the world for you till my class starts. Now why don't we take off and have
a cup of coffee?

*I realized I was desperate to break the ice at that point. It was obviously
mandatory to get out of the office, where, it seemed to me, he was treating
me as an authority figure.*

HENNESSY-GARCIA: I don't, I'm sorry. I don't take coffee, but I'll join
you, whatever ...

*Either his voice had faded out in mid-sentence or the recorder didn't
catch him. I recognize, incidentally, that in transcribing our dialogue I
shall be judged as though I am writing a play of my own. I have no ambitions in this direction, nor would I want the interview I record—either
H-G's or my own—to appear a sample of my writing skill. Anyone who
reads dialogue that has actually been spoken will always find it vastly
inferior to what he can read or hear in a good play. Certainly H-G's
speeches, even granting his natural hesitancy in speech, can in no way be
compared to what he writes for even the least eloquent character in Saul's
Fall. Let the reader tape and transcribe the next conversation he himself
participates in, and I vouch he will be shocked at the way people really
speak.*

WOLFSON: We'll try the Business School lounge. It's close by. It's a shame we're so rushed. No, for God's sake, it's got nothing to do with the Business School as such. It's just the closest place for coffee from here, though I can't say much for the coffee, but then you weren't having any, but God knows I don't want for you to be feeling uncomfortable; it doesn't much matter where we go.

There is a long silence here that took up most of our walk to the lounge. I must confess that even I of all people was too nervous for a while to keep this chatter going.

I really appreciate your looking me up and sending me that play of yours in the first place, because that play really grabbed me in a fundamental way, like nothing new I've come across in years, so for God's sake, you needn't feel so apologetic since there's obviously nothing to apologize about, so look, I'm having this coffee—

The recorder even caught the sounds of china clanking at that point— and I'm not caring what you have, or if you have nothing at all, since I just wanted the most comfortable possible situation to sit down with you and let you know that on the basis of reading that play of yours, I'm all with you, a hundred percent that is.

At that point there are some muffled sounds that turned out too indistinct to be transcribed. I am not certain if they came from H-G or from some nearby students in the lounge. As any reader can tell from my transcription thus far, I was exceedingly ill at ease and must have been speaking compulsively to keep the conversation from petering out as it was constantly threatening to do. In retrospect I realize that H-G was staying on the defensive, though he had said little more than a few words at this point. Shyness, I have heard, can tyrannize as decisively, if not quite so loudly, as the more obvious forms of controlling people. As I sipped dutifully at my coffee, whose nasty taste betrayed its brewer's failure to keep the equipment properly washed, I realized I should at least have provided H-G with an empty cup—anything to give his hands something to play with or at least hold while we went through the motions of making contact. The nervousness he showed was so all-consuming that it was not until much later that I realized he had exceptionally fine features, far better than mine in fact, though his total lack of presence would prevent anybody from noticing them. In fact he was doing his utmost to keep from being seen and would gladly, I suspect, have worn a stocking over his head if that had not added to the conspicuousness he was trying so hard to avoid. His sweater—much too warm for a Palo Alto spring day—was sufficiently baggy to hide what was doubtless an exceptionally trim build for somebody who has hit forty. His face, interestingly gaunt, with a long, thin nose, was topped by sandy-colored hair, interpersed here and there with grey, that was cut so short one's attention was called not to his natural features but to the fact he seemed a relic of a lost and quite uninteresting past. His uncommunicativeness was such that I feared he would suddenly walk away from me—until quite unexpectedly he managed to come out with some words that were intended to put me at my ease.

HENNESSY-GARCIA: It's always struck me as strange that people go to great effort to get together just so they can exchange words without any particular meaning and feelings that exist for that moment alone. I'm not saying you didn't mean what you said. I'm sure you did and I appreciate this, but I know you said what you said because somehow you weren't at your ease with me and I want to assure you—please relax!

Pause, during which I was sufficiently flustered that I don't remember what went on in my mind.

WOLFSON: That's what I was trying to get across to you all the while—relax!

I laughed, then there's another pause, and I remember at that point knowing there was a bond between us just as I had hoped there might be when I read through his play the first time. Yet nobody reading this transcript can possibly recapture what really went on between us. Something more comes through in listening to the tape, which incidentally is included with the Hennessy-García papers I have deposited in the Stanford Library's Bender room. Anyone with scholarly credentials is entitled to consult the papers and hear the tape for himself.

HENNESSY-GARCIA: I'm afraid I'm as relaxed as I ever will be.

This was followed by a nervous laugh from him that the tape picked up with frightening clarity. I have played the passage repeatedly. Everybody has some mannerism that gives him away, often even provides the key with which others can penetrate that which he is desperately trying to keep enclosed. This laugh is H-G's characteristic manner—at once his defense against the intrusions of others and the Achilles heel that reveals his inward agony with an immediacy he would cringe to know he was communicating.

WOLFSON: Listen, man, I want you to know I'm glad you sent that play. I understand exactly why you sent it to me and I want you to know your instincts were correct. I'll take care of your play, leave it to me please. I'll take care of everthing. I have lots of contacts, lots of people who are beholden to me—

I've always wondered why I would ever use a word like beholden in ordinary conversation, and I confess my embarrassment each time I hear the tape or read the transcript. I would have erased it from both if my scholarly conscience allowed me to.

—and I want you to know you can count on me. Do I make myself clear?

I don't want you feeling suspicious of me.[2] I'm totally reliable, and I'm committed to your play, which means I'm committed to you.

At this point I remember setting my hand on his wrist for a moment to demonstrate the strength of my commitment. But only for a moment, since I did not want him suddenly squirming away from me as nervousness came over him, nor did I want the students in the lounge—some of them I recognized as my own, but then most Stanford undergraduates must know who I am—to get the wrong idea of what was going on between us. (Fashionable though relations among the same sex are these days, I want everybody to know they've never been my sort of thing.) In any event, my gesture toward him, which was wholly spontaneous and despite its brevity communicated what I am sure he knew to be genuine feelings on my part, was obviously the high point of our meeting, and from here on there was no place to go except to find the appropriate words to break away from one another. He took the initiative.

HENNESSY-GARCIA (with his nervous laugh): You're going to be late for your class.

WOLFSON: You're right, for God's sake. I've got only five minutes. But I'll walk you a little ways to your car.

HENNESSY-GARCIA: I didn't bring one. I don't have a car. (Pause.) Please don't take this to be an affectation. I really don't like being burdened with things that cause trouble or uncertainty. You know what I mean.

WOLFSON: I don't quite. But I'm willing to take your word for it.

HENNESSY-GARCIA: It's *this* direction to the bus station, if I remember. I'll find my way.

I started out with him, but I saw he needed to assert his independence, and I probably should have let him off with a simple goodbye and rushed off to class. But my usual persistence came over me.

WOLFSON: Where exactly is it you go from here?

Pause, during which I remember his pretending not to hear me.
Back to Mendocino? Will I still reach you at that P.O. box?

HENNESSY-GARCIA: I'm none too sure when I go back there. It may be a while.

WOLFSON: But the manuscript? Where is it I reach you if I've luck with the manuscript, as I have every reason to think I will?

HENNESSY-GARCIA (with several words at the beginning too muffled to make out): . . . need . . . bother. I'm done with it. I thought of burning it when I finished. Or rather putting it in the garbage. People who go to the bother of burning manuscripts are striking poses. But I read it again

---

2. I refer the reader to H-G's letter of the preceding month that, as I explain in my accompanying note, I have vowed not to discuss.

and—well (now the nervous laugh again)—I liked it, to be blunt. That's when I sent it to you.

I tried to interrupt—I don't know what—at that point, but he'd gotten to talking and I happily let him go on, which is something one must learn to do with shy people, no matter how much one feels the need to say something oneself.

If something comes of it, it'll be nice, but I'll find out soon enough or be in touch with you somehow. If nothing comes, burn it—or put it in the garbage, which as I say is less trouble anyway.

WOLFSON: Wouldn't think of it and you know that. But I can see that half the task of writing is being able to market one's product and—well—

To my surprise I came out with a nervous laugh strikingly close to H-G's —to the point that when I first started transcribing the tape I attributed it to him!

—that's obviously not your baby. Now you've got to tell me where to reach you. It's not just the manuscript. I've got to see you in more detail than this. When do you think you'll be back to Mendicino? That's where my wife and I go when we want to get away from the kids for a few days. I really want to plan our next time up for when you're there. Can we make it soon?

HENNESSY-GARCIA (with panic clearly discernible on the tape): Listen, I've got to make it to that bus station and you're hopelessly late to your class.

It quickly dawned on me that I'd come on too strong again. This is a problem I recognize I always have with shy people, even when they're in much better shape than H-G. Believe me, I have the greatest possible sympathy for the fears they must constantly live with, but that doesn't deny the fact there's something inside them that wants to shrink away whenever an outwardly forceful—H-G is inwardly as forceful as any man alive—expansive human being tries to express his interest or concern.

WOLFSON: Please don't feel the need to tell me now. I get your point, and I want you to know I absolutely respect your need for privacy, I honor you for what you are, and I'll try to be more sensitive.

HENNESSY-GARCIA: Good to have met you.

Those are the last words on the tape. They were strongly put, not in the least panicky, and I remember their being accompanied by a handshake, not an entirely firm one, yet not as limp as one might imagine coming from him. Then he walked away.

*   *   *

And that was it—our one and only meeting face to face. As soon as I played the tape (I confess I let my class out five minutes early since I couldn't wait to hear how it sounded) I went into a slump wholly un-common to people of my sanguine temperament. Listening to our words I recognized how little (if anything) of substance had been communicated between H-G and me. Certainly almost nothing in the way of concrete information (I never even learned where he was headed for in the bus), and much (in fact most) of our time together was wasted on such triviali-ties as where we were going, and what we were doing there, and why. The following few hours were a dark time indeed, for I began to experience one of those losses of faith that threaten to undo a person to his very being. How, I asked myself, had I ever managed to invest my intellectual faith (as well as my professional credibility) in someone who radiated no more presence or style than one would expect from an ordinary basket-case? I found myself little short of lugubrious, and during the dinner that I had earlier hoped might include my visitor I remained so uncommunicative with my family that my wife asked me point-blank if the university had refused my promotion to full professor (they had not, of course, nor do I expect that they will). Is it possible Orlando Hennessy-García had infected me with his melancholia?

There was only one solution—to retrace the steps by which I had formed the judgment on which I had staked so much. I jumped up from the dinner table well before finishing and shut myself off in my study. Then I picked up the manuscript of *Saul's Fall* wondering whether I too might be tempted to burn it or put it in the garbage. I browsed here and there among the episodes as I had the first time. Then I read the next to last, "Endings," in which the clearly defined, yet deliberately inconsistent, emotional stances of the central character scarcely seemed possible coming from an author so tentative, so hesitant in personal confrontation. Then the last episode, "March 2," with its shrewd manipulation of an obstreper-ous crowd by an author who would run for his life if he had to address even the most friendly group. Was the man I met really the one who wrote the play? I turned to the one section in which he spoke in his own person, that feisty and fighting "Preface" full of the high spirits so con-spicuously lacking in this man I had tried to sustain a conversation with. If you repress a person enough, I thought to myself, the will, guts, energy he has been unable to exercise in daily life will manage to come out some other way. Then I set everything aside, including the lecture on dialogue as metaphor that I needed to prepare for the next morning, and I read straight through the manuscript with all the care I had given it the first time—and, I might add, with even greater enthusiasm than before. Yes, Orlando, I decided that for now I must think of you not as friend but as author, and as soon as I managed to adjust myself to this notion, my confidence was restored, my doubts were ended.

THIRD AND LAST LETTER FROM H-G TO MJW

The following letter arrived a week after our interview. Unlike the two earlier letters, it bore no return address. The envelope was postmarked San Francisco, which meant it could have been mailed from anywhere within the Bay Area.

28 April 1978

Dear Professor Wolfson,

I know I disappointed you at our meeting. Nobody can regret more than I myself do that I create the particular personal impression I happen to on people. The only way to make amends to you is to ask you to forget about my play and about me entirely. Go ahead and burn it and cast me out of your mind, and if all that sounds too histrionic, just quietly pay no more attention to the play or to me.

Apologetically,
Orlando Hennessy-García

I promptly went to considerable effort to track him down, first with a barrage of letters to his Mendocino post-office box, and then a personal trip to Mendocino, where, despite the small population of the town, few of the persons I questioned knew who he was, and even they did not remember having seen him in weeks. The old house that was pointed out to me as his was unoccupied, and its yard looked neglected. Once more I nearly gave up on him until, on 26 May 1978, I received the only communication from him up to the present time (when I am sending this manuscript to press). This communication was not in the form of a letter (I have already reproduced his last letter) but was a suitcase full of personal manuscripts and memorabilia, without any note as to his whereabouts. The suitcase was virtually falling apart and had obviously belonged to his mother, for it had on it hotel labels from the various places—Taormina, Alexandria, Malta—where he is known to have stayed with Beatrice Hennessy-García before he was sent off to Canada at age four. I shall not list the contents here (I describe them in more detail near the end of this volume) but will mention simply that I found the suitcase early one morning in front of my office door. Fully expecting, or at least hoping, that H-G would himself turn up soon after, I stayed inside my office except for the hours I was scheduled to deliver lectures (and even then I had one of the students who had seen him before our interview keep an eye out for him). I slept on a cot for five or six nights and had Luella deliver dinners to me so that I should not have to leave my post. It was all in vain, for H-G never turned up. During my long vigil I had ample opportunity to go through the suitcase. As I made my way through the various manuscripts I quickly discerned the immense and varied talents in his other writings as well as the fascinating interconnections that tied these writings to Saul's Fall. Before I quite knew it, the idea for this volume had begun to take shape in my mind. The whole job of editing—discovering and charting the analogues to the episodes from the play, tracking down Margo, commissioning the essays in criticism and hounding their authors to get them in on time—all this, in addition to my teaching duties, took so much effort that there were periods I virtually stopped worrying as to whether I should ever make contact with H-G again.

Note: On the suitcase as a device

As a device, the suitcase occupies a middle position between the letter, at one extreme, and, at the other, the foundling left on the doorstep. The letter, purloined or otherwise, has proved of the greatest convenience on innumerable occasions when an author needed a credible means of conveying information without forcing the sender and the receiver (or the interceptor, as often happens) to meet face to face. The chief limitation of the letter is the relative paucity of information it can offer: at best it can close an otherwise unbridgeable gap within a plot. The foundling, being human, offers almost infinite possibilities. As a human being it can grow, create a world around itself, and, far more than the letter, fill in whatever gaps in the plot need filling. The foundling's limitation is a consequence of the all-too-many possibilities it carries within itself. Being as human (and

H-G's suitcase with papers and memorabilia.
(Snapshot by Luella McGillicuddy Wolfson)

young) as it is, it commits the writer to center his efforts around it, often to the point of having to trace its growth for many hundreds of pages. The suitcase is a perfect compromise. Like the letter, it conveys information, but the suitcase can hold innumerable letters in addition to other documents and memorabilia of the most widely varying sort that it can use to characterize the sender, look closely into his motives, project a past and a future for him. Since (unlike the foundling) the suitcase is not itself human, the receiver can pick and choose as he will among the contents and discard whatever does not suit his needs. The suitcase, in short, is a marvelous device, and without it this book could not have been written.

LYRIC SUITE 1: LAMENTS AND REPROACHES UTTERED BY SAUL UPON THE ACCESSION OF KING DAVID

1. Praeludium

Long did I know the splendors of the throne:
Blessings poured through me to assuage the scars
I'd won for Him who, grateful for my wars,
Blinked as I gloried in myself alone.

Castles I built: pavements of glittering stone
Held gold menageries aglow on cars,
Fountains emitting light from ancient stars,
Whilst I presided like a god fullblown.

Now penury's my lot—though I disburse
Three gifts 'mongst thousands that I might have willed:
Regret to them who held my cause devout;
Envy for him who filched my power and purse;
And unrelenting hate for One who filled
My spirit with His own, then snuffed mine out.

2. Elegy in Haiku

1
The new palace guard
Parades in proud majesty;
Geese fly off in fear.

2
Turbid water seeps
From the abandoned fountain;
Steeds prance through the square.

3
Crickets in mourning—
Flower stands blazed on balconies
Under a noon sun.

4
Sumptuous hangings deck
The utmost towers; beggars crouch
Along crumbling walls.

5
He uttered no pang;
Processions of stalwarts make
Ancient revelry.

3. *Fragment of a speech from an unwritten verse drama*

SAUL (*to David*):
Though I must firmly keep to my resolve
To spare you for those irksome tasks you face,
Frankness demands I say a word or two
And treat you with the candor you'd expect
From others, like myself, who're now your subjects.
In view of what's gone on between the two of us,
My tongue balks at the thought I should admit
I'd waited years for one like you to come,
Discern those dangers snaring me about,
Protect me from the insults, mocks and wiles
With which this crafty world unhinges me.
All's said and done now. (*Pause.*) It little boots to mourn
What might have been, for with your new-won power
You'll read my simpering laments as blame,
Though nothing could be further from my mind.
You mustn't take these mutterings to heart:
They're meant for me alone, and I shall count
On you to exercise what acumen
You gained while you and I were locked in strife.
There was a time I bared my heart to you,
And that, I've come to recognize, undid me.
Not that you took me on with foul intent
(Reproaches, even *just* ones, rebuff their makers),
But that you saw (without my even knowing)
I'd left myself and all my power spread out
Like dainties laid before a starving hound.

So be it. (*Pause.*) My fall is no concern of yours
And these my plaints are simply rituals
To ease the passage to obscurity.
I've nothing more for you to overhear,
Though if in some quaint corner of this earth
You hear a bard strike up a tragic chant
Of mighty kings to mendicants reduced,
Of honors, triumphs, fervent shows of love
(Those glories that we claim as rightly ours),
Now fall'n the lot of others, do not believe him,
For, like all who tell instead of live,
He overstates the truth to stir his hearers
And utters what is best left undisclosed.
Forgive me if I've sought by indirection
To render things I'd vowed to keep untold.
Speech travesties what lurks within and bids
Us all resort to silence. My life is over.

4. Saul's song to David

David—who once risked life and limb
To calm my spirits with a hymn
      That did thy rise foresee;
Surely thou wilt not choose to spurn
Me in my wish to take my turn
      And try a song on thee.

I'll not reproach, but loudly raise
The loftiest, most exalted praise
      For traits innately thine;
No matter that this fickle throne
Which thou dost occupy alone
      Was once unstably mine.

Valiant, magnanimous and strong,
Gracious—my list need not prolong
      Such attributes well known;
The more I contemplate thy name
Most poignantly I feel the shame
      Of one by thee outshone.

Valiant—'twas thou who was the first
Through fierce Philistine ranks to burst
      With insolent display;
Whilst I, incompetent with fear,

Saw skulking in the utmost rear
    My troops in disarray.

Magnanimous—thy mercy poured
On me like blessings from the Lord
    Ere I could supplicate;
Such kindness drove me rashly mad
That in my abject state forbad
    Me to reciprocate.

Strong—in mind, and heart, and arm,
Yet loth to practice needless harm
    On those of weaker stamp;
What honor, pride, and joy I'd feel
If thou wouldst deign thy mighty heel
    Dauntless on me to tramp.

Gracious—thy nimble, dec'rous ways
Do this insensate world amaze
    With how a prince should rule,
And blot out galling memories
Of when, pronouncing brute decrees,
    I played the royal fool.

Enough—'tis futile to adore
Thy excellence and then deplore
    The king I could not be;
Instead I'll watch thee from afar
And tie my fortunes to thy star
    And live my life through thee.

5. Saul's dream song

If I were you, David, I'd wipe the slate
Clean, pick people whom you trust, erase
All memory of me.
It does no good to you or anyone
To take my own bruised feelings into account.
I wouldn't want it that way.

Of course the time may come when you're secure
Enough (that's still a long way off) to tell
The world of old King Saul.
You recognize there's something of a risk,
Since people are extremely unpredictable,
As I myself found out.

Be careful how you rehabilitate me.
You mustn't let them sentimentalize.
They'll fall for fallen heroes
(Not knowing in the least what's good for them),
Blame you for toppling me (that's most unfair!),
Then knock your proud throne over.

6. Rise and fall

Null,
Whence care
Of sheep spur
This boy with flair
To rout hordes in war,
Let none else interfere
Until, crowned king, he annul
All past arrangements, thence repair
With haughty mien to his fortress, where
He wields authority in peace and war,
Sends forth emissaries near and far
Till loss of nerve in battle, fear
Of foes among friends, annul
His hold on crown and power,
Bring defeat in war,
Cause to restore
(Without stir,
D e m u r)
Null.

7. In thanksgiving to the Lord, for his fortunes

Lord, Thou hast raised me from below
And didst foreknow
What buoyant triumphs I should feel,
And mad'st me kneel
In thanks to Thee for every gift
That did uplift
Me from a humble shepherd's state
And elevate
My spirits with bright victories,
And after these
Swell me with bounties, rich-
es, to bewitch

Me into hope they would increase
And never cease;
Large gratitude I have amassed
For favors past;
Yet once I've thanked Thee, may this verse
Record my curse
On One who raised me to the top
And let me drop.

LYRIC SUITE 2: NEW PSALMS OF DAVID
UTTERED UPON HIS ACCESSION

Psalm 1: In praise of the Lord

1 This is between the two of us, Lord, for I can bare my weaknesses only before Thee. If I bare them before others, I compound them, for these others will take advantage of every chink in my armor, keep me so frantically on guard they will not leave me the composure I need to do battle for them or minister to their needs.

2 Still, it is not easy to speak even to Thee, for the very act of baring what goes on within me clutches me up and stifles the will to speak.

3 I know I can have full trust in Thee, as in none of my fellow beings. And I tell myself that the fears and misgivings that others stir up in me have nothing to do with my relationship to Thee.

4 There shall be no reservations, then, no inhibitions, no backing off on my part, for I know Thou wilt listen.

5 Whatever I say, remember I make no demands upon Thee, neither of compassion, nor understanding, nor the granting of any specific desires I might be tempted to voice.

6 If I admit I cry out of the depths to Thee, Thou must believe me, whatever contrary impressions I have chosen to give the world (and even Thee). Although my outward fortunes are in the ascendant, I am, in short, calling to Thee in despair.

7 Amid all these preambles and excuses I see I have quite forgotten my prime purpose, which is to praise Thee.

8 I praise Thee for the unselfconscious ease of our relationship, which allows me to achieve and sustain contact with Thee without further apologies, explanations, or pleadings.

Psalm 2: In praise of Saul

1 As praise goes, this mustn't be grudging.

2 I shall praise your prowess in battle (in those days before I knew you),

and I shall praise the overpowering effect you exercised on your men as they stormed into the enemy ranks (again before I knew you).

3 Praising is difficult when one has no first-hand knowledge of the object (at least of those deeds for which one's praise is being meted out).

4 And it is even more difficult when the object of praise, at least when I knew him, was less than perfect.

5 In the process of trying to praise you, Saul, I have come to see that I have developed disgust toward you—not because of what you are or were, or of what you overtly did to me (your tantrums never had much effect on me), but simply because you allowed me to hurt you.

6 If I take up my praise of you once more, I shall start more modestly, and without straining to praise.

Psalm 3: In praise of myself

1 This must not be grudging either, though the despair I now feel can easily make it so.

2 I can praise those aspects of myself that others praise—my brazenness in war, my fairness in judgment, my general good nature (the last of these is not truly praiseworthy, for my good nature is limited only to what others observe).

3 I should like to be able to join others in praising those attributes whose praiseworthiness I can acknowledge in full honesty, yet I find no pleasure in praising these things. The very effort to do so brings despair upon me.

4 Yet I despair even more when I hear others praise me for what I recognize not to be mine at all, but only that which it pleases them to see in me.

5 I must seek out new modes of understanding and voicing praise.

Psalm 4: In praise of praise

1 I shall ignore all objects of praise except for praise itself.

2 For praise is that language through which I can come to understand and penetrate objects that might otherwise resist or repel me.

3 As I speak my praise, the resistance that once made them inimical to me and made me think to crush them begins to soften little by little.

4 Or what so repelled me and even drove me away in disgust comes to seem harmless and in certain ways attracts my sympathy.

5 To exercise its effects properly praise cannot simply be spoken, it must be shouted, sung, and others must join in the shouting and singing.

6 The power of praise is such that our voices alone will not suffice to express it. We must clap together, loudly pluck the harp, crown our song with cymbals' clang.

7 For praise can work wonders.

Psalm 5: In praise of myself

1 I praise myself for what I am, not for what others take or wish me to be.

2 I shall not praise myself for what I did well in the past nor for what, hoping that this praise may spur me on, I may do well in the future.

3 I must praise myself casually, inconspicuously, without undue preparation and in a manner far less obvious than that with which I voice the praise of others than myself.

4 Though I demand all the accouterments of praise for myself, the singing, the clapping, the harp-playing, and the cymbal-clanging must be an inner music that only I can hear.

5 In its inwardness my praise will not verbalize itself into self-congratulation, but will flow quietly, though majestically, through my body and leave me strong.

Psalm 6: In praise of Saul

1 I shall not praise you, Saul, for those great deeds that everybody knows about and that you performed before I knew you.

2 I should be the last to dispute your greatness, but coming from me such praise works simply to feed the vanity of the praiser for his rhetorical skill or his generosity.

3 I praise you only for what I know of you at first hand, even if the attributes that ordinarily define greatness were no longer evident by the time I knew you.

4 But I shall not praise you for making my own rise possible or for allowing my pride to grow at the expense of yours. Such praise is directed not to its overt object, but to the praiser himself.

5 It must surely sound niggling to dwell on that which I decline to praise, but hear me, Saul, I have some real praise for you.

6 I praise you first for having put my complacency to the test, for forcing me to confront a complex and recalcitrant world that had not challenged me before.

7 More important, I praise you for the depths of your suffering that, whatever despair I may myself voice from time to time, has demonstrated human possibilities beyond my reach.

8 I praise you for the example you have set, for reminding me that my humanity is dependent on my knowledge of human limitation.

9 I praise you for helping teach me the nature of praise—that the usual praise for obviously praiseworthy deeds and attributes is all too often empty verbiage, and that I can direct more genuine praise toward objects passed over by those who shout their praises unthinkingly.

10 My praise for you, Saul, has quietly obliterated the bad feelings I nurtured toward you.

Psalm 7: In praise of the Lord

1 I praise Thee, Lord, for giving me the language and power to praise and thus to crash through those barriers that divided me from myself and others.

2 I praise Thee for encouraging me to voice this praise toward what I had once deemed unworthy of praise.

3 I praise Thee for unshackling me from constraints of habit, cocksureness, and hate through the praising I have learned from Thee.

4 I praise Thee for the oneness I feel with Thee that is at once the oneness I feel with myself.

5 I praise Thee for creating the music of praise and allowing me to strike up a joyful noise to be heard among all my people.

6 May our shouting and clapping, our plucking of harps and clanging of cymbals return to praise the Maker of praise.

7 And louder yet, let the blare of trumpets and cornets, the roaring of wind and sea resound with the fullness of joy to praise Him who breathed His spirit unselfconsciously and bounteously into all forms of life upon this teeming earth.

Note: On the generic inclusiveness of this book

As the Introduction indicates, this book constitutes an anatomy of generic forms and rhetorical situations and, as such, includes the following forms and situations. Please note that certain of these overlap with one another and that, in a few instances, a certain passage can be classified under more than one standard designation. The list is in alphabetical order.

acknowledgments
admonishment
allusion
analogue
anatomy
apologia
architecture (in set designs)
autobiography
biographical sketch
charts (of diverse sorts)
chronology
comedy
confession
criticism, literary:
    carping
    deconstructive

impressionistic
influence, anxiety of
intermedia
intertextual
journalistic
Marxist
oracular
psychological
source
curse
dance
declamation, choral
dedication
dialogue
diary
digression

dirge
disquisition
doggerel
drawing
dream vision
elegy
epigram
epigraph
epistle:
  prose
  verse
essay:
  familiar
  literary-critical
  philosophical-theoretical
eulogy
fairy tale
farce
folktale
foreword
genera mixta
gratitude, acknowledgment of
history-play
interview
irony (of diverse sorts)
list
melodrama
memoir
monologue (of diverse sorts)
music, accompanimental (of diverse sorts)
narrative:
  first-person
  second-person
  third-person
notes (of the most diverse sorts, for they
    are my particular passion)
novel:
  academic
  autobiographical
  Bildungs-
  Jewish

Künstler-
  self-conscious
oral discourse
painting, portrait
pantomime
paralipomena
parody
pastiche
photography
plea
poetics
poetry, as divided by periods in chrono-
    logical order:
  Elizabethan blank verse
  seventeenth-century devotional verse
  seventeenth-century emblematic verse
  eighteenth-century octosyllabics
  eighteenth-century heroic couplets
  eighteenth-century sublime verse
  nineteenth-century sonnet
  early twentieth-century Imagist verse
  mid-twentieth-century metrical verse
  mid-twentieth-century free verse
prayer
preface, literary
prophecy
prose, experimental
proverb
psalm
rage
récit
satire
sculpture
self-analysis
short story
song, drinking
syllogism
symphony (cadence of)
title
tragedy
tragicomedy

The following forms are not included in this book (I strongly considered adding them, but the publisher's deadline precluded my doing so):

allegory
ballad
biography, full-scale
criticism, literary:
  Chicagoan
  New

epic
epitaph
epithalamion
fable
film
hymn

masque
narrative, verse
novel:
  family
  Gothic
  historical
  picaresque
  political

ode:
  Horatian
  Pindaric
pastoral
poetry, as divided by periods:
  ancient
  medieval
rondeau

Note: On the generic difference between notes and disquisitions

H-G, as you can see from the following section, writes disquisitions, while I write notes, and this will tell you something of the difference between the two of us. He is formal to the point of austerity, while I am open and spontaneous, the sort who likes to let himself go in all directions at once. In a disquisition such as H-G gives us, you can expect an argument precisely worked out in advance and sticking with unrelenting rigor (exemplified by his refusal to divide his material into paragraphs, which I have quietly introduced into the text to prevent readers from skipping his disquisitions altogether) to what it purported to be discussing in the first place. With me, on the other hand, you cannot predict things in advance, for almost anything might happen in accordance as the spirit moves me. But in deference to the nature of disquisitions (which is H-G's nature as well), I shall constrain myself from interrupting him with annotations (even though I have something to interject at every point of his argument) and save my ammunition till the end (though only, of course, if I should still feel like it then).

THE THREE DISQUISITIONS

1. On fashion

It is fashionable to declare one's freedom from fashion just as one is most enslaved by it. Nobody admits to being any man's slave. Yet nobody cares to exclude himself entirely from the charmed sphere that holds the people who dress for, converse with, impose themselves upon one another. Showing oneself to be in fashion is a means of creating a bond with others; but asserting one's modishness too rashly prevents any bonds from forming in the first place. The trick is to strike the current norm, though with a slight variation of one's own—a belt whose relation to what comes above or below is not immediately apparent, or a mysterious edge to the way one enunciates a commonplace phrase.

The variation one employs can deviate only so far from the fashionable norm, else those who watch or hear you will believe you never knew the norm to begin with. Sticking too close to the norm has its own quite formidable dangers, for others may take you to be lagging behind the times just as you think yourself most securely in tune with them.

Being in fashion is a matter of people sending out signs to one another. Those who observe are also observed, and each party has a huge stake in getting the signs right. There are those who pick up the right signs as though by instinct. There are others who are unable to even after the most assiduous attempts at learning precisely what these signs are and how to transmit and interpret them properly. The signs of course are constantly changing, and those who know their way with them can adjust themselves to these changes without displaying the slightest effort. A show of effort-lessness (whatever conscious effort may be hidden behind it) is essential to being in fashion. What remains constant in fashion, whatever the external changes that are always taking place, is the process by which signs are exchanged and effort suppressed. Thus those who master the process are prepared for whatever changes are expected of them from moment to moment. It is obviously foolish for anybody out of tune with the process to compete with those in fashion.

Yet fashion depends for its very existence (not to speak of its vitality) on a considerable body of persons who will not or cannot belong to fashion. The difficulty for those who deliberately refuse fashion is to convince those in fashion that they are not simply unknowing. However strongly you wish to resist them, you generally end up at their mercy. If, in the late 1970s, you dress or wear your hair the way they did during any of the preceding three decades, you subject yourself to automatic ridicule. If you note that the style of the 1930s is being revived you are subject to at least as much ridicule if you imitate it directly without observing those strictly contemporary variations on the style that are meant to signal your con-sciousness of how the seventies are using the thirties. One does not avoid the problem by escaping to some distant style, such as that of the 1830s (whatever it was they did at the time), for this would label one as bizarre to those in fashion.

Yet how to escape showing one's person in some form or other—unless by burrowing into some shelter that will shield you permanently from the world's eyes. This of course means opting out of ordinary life altogether and few if any are prepared to undertake so demanding an enterprise. Most attempt to avoid this option by cultivating eccentricity, but these do not really escape the tyranny of fashion. Eccentricity is itself a fashion that crops up periodically when the more rigid forms of fashion seem to need some loosening. Those who adopt eccentric stances believe they are flouting fashion, but they do so according to rules that are themselves a manifesta-tion of fashion. Although an eccentricity may deviate conspicuously from the standard fashions of a particular time, the amount of variation per-missible to those who opt for eccentricity is no greater than for those tied to the standard fashions. Even if the follower of standard fashion sees the eccentric as bizarre, and even if the eccentric prides himself on his bizarreness, the latter remains careful to keep within the limits of what he knows to be appropriately bizarre. Moreover, time inevitably compromises bizarreness, for during periods in which eccentricity flourishes, it gradually becomes assimilated by standard fashion, and the bizarre, no matter how threatening it may once have been, begins to lose its bite.

Our consciousness of what is fashionable is always dependent on our knowing what is not: being "in" (to use a recent fashionable word) depends on others being "out." The fashions of eccentricity are created by those who refuse to remain "out" but determine instead to make their outness a new mode of being in. Being in fashion means having at least the illusion, sometimes even the reality of wielding power over others. The fashions of eccentricity are the domain of persons who, threatened by actual or potential powerlessness, band together with other powerless persons to exclude still others who, they hope, can be rendered powerless. Although all who take themselves to be in fashion nurture a feeling of power, they also acknowledge a higher degree of power to those who serve as leaders of fashion. These, as well as the fashions they create or popularize, are praised for being original, imaginative, innovative, never having been seen, thought, done before (or whatever the fashionable word or phrase for something supposedly new is at any given moment). However justly they may be commended, their right to lead is sanctioned by those in fashion well before the contributions they make are considered acceptable as such. If an unsanctioned person conceives or creates the same fashion as one who has been sanctioned, the former cannot be credited with his innovation. Yet many who have later become sanctioned leaders of fashion were once among the unsanctioned; what they have accomplished is the persuasion (often over a considerable period of time and with a considerable expenditure of effort) of a group of allies and followers who convince still others of the need to sanction a new leader.

Just as one fashion displaces another fashion, so every leader of fashion displaces an earlier leader, and just as every fashion has but a limited time-span, so every leader is constantly aware of the precariousness of the power he wields. Thus he is always on guard against those among the unsanctioned who might seek to usurp his leadership. Whenever possible, he seeks to convince possible usurpers to become his allies, supporters, disciples. If he cannot, he must disparage them to the point that they remain conspicuously unsanctioned (though they sometimes succeed in establishing their leadership in the world of eccentric fashion).

A special suspicion attaches to those who complain not of particular fashions but of fashion in general; these persons, as often as not, turn out to be future leaders whose complaints are intended to gain the attention they need so that the fashion public may take them seriously. Since the present disquisition will strike its readers as emphatically disdainful of fashion, I must protest I pose no threat whatever, have no aspirations to leadership or even membership in that company that constitutes the world of fashion. As far as others are concerned, I have disappeared, closed myself off, burrowed my way into so isolated a hole that nobody could plausibly accuse me of seeking to lead or even to follow eccentric fashion. If my attempt to avoid fashion seems extreme, it is because I am acutely conscious of the extraordinary power that fashion wields over all people's lives. Although we generally discern fashion in relatively circumscribed areas, above all in the way people dress and speak, fashion actually motivates all our activities—the careers we choose (or think we choose), the satisfactions, material and spiritual alike, that we seek beyond our work, indeed even the ideas, the ideals, and the gods we most fervently believe in. He who would deny fashion must awaken in the morning unable to choose what to wear, eat, think, or where to go if he has the energy left at this point to leave his bed at all. Fashion gives us the choices that make existence beyond the animal level possible, brings order and composure to a world that would otherwise slip into chaos. Those rash enough to challenge its supremacy or question its value usually end up in awe of it.

I am fully aware that if I, Orlando Hennessy-García, were a name to reckon with in the fashionable world of letters, you would approach these words of mine with reverence, remark upon the originality of the form I have chosen, praise me for having given a significant new life to old ideas or shaken you to the roots with the justness of my devastating vision. I am also aware that if my name has been too much and too long known, you will remark what a disappointment this piece is, how repetitious of all that I (and others) have said before, that a decorous silence would be most appropriate to me at this stage of my life. But of course I am not in fashion, have in fact never been, and you have thus had neither reason nor motivation to read this far into my essay. Even if you should come upon these words by chance, be assured they make no claim upon you who, wherever you are, must feel yourself free at this (or any) point to go your own way.

2. On relationship

Relationship has become the unquestioned absolute within our world. Those without relationship are labeled unfortunate, and we attach to them a special attitude compounded of our pity and our disdain, as when we note somebody dining alone in a restaurant crowded with couples and gaily partying groups. We assume that those who are alone, unless they can satisfactorily explain the circumstances, have failed in relationship. If possible we rehabilitate them, a process for which our society has assiduously cultivated new and often ingenious mechanisms. Nobody need fear being without relationship any longer, for the establishment and proper maintenance of relationships, with one, a few, or many others, can be learned like any other skill. Those with special disabilities (whether of a physical or a mental sort) can find appropriate opportunities to enable them to undertake relationships.

Attaining relationship is among the most visible ways of demonstrating one's success in the world. Although it may seem immodest to display objects of wealth, you need feel no compunction about showing off the closeness you have achieved with another person or group of persons. Doing well in relationship serves as an automatic character reference and thus can be a means of gaining status, wealth, or whatever other goals society deems desirable. For those to whom status and wealth are suspect, success in relationship can serve as a worthy ideal, for it arouses envy and approbation without the taint that accrues to the more material forms of success.

Although many treat it as an end to be achieved, those credited with attaining it remain aware that, much more than status and wealth, relationship is constantly being put to the test and, as a result, must be nurtured and renewed. Thus, it is as much an ongoing process as an end to be attained. Its status as process is manifest in the fact that we have lately made a verb of it. When we say of a person that he relates well, we are voicing one of the highest forms of praise that people bestow on one another nowadays. Our capacity for relating well is observed at all stages of our lives, from nursery school to nursing home. It may seem odd that a verb depicting the interaction of persons should remain intransitive. Yet if *relate* were a transitive verb, its subject would imply his priority, perhaps even superiority, over its object, which of course would make for an unequal relationship. Thus the statement "John loves Sally" renders Sally a passive being, nor does it tell us anything about the success of John's endeavors, while the statement "John relates to Sally" tells us a considerable amount—and of the very best sort—about both parties.

Although the relating process ordinarily takes place among persons, one can also speak of relationships between a human being and some nonperson, such as a deity or an animal. We describe those relationships in much the same way we describe interpersonal relationships, though of course we rarely if ever place as positive an evaluation on them. There was of course a time when the relation between man and God had priority over all other relationships, when men who shunned relationships with persons were honored, sanctified even, by their fellow beings for the relation they had achieved with some higher power. Today those who relate to their God, or to some beloved pet, more successfully than they do to other persons are credited with at least attempting relationship, for some relationship is always better than none at all. Nonhuman relationships, however, are clearly second best, though they are considered quite desirable if they simply supplement successful human relationships.

Since individual relationships are temporally bound, they bear certain resemblances to the process of human life in general. The resemblance is perhaps least evident between the birth of relationships and individual human birth. Except for the fact that the birth of relationships is often accompanied by considerable pain, analogies cannot easily be drawn. There are of course aborted relationships, which, like an ordinary aborted birth, are characterized by pain with nothing to show for it. Doubtless the number of aborted relationships is greater than the number of aborted births, for the start of relationship is particularly subject to missteps of an often trivial or accidental nature: what might have been a satisfying relationship for both parties has been stopped short without fulfillment for either, much time has been wasted, and one or both continue to mourn what might have been. Some relationships experience a relatively painless birth process whose very existence does not become discernible to either party until the process has gone too far to stop. Yet most relationships are born with both parties quite conscious of what is taking place. Indeed, the birth process usually demands a certain amount of verbal persuasion to be exercised to induce the process in the first place.

In relationships with the deity, the persuasion often comes from a third party who otherwise remains outside the relationship. In human relationships, one party generally takes the verbal initiative and until the relationship is thoroughly established, this initiative gives that party the advantage in setting the tone of things. Many persons, of course, do not happen to be particularly verbal and they must depend on other persuasive means. A nicely shaped body has its own persuasive power, sometimes in fact compensating spectacularly for an impoverished verbal capacity.

No matter how solidly established, a relationship can never be taken for granted, and the two parties can never fully relax. The possible death of a relationship seems as thoroughly threatening in modern life as physical death seemed in earlier, less sanitary times. This does not mean that ailing relationships are inevitably doomed to imminent death. Actually whole branches of modern medicine are devoted to the diagnosis, care, healing, and euthanasia of relationships. The ills of relationships (and their cures) are so much bruited about that many persons live in a constant state of hypochondria about their relationships. They analyze ills that may perhaps not exist at all, yet, quite in contrast to its role in physical life, hypochondria all too often works to kill relationships. In the course of trying to locate and understand ills, one or both parties come to fear that the relationship is shaky, and then, through the analysis to which the relationship is subjected, they become convinced that it indeed *is* shaky, after which the relationship is allowed to die.

Not all relationships of course die in this manner, common though it is nowadays. Some die suddenly and unexpectedly at a point when one or both parties decide that the relationship has in fact been dead for a considerable time; or the sudden desire to end it convinces one or both that even while it was thought to be thriving it was never genuinely alive in the first place. People confront the death of their relationships within a large range of styles varying between the extremes of celebration and mourning. Those who opt for the latter often feel the lack of a formal ceremony such as a funeral to ritualize and redirect the terrors that accompany the end. To some degree legal divorce helps serve this function, though that device is currently available only to marital relationships.

There was of course a time when nobody thought much about the life-span of relationships, which, if they were to be called relationships at all, were of a self-evidently permanent nature. Permanent relationship, whatever it was (this was long ago) may well have been lacking in intensity, for only physical death could destroy it, and for those who nurtured ideas of immortality it doubtless seemed pretty slack indeed. Relationship as we know it today gains much of its intensity through our knowledge of its precariousness. One can speak of a certain exhilaration, unnerving even at times, in our awareness that a relationship can be destroyed at any moment, sometimes by a mere whim that nobody can anticipate or properly account for. If permanent relationship was often rather boring, it at least offered serenity and such other satisfactions as a Montaigne or a Bacon could praise in their essays on friendship, a mode of permanent relationship that no writer of any seriousness would have anything to say about today.

At least one mode of permanent relationship still exists—that of relationship with blood relations. Determined as it is by nature, this mode is immune to the whims and workings of the human will and its existence is thus generally ignored today. The one relationship by blood that is still acceptable is that between parents and their young children, but since it is ignored as soon as the latter reach maturity (or its various semblances), it has lost the character of a permanent relationship.

All relationship, no matter how temporary, demands an act of commitment. It may be objected that nonpermanent relationship is inconsistent with the very idea of commitment, but this is not really so, for the real commitment, however it may be verbalized, is neither to the other party nor to the relationship as such, but rather to one's own self.

Thus, relationship is not precisely the absolute we pretend it to be, for it remains subservient to the wiles of the self. Even when the self, moving from one relationship to another, tries out new guises, the self retains a durability (call it permanence or what you will) that no relationship could hope to emulate. Yet the self is also dependent on the availability of relationships for its satisfactions and the self will have its satisfactions no matter what. Relationship makes possible the growth and continuity of the self, though to realize itself adequately, the self must pick up and discard relationships during its various stages of growth. Relationship serves not only as a means by which the self affirms its own existence and endurance, but also as an outward and quite public symbol of the self's success. Thus we see to it that our essential humanity is defined by others through our ability at relationship, and we also see to it that those without relationship are consigned to the lower circles of humanity and shunned as lepers once were. We provide such epithets as *antihero* and *underground man* for those without relationship, we declare them beings without selves, and we symbolize their spiritual impoverishment by rendering them physically impoverished, even grotesque, when we publicize their predicament. A belief in the value of relationship is so pervasive among us that we are all of us on guard against those who might judge us failures at relationship.

If I have sounded skeptical about relationship, I do not mean for you to take this personally. We have no relationship with each other except as writer and reader, and I assure you I do not threaten you with any further relationship, nor do I know, or care to know, how you yourself fare in relationship. We must establish our distance from one another. Although I do not cultivate relationship as you do, I shall not chastise you with words, looks, or thoughts. And you in turn will neither praise nor condemn nor pay the least attention to me if I proceed to go my own way.

3. *On masturbating*

The important thing, while doing it, is not to fantasize, not to romanticize. You must think of this as a practical, quite viable alternative to intercourse, else you'll confuse the two and have to put up with all the disadvantages that go with the latter. The only way for the masturbatory act to maintain its own integrity is to exclude all those frills and distractions that have become a part of intercourse. If you have to imagine a partner, this is not true masturbating, for soon you will find yourself staring at strangers wherever you go and, once you have returned home, you will mentally plop them into bed with you. It is necessary to suppress not only fantasies of possible partners, but also all visual images of sexual organs, including one's own. Above all, one must suppress those prolonged narratives of meeting and courting that other body with which one will then seek to bring the process to its natural and slow conclusion. If you cannot do without the fantasy, then you may as well find yourself a real partner and resign yourself to all the uncertainties and caprices that accompany relationship.

Is it possible, you ask, to resolve on celibacy and avoid the whole process altogether? That would be a fine solution if your body would let you, but once you have rejected intercourse, you must still face the choice of either nocturnal emission or masturbation. I reject the first, for, being involuntary, it produces a fantasy not of one's own choosing plus a messy bed. Since masturbation is the only sensible choice, you must approach it as rationally and systematically as you would any other regular aspect of your life. Time and place must be honored. It is important, for instance, to do it in one's own house and bed and with one's usual night clothes (if one ordinarily wears any) on. Under no circumstances should one do it before a mirror (it goes without saying there must be no onlookers, including oneself). Although custom has associated masturbation with the hand, manual stimulation is distinctly inadvisable, for it calls more than the necessary attention to the act. One is best off simply by lying on one's stomach and allowing the organ to rub vigorously against some disposable rag or paper towel that will absorb any traces otherwise left on the bed or in one's night clothes.

Choosing the best time is every bit as necessary as choosing the appropriate place. For example, stopping one's activities in midday to masturbate is to inflate the activity's importance in the same way as practicing before mirrors. The least conspicuous times are just before going to sleep or first thing in the morning, though it is doubtless equally appropriate if you find yourself waking in the middle of the night. Frequency is a variable thing, depending on one's age and physical disposition. Doing it more than necessary also makes too big a matter of it, while failure to do it frequently enough invites nocturnal emissions and dreams of all those fantasies you thought you'd done away with. Above all, one must maintain one's equanimity against all temptations. Even with the rigor and regularity I have prescribed, there is always the danger of inflating one's image of the self at the moment of climax.

But does this not, you object, rob us of what we have been wont to call our basic humanity? I recognize there are many readjustments to be made in the way we conceive of ourselves, and these will take time. For now I ask only that we try to see through the sexual imperatives that others have imposed upon us, that we remind ourselves we will have no illusions, no attitudinizing about the way we conduct our sexual existence. Can we, for example, acknowledge that our genital organs are simply mechanical instruments, to be taken no more seriously than that other much sentimentalized and much abused organ, the heart? Can we acknowledge as well that the processes in which they engage are no more glorious or mysterious or even problematic than the processes by which the various solids and fluids passing through our body are flushed out? You may also object, in this time of rising feminine consciousness, how it is I dare address myself only to the needs and functions of the male. I must answer my knowledge is limited to what I have learned from my own body, but with the proper anatomical and physiological adjustments, everything I say is doubtless applicable to the female body as well.

Whatever resistance my argument may meet, I no longer feel the need to defend masturbatory activity against those who take it as a form of self-abuse and predict the most dire consequences, mental and physical, for anybody engaging in it. Whatever the condemnation to which it was subjected in earlier times, I can recommend it today as an activity much befitting puritans, since it clears the mind and body for other, more productive enterprises. Those who demand proof of its advantages might note, for instance, how much less time consuming it is than intercourse, which, with its multitude of preambles and postscripts, has kept many a person from realizing his or her creative potential.

There are some who cannot assent to any activity they take to be undignified. I shall not argue that masturbation in any way lends dignity to one's life, but I also assure you it in no way detracts from the dignity one has otherwise achieved (those committed to intercourse are of course constantly laying their dignity on the line). Its most notable virtue is that it lends stability to life, keeps an otherwise precarious self on an even keel. Once you accept the virtues of evenness, you may find a positive pleasure in masturbating. But your pleasure is ultimately dependent on your ability to rid yourself of any longings to bypass or transcend masturbatory experience. The pressure from others is always upon you, for these would have you believe that anybody committed to masturbation is a failure in relationship, while relationship as we know it today (if you will allow me to revert to my earlier arguments) is a fashion whose power few dare to resist. We are all of us afraid to go it alone. I offer no comforts, no alliances, I cast no spells, but I shall also place no pressure upon you. Let us each go our own way.

Note: In refutation of the above

Although I have deliberately refrained from interrupting the tight argument you sustained so well throughout these disquisitions, I can assure you, Orlando, that you had me champing at the bit all the while I was reading, and I can further assure you that however much I may admire your rhetoric, I disagree with you on virtually every point you make. As for your strictures against fashion, has it ever occurred to you that the vast majority of monuments that grace our culture—the various great paintings, poems, dramas, musical compositions, philosophical treatises, political tracts—were fashionable in their own time? There is no necessary antithesis between quality and fashion. I know you will want to cite a number of exceptions, and so can I: everybody knows that a few gigantic figures, such as Hölderlin, Schopenhauer, and the Impressionist painters, were insufficiently appreciated at the time they did their best work. But they are exceptions and you'd be more honest to treat them as such. Furthermore, whether you like it or not (and I suspect you do), the present volume is designed to put you, Orlando Hennessy-García, into fashion. As for your subsequent two disquisitions, the negative feelings you have aroused in me are so strong that even were I to offer logical arguments in refutation, my temper would constantly threaten to undo the calmness of spirit that logic demands. As an alternative mode of refutation, may I suggest that you come visit Luella, me, and our three children to see for yourself what contemporary family life is all about (though kindly give us a few hours notice to get things in order).

Note: On being a presence

The trouble with you, Orlando, is that you have not made yourself a presence. To the extent that you have hidden yourself from the world, you are dependent on the texts you write to exercise what presence you have. And surely you have read enough to know that a text cannot exert its power without a strong presence behind it to impose its own existence upon readers, cajole them into sharing its values, intimidate them (even at the risk of violating the acknowledged norms of civilized behavior) to the point where you can manipulate them into any response you please. Yet how can you hope to exert such effects, Orlando, when your writing keeps insisting it has no designs on anybody and demands nothing more than the freedom to let you go your own way? Frankly I've become a bit weary of having to mediate between you and your readers. It's time you faced up to your own responsibilities, you stern and masturbating moralist: break through the fortress you've reared around yourself so that you may breathe into us that bold and raging spirit that has been bottled up inside you far too long!

KING DAVID'S MEMOIR

1

I have always looked suspiciously upon old men who write memoirs. No matter how faithfully they may try to render the past, their perceptions are invariably compromised by their need to place themselves in a good light. After all, when you know there is little time left, you will work to create the most imposing possible monument by which to be remembered. Memoirs are very much like those edifices men build to commemorate themselves shortly before they die: whatever was uniquely human about these men disappears in favor of something stupidly lofty, inflated, impersonal.

It is not in my nature to leave such monuments. Those who choose to leave memoirs rather than buildings usually do so because they have specific accounts to set straight. The result is they end up making accusations against others and being apologetic about their own acts. I can say at the start I do not feel the need either to accuse or apologize. If others have sometimes been ungrateful or unjust to me, I hold no grudges. Since my lot has been more fortunate than theirs, I can easily afford the generosity it takes to ignore whatever irritations they have caused me. By the same token it would be foolish for me to engage in apologetics. I am not implying I have not done wrong in my time. The errors, injuries, injustices I have committed are doubtless greater than those of many men, for anybody who serves as a leader, whether in war or in peace, is forced by the nature of his role to make numerous decisions, and many of these, on reflection, will probably turn out not to have been the best ones. I have learned to accept my culpability, but my success in accepting it requires my refusal to become defensive. Those who feel the need to defend themselves are usually people who believe their actions have not properly been understood or appreciated. In these, my last years, my policies have achieved a degree of assent rarely attained by rulers with whose reigns I am familiar. The chief flaw I can envision for this memoir is an occasional lapse into self-congratulation, and I shall try to guard against this. If I do not wholly succeed, my people can attribute this failing to the serenity they have been kind enough to allow me.

If my reasons for writing are not primarily to pursue my self-interest, you may ask why I am bothering to write at all. I must explain that I am fully aware of the role I have played in human affairs, aware as well that this role demands I leave a few words behind. Men in later times are likely to be curious about me, speculating about my motives, wondering how it was I attained that which it has been my good fortune to possess. I shall therefore speak of those portions of my life that others will probably remember about me—my relationship to Saul, whose failure made possible my coming to power; my relationship to some of the women who bore my children; and my relationship to my son Absalom, who came closer than any person to destroying the equilibrium that I have luckily possessed since my earliest days. These are not necessarily the portions of my life to which I attach the most importance. I should much prefer to describe the challenges imposed by the battles and the affairs of state that have engaged my skill over the years. But since these are not the events that excite much curiosity for later generations, I leave them to ordinary chroniclers. Whatever fails to arouse much interest is also unlikely to be distorted in the telling.

One warning in advance: I am more impatient of long-windedness than most men. My best writing is in my psalms, whose most notable quality

is that they are short. I might point out that I call this account a memoir
in contrast to memoirs, which are generally expansive enough to allow the
author to dwell lovingly over the details of his life and times. I should
frankly feel impatient writing that sort of piece. Once I have said what
little about myself I feel needs saying, I will simply stop. Those who read
to be entertained must look elsewhere.

2

It is difficult to know where to start in telling of my relations with Saul
and his family. A simple narrative that recounts events in the order they
occurred would go on interminably and shed little light for anybody (or *on*
anybody for that matter). In all phases of life I have always preferred to
organize matters, and I shall do the same in telling my past. All aspects of
the story have their unpleasant side, and I leave the most painful part of
all, Saul's sickness and his jealousy toward me, for last.

I shall start with something that had at least its pleasant side, the story
of Saul's children. Three of these I was deeply involved with. The involve-
ment, I confess, was considerably more on their part than mine. As a
stranger in their household, I was at first reluctant to initiate actions, but
instead allowed others to give me signals as to how I should conduct
myself. Remember I was from a quite impoverished home, my father old
and feeble and without the will or energy to give his sons the push they
needed to get a decent start in the world. Though Saul had started out in
circumstances not much better than my own, by the time I knew him he
and his family had assumed all the trappings of royalty, and I admit I felt
thoroughly impressed. Saul's son Jonathan was the first in the family to
seek out my companionship, and I was content to reciprocate the strong
feelings he continually expressed toward me. In retrospect, I realize he was
a somewhat hysterical type, neglected by his father and desperate to
establish contact with whoever was willing to give him the attention he so
sorely desired. I must have seemed impressive to him on account of the
victory I had won over the giant Goliath (this was, of course, the event
that brought me into Saul's household in the first place, but I shall say no
more of it and leave it to the chroniclers, who have certainly made more
of it than necessary). Jonathan imitated me in all respects, not only my
dress, but my walk, my way of speaking, in short whatever mannerisms
(most of which I was unaware of) he could detect in me. I do not deny
feeling flattered by such attentions coming from a king's son, though I
also know that, lacking a well-defined self of his own, he badly needed
another being in whose self he could participate. Jonathan swore eternal
loyalty to me, and since it pleased him to hear me voice the same senti-
ments to him, I willingly complied. Yet I was already aware that nothing
on this earth is eternal, and that loyalty to other persons is at best a

precarious thing—indeed, that those who exact protestations of loyalty from you are usually those who are far too weak to manage their lives on their own. Still, Jonathan's loyalty stood me in good stead on several occasions when I became the object of his father's wrath. I shall always feel grateful toward him.

Jonathan's feelings toward me, I now recognize, were essentially those of an infatuated lover—no different in kind from those that his two sisters, Merab (the elder) and Michal, expressed toward me as well. The spectacle of three siblings battling over a naive young stranger has its comic aspects, and these were not wholly lost on me. Saul's household, I should explain, had a makeshift, disorderly quality that was scarcely befitting a royal court, and the schemes his children initiated to absorb me into their lives were by and large a reflection of the general atmosphere in which they had grown up. I responded to the two daughters' overtures as pliantly as I had to their brother's. With the lapse of so many years it is of course difficult to untangle precisely what my motives were, but I am certain I must have enjoyed the sense of power one feels over those who seem willing at any moment to throw themselves at one's feet. I do not believe I consciously played one against the other (in effect they were all three taking care of that by themselves), but I confess that in those days I was perhaps more liberal than I needed to be with the use of my body. Merab fell out of the picture when, it unexpectedly turned out, she became betrothed to somebody else. That left the field open to Michal, who became the first of my wives. Since my falling out with Saul had begun even before this, we were not together long. My memory of her remains dim.

My relations with Saul himself were so complex that I cannot pretend to do full justice to them in a short space—though I hope at least to do justice to Saul himself, who, whatever his many failings, has more than earned his place in our pantheon. I have often felt that Saul had more going for him than any man I have known. In certain crucial respects I must recognize his superiority over me. He possessed a brute strength in battle that I could not hope to emulate. If my success in battle has been thought to equal his (even at times to surpass it), this is only because I have managed to compensate by my sense of timing and, perhaps even more important, my ability to organize my men with maximum efficiency.

It is difficult for those who have been successful to understand why others, particularly those with a high potential, are unable to make adequate use of their abilities. As a boy I had often seen Saul distantly on the battlefield and I rejoiced in his victories with something of the same pride I was later to feel in my own victories. I found myself wanting to identify with him, praying for his future victories, mourning despondently on the few occasions the Philistines got the better of him. By the time I was introduced into his household he had every reason to feel comfortable with me. My enthusiasm for his cause was known to everybody around him, and of course I had won him the victory over the giant. Try as I will, I can honestly not remember any ambitions at the time except to use what skills I possessed to further a cause in which I believed fervently. But perhaps I am lapsing into the accusatory and apologetic mode that I promised to avoid. Suffice it to say I was dealing with somebody whose behavior could not be explained in any of the ways comprehensible within my limited experience up to that point. Still, I was the one sent in to heal his melancholy (this was the term his family, desperate for an explanation, used to describe his condition), and I devised a multitude of techniques to meet the challenge. When I was first sent to his room, he was no longer the man I had last seen triumphant on the battlefield. His body was contorted in an immobile position, and his face locked in a grimace that cannot be described with any familiar analogy. He had, in short, lost all his human dignity. I confess I felt no pity for him. Many will condemn me for hardness of heart, and I offer no excuses. Yet I also know that the successes I had (however temporary) in healing the king were largely due to the absence of strong emotion on my part. Healing a person demands a resourcefulness and an agility of mind that pity, or any strong emotion for that matter, can only inhibit.

I do not of course wish to give the impression that I am myself devoid of emotion. Although I have promised not to render yet another account of my fight with the giant, let me mention one thing the chroniclers never consider. There were moments during the fight in which I felt inwardly so shaken I thought I would die of fright. I know that the image people usually have of me does not easily allow for this admission, but I say it for what it is worth. For many people, I'm told, fear quickly leads into panic, and after that, of course, their cause is lost. For me such feelings of fear— and I assure you they occurred regularly during the years I engaged in battle—have served as a challenge to pull myself together, work up my anger toward my opponent, make me consider how I could dispatch him in the quickest possible way. I confess to a certain exhilaration that the whole process sets off.

Not so, alas, with Saul. I am not sure if he ever panicked in battle, but I suspect that when things started going badly for him they first took the form of fear that the fear he was experiencing might perhaps go on and keep him from finishing the fight. This is, of course, the worst possible reaction anybody can have, but I know it to be a common thing among all too many people. Once a fear sets in, they stop what they are doing to assess themselves, after which they start asking themselves if perhaps they might not be doing better than they are, or they worry about others who seem to be doing better, or still others who are doing almost as well, sometimes equally well. Once they decide they cannot go on doing what they do adequately, they begin to ask whether the whole thing was worth doing in the first place, if they would not, in fact, be better off, or truer to themselves, if they did nothing at all. And that's where Saul ended—doing nothing.

By the time I entered his household he was well beyond the introspective stage and totally at the mercy of his various symptoms, which ranged the scale from sloth to sudden violence. The best I could hope to do for him was give him some temporary comfort, as I did with my harp playing, or shake him out of his depressed state (this sometimes demanded a certain harshness on my part), but which also got him to function in a reasonably normal way for as much as two or three days at a time. If I had had no outside interference, I might well have effected a permanent cure, or at least one that allowed him to assume control of his realm long enough to give it some semblance of order. It is not for me to speculate what might have happened. My problem was he needed my services both as healer and fighter and I was often called from his side at the most inopportune moments to lead his troops in battle.

Again, even this arrangement might have worked but for the interference of many well-meaning people who allowed themselves to be carried away unthinkingly as people all too often do. I refer of course to that unfortunate song that made the rounds about Saul killing his thousands and David killing his tens of thousands. There have always been a few who believed I initiated this song, and many more who are certain that I at least encouraged a crowd to chant it at a time the king would be sure to hear. If I firmly deny any sort of connection with this song, I do so in a spirit that is neither accusatory nor apologetic. My reaction to the song when performed in Saul's and my presence was one of acute embarrassment, and its immediate results were so unpleasant for me it is impossible that anybody knowing Saul's condition in the way I did could wish to upset it in so brutal a way.

Be that as it may, from then on Saul's behavior toward me took a consistently violent course, and he no longer allowed me to make any serious attempts at healing him. In fact, I lived in frequent fear for my life, though as in battle I was able to use my fear as a challenge to do whatever was necessary to save my life from the threats to which it was constantly subjected. Still, nobody should underestimate the unsavoriness of an atmosphere in which weapons are tossed about without warning and death plots are hatched with the frequency of rainstorms in winter. As with all disagreeable situations that turn into a way of life, I accustomed myself, adapted myself to it as though this were the way men had been meant to live with one another in the first place. Things might have gone on this way interminably until the common enemy, taking advantage of our situation, had done us all in. As it turned out, the javelin Saul sent my way one morning gave me the boost I had needed all along. It hit the wall less than an inch from my head—it grazed my hair, in fact, and I recognized I was foolish not to flee. As everybody knows, I took arms against my former master. Needless to say, I dreaded the thought of turning into his killer, and I shall always be grateful that the lost battle that precipitated his suicide was against the Philistines and not my own men.

All this was long ago and if feelings of passion have occasionally got in the way of my telling, this is surely understandable. I was obviously too close to Saul, and at too late a stage in his illness, to give him his proper due. Looking back over the years I can even say that Saul has worn well in my memory. While he was alive his craziness and his capriciousness were constant irritants, destroying his former glory in the minds of all who had to witness his acts. I do not believe I was hypocritical (though some may choose to judge me so) when I bemoaned his and Jonathan's death with the cry, "How the mighty are fallen!" But I have nothing to say beyond these words together with those I have scribbled in this memoir. Let others write tragedies about him to place him among the immortals and give him the dignity that was never precisely his.

3

Recalling my love relationships should serve as a pleasant enough idyll sandwiched between events of a distinctly unpleasant nature. I do not deny the pleasantness of this aspect of my life, but the amount one can profitably say about it is limited. Those who characteristically suffer tormented relationships can, of course, write at great length, for their constantly recurring ups and downs easily sustain a reader's interest. Attachments have always come my way easily. Since my military fame started so early in my life, I suppose I was never in a situation in which I had to court a woman in the usual way, and I used to envy men who were forced to measure their success in love by the challenges they had managed to overcome. I have had to remind myself that for me the challenges of courting had their equivalent in the challenges I regularly met in battle, for my military success automatically made me desirable to women. It may well be they would have accepted me even had I possessed unfortunate looks (this one can never know). If I seem to complain, I in no way deny the intense enjoyment I experienced in these relationships. I knew at all times that I was being admired for the power I was thought to represent, and I admit taking full advantage of the situation. In matters of state one dare not allow oneself to enjoy the exercise of power, for one's actions would quickly assume a tyrannical nature. It is different in love, where both parties, the powerful and the powerless, have the rare privilege of enjoying equally.

Unfortunately, of course, one often finds a third person involved whose disappointment is proportionate to the happiness of the two lovers. This is what happened, for instance, in my relationship with Abigail, who came into my life when I passed through her husband's lands while doing battle for Saul. The complicated story of her husband's refusal to pay my men and me the accustomed tribute has been told often enough, and I shall not dwell on those details. When Abigail took it upon herself to deliver the tribute, she staged a scene quite worthy of royalty. I watched her walk lithely down the hill to me with her entourage of servants bearing the choicest gifts her husband's farm could produce (the very things, in fact, he had refused us!). As the procession reached us, she bowed before me with a sprightly ceremoniousness that returns to my memory like few images from the past. I became a more-than-willing participant in her spectacle. Our love was a foregone conclusion well before I was aware of the hate she bore her husband Nabal, a surly type who excited disgust from all who came in contact with him. We created a basis for our love in our common loathing of him. When he died in one of his drunken stupors some days after our meeting, we frankly rejoiced and Abigail joined my fast-expanding household.

I know it is assumed that the Lord struck down Nabal on account of his general meanness and specifically his conduct toward me. Everybody accepts this explanation, and I am not prepared to refute it. But if I too accept it, then I am also forced to accept a similar explanation, namely, that the Lord allowed my first child by Bathsheba to die because I had earlier sent her husband, my general Uriah, to what I knew would be his certain death in battle. I am not one of those who use the Lord's name to provide a simplistic reading of complex events. The Lord obviously has His ways and I am willing to abide by them. But I do not presume to understand them. I have never, for instance, allowed myself to brood about how I stood with the Lord. I have maintained the utmost confidence that whatever happened between Him and me—and let me tell you He has put me through some excruciating tests—He had no thought of abandoning me. And this has made all the difference in the world to me. If I have relatively little occasion to mention His name in these pages, this fact should not be taken as ingratitude, but rather as an expression of my refusal to interfere with what I recognize to be His proper domain.

Those intent on seeing the death of Bathsheba's child as the Lord's attempt to punish me will also have to account for the singularly fine fortune thus far of Bathsheba's next son, Solomon. But I will not press them for an explanation or they will come up with dire predictions for him. If I insist that the Lord's interference in these matters cannot be demonstrated, I do not deny the wrong I did Uriah. I regret it as I regret a multitude of other wrongs I have committed over a long reign. If I resort to such explanations as the notion that I was carried away by love, this neither explains nor excuses anything. Suffice it to say, it simply happened.

Once I became king, it was the natural thing to send out couriers to bring back whatever women had lately caught my fancy. The challenge was not to allow this to become too mechanical an operation, and I confess I came to need special circumstances to help me awaken my interest in women. By accident I spied Bathsheba (I had never seen her before) as I glanced over the palace roof toward the communal menstrual baths, where she was bent over in the midst of her ritual. I sent my men for her before she was properly cleansed, and I shipped her husband off. What more can I say, except that I recognized the whole thing for the forbidden fruit it was, and (if you will permit me to say it) I found it most satisfying.

Of my other relationships, little if anything needs to be said. None have become implanted in my memory with the precision of the two I have mentioned, though I remember that many had great significance for me at the time. As the years pass, each relationship gradually merges in one's memory with the others and one fears in the retelling that particular events and particular women may become erroneously linked. Growing old, I have all too often lost my sense of individual persons but have instead cultivated a collective memory of body rubbing against body, of plunging all too briefly into rich and undiscovered territories. To go on with such descriptions would be foolish. They create unnecessary longings in me—longings I know can never again be satisfied. I shall move to my last topic.

4

But this one is harder to begin than any. I shall not even try to lead into it, but state the main point briefly: my beloved son Absalom tried to take over my kingdom by force. Yet saying this adds nothing to anybody's knowledge. Absalom's rebellion, though now long past, is a famous incident in our people's history, and the facts surrounding it have not excited much controversy. I have not felt myself condemned by others in the matter (as I have in innumerable other issues of a considerably less important nature). You may wonder why I choose to take up a section of this memoir with the incident and I can only answer that it tapped a nerve in me that nothing else in my life ever did. Everybody knows I maintained my customary detachment in my relations with Saul and with the various women in my life. The Absalom rebellion threatened to break through the detachment I had to maintain at all costs to govern successfully.

The details are sordid. That long chain of events leading to the rebellion —my son Amnon's rape of his sister Tamar, Absalom's consequent slaughter of his brother, his setting up his own kingdom and his march upon my city, his sleeping with my concubines in an open tent for all to see—these details have been dwelt on interminably and need not be rehearsed once more. When troubles break out within a family, the high drama generated by outward events can all too easily make one lose sight of the causes behind these events as well as their larger significance. In retrospect I judge the Absalom rebellion to be a relatively minor thing among the events that have marked my reign. Its chief significance is doubtless in what it taught me about myself.

Thus, I now recognize it is sheer irrationality to exercise too much devotion on a child. I do not hide from myself the knowledge that the more devotion I felt toward Absalom, the more he was tempted to defy me. My relation to him can be looked upon as a reversal of all my other relationships, for in my devotion I allowed him an upper hand I have allowed no others before or after. Not that I was aware of this at the time. These things happen with a gradualness that prevents one's being confronted by them at a particular moment and then realizing one must take matters in hand. Although Absalom, as I say, was playing my customary role, I mean this only in the sense that he was calling the stops. In all other respects we had nothing in common. If he had possessed my strength and my detachment he would have deserved to overthrow me, and I should willingly, if also reluctantly, have handed him the kingdom I had built up.

But the children of men who have made it on their own are usually incapable of assuming their fathers' strength, and they are all too often a disappointment to everybody. This was certainly true of Saul's children, though I confess to more instability among my own. (I except Solomon, for whom I have the highest hopes.) It may be I had never sufficiently cultivated my private affairs and when I did so through my love for Absalom, I showed a naiveté and a lack of experience wholly untypical of me in public matters. In one instance after another I would let myself be hurt when I thought Absalom was not feeling grateful for what I did for him. Of course I know that gratitude is a foolish thing to demand of anybody unless one has a political purpose in mind. Many such things that I knew from difficult experience failed to do me any good when it came to my relations with Absalom.

For a short while I accepted the standard opinion that the Lord was withdrawing His favor from me as He had from Saul. But I quickly realized that to assent to this would mean I was expecting the Lord to continue drawing away from me, and I knew my own downfall would surely follow. This of course was intolerable to me and I saw to it that Absalom's army was opposed by all the force and skill I could muster.

Another, less theologically influenced opinion blames Absalom's actions on the bad counsel he received from others, above all Achitophel. I am suspicious of all such simple explanations, even if, in effect, they relieve me of the blame. As you can see I have preferred to face these matters honestly. And though I was able to crush the rebellion decisively, I am honest enough to admit I did not manage all the details with the aplomb on which I had always prided myself. For example, I begged my men to spare Absalom's life, but they knew better and they took matters into their own hands (of course I loathed them for what they did). I had obviously been unable to think out the political consequences of my request. Yet I must also not underestimate the effect that Absalom's violent death had on me. When I learned the news I broke into shrieks and wails such as I never have before or after. The particular cry I uttered, "Absalom, my son, my son," has become legendary and unfortunately has provided sanction for men weaker than myself to give in to whatever emotions come their way. Throughout the protracted rituals that followed Absalom's death I participated with a zeal I had never before allowed myself. Yet gradually, and well before the rituals were done, I found myself conscious of the theatrical quality of the role I was playing, and this was enough to set off the extrication process I needed to jolt me back into life.

But I am hedging too much, skirting an issue that even my professions of honesty have not yet helped me to reveal. I loved Absalom as I have never loved another soul, and I would once again, indeed many times, undergo the suffering he tortured me with only to have him alive. Now I have said it. It hardly matters what this may do to the image other men carry of me.

5

So here I sit, having reached an age where everybody (including myself) is waiting for me to die. They have left me the virgin Abishag to bring me what comfort she can. Although I appreciate her kindness, she will understand why I could not include her among the love relationships I took up earlier. Solomon waits patiently in the wings for his chance to take up his kingly role, and I must say in his behalf he has done nothing to rush me along my way. He knows he will not have to meet the same challenges and uncertainties that I have met, for I am leaving him a stable and finely organized state that, with the proper care I am confident he can give it, will stay on a fairly even keel. I make no pretensions of course to having created the perfect state in which everything runs like clockwork. However much this desire may come over a ruler, he must accustom himself to imperfections, temporary solutions, irritations that never seem completely to go away. I have accustomed myself, for instance, to the bad feelings that the surviving members of Saul's family have continually directed against me over the years. However unjust I know these accusations to be, I can understand the family's need to blame somebody for the downfall of their house. Nursing a state along is like nursing a human being (that's something I learned from nursing Saul). You can't predict what may happen from day to day and you learn never to expect too much. I do not know exactly what people mean when they speak of wisdom, but I suspect I do not possess it (even now in my old age). Practicality yes, but if by wisdom they mean the insights that come from prolonged and deep suffering, I make no claim to this sort of knowledge. Saul might have emerged a wise man if his destructive impulses had not finally got the upper hand. There are things he knew that I recognize I shall never know. I do not envy him. Though men credit me with triumphs of the highest order, I know I have achieved what I have to the neglect of many experiences that other men have found valuable. I admit it has taken me until now to understand that these experiences that have remained foreign to me should be treated with respect. If what I speak is in any way a sort of wisdom, I am happy to possess at least this much of it.

BACKGROUND MATERIALS

PART TWO

*Analogues to Saul's Fall
from the Author's Earlier
Writings*

Note: On the difficulty of organizing this book

Nobody will ever appreciate the difficulties I have confronted in deciding where to place the various items that make up this volume. It was simple enough to figure out where the introduction and conclusion should go (not to speak of the foreword and acknowledgements), while the conventions of a critical edition dictate that the central text be placed near the beginning and the essays in criticism near the end. Grateful though I am that H-G himself took care of the order in which the episodes of his play should appear, I had no ready-made criterion as to where to place the essays in criticism in relation to one another. Should they be ordered in ascending or descending sequence according to what I take to be the importance of each critic? Or should they be ordered temporally according to the relative contemporaneity of each critic's approach? Or temporally in the order in which I received them in the mail (that's what I finally settled for, since I'm not yet at that point in my career where I can afford to make enemies—please note as well that the dialogue I taped and the single already-published essay in criticism, Roy Curley's review of the play in the local newspaper, have been placed discretely in the middle of the section).

The greatest difficulty—and I count this among the major scholarly hurdles I have ever encountered—lay in how to order the background materials. Of course convention dictates that this section must come in the middle—that is, between the dramatic text and the essays in criticism. Yet once this convention has been met, there exists no authority to guide an editor in arranging the order of the innumerable and disparate texts that make up this section. My problem was not any fear of offending the author, who I was certain would never let any objections he might have to my procedures be known. Rather, I was much more concerned with making the order seem both plausible and handy to the reader. I early decided to print the items that H-G entitled "Saul's Fall Overflow" in the order in which he had tied them together in the suitcase. Yet I also recognized that the letters he had sent me regarding the play as well as the tape of our interview constituted a legitimate part of what any self-respecting edition would include as paralipomena to the central text, and as a result I took the liberty of interspersing these among the overflow writings at what seemed (after considerable and tortured self-deliberation) the most appropriate points.

The second section of background materials, namely, H-G's writings preceding Saul's Fall, proved a far touchier exercise in ordering. Choosing the actual texts was no great problem, for I was able to utilize an iron-clad criterion, namely, that each text had to be discernibly analogous in form or theme to an episode in the play. But what order to print these in? I should happily have solved the problem by publishing the texts in the order of the play's episodes to which they served as analogues—but since most episodes had more than a single analogue among the earlier writings, this solution was clearly impossible. Another ordering device might have been strict chronology according to the periods in H-G's life when the events he was describing occurred. But where would I place "Fairy Tale," which, whatever its psychological implications, is not autobiographical in any strict sense? And where the "Growth Paper," which, though autobiographical in the extreme, encompasses the periods during which nearly all the other texts take place? Finally, I settled on another, less tangled form of chronology, namely, the order in which H-G presumably wrote these various pieces. This still left problems: for instance, since the two uncompleted novels, however different in style, utilize much the same autobiographical material, an incident from the first such as "Three Projects," which took place when the protagonist was in his late teens, would have to be printed before "Scoldings of the Week," which took place when he was only four. The uncertainties of authorial status and intent surrounding "An Epistolary Exchange," which I discuss in detail in my note following that section, created still another dilemma that, in an unreflective moment, I resolved by simply throwing the text between the passages from the two uncompleted novels. And what about "The Margo Experience," a text that I myself wrote on the basis of revelations about H-G's oral discourse from a sometime acquaintance of his? At the time he uttered this discourse, which was also about the time of the "Growth Paper," he claimed to be half-way through a draft of the first of the novels. Was I to sandwich these two sections between the passages I have included from this novel? But what if he had not yet written the first of these sections, "Sunday Dinner at the C's," which is about halfway through the manuscript? The more introspective I became about the whole process, the more I came to recognize there is only one thing certain for an editor—that classifying with conscience results in the most profound agony.

Note: To librarians attempting to classify this book

If my own job of organizing has been fraught with difficulties, these are nothing compared with the task you are about to face. Whichever classificatory system you employ, you are assigning the book a number that will determine once and for all time the companion volumes it must consort with on its shelf. In view of the fact that the play is the centerpiece (not to speak of the title) around which the entire book revolves, are you automatically placing it in the drama section? Before you do so, I might mention that H-G's various narratives, autobiographical or otherwise, count up to more words than the play and that you could thus argue for a number ordinarily assigned to fiction. But if you disregard length and instead consider intensity of effect, you will note that the poems (not merely the "Lyric Suites" but also the "Epilogue" and "Epistle in Reply") loom more memorably in the reader's mind than any other genre within this book. Whatever the solution to these dilemmas, will the number you choose pin H-G down as a British or as an American writer? Yet what if you do not base your classification on H-G at all, but, acknowledging that his work cannot be understood properly without the diverse essays in criticism and my own copious notes, you elect to place us all on the criticism shelf? Since you may well feel ready to tear your hair out at this point, why not concoct a number unrelated to any of the above categories and simply admit that this book, by its very nature, eludes all your systems?

A HERO'S DEATH IN THE SPANISH CIVIL WAR

Note: This is H-G's only known published work. It appeared in The Scroll, *the literary magazine of Fort Edmunds School, Fort Edmunds, Ontario, in the Winter, 1949, issue when H-G would have been thirteen years old. Analogue: "Inquiry."*

The driving autumn rains in this first year of the Spanish Civil War had interrupted the only relaxation on which Don Pedro García's men had come to count. All through that first summer in the lulls between the various battles they sat at a river bank and sang together to the accompaniment of a guitar that one of the men, Pablo, always managed to carry along. It was by singing together that they were able to express their anger at the hated Fascists who were trying to take over their duly elected Republic. Many an evening near a clump of poplar trees and with the blue Duero slowly rolling by they would sing "Los Cuatro Generales," whose words, sung to a popular old folk tune that did not itself have any political meaning, were actually a scathing attack on the Fascists. Singing this song, and others too, gave them all a feeling of well-being and provided them with the courage they needed to sustain the next day's assaults.

Courage was a special problem for Don Pedro. Although he knew inside that he possessed great reserves of courage for whenever the occasion demanded, the impression he made on the men under him, most of whom had not had much formal education, was that of a thoughtful and somewhat shy person, one who might not be very well prepared to do the right thing under fire.

During one of the group's retreats along the Duero, it was discovered that they had left their flag behind.

"I feel terrible about this, for the Fascists will use it to taunt us," Don Pedro told his men.

"Better let it be," said Pablo, who probably had more fear about losing his guitar than losing the flag. "We must not be tempted to lose our lives for something that is not completely necessary to us."

Then Don Pedro, who had been very quiet up to now, spoke up in his patient but firm way: "Leave it to me. I shall retrieve our flag."

"Do not do so, Don Pedro," the men admonished him, almost in a chorus.

"I know the castle intimately, every nook and cranny of it," Don Pedro asserted. He was speaking about the nearby medieval castle that the Fascists were occupying and to which they had removed the Loyalist flag, which was now insultingly being allowed to fly upside down from the bottom of a protruding tower. Don Pedro had known the castle since childhood, often having played in it.

The men worked hard to hold him back, but he was obviously determined. It was twilight and the rain was still falling heavily. "I shall be hidden by the dark and the rain," he said to reassure his men.

They followed him a ways, but kept carefully out of sight of the Fascist sentries who were sure to be looking down from the battlements. Don Pedro García quietly gestured his men to stand back. Fear was in their eyes, but if there was fear in his, he did not allow it to show. He walked ahead in the driving rain and when he reached the base of the castle he slowly, deliberately began to climb. From his childhood he still remembered which stones on the wall protruded enough to give him a foothold, though it was harder now, for he was bigger, and what was an easy foothold for a child was not necessarily one for a grown man. Still, he persisted and despite the rain and the failing light his men, well hidden in a hole they found at the edge of the road (and which also gave them a little protection from the rain), watched him with awe as he made his precipitous way upward.

Don Pedro García managed to get very near to the jutting tower from which the flag was dangling downward so insultingly. Every move he took was careful, yet also deliberate. His men had never witnessed anything like this and they could hardly believe that a gentle person like Don Pedro would ever be able to conduct himself in this way.

When he arrived at a point from which he could reach out to a corner of the flag, he stopped a moment to stabilize his position before extending his hand. As his men looked at him he seemed to dangle precipitously, but in reality he was quite firmly placed. His one free hand got hold of a corner of the flag, and with one sharp tug he tore it off and stuffed it inside his shirt. His men cheered silently to themselves as they witnessed what they took to be a wonder from above.

Then all of a sudden, just as Don Pedro was starting his descent, a sentry appeared on top of the jutting tower. "Who goes there, friend or enemy?" the sentry asked brusquely. Don Pedro feared this would be the end, and so did his men. The big question for his men was how he would answer the sentry. At first he said nothing, but started down the wall in hopes of making it since after all it would not be easy to aim accurately at him in the rain and the impending darkness. The sentry beckoned to other towers and a number of Fascist soldiers appeared on the battlements to watch Don Pedro's descent.

"Stop or we will shoot," one of them cried out, shooting his gun in the air.

"Are you friend or enemy?" the sentry asked again.

"Look, he has stolen the enemy flag we were exhibiting," screamed a Fascist on one of the battlements. Then they all noticed the flag was indeed missing from the place where they had let it perch ignominiously.

A frightening moment of silence ensued in which the various men on the battlements took aim. Don Pedro, recognizing what was about to happen, suddenly spoke up in a loud and firm voice clearly audible to the Fascists and his own men alike. "I defy you all in the name of freedom, honor, justice, and truth!" Don Pedro exclaimed. He had hardly finished the final word when the shots rang out. The last glimpse his men got of him was of a headless body momentarily hanging to the wall, then suddenly dropping to the cold and soaking ground.

They made no attempt to retrieve the body (much as they would have wanted to), for they knew it was better for their cause that their own lives be saved.

But Don Pedro García's death was not in vain. His group of men held loyally together during the remaining years of the war, and they were known to have fought valiantly—much more so than before their leader's death. And when the summer came again, in moments between battles they sat along the various great rivers of Spain, the Ebro, the Tagus, the Guadalquivir, singing "Los Cuatro Generales" and their other songs to the strumming of Pablo's guitar. And these songs now had a new meaning for them.

*　*　*

The author is proud to let those who have read this story know that the hero is a portrait of his own father, who was killed in action early in the Spanish Civil War fighting on the side of the Spanish Republic.

Note: It is highly unlikely that H-G knew any details about his father's death at the time he wrote this story. For one thing, he did not establish contact with his Spanish relatives until after his mother's death several years later, and she had herself lost contact with the family as soon as the war began. Moreover, H-G shows virtually no knowledge of the historical and geographical details of the war. The whole valley of the Duero, including the city of Valladolid, where his father grew up, was taken by Franco's forces during the first summer of the war, 1936, and the idea of a small band of Republican soldiers fighting along the river during the subsequent autumn is not historically credible. Moreover, most of the valley of both the Tagus and the Guadalquivir Rivers was in Franco's hands well before the second summer of the war, and thus H-G's ending, which has the band of soldiers singing their songs along these streams after this time, could not very likely have taken place. One is forced to conclude that the story, which was later to supply the germ of the incident surrounding Citizen 2 in "Inquiry," is more a product of the author's youthful idealism than any attempt on his part at genuine historical reconstruction.

FAIRY TALE

Note: Typescript attached by paper clip to "A Hero's Death in the Spanish Civil War." Analogue: "Conspiracy."

Once upon a time there was a king who was always being pestered by people. Every time he wanted to sit on his throne to play with his scepter or stroke his cat's fur somebody would rush in to tell him something must be done right away or else everything would go to pot. He kept trying to ward these people off with one sly hint after another, but nobody would take hints. One day a genie came dancing in and the king was sure that here was still another person come to pester him, even though nobody had ever entered the throne room dancing. "I'd just as soon you give me a few minutes before pestering me," the king said softly. "What makes you think I came here to pester?" asked the genie. "But that's what people are for, and I'm getting mighty tired of this," said the king. "You shouldn't jump to conclusions so quickly," said the genie. "Then what are you here for?" asked the king. "To grant you whatever you wish," said the genie. "Then do something to keep people from pestering me all the time," said the king. "Will do," said the genie dancing out the door. The king waited for the genie to come back and tell him what he had done, but he didn't come back. After a while the king noticed that fewer and fewer people were coming in. When nobody had come in for a long while, he got off his throne, pulled open the heavy drapes of the throne room and looked out over the city, where there was not a soul on the streets or even the slightest wisp of smoke coming from any chimney, though it was deepest winter. "Where's that genie?" he shouted impatiently, and the genie was back in no time at all. "What have you done?" asked the king. "Granted your wish," said the genie, disappearing as fast as he had come. The king drew back the heavy drapes. He walked to his throne ceremoniously and, grinning to himself, he sat down to admire his scepter, stroke his cat till it purred, and live happily ever after.

The following hand-written note is attached to the typescript of "Fairy Tale":

This is very well written and we want you to know, Orlando, that we feel your writing skill is in no way involved with our decision not to print it in *The Scroll*. We are convinced that if you think about the story a while and look at it in a few months you will feel grateful it wasn't printed for other people to see. Incidentally, we hope you are still feeling properly proud of "A Hero's Death in the Spanish Civil War," which received a number of lovely comments from parents soon after our last issue came out.

GROWTH PAPER

*Submitted to the Bard College Committee
on Psychological and Social Development
in Fulfillment of the Second-Year
Growth Requirement, June 1956*

Analogues: "Prologue," "Battle 1," "Prayer," "Endings," "March 2."

Since your assignment assumes we are all the products of our various origins, I start by reciting a few facts about my parents. But I must warn you that these facts may not connect persuasively with the person I am today and if this paper does not successfully fulfill the requirement you have set, it is perhaps not so much because of my incompetence in self-analysis, or even an unwillingness on my part to engage in it, but because some of us, like it or not, are anomalies according to the systems of thought that prevail today. I recognize you have the best of pedagogic intentions when, in your assignment sheet, you suggest we apply our knowledge of Marx and Freud (and even some of the lesser luminaries we took up in Dr. Ohrenstein's History of Western Consciousness course) to an understanding of our own lives. It is a fine thing, I'm sure, to show how our culture's great theoretical constructs can be related to what we say and think and do, but please understand that my own life does not lend itself readily to such connections.

I forgo further apologies. My mother, Beatrice Hennessy-García, was British. She liked to think of herself as English, despite the Irish name. Her father, whom I never knew, was a colonel dating from Britain's best imperial days, and my mother grew up in various colonial domains—India, Singapore, East Africa. Her own mother died when she was a child and I know little about her except that she had inherited considerable wealth from a father who had manufactured cotton goods in the Midlands during the last century. I know you would like me to establish some connection at this point to Engels' analysis of working conditions in Manchester at that time, but I am not prepared to say anything beyond the obvious. Perhaps I should add at this point that this is the same money (what little is left of it) that is seeing me through college and may, if I'm fortunate with the companies it has been invested in, keep me from having to make professional commitments before I feel ready for them. (You may wonder if I feel guilty about the money, and I can say with some assurance that I do not. I doubtless feel a lot of guilt about a lot of things, and I cannot guarantee that perhaps some of this guilt may have some unconscious connection with what my maternal great-grandfather might have done to the women and children, not to speak of the men, working for him a century ago—I cannot guarantee this, for the selections from Freud you have had me read make it amply clear how much we have all repressed, so God knows what bad feelings I may feel lurking in my subterranean depths, or into what lofty sublimations my guilt may have transformed itself.)

But to return to my history. My father played no real role in my life. (I know this statement doesn't make Freudian sense, for even if a child was born posthumously, as I indeed was, some other person or force in a woman's life should automatically emerge to fill in the third angle of the Oedipal triangle. I really wish I could make things fit the coherent pattern your assignment calls for; nothing would make me happier, but this is not possible.) If I say my father played no role in my life, I do not imply that his absence has been a matter of indifference to me. Nor do I believe I have consciously longed for a father (God knows *what* I have longed for unconsciously), but I have had the curiosity natural to anybody who knew from the start he was forever denied the possibility of contact with half the force that created him. My father was Spanish. His family had been solidly established in the provincial city of Valladolid since the expulsion of the Moors. He was passionately committed to the history and the arts of his native region, and since he evidently did not have to work for much of a living, he spent his days supervising the local museum of polychrome sculpture, a form that had flourished in the area during late medieval times. My mother, always on the lookout for exotic things to do, came to Valladolid to study the sculptures, perhaps (if she could screw up her courage enough) even to prepare an illustrated book on them. From what

I pieced together in later years from her own testimony and that of his family, my conception came about through a series of misunderstandings that can best be ascribed to differences in national character (neither Marx nor Freud are of help here). My mother pestered my father for help in the museum, and my father, never having met a persistent British female before, took her pleas for intellectual counsel to be sexual overtures and he reciprocated in kind (or what he thought to be in kind). She in turn took his response to be simply a show of concern. In short they got their signals crossed and I was the unhappy result. To the end of her life she let it be known this was the one and only time she experienced sexual penetration.

Beyond this, I have only the slightest inkling what went on in their lives during this period. Certainly they never kept house together. She returned to England quite unaware she had conceived. Once her situation became evident she notified him by telegram, and with so discreet a touch, he absolutely failed to get the point and wired back his congratulations on the completion of her book. I gather she made an attempt or two to take her own life, then precipitously dashed off to Spain to confront him directly. To her utter surprise he married her and she returned to England never to see him again. Spaniard and Catholic that he was, he obviously made a sacrifice of the most enormous sort, for it meant that no future (and presumably more carefully considered) marriage was possible. As it turned out, it would have been impossible anyway, for shortly before my birth he died fighting on the Republican side during one of the early engagements of the Spanish Civil War. You will note I have idealized him, and I do not deny this. What to make of this fact is another thing. Can it be that in never knowing him I lacked an Oedipal rival and could thus afford to ennoble his memory? Or would you prefer me to see him as the terrifying rival after all, with my adoration of his memory simply a way of sublimating the guilt I feel for my joy in his quick and all too convenient death? Take what interpretation you will, I scarcely care.

But to return to my history (though that word implies continuities that are simply not there). If I have had a history, it is one not of continuities but of disruptions, though anybody who wishes to point out possible continuities underlying the disruptions should feel free to do so. As far as I'm concerned, everything about my background seems strange, nothing seems typical, and I have no idea how to fit myself into any of the standard frameworks, whether those lofty ones developed in Dr. Ohrenstein's course or those one finds in popular handbooks. It would be marvelous of course to have the security of a framework telling me who and what and where I am. But I have come to suspect that people's attempts to define substantial and coherent selves are simply the way they drug themselves into feeling comfortable about doing what the world expects of them. So— to return to my history, or rather my disruptions, which during my earliest years took two principal forms: first, being left for whole days, sometimes whole weeks with a nanny (she was loving, warm, and fulfilled all her traditional functions, but I could not honestly return her affection, which always seemed to me a bit contrived) while my mother was busy with her various writing projects (few of which, despite much hard work and constant attempts to impose herself upon the reigning powers within the intellectual establishment, resulted in publication); and second, being taken by my mother (sometimes with Nanny, occasionally without, which was much worse, since Nanny was a buffer between us) to various picturesque places—Taormina, Antibes, Malta, Alexandria, though never to Spain— where she sought inspiration and stimulus for her pursuits. I never had a chance to develop playmates nor to feel myself rooted in any particular ambiance, and thus I early came to see myself as a person without context. I recognize that speaking in this way may impress others that I am eliciting feelings of compassion from them. Yet I do not mean my remarks to exact emotional effects of any sort from those of you who are sitting in judgment of this paper. Please treat these remarks as a means I have sought to explain some things to myself and to you as dispassionately as I can, though I recognize that, like it or not, the words we use always have some effect on others as well as on oneself.

I return to my disruptions, which happened to take a more pronounced form after I left England soon after the start of the war. Since it was quite common at the time for English families to send their children to Canada to avoid the air raids, I should make it known from the start that my mother had genuine humanitarian reasons for sending me to a safe and far-off continent (I do not deny that she frankly felt relieved to be rid of the pressures emanating daily from a curious, precocious, demanding, and easily bored only child). As it turned out, I never even saw my mother between the ages of four and thirteen, at which point she turned up in New York and after which I lived with her sporadically between her various bouts with mental illness (no Freudian perspective, incidentally, is applicable to her, for she was no ordinary upper-middle-class neurotic with couch-curable symptoms; rather, to cite the words I once used to confront her with the truth of her condition, she was gloriously, hopelessly insane!). During the long interim before she turned up in this hemisphere, I lived with one Canadian family after another. I recently figured I averaged about fourteen months per family, though in one case relations were severed by mutual consent after only two weeks, and in another case (I can scarcely call it a lucky one, for tensions ran high throughout) I lasted virtually two years. These were all quite genteel families who were doing their patriotic duty by me—all with well-scrubbed children my age, and all connected in some way by a network of friendship or relationship (often so tenuous a social worker would have to be called in to remind us all of our bonds to one another) with my relations in England. I myself felt no genuine bond with any of them and I confess there is not a single one of these families with whom I am now in correspondence. For all I know there is not a one that even knows I am a student at Bard. You will wonder why this frequent movement from family to family, and I can only say that in every instance there developed strains that could be resolved only by a total break. You will also wonder if I unconsciously "arranged" for these breaks (this is surely where Freud could be invoked), but I can only reply that indeed they were "arranged," though by no means unconsciously on my part. It is no secret to anyone who knows me at Bard that I do not easily form relationships with others, nor was I able to during my Canadian childhood. Once I had reached the point with a family (especially with the other children) where I knew one more day would be unbearable, I systematically saw to it that some unforgivable incident (nothing ever violent, but something grossly unpleasant just the same) would occur to make a change mandatory. It always took considerably more than a day to effect the change and I learned to make the unbearable at least temporarily bearable by withdrawing into myself. Since I carried my own money, finding a family was not as difficult as it was with some of the British children who had been sent to Canada. (There might be a nice synthesis of Freudian and Marxist insights into my behavior at this point, but this I leave to others should they care to bother.)

Once the war was over I was never repatriated to England. Not that I cared, for I felt no real ties there, except perhaps to my mother, who arranged that I stay in Canada until she was ready to join me (it took her a few years to get ready) on this side of the ocean. Beatrice Hennessy-García (by Spanish custom, incidentally, she should have been Beatrice Hennessy de García, by Anglo-American custom simply Mrs. Beatrice García, or even Mrs. Pedro García, and needless to say she would have been glad to drop the García altogether, but since the seed unwittingly planted in her by Señor García had had such a public result she settled for the strange concoction Hennessy-García, which recognized her marital status while reserving star billing for her ancestral name) came to this country with high hopes of succeeding where she had failed in London, namely, in establishing herself in (as she put it) literary and artistic circles. She had been notably unsuccessful, for instance, in gaining the sponsorship of Virginia Woolf, on whom she doted from afar and who, in her one interview with my mother, was cold and patronizing. Not that New York was any improvement over London, for if she had trouble getting signals straight with people of her own background, imagine what a time she must have had with the Jewish intellectuals (I intend no slurs) who happen to dominate the circles she sought to penetrate here. As it turned out, she never had much opportunity in New York for pursuing her interests or ambitions, for a good bit of her time was necessarily devoted to wrestling with the mental disease that plagued her off and on for the rest of her life. I spent so little time with her, in fact, that you will doubtless find it inappropriate for me to devote as much space to her in this, my own growth paper. She boarded me out in several schools, none of which I stayed in long enough to break the pattern of disruptions that have come to be the history of my life (see, there *is* an underlying continuity here after all). During those periods that she was not institutionalized, I spent vacations in her apartment, which she shared occasionally with some woman friend. I kept my verbal contacts with her down to the minimum (not that I had friends of my own to talk to—I am a loner by nature, rearing, or whatever, and I am not prepared to make apologies).

This is not to say I have shunned all contact with my roots. Last summer, soon after my mother's suicide (I won't go into that since it had nothing to do with our relationship to each other) I went to Europe and introduced myself to my various relatives in England and Spain. I must have felt the need to find continuity with something tangible in my past, but if anything these visits demonstrated once and for all (though for different reasons in each country) that it was useless to seek refuge, consolation, or even pleasure in contacts of this sort. My English relatives were formal and correct, they invited me for tea one by one as soon as I announced my presence to each, and I consciously (though doubtless also awkwardly) did my best to respond to them as I thought they would want me to respond. There were of course no bonds between us. My mother had always kept her distance from them, and, for that matter, none of them were closer than cousins and, more often than not, cousins at a second or third remove. I rather doubt that most of them will remember me (unless for my awkwardness) if I should try to call on them again. Although I did not cherish the best possible memories of my nanny, I went to some effort to seek her out in the old-age home in which she had been placed; she turned out to be as senile as my mother had been insane, and throughout our brief meeting she had me confused with one of her charges from another stage of her career.

Since I have left my Spanish visit for last, you may well think I am preparing for some resoundingly triumphant ending that will compensate for the failure, or at least the barrenness, of my other family relationships. And to a certain degree there *was* something triumphant about the way I was received by my Spanish relatives. Although they had never met me, and although only two of them had even met my mother (these had served as witnesses at her wedding), they accepted me as a long-lost son whom they overwhelmed with an extraordinary warmth that I, alas, was unprepared to reciprocate. The linguistic and cultural barriers proved insuperable (I won't go into the embarrassing details), but I know that as long as I bear their name, they will always welcome me among them—and this despite the fact that I must have struck them as the coldest of fish. They will never understand how grateful I feel for the heartiness they lavished on me—though I was always aware they would have deemed any relative of theirs, be he stupid, mean, malevolent, or even insane, worthy of the same treatment.

You will wonder where I go from here. I know there is nothing you would rather hear from me than some resolution that, as a result of the insights I have gained into myself since coming to Bard, I will channel my energies to create a life bursting with high achievement. But I can chart no significant continuities in my life, no upward growth patterns as your assignment clearly seeks to have us locate within ourselves. If I admit that I am about halfway through an autobiographical (what else?) novel, you will doubtless try to convince me that this in itself constitutes the sort of growth and achievement you so badly wish to see manifested in all of us. But I should assure you, first, that my novel is not intended to be seen by anybody but myself and, second, that my purpose in writing has been to define for myself precisely what happened to me, what sort of things went wrong along the way (I am not bothering with unanswerable questions of the "Who am I?" type). My working title, A Prelude to Nothing, will hopefully frustrate any expectations anybody may have at this point that I have been priming myself for a gratifying and illustrious future. In one of his most celebrated passages, Karl Marx noted that when historical events recur, what first took the form of tragedy repeats itself as farce. My novel attempts to reconstitute the private events of my life and to transform them into something at least droll, though not precisely farcical. I do not of course pretend that the events themselves were the stuff of tragedy; at best they make for pathos and, more often than not, for something of too little consequence to be worth talking about. This does not mean my life has been wholly lacking in drama; indeed, despite my persistent attempts to withdraw from human situations, I have experienced more than a nineteen year old's fair share of dramatic moments. Sigmund Freud has written at length of the awesome consequences affecting children who witness the so-called primal scene. I confess to being one of those who was fated for such a scene—or at least a significant variation upon it. Had I been among the luckier ones, I should have seen nothing more earthshaking than a small, swarthy Spaniard clutching, as best he could, a tall and none-too-willing Anglo-Irish woman. But this, for reasons I have indicated above, was not to be. Rather, I had the misfortune, four years ago, when pushing open the wrong door in my mother's New York apartment, of witnessing two intellectual and spindly ladies locked in a ridiculous but still quite fervent embrace. I have not yet reached this scene in my novel, and I shall have to marshal all the verbal resources at my command to do justice to it.

In the meantime please note that I *have* found a way of accommodating Marx and Freud to the present paper—and in one fell swoop at that!

Still, I have doubts that I have properly fulfilled your assignment according to either the spirit or the letter of your rules. I genuinely wish I could please you, but that is not possible. Please do not ask me to start over again, for that would, in effect, be asking me to redo my life along lines selected by those who have not themselves lived anything remotely of the sort. And do not reach out to me with sympathy as well-meaning people are all too likely to do these days. I am prepared to accept whatever consequences you see stemming from my actions, even if this means that I shall never fulfill what I understand to be a nonnegotiable requirement for graduation from Bard College. And please do not reprimand me as a rebellious type, for that would imply we have entered into a relationship that will commit us both to make accommodations to one another in however perverse a style. I ask only that you allow me to go my own way.

The following handwritten note appears on the final page of the paper:

It is difficult to comment on a paper that from its opening lines is antagonistic to our mutual enterprise. We laud you for your honesty in recognizing that you have failed to carry out the assignment either in spirit or in letter. We shall take you at your word and shall not "reach out in sympathy," as you put it, or treat you as what you call "a rebellious type." We shall however—despite your request—ask you to redo the paper, but we ask that you put it off for at least six months and hand it in no later than a year from now, by which time you will have had some opportunity to reconsider the issues at which we seem to be at variance. You may also wish to avail yourself of the services offered by our psychological counselling center. Our decision to ask you to redo the paper during the coming year was reached after considerable discussion by our committee, which as you know includes two student members, both of whom are in full accord with the decision.

There is no indication that H-G ever redid the paper, for he never returned to Bard College after the time it was handed in. Several autobiographical incidents and facts referred to in the paper—among them his difficulties adjusting to a Canadian family, his mother's insanity, his visit to his nanny and to his relatives in Spain—are depicted in those passages from his two unfinished novel manuscripts reprinted in this volume as analogues to episodes in Saul's Fall. Although the incident relating to the primal scene he witnessed appears in both manuscripts (though in sharply different narrative styles), I have not been able to relate it to any episodes in the play and have thus, despite its intrinsic interest, been unable to justify its inclusion here.

THE MARGO EXPERIENCE

Analogues: "Prayer," "Endings."

Among the many mystifying and seemingly inexplicable documents I found in the suitcase was a sheet of paper with the name Margo written on it a total of seventy-four times. Perhaps the most remarkable thing about the document is that the name was not simply repeated in straight columns, but was scribbled in various directions—at diagonals, in corners, upside-down. Sometimes it was in block letters, sometimes in cursive, and once (at the lower right-hand corner) in an imitation of Gothic print. The forty examples of the name in block letters were in various sizes, ranging from one instance in which the reader needs a magnifying glass to make out the letters clearly, to another instance in which the letters measured fully one and a quarter inches from top to bottom. The thirty-three in cursive attempted a different style of penmanship in each instance —so successfully, in fact, that the viewer is likely to think they were written by thirty-three different persons. Some were relatively neat, others distinctly messy; some showed what might be taken as tender, loving strokes, others had a jerky, almost angry quality. My own suspicions that everything on the sheet was written in H-G's hand (suspicions based on what seemed to me simply psychological probabilities) were confirmed for me on scientific grounds by the noted handwriting expert Dr. Richard Kopp of the Department of Criminology, University of California, Berkeley.

I should have liked to reproduce this curious document in this volume, but I decided that in order to give the woman in question the full privacy she has demanded and, indeed, deserves, I cannot divulge her name. *Margo*, then, is a pseudonym (though I have retained the first three letters of her real name and will let the reader guess if this be a Margaret, a Marjorie, a Mary, or any of a number of others). Her last name was not written on the sheet, nor could I find the name mentioned on any other document in the suitcase.

To narrow down the period of H-G's life when the document was written, I checked the water-mark on the paper (an ordinary though by now somewhat yellowed sheet of standard white typewriter paper) and was able to establish that the paper was manufactured in 1954. Because of H-G's frequent moves during the ensuing period it seemed likely he had used the paper not too long after he had purchased it. The yellowed and brittle condition also suggested that it was at least twenty years old. I thus established a *terminus a quo* of 1954 and a *terminus ad quem* of, roughly, 1964. During the first two years of this period, H-G was enrolled as an undergraduate at Bard College. I wrote to the college's alumni office to ask what students bearing the name *Margo* (I gave her real name, of course) were enrolled during this period. Since I had made the office cognizant of the scholarly nature of my inquiry, they were fully cooperative and sent me the names (as well as the latest addresses they had on hand) of eight women who bore this name. (I felt fortunate that Bard was a relatively small college and that the name was not quite as common as Susan and some others.) Each of the eight received a letter from me explaining that I was engaged in a critical edition of a work by Orlando Hennessy-García and asking if they happened to remember him and, if so, would they be willing to share any memories of him and offer any insights into his character. One Margo did not reply at all, two had left no forwarding addresses at the addresses to which I wrote, four replied they knew vaguely who he was but had exchanged few if any words with him (they all assumed from my inquiry that he was dead and they offered their sympathy), and one replied that she remembered Orlando quite well, even though her active contact with him extended over little more than three weeks.

I jumped with joy when this last reply arrived, for I was convinced from her short note that this was the woman who had once played a crucial role in H-G's life. She offered quite readily to share her memories of H-G. Unlike the four correspondents who had assumed he was dead, she asked where he was these days and also where she could find his writings (she had called a local bookstore on receiving my inquiry and was told there was nothing by H-G listed in *Books in Print*). She asked as well (though in a rather gingerly way) if he was functioning well these days and quickly added she hoped I would convey her best wishes if, as she hoped, he was still alive. She explained she would be happy to share what recollections she had if I ever happened to be passing through her town. As it turned out, she lived in a medium-size Midwestern city that I could not imagine my ever "happening" to be in (the nearest respectable university was at least a hundred miles away). I suggested she share her memories with me in an exchange of letters or even in a long-distance call that I would gladly schedule to suit her convenience, but she replied that this was the sort of thing one would want to discuss on a face-to-face basis. From the tone of these replies I knew I was on the track of something significant, yet I also felt a certain shying away on her part the more persistent I became. Whenever I brought up the possibility of coming to see her she made the point that perhaps she had led me to believe what she had to say was more important than it really was, that perhaps I would even be disappointed, that she had no intention of making a big thing out of a trivial acquaintanceship of a quarter century ago.

The more she hedged, the more eager I became to see her. With the help of a travel grant from the American Philosophical Society, I was able to make a quick trip to Margo's town, though her reticence had by then reached the point where I had to pretend I was casually passing through between lecture engagements at several Midwestern universities. She had become so reluctant to see me that I was forced to parry back and forth with her to seek possible openings in her schedule while at the same time trying to maintain the casual air she had forced on me. As it turned out she insisted on squeezing me in between her early afternoon tennis and her duties later in the afternoon as a hospital volunteer. The rush was such that she managed to keep me off my guard throughout our brief meeting— with the result that I could not adequately check my pocket tape recorder and was left to reconstruct our meeting from memory (since accuracy is a necessity for conscientious editing, I have since changed to a recorder that needs less fussing in stressful situations).

Our conversation went on for half an hour at best. I drove my rented car to the suburban tennis club at which she had told me to meet her, spoke to her about twenty minutes in the lounge, then followed her in her own car to the hospital, where she squeezed in a few short intervals with me in the course of an hour, after which I returned to the airport in full knowledge that the lady was getting considerable satisfaction from leading me around on her own terms and telling me only as much as she chose to. Still, her testimony struck me as of the highest significance for a proper understanding of the text to whose elucidation this volume is dedicated.

Orlando, as Margo called him with what I took to be a certain sympathy in her tone, was a fellow student in several of her classes, though for a considerable time they had rarely exchanged words. She remembered him as quiet and odd. Everybody who came to Bard in those days was odd, she said, but the others were odd in predictable ways, while Orlando was odd in his own way, and this she (as well as others with whom she had discussed him) found disconcerting. In any event he called to ask her to be his "date" for a dance that served as the college's major social function of the spring term. She was caught unawares (something she said she had since learned to deal with whenever it occurred), for he phoned her well before the usual time that engagements of this sort were made. Not having a ready-made excuse at hand she accepted, and although she later had ample opportunities to be taken to the dance by several students more predictable in their ways (as she put it), she resigned herself to the commitment she had made with the thought that she would at least have a new and interesting experience—and that, she said, was something that students at Bard (though not so much at other, more conventional colleges) consciously cultivated in those days.

As it turned out, she did not much enjoy the experience. She quickly got to the heart of the matter and described a walk, directly after the dance, to a parklike area along the river to which couples customarily retired in good weather when they sought privacy during or after a social gathering. He was evidently attempting to go through the usual ritual of what she labeled as that most sexually naive period of American history. He grabbed hold of her hand as he led her down the steep path, but once they had arrived at the river she sought ways to withdraw her hand in the most inconspicuous manner (she made it clear that the last thing she wanted to do was hurt his feelings, which she assumed were rather tender). It was not that she objected to Orlando's going through the ordinary motions expected of one's spring dance escort, but his hand was so wet and he managed to exude such an air of nervousness that she felt impelled, as though by instinct, to maintain the greatest possible distance under the circumstances. Next thing she knew he had launched into a speech that, as she remembered it, seemed to go on interminably. The first two-thirds or so were in what could be called an unduly hesitant mode that gradually gave way to anger and defiance. He started by asking her why she was reluctant to give him any sign of affection, then, without so much as giving her a chance to answer with some excuse or other, went on to express sympathy for the awkward situation he knew himself to have put her in. It seemed to her altogether strange to witness so sustained an outpouring of words from someone who, from the casual contacts she had hitherto had with him, had struck her as a rather taciturn sort. Whatever sympathy he managed to express toward her situation at a certain point turned into anger at what he called her attempt to lead him on, though every single statement he made seemed to follow so naturally from the last that she found herself believing the foul motives he imputed to her.

Soon after she had begun the description of this speech I noted to myself the extraordinary parallel with the sustained speeches that H-G wrote for his title character—the first of which constitutes the scene "Prayer," the second of which, addressed to a prospective executioner, is embedded in the scene "Endings." Indeed, as Margo went on to tell the things she had heard from him, the resemblances between the speech at night by the river and the two in the play came to seem overwhelming. (I have cursed myself a thousand times for botching up the tape, for I believe there were some words, even some phrases, that the speech from real life had in common with the two fictive ones.) These resemblances lie above all in a rhetorical structure common to all three speeches: in each, the speaker proceeds by subtle gradation from hesitancy in the face of an external object to an outright defiance of this object (the Margo speech and "Prayer," though not the executioner speech, both end on a quiet, resigned note). Precisely the same rhetorical structure characterizes the "Envoi," that brilliant exercise (in five versions) that H-G evidently considered attaching to the play. Through the uses to which he put this particular structure, we discern, at least in its most skeletal form, the communications model that this volume is attempting to demonstrate: first, the source of this structure in an incident within the artist's personal life; second, its utilization, in varying forms, in an imaginative work written many years later; and third, its repetition in the relationship he sets up with the prospective consumer of his work. (The last-named includes not only those who do the actual consuming, but the producer and publisher, who make the consuming process possible, and the critic, who guides the consumer's reactions to the work.) Moreover, one might note the apparently incongruous changes in the external objects to which the author's rhetoric is addressed—young woman, deity, executioner, and consumer (the first three of these objects, one might add, were interchangeable in poetry written within the Petrarchan tradition). Note also the sharply differing contexts in which this rhetorical structure occurs—first the "real" life of the address to the woman, second the work of art in which the two Saul speeches are contained, and third the transition, as it were, between the world of art and the real world in the speech to the consumer.

Needless to say, I said nothing to Margo of these connections that were floating through my mind as she spoke, but simply let her go on. As she finished retelling the speech, she made the point that her own daughter, who is still a year or two younger than she herself was at the time, would have handled the situation with the proper aplomb, that in fact any of her daughter's friends would have known how to defuse it—with humor even— before anything could get out of hand. That's the difference, she said, between the much more enlightened world we live in now and the one that existed when all of us were in college. (I did not interject that I'm a good five to seven years her junior and that I for one never found sexual relationships much of a problem.) In any event, she was thoroughly at a loss as to how to react to Orlando, let alone help him resolve his difficulties, whatever they were. (As she reflected on it during the next few days, she said, it occurred to her she had been subjected to a kind of verbal rape.)

Her reactions by the river that night allowed no opportunity for reflection. She found her own hands getting as clammy as she remembered his on the walk down. As soon as she felt he had spent his rhetorical energy, she interrupted with what she called the usual excuse in those days of a girl who found herself in trouble on a date: she announced a headache and asked to be taken back to her dormitory. Being dependent on his flashlight, she was unable to make the trip through the bushes and up the steep path alone. She kept as great a distance behind him as the need for light allowed her. They parted with a minimum of words and without the routine good-night kiss mandatory among college students in those days. "I've told you all now, I've told you all," she added, as though trying to indicate at once that it was time for me to leave and that she fully sensed the significance of what she had been through that night. I assured her Orlando was alive and writing, but she did not encourage me to fill her in on details. Her evening with him, though doubtless one of the more irritating and perplexing memories from her past, could scarcely be said (at least judging from her present activities) to have had a cataclysmic effect on her. And it was clear she knew nothing of the Margo document that had aroused my suspicions in the first place; indeed, the first she will hear of it is in this volume, which I am arranging for her to receive no later than the day of its publication.

SUNDAY DINNER AT THE C's

Note: This passage occurs about half-way through the manuscript of A Prelude to Nothing. Since H-G attempted a continuous flow of narrative without section breaks, numbers, or titles, I have arbitrarily cut off that part of the narrative that contains significant analogues to two episodes of Saul's Fall, "Healing 1," and "Council." I have also supplied a title typical of the section titles H-G was to attach to the various episodes of Cold Clay. One might note that he used nothing from this passage in Cold Clay, though a considerable part of the latter manuscript is devoted to the main character's experiences among the various Canadian families with whom he lived during the 1940s.

I never worked up much appetite anyway all the time I was staying at the C's, but that day I couldn't help noticing the way Dr. C (he tried several times to get me to call him "Father," but something in me resisted) would stare at what was left of the roast each time he had finished cutting a piece. I asked what was the matter with it, and Mrs. C quickly interrupted to tell me that nice boys don't ask questions of that sort at table. I noticed Donald and Mildred giggling in each other's direction, but she shushed them up before they had a chance to say anything. I asked again, this time almost under my breath, and I worded it more carefully than before so that nobody would get the idea that I was trying to break the rules of their dinner table, which had something sacred about it that made me squirm the moment I sat down. Mrs. C gave me a disapproving look, and then she gave the same look to Donald and Mildred, who had started giggling again the moment I spoke up. I don't know which of them upset me the most— Mrs. C with her reprovals, Donald and Mildred making fun of me, or Dr. C giving me whatever piece of meat had the most fat and gristle on it. In fact, that was the whole point of the question I asked. I never accused him directly, though I had been noticing all the weeks I was there that whenever he carved up a roast (pretty much every Sunday), he would keep a close watch on every piece as he cut it off and carefully decide to which of us each should go. I don't know exactly what criteria he applied to his own family (they pretended of course I was a member of the family) —he tended to disburse the largest piece to himself and to Mrs. C (hers was sometimes slightly smaller, but that was understandable), with obviously smaller pieces for Donald and Mildred (Mildred, being two years younger than Donald, got the smallest piece, and that was totally understandable, just as it was understandable that Donald should get a smaller piece than Mrs. C). The trouble was not the size of my piece (I was halfway between Donald's and Mildred's age and it may well be that, being a boy, I was given a piece closer in size to Donald's than to Mildred's).

No, the trouble was not at all in the size (he knew I was a small eater anyway), but in something much more fundamental: Dr. C was aware from the first meal I had with them that the sight of fat and gristle upset me terribly and made me not even want to touch the good parts of the meat. I know it also upset Donald and Mildred and I can attest to the fact he took great pains (in a way he never took with me) to cut them pieces that they could accept with a minimum of fuss (sometimes, in fact, he cut them such perfect pieces they never fussed at all). This time I knew was going to be worse for me than ever. He cut off several heavily gristly pieces from near the end of the roast and put them on the platter. I knew that one of them was certainly destined for me. Then he stared carefully at the roast trying to figure how to cut some pieces that would give Donald and Mildred (and, I suppose, also Mrs. C and himself) the least amount of unpleasant stuff. It was at this point I asked my question and was jumped on by everybody—by Mrs. C in her polite way, by Donald and Mildred with their giggling, by Dr. C with that exasperated look that grown-up men have found a far more devastating way of putting you down than any sort of scolding or direct remark. I felt a tightness in my chest and I knew if I stayed in my chair another moment I'd feel as though some huge block had fallen on top of me. When nobody had his eyes on me, I suddenly got up in full knowledge I was violating the sanctity of their table and I dashed to my room, quickly locking the door behind me before I threw myself on the bed.

It seemed an eternity as I waited for the inevitable footsteps toward my door. I started by wondering which of them would be the first to come— whether it would be Mrs. C trying to overwhelm me with love, or Dr. C to snap me back into shape with his usual sternness, or might they be sending one or both of the children in hopes they could establish more immediate contact with me, though God knows I had managed to stay as aloof from them all this time as from their parents. If it hadn't been Sunday, I would have suspected they'd call the social worker in to force a reconcilation. But there weren't any footsteps at all—or at least for so long that I pretty soon gave up any thought that they were going to chase after me, whether to punish or mollify me or even to attempt some discussion of what we all decided would be the easiest way to control me.

At first I hoped that all of them would push on the door until it finally crashed down and then they would hand me a plateful of all the most hateful fat and gristle they could collect from the roast. I even hoped for a while they would put it all in the dog-dish and try to make me lick it up from there, and that would give me the excuse I needed to throw it back in their faces, after which they would rush away from me screaming about my ingratitude while I kept myself hidden in a closet waiting until they could finish all the arrangements (these always took an uncomfortably long time) to find still another family that would take me in.

For a while I actually believed we had already gone through the dog-dish routine while waves of anger kept passing through me to the point that I was soon exhausted and beginning to doze off. Then another wave would well up and I would feel fully alert, prepared to challenge whatever approach they would make to me and then allow myself quietly to doze off again.

It was during one of these lulls that I was startled to hear Mildred's voice singing happy birthday outside my door. I shouted back it wasn't my birthday at all, but next thing I knew the whole family had joined in singing. I tried to shout it wasn't going to be my birthday for another four days yet and I would thank them to wait and celebrate when I was good and ready, especially since they were getting their dates all wrong, to which Mrs. C spoke up so loudly she drowned me out to tell me they always celebrated the Sunday before anybody's birthday and wasn't it a nice thing she had caught me by surprise this way? I didn't say a thing, knowing good and well I was protected by the lock on the door, but next thing I knew they had managed to make their way in, and with nothing but a screwdriver, which Dr. C was holding in his hand as they all poured into the room singing happy birthday again. I tried to protest their mistake, but they kept on singing until they had been through that verse at least four times. Mrs. C, carrying the cake with its ten candles on it, was the last one in. They never really gave me a chance to protest the way I wanted to at first, but they set the cake with its candles burning right in front of me on the bedside table. I came up with a strong reaction that might have been anger but may simply have been surprise, but in any case whatever I was trying to say was strong enough to blow out most of the candles—though I never had a chance to make the usual secret wish. I don't know what I would have wished and in all honesty I could hardly tell what I was feeling from moment to moment.

When the candles went out everybody was laughing, and so was I, though I was not altogether sure at first if I was mocking them or joining them or simply pretending to join them as a way of taking the pressure off myself. Whatever faint protests I made they countered in the most un-expected ways. Mildred was tickling me and making me giggle along with Donald and her. They were stuffing their mouths with cake and I scarcely resisted, though they had to hand-feed me my first bite. Ice cream appeared, and candy too, though my birthday present, according to family custom, would have to wait for the real day later in the week. That would make it feel like two birthdays the same week, they assured me. The happier they thought they were making me, the more uncomfortable I felt. There was nothing to do at this point but ride along with the C's in the hope that maybe the next crisis would resolve things once and for all.

THREE PROJECTS

Note: This section of A Prelude to Nothing, *to which, like "Sunday Dinner at the C's," I attached a title on the analogy of the titles H-G gave to the episodes of* Cold Clay, *appears only a few pages before the manuscript breaks off. Analogues: "March 1," "Healing 1," "Healing 2," "Battle 2." The version of this episode in* Cold Clay *is considerably shorter and more cryptic, and it omits most of the passages analogous to the above scenes from Saul's Fall.*

They put a vast effort into preparing me before I went—first the psychi-atric social worker and her regular psychiatric nurse, then the resident psychiatrist, finally the male attendant who fed her hand-to-mouth and whom she believed to be Leonard Woolf. The point was I must go along in every respect with her script, I was not to challenge it in even the most trivial way, and in no case, at least not until the third project, if we needed to go that far, to let on I had the slightest doubt she was in fact the person we all knew her to be impersonating. I did my best to let them know I was here purely out of duty, that this should surely be enough to keep me in control of the situation while I was facing her, that I had every intention of maintaining the casual air that came naturally in all my dealings with her. If they felt my presence would be of any help, I was perfectly content to help out, but I wanted them to be under no illusion I was doing this for whatever therapeutic benefit it might have on me or, for that matter, that I had any real hope my presence could effect the least change in her condition.

The first of the three projects they had set up was to arrange an introduc-tion to James Joyce's ex-daughter-in-law, who happened to be a manic-depressive in the same sanitarium but who, unlike my mother, was in every respect the real person she claimed to be. Moreover, in contrast to my mother, who was constantly depressed, Mrs. Joyce was now in her annual manic stage and, as they put it (I never met the woman myself), quite compulsive about cheering up whatever fellow-patients she could. I saw the futility of this plan from the start and was foolish enough to go along with it.

"Mrs. Giorgio Joyce has asked you to have tea with her," I said. "She's staying at this resort for a few days, you know." (They had demanded I refer to the sanitarium by that euphemism.)

"Mrs. Giorgio who?" she asked in her most brittle manner.

"Joyce. Giorgio Joyce," I repeated so that she would be sure to understand. "She used to be married to the son of the writer James Joyce." I was trying to hold back my impatience, but it was not clear at first how much of what I said was getting through to her. "She wants you for tea, this lady. And she's related—or used to be, at least—to James Joyce. James Joyce."

"Joyce, yes Joyce," she said slowly, obviously mulling things over, after which she suddenly let loose with a torrent of words such as I remembered too well from earlier years. "In public I feel forced to defend him. After all, those of us engaged in modern writing, however different we may be, are so vulnerable that our survival demands a degree of solidarity with one another. But engaging in personal relationships with people the ilk of Mr. Joyce is another thing altogether—I cannot hide the fact, at least from myself, that however fervently I must defend his writing in public, I am struck by a certain meanness of vision that I frankly find irritating. This is true even in his finest passages, whose genius I don't dispute despite his meanness. I can think of only one explanation for this exasperating phenomenon. His background shows!" Having built up to this emphatic moment, she seemed about to lapse into her customary sullenness when she unexpectedly took up in a new, almost compliant tone. "You may tell the lady if she were anybody else's daughter-in-law I should be delighted to have tea with her. But you mustn't put it so brusquely. Just say I'm too much preoccupied with my new novel to dare allow myself any distractions, however pleasurable these might be." At which point she quickly withdrew into her gloom.

The second project was more elaborate and because of its relative ambitiousness they worked up higher hopes for success than they did with the first, which was partly intended as a trial-run for me to get accustomed to dealing with her directly. For weeks now the only food she was willing to consume—and even that was precious little according to all accounts—was what she took from the attendant she insisted on calling Leonard. For some absurd reason they thought she might suddenly recognize me—and, as a result, reconcile herself to reality—if I replaced the attendant during a feeding session. I was skeptical from the start, but I decided to go through the motions of anything they wanted, not certainly out of any obligation I felt toward them, but out of that abstract sense of duty one feels by definition toward someone who happens to be one's parent. I put on the same casual air I had maintained during my short and unsuccessful interview asking her to the tea they had tried to set up. I didn't care in the least whether she ate what I was assigned to feed her—any more than I cared whether she showed up to meet her distinguished fellow patient Mrs. Joyce. I simply went through all the motions expected of me: first, I tried apple sauce and I held the spoon a goodly distance from her mouth in hopes she would move toward it of her own volition. But she said simply, "I'll wait for Leonard to feed me," and I knew she would starve to death before she allowed herself to take even a taste. I was asked not to force the apple sauce, but to wait a few minutes in hope she might decide to recognize me before I resorted to sterner measures. The wait was as useless as I expected, and I proceeded with cottage cheese, which I was to reach directly to her lips in small spoonfuls. "That's for Leonard to do," she protested in a voice that bespoke her helplessness and her stubbornness at once. I proceeded, as instructed, to force the spoon between her lips and I suspect that some of it may well have made it down, though she did everything to pretend she was able to resist my attempts, and at one point she managed to cough up what looked like everything that had already gone down. Once I had emptied the dish—most of the cottage cheese had ultimately landed on the floor in one form or another—I quietly put the question they had planned for me if I had even the slightest degree of success. "Is there anything I can get for you, Mother?" I gave the final word the special emphasis and warmth they had suggested. It was of course no surprise to me that she failed to respond to the question, but said simply, "I wish you'd call Leonard so I can finish my meal." Convinced, as before, that they had forced something on both of us that was doomed not to work (though I won't go as far as saying it could have made her condition any worse than it already was), I decided it was useless to pursue the session with the various improvisations they had sketched out for me. And since these improvisations were to follow from that recognition that she never gave me in the first place, I knew they could expect no more of me that day.

The third project took the most rehearsing, and it involved not simply learning their instructions, for these instructions were themselves dependent on their (and my!) discovering the various interchanges in which she and I had engaged during my early years with her before I was sent off to Canada. By the time I entered her room I had memorized a series of ploys I was to take, not necessarily in the same order in which they had taken place when I was three or four (God knows how anybody, no matter how much external prodding, can recapture those things exactly), but in an order plausible enough so that they might rouse up whatever was suppressed in her memory. Let it be said I had no more faith this would work than the two earlier projects. And I suspect my confidence in the stubbornness of her stance was the only thing that allowed me to take up the histrionic gestures they had assigned me and which I was scarcely the sort of person to practice without the most forceful coaxing. I paid little or no attention to her as I entered the special room they had set up to resemble an old Italian resort hotel. All I remember now is that she was sitting passively in a straight-backed chair next to a window looking out on the sanitarium's rose garden, but her eyes were turned down to the floor, as though she had committed herself to a world of thought as far removed from ours as some foreign planet. "Come out of it, Mum. Come out of that slump, Mum," I said with the quiet firmness they had suggested for my opening statement. (The "Mum" was a deliberate reversion to the term I had used as a small child before she sent me off.) I repeated it several times on the off-chance it might work right away and relieve me of the need to take the next step, which I dreaded so fiercely I was willing to do anything to put it off. After five or six tries, I knew I could no longer delay and I started to simulate the tantrum they had worked out with me in rehearsals and which in turn had sought to simulate the tantrum I had staged for her when I found her in that same uncommunicative state late one night while my nanny was away and she never lifted a finger to put me to bed. I started by bursting into tears, though in the authentic version I may well have started tugging at her dress before setting off the tears, but we had all decided that starting with tears would create a more natural intensification and keep her from freezing up again in case the breakthrough they were hoping for should start too early. So I let my throat clutch up as they had taught me, and then I threw myself to the floor and gradually allowed the sobs to come through. In some ways I was less conscious of her presence than of the others whom I knew to be sitting tensely in their booth behind the one-way glass. Of course there was no way they could give me the signals I had come to depend on during the rehearsals, and I did my best to remind myself I was on my own and would have to manage unexpected developments with whatever good judgment I could muster up at the time.

The great unknowable remained how and when she would break down in response to the stimulus I was giving her. But then I was certain none of my ploys would work and I went through my motions unconcerned about how I should have to react to new situations. Once the sobs were well started I crawled over to her and started the dress-tugging, though I was careful to avoid inflicting any physical discomfort in this particular encounter. I moved to a spot where my eyes could meet hers if she chose to return a glance, and in fact I continued moving back to this position (a most awkward one since I was half on my side, half on my back) periodically while allowing the sobs and the tugging to intensify. A time or two I noticed a glint that might have sparked off that moment of recognition that those in the booth were awaiting so avidly. From where they sat, there was no way they could see the glint, and I admit I did nothing to encourage it to catch fire. I let the sobs reach their natural conclusion with a long wail that left me temporarily collapsed on the floor and then I quietly got up to start the next (and last) of the strategies we had worked out. For this I needed a prop, namely, a palm frond I had set down next to the door when I first entered and which I would not have had to use if either of the other two ploys had worked that day.

I won't go into all the problems they had had locating a palm frond on Long Island (a conservatory in Brooklyn finally came to the rescue), but since the original incident they had dredged up from my childhood involved a frond I had found while we were in Taormina the winter before the war broke out, they insisted on my using an object that had a chance of awakening some recognition on her part. I started gently: here the natural intensification they demanded corresponded precisely to the order of things as I remembered them. It began with some light scratching, almost tickling, of the frond against her thigh. From the start my laughter accompanied whatever I did with the frond—first some short giggles and then, as I began to pat the front of her shoulder, I allowed the laughter to come from increasingly deeper levels of my throat and chest. It was all so much easier than the earlier sobbing scene that I found myself virtually unaware either of her or of those who I knew were watching us. By the time I got to the point of slamming the frond across her body I was quite unaware of any reaction that might be coming from her and I allowed myself to engage in the most hearty laughs with a minimum (perhaps by now an absence) of inhibition. Only gradually, and doubtless well after it had started happening, did it dawn on me I was no longer the only actor in motion. My laughter had got so loud and so sustained that it was probably drowning out whatever other sound I should have been listening for. By the time I was aware she was trying to laugh along with me I found myself unprepared how to react. I got one quick glimpse of her face, which was staring directly at mine as though she were waiting for me to give her whatever encouragement she needed to keep up the laughter. Don't ask me what went wrong. It may have been my having to share this with those in the booth who were doubtless rejoicing at the breakthrough they had so skillfully arranged. Or it may have been simply a fear of how I would manage the next and unrehearsed steps and, after these, the long, slow process of creating a relationship where none had really existed before. Be that as it may, my laughter stopped abruptly as soon as my eyes met hers, and although she laughed a time or two after I had stopped, she too stopped once it became evident I was pulling the ground out from under her. In fact her expression rapidly returned to its frozen state and I was left holding a silly and useless frond that I dragged nervously along the simulated marble floor while wondering what to do next. But of course there was nothing more to do—at least not in this room that had now become as oppressive to me as it must have been to her. I dropped the frond and, carefully turning my face away from the faces I imagined looking disapprovingly at me from the booth, I hurried out the door.

AN EPISTOLARY EXCHANGE

The following items can arguably be identified under either of these categories: letter written by Beatrice Hennessy-García in the guise of Virginia Woolf, with reply by her son Orlando; letter written by H-G for his character Angela Fitzgerald-Calderón in the guise of Virginia Woolf, with reply by her son Roland and intended for possible inclusion in Cold Clay. *Analogues: "Battle 2," "Proclamation," and "Execration."*

London
13 February 1937

Dear Friend,

Your letter is a most difficult one to answer, for I am uncertain precisely what your motives were in addressing yourself to me as my son. It is possible, of course, your letter was intended for somebody else, and if that was so, you need not read on. Unfortunately, the manner in which it was delivered gave every indication that it was, in fact, meant for me, and I have therefore been forced to speculate about your motives.

I start with the worst possible: if your letter was meant to chide me for my failure to become a mother, be warned that the decision not to bear children was made by others, not by me, that any admonishments, reproaches, or castigations you wish to level against my act of omission should more properly be directed against those who made the decision in the first place. I can tell you how and where to contact these people if you care to. Let me know.

There is of course the possibility that you had a less malign motive in mind. You may well have conjured up the desire to receive a private letter from a famous personage, and if this is true, I have obviously proved unable, irked though I am, to prevent you from achieving your goal. Or perhaps you have fantasized that your actual mother has, by some mysterious process, been metamorphosed into the writer Virginia Woolf. I do not like to disturb private fantasies and shall leave well enough alone without further comment.

The least objectionable motive I have left for last: your letter was intended as a sly hint that you wish to establish some sort of mother-son relationship with me. If this was your intention, I must reluctantly shatter any hopes you may have fashioned for yourself. As everybody knows, what I give birth to takes the form of books alone, and I can assure you no woman who has borne children ever experienced anything like the birth pangs my books cost me. They cost me so dearly, in fact, that I have felt impelled to cast them away as soon as my labors were completed. Yet each time nature has seen fit to spread a welcome fog of forgetfulness over everything I had been through, and before I was fully aware of what I was doing, I would find myself with still another book struggling to be born. Small comfort all this is to you, dear friend. Yet I am confident that some place in this large world there is a woman who does not make castaways of her children and who will have little else to do but take you to her bosom. Find her.

Yours sincerely,
Virginia Woolf

Epistle in reply

Dear Lady, do not think the worse
Of me for answering in verse.
Your prose is of such elegance
I wouldn't want to take the chance
You'll think of me as unrefined   5
If I talk back to you in kind.
Allow me, then, to pick a muse
Who's coarse enough to share my views
And fashion me the sort of style
I need to properly revile   10
You. Do not think I mean to thump
A creature clearly in a slump.
Let's leave past grudges out of this
Or else we'll head for an abyss
Whose awesome depths I'd frankly hate   15
To feel the need to extricate
Ourselves from. We'll stick to safer ground:
I understand what you propound
So cogently I'd be hard put
To use my reason to dispute   20
The arguments that you propose
To bring our kinship to a close.
If, then, your style does not permit
That I reply to you with wit,
I'll introduce another ploy   25
Which, though it's likely to annoy,

At least allows me to contrive
A way to keep some tie alive.
I'll dole you out some pity then,
In hopes you'll seek a regimen   30
Of anger, self-reflection, prayer—
Whatever quashes your despair.
Though you may find this process rougher,
It should diminish what you suffer.
Compassion bids me to confer   35
Some love despite your stern hauteur.
Break out of that protective shell,
So I may tenderly dispel
The fears within your soul that swirled
To make you flee this threatening world.   40
Poor Mother, Friend, Virginia Woolf,
Whichever name I use, the gulf
That gapes between us gives me pause
To wonder how I'll grant your cause.
My understanding of your plight   45
Does not itself make matters right.
If wit and pity aren't enough
To hinder still a new rebuff,
I'd think of trying ridicule,
But that would render me a fool   50
To one who's made herself unhecklable
By writing in a style impeccable.
Still, I'll attempt another stance
In hopes this last one may enhance
What little pride you've left me. Hear   55
Then, I propose to domineer
You in the contacts we pursue,
And thus proclaim my hope you'll stew
Deliciously in your own juice
(Which, if your inner heat reduce   60
You to a mass of morsels and we
Keep strictest vigilance and see
That no one open up to probe)
Tight-sealed like Mrs. Ramsay's *daube*
You'll crown your life the choicest dish   65
That any royalty could wish.
Yet I'll not let a soul devour
It, but place it on a tower,
Where it will stand in isolation

(With no one near for consolation)   70
Until it turn so stale and rancid,
Sour, mouldy, foul, and putrid
That the rotten, piercing smell
It powerfully sends forth expel
The citizenry puking. How   75
Better make my point for now,
Except to urge you to reflect
A bit the next time you reject?
With that, dear Friend, I bid adieu
And proffer thee a fond fuck-you!   80

Note: The specific occasion for including the above exchange of correspondence lies in the fact that the first letter, in its rejection of a closely
related kin, is an analogue to "Execration, while the second, especially in
its overt attempt to proclaim the expulsion and isolation of another (from
line 58 onward), is an obvious analogue to "Proclamation."

Although the relationship of this exchange to these episodes is in no
significant way problematic, the precise origins and intentions of the exchange posed greater problems for me than any single item I have reproduced in this volume. Unlike all the Virginia Woolf material I found in the
suitcase, this exchange was not attached to the manuscripts of either A
Prelude to Nothing or Cold Clay: it had come from a different typewriter
altogether, its paper was considerably older than that of the two novel mss,
the "Epistle in Reply" was in H-G's handwriting on five sheets of yellow
copy paper clipped to the Woolf letter, and the two letters were tied in a
bundle that included such miscellaneous items (none of them part of the
novel mss and all from a relatively early stage of his life) as the "Growth
Paper" written for Bard College and the short story on his father published in his school literary magazine.

My initial thought (and hope) was that the first letter might conceivably
have come from the typewriter of Virginia Woolf, that is the real-life Woolf
and not H-G's mother (or her fictional surrogates) in the guise of this famous
author. It was clear to me that if this were a genuine Woolf letter it would
constitute a literary find of the highest order. Not only is Woolf among the
undisputedly major writers of our century (Beatrice Hennessy-García in her
madness at least showed good taste in assuming Woolf's identity), but the
attitude toward child-bearing that the correspondent displays here provides
a unique perspective on the attitude she took to her husband's and her
physicians' decision that she not attempt motherhood.

Although I recognized that in view of Beatrice Hennessy-García's im-
personation of Woolf during her madness the chances that this was a real
Woolf letter were minute indeed, I refused to discount the possibility

entirely. In fact, I vowed that if this were the genuine article I should temporarily cease work on this volume in order to publish the letter with all the ceremoniousness and annotations it deserved. No scholar or scientist should discard a possible discovery simply because it seems at first implausible: would we accept the earth's revolution around the sun, nuclear fission, Hölderlin's "Friedensfeier" hymn, penicillin, or, for that matter, the existence of the western hemisphere itself if their various discoverers had not risked their all to pursue a notion that their contemporaries stood prepared to deride? And I was even prepared to stage the scholarly battle of the century with the Woolf establishment (they wield considerable power these days) if they did anything in the least to prevent my giving the world an image of their heroine that might in any way tarnish the one that they have labored to disseminate.

As it turned out, my brief dreams were quite in vain, for the watermark on the paper made it amply clear the letter could not have been typed before 1951, fully ten years after Woolf's famous suicide. Still, I take some pride in my initial attitude and hope that I may retain the courage to pursue similar possibilities at the next opportunity that comes along. I confess that even after checking the watermark I toyed with the idea that this was perhaps a later transcript of a letter Woolf had actually written, and after consulting my senior colleague Professor Lucio Ruotolo, a major authority on Woolf, I learned that any typewritten letter would have to be a later transcript, for Woolf, as he pointed out, wrote out her correspondence by hand, but Professor Routolo quickly deflated any new hopes I had conceived by reminding me that on the day the letter was purportedly written, 13 February 1937, the Woolfs were not in London, as stated above the date, but at their country house in Rodmell.

This left me with only the two alternatives that I stated briefly at the head of this exchange: either this was a real letter composed by H-G's mother together with his reply, or it was a letter composed by him for possible inclusion in Cold Clay to better fill out the character of Angela during the period she took herself to be Virginia Woolf. There is still a third alternative—in a sense a fusion of the two—namely, that the first letter was actually written by Beatrice Hennessy-García to her son and that he was uncertain whether or not to include it in his novel. This third and, to me, quite satisfactory alternative would also explain the fact that the paper and typewriter differ from those in the remainder of the ms.

But innumerable questions remain: If the first letter was indeed written by Beatrice Hennessy-García, was the second given to her to read, and what could her reaction have been? Or was H-G's reply actually written after her suicide as a means of coming to terms with the event (the yellow paper bears no watermark and I have been told there is no means of analyzing it chemically to demonstrate its age without at least a seven-year margin of error)? If the first letter was composed by H-G, did he do so during her lifetime (for instance, after a visit to her sanitarium at a point when she was unresponsive to him), or after her death? And if the former of these two alternatives is the correct one, might he have sent her both the letter he composed under her assumed name together with his reply? Or if he composed it after her death, did he do so before he started work on Cold Clay, or was the letter originally conceived as a part of the novel and then discarded? Could it perhaps be the seed out of which the objective, third-person style of Cold Clay emerged? Did his writing of the first letter (or his receipt of his mother's real letter) perhaps give him some inkling that the subjective, first-person mode of A Prelude to Nothing was inadequate to his psychological needs or artistic purposes? These are of course large questions and can scarcely be answered with any accuracy at present. Yet the existence of this document (whatever its origins) and the questions it raises provide a component to our communications model different in kind from any of the others that compose this volume. May those who consider utilizing this model profit from my speculations and errors, from my hopes and disappointments, from the kinds of questions I have learned to raise and my reticence in jumping to conclusions—above all, may they gain courage, caution, and instruction from the example (imperfect though it may be) that I have set for them!

Additional Note: The daube in line sixty-four of "Epistle in Reply" refers to the French stew that Mrs. Ramsay, the heroine of Woolf's To the Lighthouse, is busy supervising and serving during much of the central part of the book (sections 16–17 of "The Window"). The chief principle underlying a daube is that it cook slowly under a tight seal so that the juices may be preserved and absorbed within the meat. According to the various cookbooks I consulted, the exact ingredients and their proportions differ from region to region in France, but the principle remains the same.

Note: On the quantity and diversity of detail

It may well be that some readers will object to the amount of detail that the editor has seen fit to include in this edition; to which I can only reply, better too much than too little. An edition is like a feast. Not every detail that the editor has dug up may seem relevant to every reader. But as with any good feast it's better to err on the side of leftovers than to run out of food while the guests are still hungry. An editor's zeal to get at all the facts, relevant or not, may strike some as a mania of sorts; to which I can only reply better to err on the side of madness than that of sobriety. Since he can never really know in advance whether the information he seeks will help illuminate the text he is editing—or whether he will even be able to *get the information—he must be irrepressible in his efforts to seek out whatever may strike him as potentially promising. If people find me irrepressible, I answer, first, that this probably has to do with my body chemistry, and, second, that this also makes me a good editor.*

SCOLDINGS OF THE WEEK

Note: Number thirteen of the Cold Clay manuscript. Analogues: "Healing 1" (Monday and Tuesday), "Intermezzo" (Monday), "Prophecy 1" (Wednesday and Saturday), "Battle 2" (Saturday), "Prophecy 2" (Tuesday, Friday, and Saturday), "Execration" (Saturday), and "Epilogue" (Saturday and Sunday).

Roland was too worn down from these memories to intersperse his reactions. He simply recorded Angela's words as he remembered them:

Monday

I am whispering because I know if I speak to you in a normal voice you'll shout back before I've even had a chance to say what I have to say. If I whisper, at least you're more likely to speak to me in a normal voice, and that's all I ask. Remember I'm not asking very much of you. Most people would ask a good bit more of a four year old, but I decided to keep my requests minimal—that means modest, yes—or very little—in other words, I'm asking very little of you compared to what other mothers ask a little boy your age. In fact, I'm not even asking you to do anything. All sorts of other little boys, nearly all of them, I can assure you, are constantly being badgered—yes, that means nagged—to do this, do that, do this, do that. But it isn't my way at all. I am simply asking you *not* to do a few things here and there. There aren't many of them, and you should feel fortunate —lucky, that means—I'm as selective—choosy—as I am deciding what not to ask of you. As I said, there's nothing I'm asking you to do, nothing at all. Those things are for Nanny, and you should feel fortunate—lucky— we have her with us. Not every little boy has a nanny all to himself. But I won't keep reminding you how much luckier you are than most little boys. It'll go to your head and you'll end up expecting everything to come to you much more easily than it ever does to other little boys. No, I'm not going to do anything to make life harder for you than it's certain to be anyway, for there isn't any way possible not to keep it from being hard, even if a little boy your age couldn't believe what things are bound to be like when you're as old as I am. No, I won't even try to tell you, I just want you to count your blessings for the moment and remind yourself how lucky you are before you start raising your voice on me again. You see how well this

whispering is working. You've kept your voice down to the way normal—
that means nice—people talk for at least ten minutes now and I suspect
that's a record for you. No, you don't want to break the record now, you
don't want to make it bad for yourself. I said no, even if you're forcing me
to raise my own voice to a sound that I'd be the first to find irritating if
anybody talked to me this way. I can see there's nothing more for me to
say.

Tuesday

I've decided it's better to talk to you in a normal tone of voice and also
to tell you directly what it is that's bothering me. It's useless trying to get
to you in indirect—that means roundabout—ways. For some children,
probably for most of them, I'm sure it makes things easier, but you're
different, and there's no way to hide that fact from either of us. So I'll
tell you directly—I'm frankly angry at you and you might as well know my
feelings. Just because I'm not shouting at you doesn't mean I feel any less
strongly about it. It's just that that isn't my way at all and you should feel
fortunate—that means lucky—you have a mother who'll talk to you in a
normal tone of voice when anybody else's mother would be shouting her
head off at you or beating you down with God knows what. Don't think
you've not been tempting me to do things that way, but I've managed to
remind myself I'm not the sort of person to do things that way. I know it
would be easier for me to shout, but that isn't going to make it any easier
for you, and it's you, not I, whose welfare—that means well-being, yes, or
feeling good—is what's most important. You see, I want you to think out
for yourself—quietly and without a lot of fireworks to distract you—I
want you to think out quietly just what you've been doing to me. Not
that I can't take it. I've learned to take a lot of hurts along the way, and
if it were anybody else doing this to me, I'd let myself feel bad quietly
and never let the person know. But I have a special responsibility to you—
that means I'm in charge of making you turn out to be well and happy—so
I'm going to make you think out the consequences—that means the bad
effects, the results—of what you're doing to me. And I don't think it does
you any good for us to talk about it any longer. I just want you to think
quietly about it in your room and stop all this protesting and asking of
questions. I have nothing more to say.

Wednesday

(in the form of separate notes that she requested Nanny to read to him)
    7:30 A.M. My lips are sealed today.
    8:00 A.M. Just because I write this note to you does not mean I am ready
to speak to you.
    9:30 A.M. Do not poke me. It will do no good.

10:30 A.M. Precociousness will not get you anywhere.

10:45 A.M. I know you can understand that word since you have heard it used of you ever since you began to understand English. You can always ask Nanny to explain a word you do not understand. She is allowed to talk to you even when I cannot.

1:30 P.M. Again I say do not poke. I am still not ready to speak to you.

4:00 P.M. I am willing to drink my tea at the same table as long as you do not expect me to look at you or speak to you.

6:00 P.M. Just because you hear me speak to somebody else does not mean I am ready to speak to you. My lips are still sealed.

7:30 P.M. Not tonight, but the next night after you have been good all day there will be a goodnight kiss for you.

Thursday

You must understand why there's not much I care to say to you today. It takes me a while to get over these things, but at least you can see that I am able to talk to you a little today. Not very much, but a little.

Friday

I don't know why you still go about hounding me every place I go in the house. I've told you a hundred times already I forgive you, so there's no reason you should have to go on pestering me, but I'll tell you for the hundred and first time if that will finally do any good. I assure you I'm very happy with you today. You are being a good boy and I can't see why you need to have me keep telling you. There are lots of times when something comes over you and you're not a good boy at all and believe me, those are mighty awful days for all of us, for Nanny too. But as I say, today you're being good and I hope you keep it that way. Maybe if I tell you a hundred and second or a hundred and third time the idea will sink in and you won't have to keep following me around this way. I'm willing to tell you once or twice more, maybe an extra time in a few hours if need be. But unless you stop persisting—that is, keeping up your pestering —this way, I'll begin to think you're not being a good boy after all, and then we'll be back to where we've been all the past few days. All right, I'll say it. You've been quite good today, except of course for the pestering, and you can pride yourself on the fact that you've been a good bit better today than any time I can remember in weeks. That doesn't mean I'll still be feeling this way about you by the end of the day—that all depends on how long you can keep your good behavior up—but I'm willing to feel optimistic—that means good about it—if that will be anything of an incentive—that means hoping for a reward—to you. Yes, I'm very, very hopeful, and I'm beginning to think maybe I have the best little boy in the world. That's mighty high praise coming from a mother who's as fussy as I am. But I mean everything I say, and I'll mean it even more if I don't have to answer any more questions today on how I'm feeling about you.

Saturday

I want you to listen closely, Roland, as I vent my rage. I mean really hear me. I wouldn't try hiding behind the chest or slipping off to the privy since I'm already accustomed to those tricks and I assure you they are not going to work with me any more. If anything they'll only make my anger worse, and that's the last thing in the world you'd want at this point. Don't interrupt—that makes it much much worse. There's no need for you to try to explain what you've been doing. You can be sure I know why and nothing you say is going to change my mind. No, there's absolutely nothing you can do at this point except sit still and listen to me vent my rage. It's certainly no time for apologies. Those are for little things, and God knows you do enough of them, and even there I feel lucky if you apologize for only half the things you do to me. And it's no time to start putting the blame on other people. Whatever you try to tell me, I know exactly who's to blame for this, and you know too. I'm certainly not blaming Nanny—even if she sometimes is a good bit nicer to you than you deserve. But I've never objected to that, I've never interfered, and when she goes too far pampering your whims I figure that's like having a little sweet after a heavy meal. I can put up with that. And I'm not blaming your father either. He isn't with us any longer, but then I've explained to you he was never really with us, even when he might have been. I suppose if you'd had a father around he might have helped keep you in line and exercise some of the rage that, as you can see, I'm forced to vent all by myself. Just because I'm not shouting steadily doesn't mean my anger's any less intense—that means strong—than it's been the past two hours. One has only so much voice left for shouting and surely you know by now that when I speak to you in this icy tone of mine I'm considerably more angry than other people are when they shout their heads off. I should warn you, you've not seen my full fury yet and frankly I hope you never have to. What you've done is bad enough, and I'm very, very angry, but you've not reached an age yet where I can let my anger out in full force and I've learned to control myself accordingly. I don't want to see you fool yourself into thinking I'll always let you off this easily, for if you're going to grow up to be the good and decent sort of person I still have reason to hope you may be, you'll have to learn to measure up a lot better than you have lately. I warn you, once I feel you're ready for the full force of my rage you won't like it at all. It'll be a lot more scary than the bulldog down the road that sends you running under Nanny's skirt, and more than the thunder that even though it's high time you were used to it by now, still leaves you sobbing in the middle of the night and waking us up. As you can see I really have some hope it'll never have to get that far, even though each time I think of what you've been doing to me a terrible rage comes over me and I have the urge to do things that you're lucky I'm able to keep myself from doing. But as I say, I still keep up my hopes for you, I keep them up even when the things you do are constantly telling me otherwise. I keep reminding myself it's just your age, that you'll be doing these things fewer and fewer times as you grow older, yes, I'm very careful to remind myself of that, for if I don't, I have to face the fact that you have no character, that's right, no character at all. Don't interrupt, you know exactly what I mean, I have said this hundreds of times before. You have no character, and however else you may develop—you may very well turn out to be good at lots of things—you and everybody around you will always be up against the fact you have no character at all. God knows, I never thought this could happen to anybody in my family and it's unfair to blame your father's family since there's ever so little I know about them anyway. It's no use blaming anyone, so we might as well just face the fact you have no character at all and since that's the case it's not worth my while wasting all this rage on you. That's all I have to say and don't ask me to elaborate—that means explain more than any human being should ever have to explain.

Sunday

There are times I have to be left alone and that doesn't mean I'm either angry at you or not angry at you. It has nothing to do with you, except maybe indirectly since you've worked pretty hard at wearing me down all week. But the main thing now is to leave me alone for a while and you'll find me a much cheerier mum tomorrow once I've got some rest. There's no reason I should have to keep telling you I love you. You're making a racket out of this and I'm the first to see through what you're up to. I'll say once and for all I still love my little boy, but if he goes on giggling or tugging at my dress to get my attention when I've told him this is my day to be left alone, I don't know what I'll do. I don't know what at this point.

HER THREE ATTEMPTS

Note: Number seventy-seven of the Cold Clay *manuscript. Analogue:* "Endings."

Number one:

This one was not thought out properly. It was conceived as an act of simple imitation, as though a polluted river in a suburban area of Long Island could simulate that rural English stream that had served her model so obligingly. She proceeded with her usual meticulousness in such matters—wrote a note addressed to Leonard Woolf, which she left where she knew the owner of the half-way house would see it, walked briskly the mile or so to the river, and, once there, dutifully sought out the largest rock she could find, placed it in her coat pocket, and stepped into the water. It was unclear what precisely went wrong—whether the rock was too light in weight for her body, or whether it was simply that the surrounding population was large enough to assure someone's seeing her before the act could reach its intended conclusion. In any event she was scooped up breathing.

Number two:

This one was rash. Doubtless she was convinced the trouble earlier was due to insufficient weighing down on the part of the rock. So she changed the proportion between the weights of the foreign object and herself. What she failed to consider was the possibility that the trouble might just as easily have been due to her being seen too quickly and easily. She appeared this time with a rusty anchor tied to her body with ship's rope. Although it was by no means huge, its weight was close enough to her own weight so that her walk to the river was considerably slowed down. At least five persons reported seeing her and one snapped a picture. They waited until they were sure where she was heading and were able to grab hold of her before she was even down to her knees in the water.

Number three:

This one worked. She started with an altogether new principle, one which would not have been technologically possible in her model's time. She swallowed what was left in the tranquilizer bottle, then rushed to the river and executed her performance with a minimum of fuss. Those who saw her reported everything happened too fast to save her. It may be she was dead from the pills even before the water could get to her. That we shall never know. But to all appearances, except for the absence of a pocketed rock (or any other weight, for that matter), she managed to stage the perfect imitation.

CALLING ON NANNY

Note: Number eighty-two of the Cold Clay manuscript. Analogue: "Healing 3."

"I am not a crybaby," she demanded he repeat after her.

"I am not . . ." Roland said obediently, then broke off abruptly. "Nanny, can't you see I'm grown up now? I'm just calling on you to say hello."

"I am not a crybaby," she said even more sternly than before.

The nurse who had let him in suddenly appeared and tugged at his elbow. "Just go along with her," she whispered. "That's the best way to handle them, just go along whatever it is they say." Roland looked around and quickly realized his nanny was now every bit as incompetent as all the others who filled up the dilapidated ward.

"I am not a crybaby," she said again, this time not only more sternly but also considerably louder.

Roland took a deep breath, then quietly repeated her words.

"I am very proud of you, Giles. You're turning into a very good boy."

"I'm not Giles, by the way, Nanny. Remember, I'm Roland, the one you had just before the war—for all of my first four years."

"I won't have you telling me fibs, Giles. We have punishments for boys who tell fibs."

"Just to get the record straight, Nanny," he patted her on the shoulder in a show of tenderness, "just to get it straight, I'm Roland, I'm Mrs. Fitzgerald-Calderón's son and you went to Taormina with us—I remember that myself even though I must have been three—you went to Taormina and also to Alexandria and I was very, very fond of you. You hear that, I was very, very fond of you." He patted her on the shoulder again, though he knew his last statement to be something of an exaggeration.

She paused a moment before speaking, but her eyes looked fiercely into his and her face flushed red. "You are Giles Wentworth, and I will not stand to have you lying to me."

"I'm *not* lying, Nanny, I just want you and me to get things straight before I have to leave."

"Go easy on her," said the nurse, tugging at his elbow again.

He paused a moment, then spoke up in a soft but firm voice. "I'm Roland, and that's the only thing I want you to remember. You can forget everything else as far as I'm concerned."

Her face flushed redder still, and she lifted a hand weakly as though to box his ear.

"Tell her you're Giles, for God's sake," the nurse whispered. "We've all had to learn to handle these people." He paused again, allowed his eyes to meet his nanny's eyes, which seemed even fiercer than before. "Please go along with her," said the nurse, "else I shall have to ask you to cut your visit short."

He bit his lower lip, then spoke up quickly. "I'm Giles," he said almost in a whisper.

"I want to hear that once more," his nanny said.

"I'm Giles—Giles whatever that last name you said is."

The nurse gave him another tug.

"I am happy to see you, Giles," his nanny said in a more amiable tone than any he had heard from her thus far. "Now I want you to repeat after me, 'I will never tell another lie'."

"Go along with her, you won't regret it," the nurse whispered insistently.

"I will never tell another lie," his nanny repeated.

"If you don't go along with this," said the nurse, "you'll force us to spend five hours calming her down. Have some respect for our patients."

Roland gave the nurse a look every bit as fierce as the ones his nanny had given him.

"I will never . . . ," his nanny spelled out didactically.

"I will never . . . ," Roland repeated.

". . . tell another lie," his nanny went on.

". . . tell another lie," Roland said.

"The whole thing now," his nanny insisted.

"I will never tell another lie," Roland said quietly.

"That's a good boy, Giles."

He skipped all the usual formalities as he rushed out of the ward.

A NIGHT OUT WITH COUSIN PACO

Note: Number eighty-nine of the Cold Clay manuscript. The puzzling fact about this section is that the commentaries to the various subsections give every indication of being a regular part of the manuscript, as though each one is to be read before the reader goes on to the next subsection of narrative. Although it is possible that H-G meant these commentaries as private notes to himself, the fact that these commentaries are numbered and cleanly typed out, as well as the fact that they continue the third-person mode of the narrative, leads to the conclusion that he was playing with the reader's notions of narrative illusion. Like "Four Poses" and several other sections near the end of the manuscript, this section is far more experimental in nature than the earlier ones. Analogue: "Battle 1."

The barrier

This was the language barrier, and it was formidable. Despite the year's work he had put in on his own before he went to Spain, he could participate in conversation only in a peripheral sense. It was one thing to do exercises in a book or to listen to the carefully enunciated conversations on instructional records, but it was quite another thing to sit around a table with people who themselves spoke no foreign language and who had no idea what it meant for somebody to have to manage in a language he had learned artificially. Part of the problem was doubtless that they didn't really think of Roland as a foreigner. He was related to them by blood, he bore their name (after the hyphen at least), and so they went right ahead speaking to him at their regular pace, swallowing words and indulging in local expressions without the slightest notion whether he understood them or not. Fearing to offend them, he pretended to understand considerably more than he actually did. He interjected a sufficient number of bookish phrases for them to assume he could follow them and to keep treating him as one of the family.

Commentary 1

What an austere way to introduce the Spanish part of the book! There's no description of the family household, no vignettes on his individual relatives (their real-life peculiarities were fully worthy of any novel), not even any background material on how his mother had got mixed up with them on her study trip to Spain. Some of the best pages of the early version have had to be thrown away, for everything must be subordinated to the episode about to take place.

The rapprochement

Cousin Paco was patting him on the back and making one joke after another that he failed to understand. It was easy enough to figure out they were talking about the wine, that they were pleased he liked the wine they had opened in his honor, that above all they wanted to convey their familial good will to him as infectiously as possible. He put on the best front he could command.

Commentary 2

He couldn't leave out the local detail entirely. The back-patting and the wine-drinking and the mutual reassurances around the table are peculiarly Spanish (or at least Latin) traits, and he could salvage them because Roland's inability to pick up the signs is central to the problem in which the episode culminates. But he mustn't let the detail get out of hand. Anything more than a few hints would amount to self-indulgence.

The conspiracy

Cousin Paco tittered as he whispered in his ear. Nobody in the family was supposed to hear what he said, though they were all shouting their advice to him—or rather negative advice, since a chorus of *no's* rose up in Paco's direction. Paco was being conspiratorial with him, but Roland had no idea what he was being conspired into. Except that the general subject was clear, for Paco kept using the word *aventura* amid a barrage of sounds that drifted meaninglessly in one ear and out the other. Once the family turned its attention away from them, Paco quietly nudged him out the door.

Commentary 3

The unfortunate phrase "Cousin Paco tittered" points to the essential falseness inherent in the retelling of an event. The writer is considerably less concerned with representing an action than with wooing the reader (whom he has never met and never will meet) into a forced intimacy. It should be evident from the context that Roland never felt sufficiently close to Paco to think of him as Cousin Paco (even if he was aware of the technical aspects of cousinness): but the term *Cousin Paco* exudes the warm feeling readers associate with family novels or tales of local life, and the narrator must have felt the reader needed to be indulged in this feeling to keep on reading and, even more important, that the reader, as a result of this process, would flatter the writer's own ego by reciprocating with a correspondingly warm feeling. Similarly with the name *Paco*: doubtless Roland quickly learned to think of his cousin as Paco, though the reader, if he ever went to the trouble of seeking him out, would know him only as Señor García. If Roland referred to him that way, or even as Francisco (which is the only name by which he would be recognized among the officials who made out his birth, baptismal, marriage, and death certificates), the reader would fail to view him through Roland's eyes, and this of course was necessary for the intimacy the writer needed to achieve. As for *tittered*, its near slang effect adds unnecessarily to the intimacy the writer has already overwhelmed the reader with, but in its attempt to give Paco a childlike quality it seeks to endear him to the reader despite the fact that nothing in the surrounding context supports this conception of him. Writing tries to get away with anything it can.

The descent

Where they started from, the streets were relatively straight, for this was the newer part of town, but with each street they crossed, their route became windier, the houses older and dingier. Paco kept up an interminable monologue on local history, explaining what happened at various plazas and within particular buildings over the centuries. Roland was aware he was citing dates and names of nobility (he got the gist though not the precise content) and whenever they passed an area for which he had no information, he interspersed his monologue with references (always with a laugh) to the *aventura* they were to look forward to. As they reached the innermost part of the old town, Paco slowed down, lights were dimmer, street noises seemed more muted than before. A policeman suddenly emerged out of a dark doorway. Roland, jolted, darted backward, but Paco grabbed him by the arm before he could run away. Next thing he noticed was a loud and hearty greeting between Paco and the policeman, who unlocked the door for them.

Commentary 4

It is full of pretenses. It pretends to record a series of external actions—a walk to the oldest part of town, Paco's talk, an encounter with a policeman—while actually wanting to reproduce what goes on internally within the main character—his fear of the unknown world toward which he is being led, his passivity when acted upon. The very title is fraught with possibilities of meaning that the text never actualizes. It is too much to ask these external actions to tell us all these things.

The selection

In the main room upstairs there was a constant coming and going. Paco was so busy at first greeting acquaintances among the men that Roland thought himself forgotten and retreated to a corner. Each time Paco saw somebody he knew he would say (almost in a joking tone) what Roland took to be "And what are *you* doing here?" This was usually accompanied by that characteristically Spanish way of greeting in which each man moves toward the other as though about to hug him, but actually to pat the other on the back while each face looks straight ahead. A priest in cassock was there, but Paco greeted him less heartily than he did the others. While the men were moving about, the women sat quietly in a semicircle. Every now and then a man would extend an arm to one of them who would then lead him out the room up another flight of stairs. Roland kept waiting for Paco to give him some signal on what to do next, but by the time Paco came back to him, he seemed reproachful, as though Roland should have been participating more actively while Paco was preoccupied with his greetings. Unfortunately Paco was speaking so fast to him that Roland phased out and simply assented with a nod each time Paco paused. He felt himself hopelessly confused. Paco was marching him around the semicircle, pausing briefly with him to look over each woman. The next time Roland nodded in assent, Paco suddenly stopped, extended an arm to the woman who happened to be sitting at that spot, then beckoned her up and placed her arm in Roland's. Roland had not had a chance to notice this one, but he did his best to look approvingly at Paco and her. Before he was quite sure what the next step was, Paco had handed her some paper money and shunted the two of them upstairs.

Commentary 5

The problem in telling it is symbolized by the difficulty in choosing what to call the inhabitants of the house. There are at least five words with which he could designate them—*girl, woman, prostitute, whore, mujer de mala nota*—and each was unsatisfactory in its own way. *Girl* sentimentalizes: it gives them an aura of innocence (after all, must one not blame a corrupt society for their fate?), and it also flatters them with a youthfulness possessed by few if any of those whom Roland noticed. *Woman* begs the question through its refusal of specificity; it is as though the writer advertises his unwillingness to designate them by lumping them indiscriminately with half the world's population. *Prostitute* is too antiseptic: neither she nor her customer would refer to her by this name, which is normally reserved for police records and newspapers. *Whore* is too abrupt for the context he had established: it creates an air of contempt and even if no contempt were intended, it lets the writer call attention to the fact he is sufficiently liberated to call a spade a spade. *Mujer de mala nota* would be an easy way out, for it is a term that genteel Spaniards use and a foreigner would be unaware of the genteel coloring; indeed, any foreign term deflects the problem, for all it does, whatever else it may do in its natural environment, is to lend an exotic note to the text in which it appears. In fact even if a foreign term denigrates, it generally acts like a euphemism. The contemptuous Spanish term *puta*, which he never even considered using, might well sound pleasantly foreign within an English sentence.

The encounter

The first real look he had of her was when she closed the door to her room (or at least the room assigned to her for the occasion). She was by no means young, she was distinctly chubby, and she had a long scar on her cheek that she had almost succeeded in hiding by heavy powdering. He hoped she would find a way of giving him the appropriate signs. Was he to approach her first and offer her a kiss? Or would she make the first move? Or was he expected to make some conversation, even in formulas? She mumbled some words not a one of which he understood. He replied in unconnected phrases to stress the fact of his foreignness. She came back with a hearty laugh that he decided to accept as a gesture of friendliness (he knew there was always the possibility—though in this instance it was certainly not a probability—that she would make fun of him). She gave little tugs at his shirt sleeves and pants from which he assumed it was time to take things off. Still, he pretended not to understand just in case he had got the signs wrong. Next thing he knew she placed her fingers at the buttons of her robe, which she proceeded to open with a slowness and a ceremoniousness one associates with the opening of a curtain on a play. He stared with awe. It didn't matter in the least that she couldn't conform to the usual standards of beauty or even that she was awkward the way she removed the tight brassiere that covered an overly pendulous pair of breasts. In fact it was even better if she couldn't measure up to the best, for this way she was in no position to expect too much of him. He started, hesitantly at first, to remove his shirt, and he noticed she flexed her arm muscles, which he took (or at least hoped that was how she meant it) as a statement on his manliness. He removed his pants, but before he could get to his underpants, she moved closer to him and placed herself directly in front of him as though trying to tell him (he hoped) he could feel free to touch anything. He reached for her breasts, stroked them gently, stopped a moment to make sure she approved his move, which she obviously did, for she quickly pulled him down on the bed. Suddenly confident he was getting the signs right he grabbed greedily at her breasts and made his way downwards. She in turn grabbed at his underpants and, starting to slide them down, she whispered the single word *francese* in his ear. This confused him, in fact caused a sudden nervousness to come over him—was she proposing to suck him or asking simply if he was a Frenchman (and if the latter, what did she mean by that?). His confusion was so great, in fact, that he climaxed too soon, so soon that he left the traces in all the wrong spots—his underpants, the bed cover, her wrist and knee. She reached under the bed for a rag to wipe herself off, and although she tried not to show her disapproval he had no illusions about what she must have been thinking. He stroked her breasts lightly to indicate he understood how she felt. She took her time tidying things up, then patted him on the rear as though to say better luck next time. He reminded himself she was not to blame, and he hoped she would not make too much of it when she faced Paco. He tried not to look at her as they put their clothes back on.

Commentary 6

Anybody reading this in our liberated time will notice the conspicuous refusal to name sexual organs. Naming the more sensitive parts of the body poses much the same problem as naming the members of the profession (since there was only one member in "The Encounter," he could get around that problem by calling her simply "she"). To take one extreme, if you say *penis, vagina,* or even *male* or *female organ,* you willfully interject the vocabulary of a medical book into a relatively informal narrative style. You also advertise your coyness and fear of offending anybody. At the other extreme, if you use *cock, prick, dick, dong, pussy, cunt, twatt,* or whatever goes with current fashions, you are forcing slang terms into a style quite unable to digest them, you self-indulgently call attention to your liberated-ness, and, perhaps most reprehensible of all, you excite your reader sexually to the point where he may well be unable to listen to what you are really trying to say. Yet your refusal to name the organ is itself a distraction and an attention-getter. Whichever way one goes in writing, it's hard to win.

Epilogue

He did not find Paco in the main room, but in a small one several doors down from the bedroom in which he had just enacted his failure. It was a room where the regular customers seemed to gather when everything was over and they could enjoy some relaxed conversation with the girls (women, prostitutes, whores, *mujeres?*). (It was like an audience's being invited to party a bit with actors they had just seen in a play.) Paco, stretched out on a bed with a girl sitting on each side of him, was regaling everybody with jokes Roland had no hope of understanding. Another customer was pouring red wine for everybody, and another strummed lazily at a guitar. Roland sat as inconspicuously as he could in a corner and hoped Paco was not planning to keep him there all night. Everybody was good about leaving him alone, but then the girl that Roland had been with walked in, and it was clear to him (though he understood scarcely a word) that Paco was now directing the jokes at him. She gave only short answers to the questions Paco put to her, and her expressions and gestures told him she was gallant enough to cover up for him. He would have rushed to hug her in gratitude if there had been any way to. But it was best to pretend he wasn't really there at all, that he was simply watching a film or play about doings in some exotic foreign country where people played guitars, clanked wine glasses, and joked unselfconsciously about matters that, in one's own life at least, would seem altogether devastating. He remained in his corner in full knowledge that this first time would also be his last, that by any usual definition, this wasn't even a first time at all and therefore he needn't even think it a last time or any time at all.

Commentary 7

How would you wind up an incident like this one? You have to give it some finality, make your readers feel they have come to the end of something in order to get a fresh start with the next incident. But does this finality not exaggerate what really happened, make it seem more catastrophic than it really was? And how does one judge the "really was"—by the way it felt at the time or the way it seems in retrospect? And since one is always writing in retrospect (unless you scribble in your diary all the while things are happening to you) nobody, least of all oneself, can ever know what it was like at the time. But that's only the start of the problem, for all subsequent incidents must seem to be generated out of this one, so while you write you are stressing only those details and striking those attitudes that will generate what you plan to develop afterward. Furthermore, everything written before this incident has already colored the way you tell this one, even to the point of falsifying significant moments to maintain some sort of continuity with those horrendous earlier experiences that must have generated everything that came after. And what if you defy these continuities, treat this episode as a discrete entity deliberately inconsistent (at least by common-sense standards) with all the others, allow the next episode to show Roland Fitzgerald-Calderón pounce like Zeus the Swan upon some young Spanish princess whom he had followed to her palace after watching her try out some boots in an elegant Madrid shop? All story telling, whatever one's intentions, ends up being a lie, and above all if it's your own story!

Note: On the respective roles of editor and author

An editor is like the baritone in an Italian opera: he has ample opportunity to make his presence felt, and he often has some interesting music to sing, but he must always relinquish his claims to the soprano for whom he has been pining all along. An author is like the tenor, who, even if the presence he creates is a bit on the wooden side, is authorized to woo, conquer, and die in the arms of the soprano simply by right of the voice range he was born with. Since you are the tenor of this book, Orlando, I must remind you it is both your birthright and your duty to play the role assigned you to the best of your ability. I do not expect you to woo some fat soprano (or even a thin one, for that is scarcely your style), but you must take pains to woo your readers, for these are the only partners you can hope for in view of all the other relationships you have shunned these many years. You should neither approach them full of excuses, as you all too readily do when you assure them you have no designs on them whatever, nor should you come on so strong at once (I frankly don't worry about you on this score) that they close the book on you before you've even begun to woo. What you want is to insinuate yourself into their affections step by step, pausing now and then to make them wonder what your next move will be, then perhaps move in with a short whisper in the ear, followed by a gentle stroke of the hand over some especially sensitive spot, and soon, without even a word in return, you will feel them responding to you as though they are telling you, "This is glorious—nothing's felt so great in years!" All the while you'll notice me in the wings watching you play out a role that, though I wish it were mine, at least leaves me with the consolation that I shall still be around to comment wrily once you and your readers have brought your passions to their natural crescendo and endured them to their all-consuming, inevitable end.

FOUR POSES

Note: Section ninety-four of the Cold Clay manuscript, which breaks off at this point. Nothing in the preceding episodes serves to introduce its setting or the circumstances surrounding the central character. Moreover, it is the only passage in Cold Clay that contains any first-person narrative. After

repeated readings, it becomes fairly obvious what this setting and these circumstances are, but I have decided to forego commentary and explanation
for two connected reasons: H-G did not volunteer information on this segment of his life either in his interview with me or in any other writings
included within the suitcase; and he is still presumably (and hopefully!)
alive and should be spared any embarrassment that might come from too
overt an identification of the setting and circumstances. Since he has made
it clear in many passages included in the suitcase that both novel manuscripts are autobiographical, I leave it to the reader to reach his or her own
conclusions. Except for this section, there is no record among the writings
in the suitcase of the decade of his life between his departure from college
in 1956 and his settling in Mendocino in the mid to late 1960s. Note the
extraordinarily large number of analogues between this relatively short section
of the novel and Saul's Fall, in which six episodes—"March 1," "Healing 2,"
"Prayer," "Conspiracy," "Inquiry," and "Endings"—contain distinct echoes
of "Four Poses." Those who have a difficult time understanding this section
even after several readings might wish to refer to the pose of painting no.
two in the episode "Endings" (I do not feel I am violating discreetness in
offering readers this hint).

Pose 1

Left arm: up 30° and pointing NNW.
Right arm: level and pointing SE.
Head: up 60° and twice as close to the right arm as to the left.
Left leg: knee up at a 15° angle and foot pointing NW.
Right leg: flat on floor and pointing ESE.
Much white flashing past, not slow enough to get fixed. Some pinching
along with it. Nonwhite shades flashing past, some floating loose, some
tight and rigid. No consistency again. Top of loose blue gown getting fixed.
"What's your name? See if you can tell me your name." More colors
floating past, white T-shirt getting fixed. "Who's the president these days?
Know his name?" Fixed so long this time that wetness oozes out the shirt
and makes a small blob bigger. "Tell me who's president of the United
States or you'll see what I can do to that silly pose of yours." Open hand
flashing past from left to right.

Pose 2

Right arm: up 20° and pointing SSE.
Rest as before.
He saw a white one—the tight kind—flashing past, then get fixed. "Does
it hurt here, or here, or here?" He knew there was pinching going on, but
the connections were hard. It was hard to know where exactly the pain

started out from, where the center was, if it was really still there, or if perhaps it had been there and worn away. "You don't have to tell me in words—I know that doesn't come easily. Just a blink of the eyes or a muscle twitch, any sign you can give so I'll know where the pain is." He knew the pinches for what they were, but they were hard to connect with what was already happening in his body. He saw the white move, unfix itself, and he felt a sharp knock on his knee.

Pose 3

Right knee: at a 25° angle with foot pointing SSE.

Rest as before.

It doesn't really matter to me if they flash past or get fixed or if nothing happens at all. I fix on a flowing one in several colors, and I know I have no choice, I cannot even close my eyes to it. "The point is, I can wait, and there aren't any others around here willing to do that for you." I know it's fixed and there's no way I can loosen it and get new ones flashing past. But it doesn't matter, they don't make that much difference. "You can keep up that way forever, but I want you to know I'm parked here till I get some response out of you." This one flashes past a ways, gets fixed again, loosens, gets fixed with the colors a little different. "Since there's no other way of getting to you, here's one that will!"

Pose 4

Left arm: up 20° and pointing ESE.

Right arm: down flat and pointing NNW.

Head: down flat and twice as close to right arm as to left.

Left leg: knee up at 90° angle and foot pointing WSW.

Right leg: down flat and foot pointing due W.

You come and go flashing past all day and sometimes you get fixed, more often not. I don't notice much of you, only the part that flashes past and those that get fixed. Sometimes, like now, very little flashes past and nothing gets fixed. I notice, of course, when you knock, poke, pinch, scratch, twist, kick, but perhaps I should add I don't really much care, and I don't even try to connect it with what's been flashing past or getting fixed. I can tell you think I defy you when I don't respond, but that's not true at all. In fact there is curiously little connection between the efforts you put into getting a response and the way I feel about what you are doing. The point is, I don't feel anything about you even when I am aware my not feeling anything makes you try all the harder to get to me somehow, some way. Be advised you can do what you want to my body, though it is only fair to tell you that, whatever you do and however long you persist, my mind through no particular will of its own continues to go its own way.

MENDOCINO DIARY

Note: Among the manuscripts in the suitcase this is the only one in diary form and it covers only seven successive days of H-G's life. It is handwritten in a spiral notebook the remaining pages of which contain first drafts of two scenes from Saul's Fall, "Healing 3," and "Conspiracy." Since the notebook was not attached by rubber band to the paralipomena to Saul's Fall, I decided not to print it within that section of this volume, even though the end of the diary records the origins of the play. Instead I am printing it directly after the autobiographical writings, for H-G explains in the 27 May entry that he started keeping the diary in order to find material with which to bring Cold Clay to what he saw as its natural culmination. Indeed, the diary clearly provides the transition from the novel to the play and, in addition, gives ample evidence for the way he intended to use material from the two unfinished novel manuscripts in the play. It is instructive to note that what were presumably the two first scenes he wrote, "Healing 3" and "Conspiracy," remain closer in form and theme to their respective analogues, "Calling on Nanny" and "Fairy Tale," than any of the episodes he was to write later. I am unable to supply an exact date for the diary, and H-G, as the reader can see, failed to fill in the year after the various dates. A school notebook of this sort does not contain watermarks to help in the identification of dates. Fortunately, H-G never removed the price tag glued to the notebook, and after checking with the manufacturer, the National Blank Book Company of Holyoke, Massachusetts, I ascertained that the price of the notebook, $0.35, would have been too low for any retailer to charge after the inflationary trend that began in this country in 1974. From remarks within the diary it is clear that H-G had been in Mendocino for several years at the time he wrote the diary, and since we know that he moved there in the mid to late 1960s, I judge the diary to have been written some time during the early 1970s. Analogues: "Preface," "Prologue," "Endings," and "March 2."

23 May

It's my day for blanking out all meaning. There's only the doing of things without any attempt on my part or that of others to read anything into it. Started out with the usual early morning walk, making a loop up Williams Street and back around over Heeser, which meant I could avoid Osborne altogether (even though that's the quickest way to the water), and nobody would have the slightest idea I was going anywhere regularly at a regular time. (My saying this is in no way an attempt to invite an interpretation of my behavior, but it's as close as I can come to saying straightforwardly that I don't want to call attention to myself.) I tried out the wildflower book I'd bought yesterday since this is the best year, according to the weekly paper, since I came here and even after all this time I'd never bothered trying to learn the names. What you find on the ocean cliffs is different from what you get just a short ways inland, and the number of varieties is strictly limited, so here was an easy way to start. I quickly identified the seaside daisy (I decided to ignore the Latin names they placed in parentheses). This was an obvious one since it couldn't be confused with anything else. The blue iris was easy too and so was the coast morning glory—to the point that I was quickly—too quickly in fact—gaining confidence in what I could do going between the book and the flowers. (I'm close to something interpretable again, and will be more careful from here on.) I identified the following:

Bluff lettuce, classified as a kind (genus or species?) of stone crop;

Gum plant, a kind of sunflower that you identify by the stickiness of its unopened buds (let's not read any meaning into this, I told myself);

California poppy (so common I shouldn't list it among those I identified, but omitting it would be reading something into the matter);

White nightshade;

Owl's clover.

Trouble started with the wild buckwheat, or at least with what I thought was wild buckwheat until I realized it might be what the book called sea pinks. The buckwheat was classified as red, but the color photograph made it look pink—just as pink as the sea pink, which the book classified as pink. I should have been able to tell them apart from the leaves, which the book analyzed, but somehow all I could find were stems without leaves. The problem repeated itself with other flowers: I would decide some specimen was blue, look vainly through the book's blue section, then wonder if the slightly reddish hue didn't qualify it as purple, then look through the purple section and think I had identified it until suddenly I noticed the leaves looked entirely different from those on the picture. And sometimes I was sure I'd made the perfect identification, everything cohered, and then I would note in the description that the flower wasn't due out until mid June! Where to go from here? There were moments I thought simply of throwing the book over the cliffs, but chances were I'd be noticed and half the town would be remarking on this, yet even if nobody saw me the book was sure to wash ashore immediately and litter up the beach (and with my name in it too!). I quietly hid it away in my coat pocket. I kept on walking along Heeser to the northwest end of town and started looking at the flowers as unreflectingly as I could, as pure images without names or connections. I tried to relax enough to allow the shapes and colors simply to impress themselves on my mind at one moment individually, at another in large groups that I would try to absorb as a whole. Next thing I knew the effort of taking in images had come to seem as taxing, confusing, and

purposeless as that of working out the classifications. There was once a
time, I'm sure, when the naming and classifying of things could be com-
bined unselfconsciously with experiencing them, but this is no longer
possible. I decided to ignore the flowers even if everybody in town was
swearing this was the greatest wildflower year of the century, and I
wandered down the path to the rock pools to look at things where no
prejudices or meanings had built up for me today. I reminded myself not
to make associations with the rock pools I remembered from Sicily when
my mother dragged me there at four, nor would I even make associations
with any of the innumerable earlier times I had been down this particular
path to these particular pools. It was best simply to sit down and stare
unthinkingly as the waves kept filling and emptying the pools with their
changing rhythms. I picked up a stick and poked gently, casually at
pebbles, seaweed, whatever else of sea life I could get within reach. I
noticed an anenome closing in on the stick even with the light touch I
gave it. Without thinking why, I dropped the stick and moved my right
middle finger over an anenome, stroking its furry surface softly as I watched
it close in on me. Soon I was moving from one anenome to another,
sometimes lingering a while with my finger embedded tightly within—
until I suddenly noticed what at first sounded like a cackle coming from
behind me: some high-pitched sea monster, I wondered, though a quick
glance backward showed two teen-aged girls imitating the motions of my
finger. There's always somebody, I told myself, to read some sort of
meaning into your every action! I fled as unobtrusively as I could to keep
them from suspecting I was fleeing from them.

24 May

This one started out well, just as the last one did. I decided to walk
down each street systematically and see how many of the houses I could
identify by the names of the families that had originally occupied them. I
did pretty well as far as names go—the Brown house with the scallops on
the front, the Hayden house with the three Gothic windows and its
board-and-batten walls, the Bowman house with its L-shaped front porch.
But as far as remembering what family had come here at what particular
time, who traded in the local lumber, or started the weekly paper (that
was a member of the Heeser family, something in my brain clicked off
automatically), or who married the school marm from Maine before the
Civil War—all this was so thoroughly mixed up in my mind by now that
I made no more effort to piece it together than to identify the wildflowers
after I'd decided to stash the wildflower book in my coat pocket yesterday.
I said a decent hello when any of the old-timers passed me by, but not so

heartily that it would encourage them to engage in conversation as my greetings had during my first year or two here. The danger was always worst when I passed one of them puttering in the garden. They were ready to spout local history at the drop of a hat, and a single question would get an hour-long answer so full of digressions that I would end up forgetting the main point (as would they). I am no longer able to absorb the local lore any more than I can the wildflowers. So why did I take this systematic walk? Not, certainly, to try to set up some continuity between myself and the town's history, as I had briefly when I first came here. Why should I feel any more involved with what went on here than in some common- place inland town—after all, I came here for the setting and climate, which are unique (if not to everybody's taste), while the local doings, whether now or in earlier times, were little different from what you would find in almost any American place this size. Of course I could acclaim the repre- sentativeness of Mendocino life and treat the town like a book I was reading. That possibility had also intrigued me for a while, though it didn't last long. So now there was nothing left except to try to cover the grid on which this town, like thousands of others, was laid out. The point of each walk is to vary one's pattern—not just starting in a different direction, but constantly changing the shapes of the squares and the rectangles you make. You don't have to read any meaning into anything, for the names of the houses if I can (or choose to) remember them, are simply points on the pattern to guide me through my maze. The more I vary the route, the less chance anybody will dub me the local eccentric who takes his solitary stroll past a particular house precisely at 9 a.m. on a particular day, fog and rain notwithstanding. Everything worked beautifully today until I came past the old carpenter's shop with its scrawny black mut always sitting in the open doorway. In the past I'd always known better and managed to keep to the other side of the street even though it had no sidewalk there. It was time to vary, I thought, but with the dog's first growl I made a careful semicircle around the shop, virtually cutting half way into the street to keep a sufficient distance from the dog. I obviously didn't carry it out with the necessary aplomb, for next thing I knew the carpenter was shouting after me with a sarcastic edge to his voice, "Think that bit of a thing is going to hurt you?" I should have known better than to make myself so conspicuous. From here on (except for Sundays) I decided to cut that block of Evergreen Street out of my walk.

25 May

I'm staying in today seeing to it that nothing unexpected can happen. The important thing is evenness. I must keep to a routine and not take chances on anything getting out of hand. I'm tinkering a bit with the sanitarium passages in *Cold Clay*—not that they still absorb me, but precisely because it doesn't absorb me so much anymore that it can interfere with the need I feel for evenness. Right now the task is to make myself uninteresting, not only to others, but to myself as well. There mustn't be a search for high moments, nor low ones either, for eliminating the high ones insures me against the lows—no big hopes and thus no disappointments. I refuse to dramatize myself—there will be no histrionics, no mysteries, none of that stuff great dramas are made of, no attempt to center a comedy or a tragedy around myself, or even an unstructured chronicle play. I mustn't try to charm myself any more than I should try to charm others—yet at the same time I mustn't be abrasive with myself any more than I ought to with others. Straightforwardness is all. I must stamp out any temptations to organize my life according to rules and conventions derived from narrative. There must be no beginnings, middles, ends in which I am always looking forward to something, then trying to figure out why I am where I am in terms of what happened in the past. As I look over the preceding diary entries I can see I was allowing myself into precisely those situations the last two days, but today is different—without any real planning I go casually back and forth to the manuscript, play some classical chamber music in between, or take a quick trip to the grocery (despite my earlier thought of not venturing out at all), or play a twelve-tone wind quintet (unlike the Mozart, I do this on earphones since it would otherwise call undue attention to myself from next door). There are times I simply stare —at the old furniture that came with the house (the style is supposed to be getting fashionable again, though these pieces are hopelessly run down), or now that it's getting dark, I notice (as casually as possible) the light that just went on in the Adams house across the street. It's an unfamiliar face in the kitchen, so they've probably rented it out to tourists again for the week—bent down over the stove, a tall, earnest, moon-faced girl with long black hair that she's allowed to flow around the edge of a pot she stirs with inordinately vehement motions. It's time to draw my blinds, not just so I won't be seen, but to keep me from looking out, participating (however distantly) in her life, reading things into it (or mine), seeking out meanings that have no business existing.

26 May

Disparate perceptions that must exist disembodied from any person, time, or place and whose only reason for being in a diary is that they occurred to me (or him, since I must expunge myself) in the course of this particular day (whose date should also be expunged) while sitting in this ancient and disintegrating Victorian parlor (which should also be part of the expunging process) doing nothing:

1. Does one write things down because they are intrinsically interesting, or because they do something for oneself, or simply to keep in practice writing (like keeping one's body up with calisthenics)?

2. Even if you do it only for yourself, writing remains a social activity to the extent that you conjure up a relationship with an audience every time you put language to use.

3. Imagining an audience means imagining the intrigues, alliances, and cabals that have always been central to literary life.

4. Those who wish to pursue any audience outside the one in the writer's imagination must be prepared to eat, drink, sleep (and God knows what other forms of conviviality) with those who wield the power necessary to fetch them an audience in the first place.

5. He who assiduously avoids human contact also avoids a whole range of maladies from paranoia to the common cold.

6. Since he had hated the young when he was himself young, he saw no reason (despite current taboos) to change his mind about them now, and by the same token he saw no necessity to nurture good feelings toward his fellow adults, or, for that matter, to change his mind in later years once they tossed him into a nursing home with others about to die.

7. Anguish is a pity since it is soon forgotten.

8. It is fortunate that the conventions of language rarely require a person to speak his own name, else he would constantly feel embarrassed about the fact that he exists.

9. The trouble with writing that proverbial last letter is deciding to whom to address it—if it's to a specific person, it'll be sentimental, whether in the vengeful or the self-pitying mode; if it's to the police, it's a cold exercise that will end up routinely nodded at, then filed away; if to the world at large, it will have no readers at all.

10. Extreme psychological states are interesting not for what they tell you about the human mind in general, or about any specific person, but for the opportunities they offer to see what writing is all about.

11. Ten would have been a good number to end with, so let's not call this eleven, but simply an epilogue: There is nothing that people can do, or say, or think—no matter how privately, impersonally, and without overt connection to anything else—that does not exist within some context that colors and gives meaning to their various actions, utterances, and thoughts. In other words, nothing of me has been expunged.

27 May

What's a diary for anyway?

(1) As far as the diarist is concerned:

(A) To remind you what you did a few days or weeks or months or years ago in case you've forgotten.

(B) To give a sense of importance to things while you are doing them (and even influence the way you do them).

(C) To winnow material from your raw experience for use in future, more formal writings.

(2) As far as the reader is concerned:

(A) To experience another person with a higher degree of spontaneity and intimacy than one can in other forms of writing.

(B) To supplement, even subvert the standard knowledge surrounding some famed person.

(C) To lose oneself in the real-life details of some distant world, whether that of an ancestor or some figure whose doings others have pronounced exemplary.

As I look back over the entries thus far, I see I have fulfilled none of these functions. From last to first: (2, C)—I have not created enough of a world to give anyone in the future the slightest sense of what life in Mendocino is like these days; (2, B)—I am not famous anyway, nor intend to be; (2, A)—the spontaneity and intimacy of my diary entries are as conventional as the high rhetoric of epics or the rhyme schemes of sonnets—note, for instance, how I constantly fall back on such diary conventions as (1) alternating between "I walked down the street" and then reflecting on my action or (2) letting each day's entry culminate in some event or reflection that pulls things together (the anenome and dog incidents, the image of the girl stirring her pot, the epilogue that undercuts the idea behind the earlier epigrams) while pretending not to be an ending in any ordinary narrative sense; (1, C)—I had of course (the "of course" is a diary cliché to suggest that I am talking to myself and can thus unselfconsciously take earlier events for granted) intended these entries as raw material toward a closing episode for *Cold Clay*. If *Cold Clay*, according to the plan I have adhered to unthinkingly all these years, was to consist of a series of disparate, objectively narrated episodes drawn from my own life, then I would surely need to round it out with something— an incident, episode, description—of these years in Mendocino, deliberately uneventful though they may be. All I'd have to do, I thought, was jot down my daily routine for a few days, translate the "I's" into "he's" just I transformed *A Prelude to Nothing* into *Cold Clay* by changing from first to third person and cutting out the continuities. Yet as I reread the entries I know I haven't the slightest desire to transform them into anything and am even wondering if what's happened the last four days wasn't a signal that I'm ready to abandon *Cold Clay* altogether; (1, B)—though I tried to arrange my doings and my descriptions of them in such a way that nothing would have any undue importance, the very process of doing what I did and knowing I was about to write it down blew everything up out of

all proportion, which I suspect is what diarizing has always done, and I find
the whole thing appalling; (1, A)—I don't care to remember what I did.

*　*　*

The ideal diary is one that would simply record one's actions, thoughts,
intuitions precisely as they occurred without any conscious intrusion on
the diarist's part. This would necessitate a special, still uninvented form of
recording equipment that would be so unobtrusive the diarist would remain
unaware any switch was on at all. Of course he should never have to read
any of the print-outs: not only would they fail to give the proper shadings
or emphases, but once he is aware that he has been recorded, he would
henceforth selfconsciously dramatize his every move. Down with all diaries!

28 *May*

The whole point of this was to objectify myself, clean myself of meaning.
I had moved from *A Prelude to Nothing*, which tried to render a continuity
I imagined in my life, to *Cold Clay*, which, with its unconnected episodes
and its coldly distant third person narrative, still ended up being fraught
with meaning. From here on I'll stick to words and sounds alone and see
where they take me. I'll start with *diary* since that's the closest thing at
hand:

Words suggested

journal
notebook
annal
record

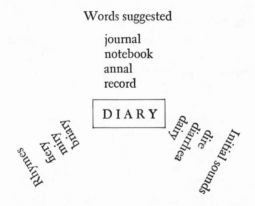

Dear Diary, You're a failure and a dud,
Your banalities appall,
Though I'd rather drop you with a thud,
I'll settle for a dying fall.

Note the word *fall*, just the opposite in sound from *diary*, and note also
the various gradations in sound between these words in *failure, dud,* and
drop.

"A Phonetic Comparison of *Diary* and *Fall*"

Diar-y	Fall
D voiced high on the alveolar ridge	F unvoiced on the lower lip
I sounded near lips	A sounded deep in the throat
R a liquid that's retroflex	L a liquid that points forward

29 May

I wouldn't have started a new diary entry if I weren't sure this is the last one forever (and it neatly rounds out the week to boot!). All night I brooded about what to make of the word *fall*. First, though I had come upon the word accidentally, I could describe it soundwise through its opposition to *diary*. Second, I'm making my New Year's resolution seven months in advance, and will really go through with this one: I'll objectify whatever material I can from A *Prelude to Nothing* and *Cold Clay* (or anything else I ever wrote) and in the least personal of forms, namely, drama (and me of all people who's not been inside a theater, movie, or public performance of any sort in ten years!). Third, I'll chart words out of *fall* the way I did yesterday out of *diary* and everything in the play will be generated out of these words.

Words suggested

overthrow
regression
dying
autumn
dropping
cadence

FALL

Diagram of words radiating from FALL:

Initial sounds: file, full, fill, feel, fool, fell, fall

Rhymes: ball, tall, hall, appall, maul, crawl, wall, Paul (always) falls, Saul (early) falls, Testament king who fell, Read up high on him right away, of Paul, so won't, do any good, but also an Old, always on the ascendant, never

Note: An explication by MJW *of "a generative chart for the word* fall"

I have withstood the temptation to comment in detail on the diary, for I believe it speaks for itself. Yet as a scholar I cannot resist demonstrating how much of the chart in the last day's entry suggests specific aspects of the play that H-G, keeping to his seven-months-early New Year's resolution, subsequently wrote.

Rhymes:

tall—the giant Goliath in "Battle 1."

hall—I am uncertain at this point how H-G meant to use this word.

appall—the tone of many scenes, for instance "Intermezzo" and "Execration" (above all the scenes dominated by Saul's daughter), is surely meant to appall the reader or audience; note as well that H-G used the word appall in the diary entry of 27 May as well as in the doggerel verse in the 28 May entry, where it is made to rhyme with fall.

maul—Saul in his madness (see Daughter's speech in "Healing 1") was known to maul others.

crawl—Saul crawls like a dog in "Healing 2"; note as well H-G's fear of dogs manifested in the diary entry of 24 May.

wall—this may well have suggested the barrier against which the Daughter pits herself in "Execration."

gall—a word that must have suggested something of the Daughter's character.

Paul—the first proper name that came to mind, but rejected by H-G in his parenthetical remark because Paul was too obviously a model of success.

Saul—the second proper name that came to mind and the one he settled on; through the parenthetical note it is evident that he remembered very little about the Old Testament story at the time he determined to write on this subject. What looks like a facetious remark at the end of the "Preface," that "one could justify using the story of Saul simply by virtue of the fact that the hero's name rhymes with the word fall," turns out to be the actual origin of the play's theme!

Meanings:

overthrow—H-G chose the traditional form of a play about the overthrow of a ruler by his successor, as in Shakespeare's Richard III and Richard II.

regression—under stress, Saul regresses to immature stages of development, most obviously in "Healing 2," where he starts out having regressed to the animal stage and gradually makes his way back to heroic action.

dying—the scene "Endings" concerns itself with several distinct ways of dying before Saul finally puts an end to his life.

autumn—I am unable to make a connection here. One would think that with all his systematicness H-G would have planted some allusion to this season in the play.

dropping—note the occasions when Saul is in what H-G calls a "slump,"
   especially his dropping into this condition at the end of "Battle 1" and
   "Healing 2"; also note the Daughter's "plopping" to the ground at the
   end of "Execration" and Saul's dropping on the bed when he kills
   himself.
cadence—major premise: ". . . each episode was conceived . . . with a distinct beginning, middle, and end" (from H-G's "Preface"); minor premise: ". . . he conceived these episodes after the model of musical composition" (again from H-G's "Preface"). Conclusion: H-G conceived the end
   of each episode as a musical cadence.

Initial sounds:
fail—the play is concerned from the start with Saul's consciousness of his
   failure and its relation to his fall.
fell—one can speculate that since Saul's fall had in a sense taken place
   before the play began, the play treats the notion of falling essentially
   in the past tense.
fool—Saul often is shown having the attributes of the traditional fool and
   is treated as a fool by his Daughter and by David.
feel—this word is hard to place precisely, though the presence of the word
   in the generative chart may have influenced the self-consciousness with
   which Saul and his Daughter express their feelings in such monologue
   scenes as "Prayer" and "Execration." Note also Saul's stuttering line
   "You don't know what goes on inside there" as he points to his heart in
   "Healing 2."
fill— ⎫
full— ⎬ these words are even harder to place. They may well have suggested
   the principle of plentitude whereby each scene was designed to have
   analogues both in known literary works and in H-G's autobiographical
   writings.
file—here I am really at a loss, though as a scholar I confess this is a word
   dear to my heart. I shall file it away for future investigation.

Note: On editorial self-restraint

It has been said of many books that the notes and various forms of editorial commentary are more arresting than the main text. I have always had
a soft spot for that kind of book, and if this project were completely my
own, I should outdo myself concocting the most ingenious commentaries
that I could well imagine taking up the better part of the book. Such at
least is the book I envision writing some day, but not this time around, for
the present book, dedicated as it is to the understanding of a text solemnly
entrusted to me by its author, must maintain a certain chasteness and
restraint in harmony with the rigors of the author's own personality. As a

result, whenever the passion for commentary comes over me, I tug at some part of myself and ask "is this really in tune with his spirit?" Please note that I have restrained myself enough to reproduce my author's play without a single intrusion. Though my self-restraint has proved less notable in other sections of this book, you can be sure that, out of deference to the author and to the various writers who have contributed to this volume, I have provided only a small fraction of the commentary that was threatening to burst from my pen. Yet be warned that my next book may well consist of notes alone without even the semblance of a text on which they purport to comment.

ESSAYS
IN CRITICISM

PART ONE

*Contributions by Fellow
Writers*

STATEMENT FROM THE DRAMATIST FREDRIC SACKETT

It belabors the obvious to remind anyone today that Fredric Sackett is the commanding dramatist of our time and one of the indisputably classical authors of this century. Since he is notorious for the rarity of his public pronouncements, it seems to me of the utmost significance that he was willing to remark—and most favorably so!—upon the text around which this volume is centered. Although his statement lacks the specificity one demands of ordinary commentators, it is abundantly clear that Sackett recognizes Orlando Hennessy-García as a kindred spirit. Let us remember that a few oblique and metaphorical lines from a great writer can often tell us more about a kindred author than many volumes of learned commentary.

What is asked is considerable, more than my fading voice is prepared to respond with—

Still, I have taken it upon myself to peruse here and there, well known though it may be I no longer command the concentration necessary for sustained reading—

Yet I have read enough to recognize a presence in touch with what was once all too confidently called the human condition—

And I can say I welcome all who are willing to confront, immerse themselves in, drink down the dregs of our common misery—

I welcome all such, including this young author, whoever he may be—

I have little more if anything to say—

LETTER FROM THE NOVELIST SAMUEL SCHRIECKER

The distinguished novelist Samuel Schriecker needs no introduction for those seriously interested in the literature of our time. It will be evident that my good friend Sam Schriecker and I disagree on the relative merits of the play to the understanding of which this volume is dedicated. Such disagreements are natural during the early stages in the reception of any innovative work and thus provide an invaluable contribution to the communications model that this volume constitutes. When a major writer

195

resists a new work by a fellow writer, we can generally attribute this resistance to the intense and singleminded vision through which he must needs approach any external force in order to maintain his own creative integrity. The reservations about genre and theme that Samuel Schriecker voices are expressions of his own very laudable concerns, which, as everybody knows, include the exploration of new novelistic forms to accommodate what he terms the "Jewish matter" in a manner that is both local and universal at once. It is a tribute to Sam Schriecker's integrity that he is willing to express these concerns honestly and directly in this particular volume.

Dear Milton,

Hearing from you reminded me that I never properly acknowledged the fine hospitality you arranged that time I spoke at Stanford. You can see I do indeed remember you, and with warmth. My favorable memory of you is confirmed by your recent communication, for your championship of an unknown writer (which one does not ordinarily expect among members of your profession) is something I find most creditable.

If I reply to your request in the form of a personal letter rather than the full-blown essay that I know you'd prefer, I hope you will appreciate the dilemmas that afflict a successful writer (which, for better or worse, I must consider myself these days). You may think that my refusal to contribute a formal paper stems from the expenditure of time that such a venture would assume, but that, let me assure you, is only the least of my concerns. Once I put my thoughts in the mold of a formal essay, this inevitably involves my agent, who would hold up your project interminably to argue the best possible terms for me (not to speak of himself), and it would also commit me to including this effort in my forthcoming volume of collected essays, which as I see it now is taking a shape that could not easily assimilate a piece on your Mr. (or should I say Señor?) Hennessy-García.

This is not to say I have failed to take the task you request with my usual seriousness in such matters. I have in fact pondered considerably over his manuscript—to the point where it slowed down my pace (from four to two pages a day during the two days I read and pondered) on the embryo that is destined to be my next novel. (Please do not get the idea I am objecting to this expenditure of writing time. I see this as part of my normal duties, just as every successful doctor—and everybody knows my family sorely wanted me to enter that profession—devotes at least part of his practice to the treatment of less advantaged patients.)

Nothing would of course make me happier than to give your author the clean bill of health that I know you wish for him. But this, alas, I am unable to do and as a result of my ponderings I must say in all honesty that what you sent me is at best a mixed bag. My objections lie in three specific areas—the pretensions that the author assumes, the genre he has chosen to work, and the content he is presenting to us. I take these up in order.

1. Pretensions

From the preface, the scene titles, indeed the very nature of that which he dared to treat (a dialogue with the deity, a formal death speech, that whole huge choral apparatus) it is clear that the gentleman is setting up shop in competition with the very great. But it is also clear that he can by no stretch of the imagination be considered Nobel Prize material, that he is not even Nobel-nominee material (there are some who take a perverse satisfaction in their always-the-bridesmaid-never-the-bride status, but your author does not merit even this quite circumscribed form of happiness), that he'd do well to deflate his lofty pretensions to bring them into some sort of accord with what reality is prepared to offer him, which, as I tend to see it, is none too much.

2. Generic considerations

How is it a self-respecting young writer (is he really that young?) would test his wings on the drama of all forms? Surely he must know that the mode in which the human spirit is most likely to reveal itself in our time is not the drama (though the world well knows I have tinkered with it at moments in my career), but the novel! To commit one's profoundest thoughts to the dramatic mode these days seems at best a rash and willful act that flies in the face of all we've discovered about how the mind can manifest itself in the most vital, liberated way. Choose the wrong genre, and you're lost from the start. What more need I say?

3. Thematic considerations

This is a ticklish subject. Not that I've ever shied away from the ticklish, but some persons will doubtless take what I say in the wrong spirit, and I must make it clear I have no objections to anybody of whatever racial, religious, or sexual orientation plundering the Bible. I recognize the Bible as common property and make no special claims on it in the name of our particular tribe. This said, I must cite a certain inappropriateness in the author's use of what one might call the "Jewish matter." Again, let me repeat I do not mean his use of the Old Testament as such, but rather a certain Jewish coloring that he has seen fit to apply with all too bold strokes. Let me refer, for example, to the scene with Samuel and the Witch of Endor. Before finding fault, incidentally, I should express my delight that your author found room in his composition for my namesake the prophet, even if only in this single scene. Samuel's been unfairly neglected by writers and artists over the millenia, and any rehabilitation he can receive rates a plus in my judgment book. But to return to less pleasant things, I must say your friend has simply not mastered the ethnical situation he attempted to portray, nor could he be expected to have. This scene (I forget its name—the names of the scenes are rather confusing, and he should instead have used an old-fashioned act and scene numbering, which after all was good enough for some very great writers) attempts quite obviously to capture the primordial Jewish family drama, composed as it is of the son (Saul) who can never measure up and the reproachful parents (Samuel and the Witch) who outvie one another in the verbal might of the reproaches they level at him while he in turn enters the battle to outdo the two of them with the most devastating yet also pathetic reproaches of his own. Glorious drama this—and how great the execution might have been by someone who'd had the chance to suffer it at first hand. There are moments, certainly, when the author manages to strike the true ethnic note. I think of the opening line from the scene I discuss above, "So what's the great Witch of Endor for. . . ." To be sure, the line as a whole is not sustained (and there's a deplorable drop in authenticity in subsequent lines), but for a moment at least we experience that curious mixture of reproach, submissiveness, skepticism, and awe that marks the Hebraic sensibility. Indeed, it is at individual moments like this (there *are* some others, though none too many) that I suspect the García side of our author has absorbed a few drops of that Jewish blood that, according to the notable theory propagated by the great Hispanist Américo Castro, has flowed since early times (despite innumerable dilutions) throughout the Spanish population. But the author tempts us with such morsels only to remind us soon after that he is unable to provide us the feast toward which he has whetted our appetites. Far be it from me, offspring of the most persecuted race in human history, to deny others the right to pursue what they will. Yet if he cares to overwhelm us with his authenticity, let Hennessy-García work up his Irish matter, his Spanish matter, and whatever else may help him liberate the creative impulses he has so energetically sought to set free within himself. Each to his own. Send him my encouragement, if not precisely my admiration.

To reiterate, I find it commendable in every way to see an academic wanting to help an unknown writer, though as you can tell from my remarks on the Señor, I'm not at all convinced you placed your bet on the most promising possible horse. Next time you're in a betting mood let me know and I'll put you in touch with some of my younger friends who badly need (and deserve!) the promotion you've so superbly lavished on the gentleman in question. My best wishes in the meantime. And do convey my greetings to the many fine persons you introduced me to my last (and all too quick) visit to Stanford. Remember you can always count on a substantial reduction in my regular fee for any future lecture you might care to arrange at your lovely campus.

Sincerely yours,
Samuel Schriecker

A MESSAGE TO MESSER ORLANDO
FROM GEORGE JOHNSON

Since poetry does not enjoy nearly as large an audience these days as fiction and drama, George Johnson's work is not as well known to the general literary public as that of the dramatist and novelist whose comments on Saul's Fall are recorded in the present section. Yet for readers deeply concerned with the directions that poetry in our language is taking, no name commands more respect (whatever disagreements one may have with him— for his personality by its very nature invites disagreement) than that of George Johnson. He is not only a poet of the most considerable stature, but a teacher and theorist of poetry whose ideas of where poetry should be going have had a profound effect on some of his most distinguished contemporaries, several of whom he mentions in his present statement. Needless to say, the most serious poets these day have maintained an antipathetic attitude toward the drama, which they see as lacking sufficient concentration of language and effect, and it is only natural that George Johnson should view the work around which this volume is built from the point of view not only of the genre he himself practices but above all of the theory he has voiced with such fervor in his prose writings and lectures as well as in his celebrated role as conversationalist. Yet despite the profound differences that separate the two writers, it seems to me remarkable what deep affinities George Johnson obviously feels with H-G, especially with his theories if not so much with his actual artistic practice. If I had had the foresight to send him H-G's "Mendocino Diary" together with the play, I believe Messer George (as he obviously likes to be called by his fellow writers) would have discovered even deeper theoretical affinities than he has with the text he examined. And if I may bring up a far more significant "if" situation, what if H-G had stayed at Bard College at least another year instead of departing abruptly in 1956? As is well known, that is the very year George Johnson came to teach at Bard and founded what has since become known as the Bard school of poets. Might H-G, like Jasper Bernstein, have turned from fiction to poetry under Messer George's powerful tutelage? Or might he have turned to drama anyway, though to a more poetic and, to use one of George Johnson's favorite terms, "high voltage" form of drama? Such questions can of course never be answered, for they exist in the "might-have-been" world that H-G created with such poignancy in "Prophecy 1." It is also possible, perhaps even probable, that H-G, loner that he has always been, might have chosen to resist even as charismatic a force as Messer George, whom he might have subsumed within the theory of fashions he was later to enunciate in the first of his three disquisitions.

Come off it, Messer Orlando, too much is too much and anyway y're not a member of our guild. But I have hopes for you, esp. what you say y're getting at in that preface of yrs which at moments really grabs me. (I don't say it quite grabs me by the balls, but it grabs me just the same.) And that prologue too, where you bring up all those hifalutin terms tragedy/comedy/ history/and/the/like and then after each of them you say "but this is no longer possible," all of which means you figured out for yrself that all the old forms are dead and done with. Yep, th're dead all right, and it's great to hear this told by somebody from outside the guild. So let me say I recognize yr heart's in the right place, and if y'll let me instruct you in a few central matters, Messer Orlando, I suspect we might build a pretty good base for communication. So here goes!

first rule:

IT MUST BE REAL

Now real to me doesn't mean any of that realism/representation stuff that has haunted our kulchur a few thousand years too many. Though I can see y're trying to get away from the story-line idea, y've not really managed to get that imitation notion out of yr system. Take an emetic from Messer George, and y'll be rid of it all in no time flat (you may feel crampy for a moment, but just imagine the relief y'll feel afterwards). Then y'll ask yrself why you had to stick to that Saul story all the way. Who the hell wants to plunder that creaky old bible nowadays? I don't mean you shdn't use it here and there, but if yr central field of force is generated by the image of falling, then you shd be ramming together a whole large batch of those who fell—a Sumerian king, a Pharaoh, young Icarus, some Mayan god, Richard II, Richard Nixon, and if you can concoct yrself a decent stew out of all these, I've got nothing against yr throwing in a dash of old King Saul for a little extra flavor.

second rule:

IT MUST BE ORACULAR

Here's where the preface really lets me down. Y're satisfied simply with "frustrating traditional expectations," as you put it (I'm all for that) and by this means you want us to "never feel quite sure about where we stand." That's all well and good, boy, but it's just a starting point. Yr program never gets beyond the negative, or to put it in my sort of terms, all y've told us so far is y're willing to help the rest of us shovel up the old shit. Now when I leafed through the play I got glimmerings of something bigger, something that, for a moment or two, would get those chthonic soundings that some of us are after these days. I never felt those glimmerings if I tried to read straight through a page, only when I let my eyes wander, esp. in those rages that sporadically pour out of Saul and his daughter (though in no way from that asshole David, who's got no business at all intruding into poetry). Trouble with those rages (and that's also the trouble with everything else) is that as soon as anybody tries to read down a page, all he hears is a torrent of words. "Words, words, words," as Lear put it so desperately (no wonder he went mad!). What's wrong here is too much logic, too much in the way of connectives pretending to hold everything together. It's that old Western hang-up, Messer Orlando, all that crap that started with Socrates, and after 2,500 years the pile's too high for you or any of us to shovel away in a single generation. But w're making a start, some of us at least, Jordan and Carsten and Bernstein and myself (plus a flock of young ones w're in constant communication with) and before us of course Wms and old Ez. When y've had several millenia of getting things wrong, it's only natural if it takes a while to set things right. But I'll get down to brass tacks and leave you with something positive to think about. Why don't you take a few lines from one of those pages and

(1) Calculate the parabola that'll give you the rhythmic curves you need (ours is a scientific enterprise—more scientific in a fundamental way than what those birds who call themselves scientists piddle around with);

(2) and don't be ashamed to use yr logarithm table to figure out the length of yr open spaces. What's left unsaid between breath-groups (whether to the right or left, or above or below lines) is the key to the effects y're creating and matters like these must be calculated with utmost precision.

third rule:

IT MUST BE CHARGED

Here again y're on to something in that preface even if you never really carried it out. It's when you say "Each episode may be viewed as one of those highly charged images—independent, yet related closely though without overt explanation to the other images," etc., etc. That's straight out of Ez, boy, and I bet you never even knew it. The trouble is, none of this jibes with all that other talk of yrs about beginnings, middles, and ends, and all I can say is y're caught up in that old Western hang-up again, Messer Orlando (the only ends I happen to recognize are those between our legs). I can assure you that three lines by old Ez (*any* consecutive three laid out on the page the way he intended) generate more real drama than all yr seventeen episodes put together (what's an episode supposed to be anyway?—I always connected the word with things like hiccups, diarrhea, epilepsy). No, if you want to hit the really high voltage, Messer Orlando, you may as well add yr episodes with their beginnings, middles, and ends to that old crap pile we were talking about and start afresh. Or not completely afresh, since I've got a salvage operation in mind (Messer George is patenting his own machine to turn crap to good uses). The point is, y've got to learn to organize yr stuff not in episodes but in short breath-groups, for these alone are capable of giving off the electrical charge y're after. So here's a little experiment I tried: I opened up each of yr episodes, plus yr prologue and epilogue, and I chose a single breath-group from each *at random*, and then I placed them carefully on a single page in the original order of the episodes th're drawn from. Finally I calculated the open spaces, and this is the result:

                       To reassure their spectators

           (*Short fanfare*

A good bit mightier than his bite

    I'm immovable (*sd Saul*)

    (*Somewhat louder growl/*

    It's only a small sky,

         after all

For my sake and David's

    /this is a matter of

        Not a paranoiac

                   (*Moving close to Saul again*

        I defy you!

               (*Same sound from sinkhole*

     This hypocrite who professed

        to heal me once

Nothing's fated in the least

             (*Starting to dictate again*) (

Such quakes to test the earth's thin crust

                  without any fuss

       Mourn our dead king/

          into postcathartic calm.

Put your nose to this, Messer Orlando, and y'll get a pure whiff of muses cunt. Come to think of it, I'll go ahead and print it in the coming issue of *The Dry Heaves* and as far as I'm concerned that'll make you eligible for the guild (and better start subscribing: send $20 for a year's subscription—anywhere from 2 to 4 issues depending on how horny the muse feels—to Burning Tiger Press, P.O. Box 9669, Framshaw Station, Mich. 49132).

MEANWHILE:

it's time

you started

reading

Carsten on/

Bernstein

(that's the elementary

Step

after which Bernstein on

Johnson

(not Procrustean old Sam-u-el,

but Messer George himself

who'll give you

INKLINGS

how to:

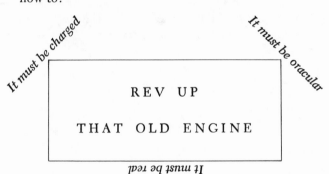

REV UP

THAT OLD ENGINE

Yrs,

Messer George

Note: If I mention that the famous Shakespearean phrase "Words, words, words" is from Hamlet (II, ii, 194) and not from King Lear, I recognize I am engaging in a form of pedantry endemic within my profession. I do so not in order to show up George Johnson, whose breadth and depth of learning would put to shame nearly all academic persons of my acquaintance, but because this little slip tells us something about how a poet's mind works. It is the same phenomenon precisely as Keats' confusing Cortez and Balboa in his great sonnet on Chapman's Homer.

Note: On notes

The purpose of this note on notes is to defend what the reader may judge to be a disproportionate and insufficiently justified number of intrusions on the editor's part. To which I reply, a good book should be like a dialogue with a number of voices engaged with one another in such a way that one questions the other, or eggs the other on, or occasionally one-ups the other. Too many books are written in a single voice that the author manages to sustain with the most willful artifice while the poor reader remains subjected to an unending barrage from a single direction. As you think about it, most such books (and the list includes many famous ones) leave something to be desired. And that is what this book, with its constant editorial intrusions and its multitude of eminent voices commenting in the most varying and often conflicting ways upon a single text, seeks to rectify. And so, I might add, does the text to the understanding of which this book is dedicated: note the scene "Endings," in which a variety of voices is assumed by a single character; or note the Author's statement in his "Preface" that "our perceptions, as we move from one episode to another, are meant to be jarred so that we must never feel quite sure about where we stand." This edition is thus conceived fully in the spirit of the play itself. I am confident I speak for H-G as well as for myself when I say—NO MORE ONE-DIMENSIONAL BOOKS!

ESSAYS
IN CRITICISM

PART TWO

Contributions by Literary Critics

SAUL'S FALL AND THE SAUL TRADITION

R. Passmore Smith

When I told my retired colleague Passmore Smith about this project he immediately volunteered to read the play and provide a study of its sources not only in the Bible but in the depictions of Saul within subsequent literature. The choice of Professor Smith for this task seemed most appropriate, for those who attended Stanford during the last half century retain a most affectionate memory of his course "English Literature and the Biblical Tradition," which, through his jovial manner of presentation, succeeded in making difficult and often obscure matters thoroughly entertaining to the thousands who packed his lectures. The briefness of Professor Smith's contribution to this volume is in no way proportional to the length of time he devoted to the project, for after spending several months reading innumerable versions of the Saul story he reluctantly concluded that H-G utilized nothing but the original Biblical version and even that in the most sketchy of ways. Such are the hazards of scholarship.

Since it is frequent within the sciences for researchers to spend months, even years, in their laboratories, only to find that the experiments they have been running do not yield the results they expected, it is surely no disgrace for a literary scholar to expend considerable time tracking down the sources of a work without much to show for his efforts. When I undertook the task of seeking out the depictions of Saul in those earlier literary works that I assumed stood behind Orlando Hennessy-García's play *Saul's Fall*, I assumed that, like nearly every author of note who has dealt with Biblical materials, he had steeped himself not only in the Bible, but in those particular embodiments of the tale that other writers have treated before him. My assumptions proved wrong, for after studying his play in conjunction with virtually every well-known literary work on the subject of Saul, I was forced to conclude that he used no source but the Bible, and this in only the most tangential (shall I say cavalier?) of ways.

I shall return to the Bible later, but must first indicate some of the literary treatments of Saul with which one might have expected an aspiring young author to be familiar. The most distinguished of these treatments is Alfieri's neoclassical tragedy *Saul* (1782), which, even if Mr. Hennessy-

García did not know Italian, he could easily have found in English translation. French writers have displayed a penchant for the Saul story, as witness the early tragedy by Jean de la Taille (*Saül le furieux*, 1572); the mock tragedy *Saül* supposedly by Voltaire (1763), whose Enlightenment bias against religion it is just as well Mr. Hennessy-García did not attempt to adopt; Lamartine's Romantic tragedy *Saül* (1818); and Gide's early play *Saül* (1895). In English one can cite Cowley's now little-read epic the *Davideis* (1656) and D. H. Lawrence's charming play *David* (1926), which, like Gide's play, is refreshingly free (except for occasional hints that something is going on between David and Jonathan) of the perverse obsessions that all too frequently mar the work of these controversial authors. As far as I can tell, Mr. Hennessy-García's play shows not a single verbal echo, allusion, or thematic adaptation of anything in these works that could not more easily be traced to their common Biblical source. I should certainly have expected him to make use of Robert Browning's famed dramatic monologue "Saul" (1845), but here again the results were negative. (Had Browning rhymed Saul with "fall" instead of with "all," as he did, I might have argued for Mr. Hennessy-García's knowledge of this poem.) Since the author makes much of the influence of music, particularly opera, in the preface to his play, I consulted the libretti of Handel's great oratorio *Saul* (1739) and Carl Nielsen's opera *Saul og David* (1902), the latter of which I made my way through in Danish, which I quickly concluded Mr. Hennessy-García never bothered doing. As for Handel, I could find no influence except of course for his use of the hero's Dead March (to be played on a hand organ, no less!) in the scene entitled "March 2." His use of this passage, which is often played as a concert piece, would not have necessitated his knowledge of the oratorio as a whole.

Regarding the Bible, Mr. Hennessy-García's deviations from his source are so extensive that I shall limit myself to but a few typical examples. For instance, whereas the Bible has David himself volunteer to fight Goliath (1 Samuel 17:31–38), Hennessy-García allows Saul to conceive the idea of the young man's combat with the giant ("Battle 1"); moreover, whereas the Biblical David does not attempt to heal Saul until after the combat, the play's David starts the healing process in the scene preceding the battle with the giant. Jonathan, a major character in the Biblical story, is wholly omitted in the play (if the author did so to avoid suggesting homosexual overtones, I can only commend his omission), whereas Jonathan's sister Michal, whose role in the Bible is at best peripheral, not only assumes a major part, but her characterization in the play has not a jot in common with that in the source. Whereas Saul's suicide in the Bible (1 Samuel 31: 4–6 and 1 Chronicles 10:3–5) achieves a nobility comparable to that of Brutus' in *Julius Caesar* (Saul falls upon his sword only after his armor-bearer has refused to do the job for him), the play's Saul kills himself after trying out a grotesque succession of the most histrionic poses imaginable. Finally a word or two about the Biblical place-names—Siphnoth, Gilgal, Michmash—which are strewn about so liberally in the scene "Battle 1." Although the author would have found all these places mentioned within the Biblical account of Saul, none is used in connection with the particular battle Mr. Hennessy-García purports to describe. I can only conclude that the author was exploiting these Hebrew names (which doubtless sound exotic to the English ear) for what he hoped would have a comic, even ridiculous, effect.

Artists have of course always been jealous of their freedom to do what they please with their sources (no matter how sacred these may be) and we should not begrudge them this privilege. Since we easily forgive Shakespeare for setting a scene of one of his most mature comedies on the Bohemian seacoast or for transforming a middle-aged Hotspur into a vigorous young man in a play that calls itself a history, the attitude of charity that the Bible intends us all to practice encourages me to voice my complaint about our young author's use of Scripture with the minimum of rancor and ill will.

ORLANDO HENNESSY-GARCIA AND THE AVOIDANCE OF SHAKESPEAREAN EPHEBICIDE

Sidney Rose

Sidney Rose, distinguished occupant of the Mrs. J. Chauncey Cheshire Chair of Rhetoric and Declamation at Princeton, has forged together a critical system that, though it contains elements adapted from such eminences as Hegel, Nietzsche, Freud, Northrop Frye, Kenneth Burke, and Jay Grossberger (the last of whom is himself a contributor to the present volume), has achieved an authority of its own comparable to few in our time. Although his central theme is the difficulty that dramatists face in overcoming the influences of the great writers of the past, through the daringness of his own thought he has liberated himself more successfully from the major influences upon his own system than have the dramatists whose valiant but all-too-often unsuccessful struggles with their precursors he writes about so movingly. Professor Rose, who has averaged four elaborately argued books per year over the last five years, is to my knowledge unrivaled in the history of literary criticism for writing more rapidly than even his most fervent followers can read him. Although I was aware he would not have time to read any of H-G's writings except for Saul's Fall, his intense concern with a dramatist's relationships to his predecessors made it seem advisable to send along the column of public analogues from the "Table of Analogues" that I had compiled. Although the list contains a variety of dramatists, Professor Rose has chosen to concentrate on H-G's problematic relation to Shakespeare, whom he considers the only one of these dramatists to possess a sufficiently dangerous power over his descendants to make it worth his while fitting an essay on Saul's Fall into his busy schedule.

In one of those prescient remarks whose casualness of tone masks its underlying profundity, the young T. S. Eliot long ago wrote, "Shakespeare does not lend himself to genealogies." Ruminating to himself over this insight in the succeeding decades, Eliot obviously took its import sternly to heart when, in middle age, he himself turned to the drama and, recognizing his status as a weak poet with his customary honesty, he carefully, cautiously veered away from all Shakespearean influence and contented himself skirmishing with what he could acknowledge as mercifully lesser talents, namely Euripides, Shaw, and the anonymous writers of medieval mystery and morality plays. Not so Orlando Hennessy-García, who, in the unthinking intrepidity that characterizes the Biblical (if not precisely his own) version of David when the latter sought battle with Goliath, took on the giant among giants among dramatists. Shakespeare has proved an unusually cruel and demanding father-figure to the various ephebes who have sought to plunder his wealth. If one looks at the history of his imitators over the centuries—Middleton, Otway, Dryden, Rowe, the young Wordsworth of *The Borderers*, plus a host of Victorian closet dramatists—one recognizes that he has consistently practiced that infanticide which he himself portrayed so ghoulishly in the murder of the little princes in *Richard III*, a play which, incidentally, has obsessed Hennessy-García more than any of his others.

If Hennessy-García did not exactly perish in the ensuing struggle with his ruthless precursor, his was also not that clearcut victory which, though possible in such arenas of action as science, sports and war, is that never-to-be-achieved goal which gives writing its peculiar though also privileged status in our culture. The record of struggle between the ephebe and his overbearing precursor—the search for appropriate areas of emulation, the occasional shows of one-upmanship, the deliberate (though unconsciously conceived) attempts at misunderstanding—all these provide a humanly more poignant document than those facile narrations of victory or defeat that mark activity outside the humanistic realm. I shall describe Hennessy-García's encounters with his master according to five of the twenty-three precursor-ephebe ratios that I have worked out in my last six volumes to depict the stages of struggle between a later dramatist and his predecessors. The five I have found most relevant to *Saul's Fall* are, in order of increasing success in the struggle (one must not, of course, confuse this mode of success with what conventional evaluative criticism calls artistic success) μίμησις, Anspielung, остранение, 変 , and שׁבר (I should like to have included a section on οὐσία, but my already over-committed schedule does not allow me sufficient time to apply a sixth ratio).

1. MIMHΣIΣ (Mimesis): "Battle 2" and Richard III (oration scene before the final battle).

This is of course the simplest possible relationship between precursor and follower and, as I have developed at length in *Dark Realms of Origins*, it must be classified as a too easily earned defeat. Although *Saul's Fall* includes several examples, the one most quickly evident to any reader or audience is the imitation of the speeches enunciated before battle by the two contenders Richard III and the Earl of Richmond. In each play the speeches are symmetrically linked to one another; David, like Richmond, establishes his opponent as a tyrant and himself as the restorer of his followers' lawful rights; Saul, in turn, characterizes his challengers as "rebels, curs, ingrates," words comparable in intent to Richard's "vagabonds, rascals, scum," but thoroughly lacking their predecessor's bite. Such is the price of mimesis—for in this stage the ephebe has not really begun his struggle with the precursor.

2. Anspielung: "Healing 2" and Beckett, Waiting for Godot and Endgame; Milton, Samson Agonistes; Shakespeare, Othello (farewell-to-war speech); 1 Samuel 29:5.

Anspielung represents a distinctly higher stage in the struggle even though, to the extent that this reproduces the exact, or nearly exact, words of the precursor, it can be seen as a purer form of Mimesis than Mimesis itself. Yet Anspielung can succeed to a higher degree than Mimesis through the playfulness with which the quotations are ordered within the later text. (As I indicated in *Wrestlings with the Angel*, I prefer the word *Anspielung* to our own word *allusion*, for the idea of play [Spiel] comes through with more trenchant effect in the German than in the Latinate form *lusio* so obscurely buried in the English.) It is precisely in the act of playing with and against the precursor that, in contrast to ordinary Mimesis, Anspielung allows the ephebe to avoid the full force of the father's wrath. Though Anspielung alone cannot prevent the father's act of infanticide, it can, like Scheherazade's postponement of uxoricide through her relentless telling of tales, at least put off the fatal act until the ephebe has been able to bring other, more potent ratios into play.

Much of the charm of the game here comes from the fact that we find Anspielungen to five texts by four different authors, that the Shakespearean Anspielung is in fact saved for that climactic moment when Saul recognizes the heroism incipient within himself, and that this Shakespearean Anspielung, unlike all but the one to *Waiting for Godot*, does not contain an exact quotation but is a deliberate translation of the Shakespearean text, in which Othello bids farewell to his heroism, into its opposite. Thus we go from the predecessor's "Farewell the tranquil mind! Farewell content!" to the ephebe-now-turned-rebellious-adolescent's "Welcome the clear mind, welcome content." If one looks closely at the order of the Anspielungen, one notes that Hennessy-García has, in the course of a few pages, taken us up the chain of being from the groveling animal stage of Lucky in *Godot* to the antihero stage of Hamm in *Endgame,* to what Northrop Frye would call the high-mimetic stage of Milton's Samson and thence to the transformation of the high-mimetic Othello into a figure wholly out of romance. And then the sudden collapse created solely by means of the Anspielung "Saul killed his thousands; David killed his tens of thousands"—incidentally the only direct quote from the play's Biblical source. As always in the Anspielung stage, the ephebe has shown considerable cockiness throughout, yet the master can afford to ignore him.

3. остранение *(Ostranenie): "Healing 3" and* Henry IV, Second Part *(Prince Hal's borrowing his father's crown).*

As my readers well know from my earlier books, I am adapting Šklovskij's term, which means "making it strange" or "defamiliarizing the familiar." Whereas Šklovskij, like Aristotle in his use of Mimesis, was referring to a writer's treatments of the so-called real world, I of course refer to the way a writer defamiliarizes not the world, but an earlier and well-known text. As my colleagues Jerome Hochberg and P. Horsley Foster have demonstrated time and again in innumerable writings, the Aristotelian notion that a critic can presume to postulate a relation between art and external reality should have been laid to rest long ago with such other antiquated notions as the four humors and the sun's supposed revolution around the earth. Yet I contend that the older rhetorical terms (see my *Prophecy and Purgation*) deriving from this relation can be useful to us if we simply substitute the term *other art* for *external world* or *reality.*

Thus Ostranenie in "Healing 3" derives from our recognition that David's accidentally removing the crown from Saul's head is a redoing in new and seemingly inappropriate terms of one of Shakespeare's most memorable images, namely, Prince Hal's deliberately removing the crown from his father's sleeping head and trying it out in too hasty an anticipation of his coming kingship. The ephebe at some level of consciousness has chosen to misread the master: what was deliberate in Shakespeare is wholly accidental in Hennessy-García; whereas the Shakespearean king is still master of his domain, Hennessy-García's is already at the mercy of his healer, whose accidental act sets off still another fit of the paranoia that, under the healer's patient tutelage, he had managed to get under control only a few moments before. As a result of this Ostranenie we shall never again be able to read or see the Shakespearean scene in quite the same way again, but shall in fact read our experience of the later scene back into it. In Ostranenie, far more than in Mimesis or Anspielung, we are aware of the agony of struggle against that mighty force which threatens to inhibit the ephebe, engulf him, all too often crush him totally. And yet in his outward stance the ephebe in this scene has managed a casual air that virtually dissimulates the fearsome process transpiring within; he has, as it were, quietly stood back and warned his master not to take him too lightly.

4. 諞 (Pien): "Execration" and Richard III (Queen Margaret's curse).

As I have explained at length in *Paradigms of Perversities*, the term *Pien* from classical Chinese literary theory connotes a deviation from the norm, often of the most disastrous sort, and it implies as well that in abnormal times one can expect abnormal forms of literature. The original formulation goes back to the third century A.D. and, like the original uses of Mimesis and Ostranenie, takes for granted a relation between literature and the "real" world. Again my own reformulation has attempted to de-antiquate the term: thus the "abnormal times" that Pien connects to "abnormal forms" need not take place in some naively constituted outward reality, but in the consciousness of readers and audiences that older forms can no longer elicit the same responses they were able to from an earlier public.

In pitting the Daughter's curse against Queen Margaret's curse in *Richard III*, Hennessy-García keeps us more constantly aware of the Daughter's deviances from traditional cursing than he does of her conformity to it. When Margaret reproaches all around her with her curses, we recognize her as engaging in an age-old ritual that, to a contemporary audience at least, seems to go on interminably. No matter how fervently or powerfully she shrieks, she never surprises us. Even if we could not hear her words, we would know their import from her gestures alone. By contrast, the Pien that Hennessy-García strives for in the Daughter's execration scene is abundant with surprises. She worries constantly that she will lose her rage and busily thinks up new reproaches to restore that primal outrage which is at once her reason for being. The actual curse is saved for the final moment, and everything about it consists of surprise, for it is directed not at the characters she has been reproaching all along, but at the audience; indeed, this is the only moment within the whole play (except for the prologue and epilogue, where one expects such things) that the audience is addressed directly. If anything in this scene is ritualized, it is not the curse or its attendant reproaches, but the actions of the two mimes who act as a silent musical accompaniment for the Daughter. Ritual has thus been deflected by a further movement of Pien from the speaking of the curse to "outsiders" (they stay literally outside her oval compound) who essentially mediate between her and an audience that, living in a post-Enlightenment world with its pretenses of benevolence and its demand for certain behavioral niceties, is unprepared to accept an unmediated curse. As so often when Pien is operative, we are made to recognize that a mode of discourse which was natural within an earlier time can communicate within a later, seemingly foreign context only through the maximum of deviation and surprise. The ephebe has snubbed his precursor simply by recognizing that he must write for an audience with a totally new set of preconceptions and expectations.

5. שבר *(Shabar): "Endings" and* Richard II *(final soliloquy and meeting with executioner).*

The Hebraic concept Shabar, which, as I have developed at length in *Sublimations of Sublimity,* means shattering, or fragmenting, remains the most radical of the ratios employed by Hennessy-García in this play, though it is by no means the most radical among the twenty-three possible ratios described within my other writings. Not that I can point to actual examples for all twenty-three in particular literary works, for some—above all Procreatio-ex-nihilo—exist primarily as conceptualizations of possibilities, extrapolations of the destructiveness that some future writers, combining the utmost boldness with the utmost verbal resources, could wreak upon the giants of the past. Let me extend Jerome Hochberg's famous insight that criticism has now come to rival art in the intensity and complexity of its vision. To cite the terms with which I have expanded this concept in *The Catastrophe of Consciousness,* criticism, at least when practiced by the few truly strong critics among us, has the power to generate new and more compelling forms of art, not to speak of new and more compelling forms of criticism.

Still, though Hennessy-García is not a critic (except in his preface, prologue and epilogue, all three of them texts of considerable suggestiveness which, time permitting, I should have welcomed the chance to discuss), the Shabar that he effected in the fragmentation of his hero's dramatic character in the scene "Endings" is an achievement we can by no means take lightly and one which, more than in his use of any of the other ratios I have described in this essay, leads me to believe he more surely possesses the makings of a strong dramatist than any beginner I know of writing today.

In the opening lines of the monologue that constitutes the scene "Endings," we immediately sense the affinities with the introspective monologue (by far the most introspective piece of writing Shakespeare had accomplished at that point in his career) spoken by Richard II in prison as he awaits his executioner. Yet Saul has scarcely begun his monologue before the author shatters his character into fragments, each of which is temporarily frozen for us in a separate portrait of the king that appears on an easel behind him. Thus we experience each fragment of his character (if there is such a unitary entity as character at all!) in single and separate compartments—Saul successively as stoic, catatonic, military brute, masochist, existential hero—and all of these finally rejected in favor of a pose that eschews all poses (and is no longer even illustrable on the easel!). Shakespeare's Richard, like all his great figures, is by no means made of cardboard, yet Shakespeare holds the various phases of his personality together with an illusion of continuity and a refusal to disrupt unnecessarily. With his bold act of Shabar, the youthful author of *Saul's Fall* now forces us to penetrate behind the frail continuities that veil the disruptions implicit in Richard II and Shakespeare's other great characterizations. The ephebe has dealt his precursor a knock-out blow (though the struggle will and must begin anew with the very next word he attempts to set down).

Note: *After receiving this fine essay, I felt it only fair to inform Professor Rose, whom I had earlier feared to bother with unnecessary details, that although Saul's Fall is H-G's first play, the author is scarcely an ephebe in Professor Rose's special sense, that he has in fact been writing for years and has reached that stage in life people ordinarily call middle age. I received the following letter in reply:*

Dear Professor Wolfson,

Your belated divulgence of the author's true age has forced me to reduce considerably my judgment of the degree of success he achieved in his agon with his great precursor. I confess I had been looking forward to a personal encounter with Mr. Hennessy-García, whom I hoped to salute with those fateful words "I greet you at the beginning of a great career" that Emerson conveyed to Whitman on receiving his copy of the first *Leaves of Grass*. This is now no longer possible and I shall forego the considerable pleasure that such a meeting would have given me (though I recognize that, to the extent I would have become still another inhibiting influence for him to struggle with, my own loss will at least spare him some additional anxiety). Although my present writing commitments do not permit revision of the essay I sent you, my application (if not precisely my evaluation) of Hennessy-García's use of my five ratios remains valid. It goes without saying that my general pronouncements about writing (which, after all, are the chief goal of strong criticism) are in no way altered by the disappointing news you passed on to me, and I can report with pleasure that some of the thoughts which my examination of the play stirred up in me will find their way into my forthcoming *Spectral Speculations*. Still, as a result of this incident I am confident that in your future contacts with busy colleagues at other universities you will surely be considerate enough to supply all the relevant information at the start.

Sincerely yours,
Sidney Rose
(Mrs. J. Chauncey Cheshire Professor of Rhetoric and Declamation)

Note: How one goes about rounding up the great

Readers may wonder how I, who have not yet arrived at that stage of my career where I am a household (or even an office) word, have been able to get persons the likes of Fredric Sackett, Samuel Schriecker, Sidney Rose, and Jay Grossberger et al. to grace these pages. I offer the following suggestions for anyone who might seek to follow my path:

1. Keep a correspondence going with everybody you admire as well as those whom other people you admire admire (don't be concerned if your letters don't always get answered);

2. Use any excuse you can to maintain telephone contact even if all you do is check on your respondent's availability for lectures, readings, conferences (if the plans you discuss don't work out, you can always plead an unanticipated lack of funding);

3. Hound editors to let you review the books or tape interviews of those to whom you care to mete out praise in public;

4. Have a wife like Luella who will feed and pamper any visiting dignitaries you happen to bring home.

Moral: Contrary to the old adage, flattery will always get you somewhere.

ON THE OVERT ABSENCE OF SEXUALITY IN SAUL'S FALL

Eric Goldblatt, M.D.

The psychiatrist Eric Goldblatt is well known in the Palo Alto area for helping hundreds of persons negotiate the crises that afflict the lives of tense and busy people within a community with more than its share of competitive, highly motivated professionals. I deliberately told him nothing about H-G when I requested him to comment on the play, for I recognized that, unlike works by already well-known authors, Saul's Fall offers a unique opportunity to observe what a text reveals about psychological phenomena without the inevitable intrusion of information about the writer that, no matter how much we may seek to ignore this information, somehow ends up coloring our sense of the text. Special thanks must be accorded to Dr. Goldblatt for his willingness to expend considerable labor on this project without a fee. Whereas the academic contributors can count *on professional advancement (which includes salary raises) as a result of publishing their efforts in this volume, Dr. Goldblatt, whose time in monetary terms is worth more than that of even the world's most prominent literary scholars, can derive no advantages except for his readers' gratitude (to assuage my guilt he promised to tell his accountant to claim a tax deduction for his time as a contribution to an educational charity). Incidentally, just in case some readers entertain any suspicions about how I came to choose Dr. Goldblatt for this volume, I can assure them that my relations with him have been of a social and not a professional nature.*

My days are taken up talking to patients, and I make no pretense to being a writer. I therefore hope that my academic friends will not object if my remarks on *Saul's Fall* appear not as a sustained essay (a form the very thought of which creates anxieties for me), but as the rambling thoughts I am accustomed to setting down during and after sessions with my patients. Mind you, I have no intention of treating the author of this play (whom I have never met and whom I know nothing about) as a patient. Nor do I intend to look at his play as a means of discovering insights into his personality. I have been made amply aware by those of my patients who teach literature that drawing conclusions about a writer's psycho-history on the basis of his artistic work (something that we have all done informally on numerous occasions) is much frowned upon these days. (My strong feelings about the need to maintain confidentiality forces me to mention at this point that my literary patients are not necessarily members of the Stanford faculty, but come from a number of the many colleges located between San Francisco and San Jose.) I thus limit my remarks to one particular thing that struck me in reading the play, namely, the conspicuous absence (all the more conspicuous for its all-pervasive presence in our contemporary world) of sexuality in *Saul's Fall*. Except for the one short and undeveloped remark by the Daughter about David's pinning her to the floor (in the scene called "Execration"), I can find no overt mention of sexual desire or activity anywhere in the play. This is all the more surprising since the original Biblical account assigns a large role to Saul's son Jonathan, who has been totally eliminated from the play, yet whose intimate friendship with David has often been viewed as containing homo-erotic overtones. Since I have promised to refrain from drawing conclusions about the author's psyche, I shall not inquire as to why he thought it necessary to suppress the Jonathan-David relationship. Instead, as I have said, I shall concentrate on what I see within the play—or perhaps I should say I am concentrating (excuse the indirectness of my speech, but this is how psychotherapists, through the very nature of their duties, are forced to deal with touchy human situations) precisely on what I do *not* see in the play, namely, sexuality. Yet sexuality is always present,

though in the most suppressed of ways. Let me call attention to the scene
entitled "Conspiracy" in which the king is stroking a cat he keeps on a
leash. How many of us have ever seen a cat on a leash, and above all when
its master was stroking the animal on his lap? Surely nobody will think it
farfetched (my literary patients always use this word when they complain
I sound like a Freudian critic in analyzing their behavior)—nobody will
find it farfetched to note that a common word for *cat* is *pussy*, which as
everybody knows is one of innumerable slang terms for the female sexual
organ. Thus Saul is in effect achieving a surrogate sexual experience. And
note the leash: it is as though he can only manage this experience when
he has total power over the movements of his surrogate. Yet we also know
that a leashed cat, unlike a dog, is quite likely to lash back at its master
by means of scratching and other forms of violent behavior. The danger to
which Saul subjects himself here is fully in tune with the masochistic
tendencies that he displays throughout the play. The unnamed Daughter
also manifests behavior patterns that can only be attributed to a suppressed
and, for that matter, displaced form of sexuality. Her attitude toward Saul
is not that of a daughter, but rather of a mother, as in the scene entitled
"Intermezzo," in which she talks him out of his suicide habit in precisely
the same way that a mother would try to talk her child out of sucking its
thumb or biting its fingernails. In the scene entitled "Prophecy 2" she
allows him to play the weak little boy while she tries to screw up his
courage so that he will ignore the gloomy predictions they both hear the
chorus pronounce about his impending fall. The unnatural family role
into which she is forced at the expense of her natural feminine desires (I
recognize that some of my younger female patients disagree with me as to
what is distinctly natural to men and women) can have only a single
result—namely, the rage she expresses with such utter vehemence once she
is separated from her father and her temporary lover. Behind these various
examples of sexual suppression and displacement I discern a sexual event
that, fairly early in the play, is told to us in the guise of a military event. I
refer to Saul's monologue entitled "Prayer," in which he describes his early
success in war, the fears that began to come over him in battle on a
particular day, and his subsequent failure of nerve that came to prevent
future military victories. The story that Saul tells is one that I have heard
innumerable times from male patients, not about their problems in battle
(I do not ordinarily see many patients from the military), but about their
failure in maintaining sexual potency. Translate the military terms into
sexual ones and I believe you have the key to Saul's behavior in the play.
(I say this in full knowledge that I have not been trained as a literary
critic.) The depression that results from Saul's failure, as well as the
paranoiac behavior and the capricious, often tyrannical acts that follow, is
a most frequent consequence of sexual failure among many males I have

treated. (These problems can in most instances be treated successfully these days, but the play concerns itself simply with a description of the problems, not their treatment.) The unnatural role into which the Daughter is forced is itself a consequence of the behavior pattern the father has fallen into as a result of his failure. It seems only natural that the family breakdown we witness should be resolved (even though no cure takes place) through the ascendancy of a character with the flexibility, shrewdness, and psychological insight of David.

Readers may well wonder why I offer no elaborate analyses of the various acts of violence and perversity with which the play abounds. Let everybody feel free to work out his/her own interpretation of such matters as the stomping on a supposed corpse in "Battle 2" or the desecration of a coffin (in "March 2") by all manner of abuse from kicking to urinating. What interests me in such passages is not the more lurid things one might wish to make of them (this is very easy), but rather the author's refusal to hint directly at the obvious sexual overtones they suggest. In the urinating scene he is willing to tease us with a penis in all its visual presence, yet at the same time to limit its activity to what any viewer will recognize as considerably the less cogent and arresting of its two quite diverse physiological functions. As should be amply evident by now, Saul's Fall is very much concerned, even obsessed, with sexuality in spite of its overt absence that I indicated in my title to these modest remarks. And as I never tire of reminding my patients, if you suppress anything long or deep or far enough, it's bound to come out the other end.

SAUL'S FALL AND MUSIC: A DIALOGUE ON THE INTERRELATIONSHIP OF THE ARTS

Francis Heston and Arnold Robins,
with MJW as Moderator

One of the most promising areas of inquiry these days, especially among specialists in literature, is the interrelationship between literature and the other arts. Because of the analogies to music to which H-G devotes a substantial part of his "Preface," Saul's Fall provides a unique opportunity for the examination of how two quite different media interact with one another in a single work, or, to be more precise in regard to the work under consideration, how a writer's interest in another medium can influence and give a peculiarly individual shape to his own literary composition. After the first of the three workshop performances of Saul's Fall staged by the Stanford Drama Department, I arranged a panel discussion on H-G's use of the musical analogies in the composition of his play. All but a few members of the audience were willing to stay for the discussion. Each was given a copy of those parts of H-G's "Preface" that discussed the use of musical analogies. (To prevent any prejudicial biases from interfering with the discussion, I omitted that early portion of the "Preface" in which H-G expressed his contempt for the contemporary theater.) The panel consisted of two distinguished Stanford colleagues of mine, the musicologist Francis Heston, a specialist in music of the Renaissance, and the literary critic Arnold Robins of my own department, who is currently at work on a theoretical study of intermedia communications in which he deals not only with the relations between literature and music, but with the complex interrelationships among such media as photography, painting, sculpture, architecture, and film, as well as various mixtures of these media at various moments in the history of the arts. The following dialogue is a transcript of the tape made at the time. I have omitted my introduction (most of what I said has been condensed into the present introductory note) and start with the first presentation, that of Professor Robins.

ROBINS: As Professor Wolfson has indicated, and as you can see from the preface before you, the play you have just seen offers us a unique opportunity to observe how techniques and conventions that were developed in one medium—namely, music and specifically opera—have been adopted within a nonmusical drama and in such a way, I must emphasize, as to give the composition you have witnessed a character considerably different from that of other dramas you are familiar with. As Hennessy-García put it in the opening sentence of the text you have before you, he "conceived these episodes after the model of musical composition." And a page or two later he gets more specific and tells us he is following what he calls "the dramatic method peculiar to opera—not the Wagnerian music-drama or the styles that derive from it, but the older opera in which each segment maintains its distinctiveness in relation to every other." And note the next sentence—"certain passages strive to create the effect of arias, duets, or ensembles—to the point that a set speech may, like certain famous arias, assume and explore a single-minded attitude such as pleading, praying, raging, or admonishing." Now—what I'm going to do tonight is try to demonstrate how the method peculiar to opera, and particularly the opera of the early nineteenth century, before the advent of Wagnerian music-drama, helped the writer of this play create a distinct style of his own. Rather than speak in general terms, I shall look at a single episode, the one which, as you'll notice on your program—it's the fifth of the seventeen episodes—which he calls "Prayer." Could I ask some help in passing out copies of this scene?

[At this point there was a pause in the tape while photocopies of "Prayer" were distributed to the audience.]

As you can see from the title of this monologue scene, the author is working out what he calls one of those "single-minded" attitudes peculiar to operatic arias and in this case it's one of the four attitudes he specifically mentions, namely, praying. Now if I can ask you—at least the opera buffs among you—to call to mind some of the more famous early-nineteenth-century operatic arias, for instance the "Casta Diva" sung by the title character of Bellini's *Norma* soon after her entrance, or the "Tacea la notte placida" sung by Leonora at her entrance in Verdi's *Il Trovatore*, you'll notice that these arias are highly conventionalized in form. They generally start with a recitative, then they move to a relatively slow and quite melodious portion in which the single-minded attitude is stated and then, often with a change of key, they end in a fast and furious finale called the cabaletta, in which the single-minded attitude of the cavatina is in one way or another questioned, subverted, answered, turned upon itself. Let me play you an operatic prayer, the "Casta Diva" aria I mention.

[He then turned on his cassette and identified each section of the aria, first the recitative, then the cavatina, and finally the cabaletta, though there were also some transitions and choral additions that, for the sake of simplifying matters, he chose not to mention.]

Now, I submit that this speech of Saul's is no ordinary dramatic speech—it is certainly not like anything I can think of in modern drama—and I submit that it owes its peculiar character to the type of operatic aria I have just played. Note, for example, the recitative-like quality of the address to the deity in the opening lines, which is then followed by a long, slow, cavatina-like depiction of the history of his relations with the deity. The pauses, to which the author attaches short musical phrases—squibbles, he calls them, and I suspect he made the word up, for I couldn't locate it in any dictionary—anyhow, these pauses are like the pauses between the stanzas of a cavatina, each of which repeats the same melody with occasional variations. Then note the stage direction—"Pause, then speaks up suddenly"—which, followed as it is by Saul's defiance of the Lord, is where I see the cabaletta starting. And the marvelous thing about it all is that if you'd never read the author's preface, you wouldn't know he was writing an aria in words and yet as I'm sure you must have felt as you watched Larry Friedlander's wonderful job of acting, the whole speech works itself out in the most moving and natural-seeming way.

WOLFSON: That was a most illuminating analysis demonstrating the confluence of two artistic media within a single speech whose complexities, as Professor Robins reminds us, we were surely not aware of as we listened to it spoken with such pathos and anger in the context of the play. I shall now turn to Professor Heston for the special perspective that a musicologist can offer.

HESTON: Let me remind you, first of all, that I am a specialist in the music of the Renaissance, a time when opera did not yet exist, though I am of course thoroughly familiar with the theoretical discussions of opera that took place in Count Bardi's circle in Florence and that helped make the development of opera during the subsequent century possible. Although I must therefore speak as a nonspecialist if I am to comment on the particular example that Professor Robins has introduced, I must ask him to account for the memorable final passage of Saul's speech that follows his defiance of God with the quiet and resigned words, "I suppose it wasn't much use after all." Can this quiet passage, which to me at least sounds considerably more like what he calls the cavatina passage—can this passage by any stretch of the imagination be accommodated to the rousing cabaletta that concludes the aria form in which he has sought to fit Saul's speech? In fact, with this quiet ending so reminiscent of the quiet early parts of the speech, might one not more appropriately claim that Hennessy-García was imitating another type of aria altogether—the A-B-A *da capo* form of eighteenth-century *opera seria*? I am speaking as a nonspecialist of course and would like to hear what Professor Robins has to say to this suggestion.

ROBINS: I'm sure a very good argument could be made for the analogy to the *da capo* aria, though if I remember correctly, the repeat of the A section after the B in this type of aria is just as long as its initial rendition and the second time round it's subject to extensive ornamentation, whereas the quiet ending to Saul's speech, which I'll be the first to admit can't quite be fitted into the early-nineteenth-century pattern, is much shorter than the early quiet section and too simple in language to be considered ornamented in any way. But perhaps I should remind you of a line in the author's preface that tells us he did not intend the model of musical composition to be used, as he put it, "in any strict or literal sense."

HESTON: And that's precisely what I was about to quote back at you, Professor Robins, for I believe that in setting up a strict analogy between two quite different forms of artistic communication you have violated both the intent and the spirit of the author on whom you claimed to be giving us information.

[At this point there was a pause, during which Professor Robins sipped quietly from his water-glass while obviously preparing a reply.]

ROBINS: All right, Heston, so we're agreed that at best we can set up some not-altogether-precise analogy, but you must remember that the author specifically tells us he is writing a play that is meant to be operatic in nature.

HESTON: That *ic* suffix bothers me. Although I don't pretend to be a specialist, I can scarcely see how one can make an adjective out of such a noun as "opera," which is by no stretch of the imagination a monolithic form. One can speak of French opera of the late seventeenth century, and this is a very different animal indeed from French grand opera of the 1830s and 1840s, while the latter is different—despite some mutual ties— from German and Italian opera of the same period.

ROBINS: I don't deny anything you say, but if an author says he's trying to be operatic, however vaguely he may use the word, we might as well figure out what he means by it. And surely you will admit that the play we have just witnessed is considerably different in style and tone from anything else in contemporary drama.

HESTON: I am not a specialist in contemporary drama or, for that matter, in any other form of drama.

[*At this point there was a long pause while both participants sipped water, and I realized it was time for me to step in.*]

WOLFSON: It's really quite a healthy thing, I'd say, to voice disagreements of the sort we are hearing tonight. It's only out of such fundamental disagreements that we can hope, if not tonight at least at some future time, to arrive at a dialectical resolution of these sharply opposed viewpoints.

HESTON (*Looking at me*): I hope you remember that the word "dialectic" had an entirely different meaning during the Renaissance than it came to have after the time of Hegel and Marx, whose vague and sweeping use of the term has given generations of students license to bring the most diverse and incongruous phenomena together.

ROBINS: Let me remind you, Heston, that neither Professor Wolfson nor I are students, that we are in fact colleagues of yours, though admittedly in different but not wholly unrelated disciplines. And I'd like you to know that I myself am making a speciality of drawing analogies between various art forms, since they can often help illuminate one another, especially when their practitioners had analogies in mind such as the author of our play has openly advertised.

HESTON: Might I make a little suggestion to you, Professor Robins? Whatever an author or composer says about his intentions, perhaps you should exhaust the resources within your own discipline before you turn to others for aid. If you want to explain the background of that speech "Prayer," for instance, you might do well to seek out the sources of Hennessy-García's technique in handbooks of rhetoric that he is likely to have used in school or college. When a musicologist—especially one working on the music of the last five centuries—wants to find out why a composer employed the style he did he can usually find some rather telling evidence in the standard handbooks on harmony or counterpoint that circulated during the composer's youth.

ROBINS: As it happens, the author of this play is not much older, I'm told, than I am, and I suspect that he and I were subjected to much the same sort of English instruction. I can assure you that your suggestion does not seem in the least promising to me.

[At this he paused and sipped water, then turned to Heston for a reply, but Heston did not look either at him, at the audience, or at me, but looked down at the table and himself started sipping water. I realized it was time for me to step in again.]

WOLFSON: We're a bit at loggerheads for now, but I believe this can be very instructive to all of us, for what we are witnessing are some essential differences between two respectable disciplines within that large but diverse area we call humanistic study. Whereas literary scholars tend toward the interdisciplinary these days, musicologists are remaining proudly *intra*-disciplinary.

ROBINS: But isn't opera itself—and from whatever period, I might add—something interdisciplinary in its own right? Why don't we have an opera specialist on this panel? The only explanation I can think of is you don't have any around in your department, since opera, participating as it does in such diverse fields as drama, dance, painting, architecture, just isn't pure enough for you to bother with. I can see you look down on it as a bastard form and you're ready to condemn this play as doubly bastardized for coupling literature and opera in what must doubtless seem a shockingly promiscuous thing to you.

[At this point I poured some water from the pitcher into both their glasses, for I could see they both needed a bit of sipping time to mull this one over, but before he could take a sip, Heston spoke up in a quiet and firm voice.]

HESTON: I think it might be appropriate to quote a saying I often heard from my old professor, the great musicologist Wilfried Eggenthaler, who himself got it from his own mentor, the legendary Grobius: "Wovon man nicht fachmännisch sprechen kann, davon muss man schweigen," which in my admittedly rather awkward translation means, "Of that on which one cannot speak with authority, one must remain silent."

[At which point he himself lapsed into silence and started sipping water again while staring down at the table. I was about to intercede once more, but was beaten to the draw by Robins.]

ROBINS: It's people like you, Frank Heston, with your literal-minded, purist, anal mentality who have given the word "academic" the bad name it enjoys today among all those—and there are lots of them—who associate our work with barrenness, pedantry, sterility, irrelevance. As I watch you sipping away with that smug, superior look of yours, I realize we could go on panel-discussing for five more years and never get anywhere. In fact the only way I can conceive of waking you out of those dogmatic slumbers of yours is this—

[At which point, and before I could do a thing to stop him, Robins got up, lifted the pitcher, and poured what water was left in it directly over Heston's head. I pulled out my handkerchief, as did several persons in the front row of the audience and we all—except for Robins, who stood back watching— engaged in a mopping-up operation on Heston's bald head and dark wool suit coat. I brought the discussion to a close while continuing to mop.]

WOLFSON: Although the time has obviously come to end this session, let me say it's encouraging to know that abstract ideas can bring out such passions as they have in these two fine colleagues of mine. I'd say it's positively remarkable that in our academic pursuits, to which the adjective "dry" is all too frequently applied, we have now witnessed an honest show of wetness. As you can see, gentlemen, there has been nothing in the least dry about your discussion, and I congratulate you on helping us all re-evaluate the view of academic work that prevails among the general public these days.

[Then I wrung my soaking handkerchief over the floor, on which I let it drop so that I could shake hands with the two participants and try to create a more jovial atmosphere as the audience walked out. Next day I quietly though regretfully cancelled the panel discussions scheduled to follow the remaining two performances of the play—the first "Saul's Fall as a Historical Drama," with my colleagues David Riggs and Herbert Lindenberger, both of them recognized specialists on that genre, and the second on the pathological aspects of Saul and the Daughter, with my eminent colleagues from the Department of Psychiatry, Professors Herant Katchadurian and Irvin Yalom. This volume would have been the richer for their contributions.]

Note: On disjunctiveness as a legitimate principle of writing

Everybody who has used this book in the way it was intended must recognize that it is organized in a spirit of disjunctiveness uncommon even among the many disjunct books that have flourished during the last few decades. To those readers who object that this book goes too far in this direction I offer this reminder: very little writing is truly conjunct, but only pretends to be by means of various tricks of plot and rhetoric that writers have cultivated over the years. Only those writings are conjunct that mercilessly hammer away at a single point—a legal brief, a few short lyrics and tales, the directions for assembling some household object you have bought in a space-saving box in the local hardware store. Once you have accustomed and committed yourself to a disjunct book you unconsciously fill in the breaks and assume it to be properly conjunct. Nearly all the world's best books are disjunct, and so is this one.

THE STANFORD DRAMA DEPARTMENT HAS DONE IT AGAIN

Roy Curley

If H-G's piece of juvenilia, "A Hero's Death in the Spanish Civil War," is the only writing of his to have appeared in print before the present volume, the following review of the Stanford Drama Department's workshop production of Saul's Fall is the only commentary on H-G's work published in advance of the volume, and as such, despite my obvious disagreements with its conclusions, it deserves a place here. Normally critics are not invited to workshop productions, but Roy Curley, who has applied his considerable pressure as drama critic of the Palo Alto Times to convince Stanford to produce plays of a more popular nature than it has done, obviously smelled a rat when he heard about the plans for Saul's Fall. After years of reviewing Stanford productions (ninety-eight percent of which have received his negative judgment), he knew the dark back corridors of Memorial Auditorium well enough to make his way into the Little Theater without having to pass the usher collecting the invitational tickets. Evidently he left before the panel discussion featuring Professors Heston and Robins, else he would surely have made a front-page story out of what he witnessed. It might be well to remind those who object to his judgment of the play that from all accounts Roy Curley is a superb family man and a hard and conscientious worker who maintains a commendably unswerving loyalty both to his employer and to the ideals in which he so heartily believes. In short, he is what he is and none of us would want him to be other than what he is.

A new play based on the Biblical story of Saul and David received the first of three invitational performances at the Stanford University Little Theater last night. The title of the play is "Saul's Fall," its author is Orlando Garcia, and this was its world premiere.

I have presented what objective facts I could about this event and would be content to treat this as a simple news story that, with the addition of the names of the three chief actors and the director, could just as well end here. Indeed, as one who considers himself a compassionate human being, I should be happy not to write further about the event. I do not like to destroy, but I am forced by the nature of my work to destroy the efforts of well-meaning people whom I should rather leave to their own devices.

At the start of my career as a newspaper critic I felt frequent pangs of guilt for what I was forced to do, but gradually I came to realize I myself had nothing to do with the bad fortune of others, that they had simply, on their own, chosen to display whatever thoughts were straying through their minds before any audience willing to witness the display.

Those familiar with the original Biblical story will occasionally recognize a scene or character they remember—the depressed King Saul whom the nimble and quick-witted young David attempts to cure with his harp playing and whose enmity he incurs. Yet most of the playing time is taken up with unfamiliar and often quite incomprehensible actions.

Here are a few examples. In the space of scarcely six or seven minutes some two dozen messengers rush in one after the other officiously delivering messages that neither the recipient nor the audience is prepared to act upon or comprehend. Soon after this a broken hero humbly prays to God, only to defy Him blasphemously a moment later while his speech for no apparent reason is interrupted by fragments of notes from some none-too-well-tuned woodwind instrument.

Somewhat later the king is postured on his throne stroking a leashed cat for no better reason, one assumes, than that the audience would more naturally expect him to stroke a leashed dog, though as it turns out, there is no reason to be stroking anything at all, for the king is all this while exchanging cryptic remarks with a would-be assassin in the guise of a ballet dancer who is prancing back and forth in a most effeminate way to the accompaniment of squeaking notes from an offstage violin.

A few scenes later we see an oval compound enclosing a hysterical female raging at high pitch while two pantomimists outside the compound act out her complaints, ridicule her, and finally applaud her. This is followed by a prolonged suicide scene in which the hero undergoes a series of rapid and violent personality changes all of which are reflected or perhaps caused by a succession of portraits of him that are dropped, one after the other, from above the stage to an easel placed behind the bed on which he is supposed to knife himself in the chest.

There are many more such scenes one could describe, but the account I have given tells us far more about this play, if it tells us anything at all, than what we might imagine from reading the Bible before leaving for the theater. As is evident from this description, Mr. Garcia's play is in what today is fashionably called the experimental style. This is the style

Note: I interrupt Mr. Curley's review with a blank page so that readers may take this opportunity either to reflect upon the critic's words, or to seek a moment's distraction from his strictures, or, if they choose, to use this space for relieving themselves in any way they see fit. (I offer no more suggestions, else there'll be no blank space left.)

characteristic of virtually all Stanford drama productions, even those of such fine old plays as "She Stoops to Conquer" and "The Importance of Being Earnest," neither of which, though long familiar, were recognizable to me when I saw them at Stanford.

Doubtless the acting and the directing last night were as skillful as could be expected under the circumstances, and I cite the names of the three principal actors, Larry Friedlander as Saul, Tom Eoyang as David, and Portia Perkins as Saul's unnamed and hysterical daughter. The director is Antonio Raviola.

Although I have attempted to render an accurate description of what I witnessed, I cannot resist the temptation to advise Mr. Garcia, who is presumably still young, and ask him if he has seriously considered whether in writing this play he has done anything to make life a little better or easier for his fellow men. Even if he can offer them nothing more than an evening of relaxation, he would have ample reason to take pride in his accomplishment.

If Mr. Garcia is not too prickly to take a suggestion or two, I should advise him to stop trying to imitate the experimental style in fashion these days, but to look instead into the stories of his own people and to consider establishing a theater in which he can communicate with them directly. A healthy communal relationship between an author and his own people is far more likely to produce significant drama than the attempts of an isolated young writer trying to please a few esoteric minds. Surely our thriving Chicano community would welcome whatever talents Mr. Garcia has to offer.

Note: Although I refrained from replying to Mr. Curley's strictures against the play, I sent him a short note explaining the exact nature of H-G's national background.

SAUL'S FALL AND THE REIFICATION OF HUMAN RELATIONSHIPS IN LATE CAPITALIST SOCIETY

Henry Plotsky

Henry Plotsky, who refers to himself disarmingly as "the University of Oklahoma's token Marxist," has rapidly established himself as one of the most formidable Marxist minds within contemporary American intellectual life. In the academic turbulence of the late 1960s he had the rare distinction of occupying the president's desk at two universities that he attended successively. During the quiescence that has marked the 1970s he turned from activism to steep himself in the study of the philosophical bases of Marxism and their application to the arts. Although the heavy teaching duties imposed by his university have delayed the completion of the treatise he is preparing on modes of reification in modern literature, as a self-proclaimed heterodox Marxist he has gained a respect among academicians seldom accorded to those who challenge the assumptions dominant within their world. Since a variety of critical approaches is essential to the understanding of any literary work, the intellectual integrity I have sought for this volume demanded the inclusion of a Marxist-minded essay. Few if any American Marxist critics (there are of course some very distinguished ones on the Continent) could fulfill this function with finer credentials than Professor Plotsky.

It has been fashionable of late to deny the imitative function of literature. Works are praised not for what they can tell us about the world around us, let alone how they can help us change this world, but precisely for their ability to distance themselves from this world. The highest praise that can be meted out to a literary work these days is the success with which it is able to refer to itself, question itself, implicitly explore its status as what in fashionable circles is no longer called a novel, an autobiography, or a play, but simply a "text." It is no accident, of course, that such a mode of inquiry should have come to prominence in our time, for critical writing has always served as a reflection of, an accompaniment to, and even an influence upon the artists of any particular epoch. If self-referentiality has become the order of the day, and "What is a text?" the most burning question that the most brilliant younger minds can put to one another, this is to be expected in an age that has espoused Beckett, Nabokov, Barth, Pynchon, and the French New Novelists as the classical writers by whom it hopes to be commemorated among posterity.

At first glance *Saul's Fall* would seem to fit quite naturally into the aesthetic ambiance defined by the writings I have cited above. Indeed, an older form of Marxist inquiry, founded on the normative standards set by the great realist writers of the nineteenth century, would have rejected it out of hand. Everything about this play belongs to that world of decadent modernism (or postmodernism, to cite a fashionable term for the latest and stylistically most "radical" forms of art—surely a gross misuse of the word *radical!*) that the great Marxist critics of the past roundly condemned as reflections of a dying capitalist order in which art had lost all touch with social realities and refused any participation whatever in the development of a new and more humane order of social and economic relationships. Before one looks at the play, one need only consider the life of its author, who as Professor Wolfson has informed me, is a recluse subsisting on a private income and fearful to the extreme of contact with his fellow beings. And before looking at the play one need only glance at the preface, with its blatant admission that the subject suggested itself by means of an accidental rhyme, its proud identification with the most decadent aspects of modern music and poetry (whose modes it consciously seeks to imitate), above all its contempt for potential audiences whom it wishes to jar from one moment to another "so that [they] must never quite feel sure where [they] stand." By this point one would scarcely want to look at the play at all, and even a cursory reading will reveal parodistic techniques of the most extreme sort, stylistic changes and disjunctive breaks in plot that would dizzy all but the most esoteric of souls (of whom our culture boasts more than its just share today). Had these parodistic techniques and these disjunctions been intended as Bertolt Brecht employed them—to jar audiences out of their bourgeois preconceptions and to encourage them to rethink the socioeconomic relationships they had too easily taken for granted—then one could hail this play, forbidding though it may be to the uninitiated, as a progressive gesture in a world that grants its highest rewards to those most adept at displaying their regressive tendencies before their contemporaries.

Although I am tempted to condemn Mr. Hennessy-García for the obscurity of his writing as well as the style in which he has chosen to live, I am not prepared to reject his play in the cavalier manner that Marxist critics of an earlier time (of which they were themselves a product) would have done. Indeed, as a Marxist humanist contemplating the world during our present late phase of the capitalistic process, I view *Saul's Fall* as a serious critical mimesis of certain tensions central to this phase. However accidental the choice of the Saul-David story as the subject of this play, the preface makes clear that "the primary fact remains the fact of fall." As such one can read the play as a dramatization of the transition from one order to another, each of which contains its own system of values attached to that particular stage of the historical process. Thus Saul attempted to exert leadership by means of heroic acts and the loyalties that he could demand from his people through the adulation he expected them to award him for these acts. Whether the author intended Saul to represent the world of feudalism is unclear: if he did, one can surely fault him for his inability to grasp the socioeconomic bases behind the bonds that tied a people to their leaders in medieval times. What we must discern above all in the downfall of Saul's regime is that the king's psychological crisis—his failure to make contact with his deity whose chosen one he takes himself to be, his depressions, his paranoia, the irrational tyranny he exercises—are not causes in themselves, but rather the symptoms natural to a leader whose basis for ruling has become antiquated and who must be replaced by one who is more in tune with the developing historical process.

However unclearly the social basis for Saul's rule and its failure are portrayed, the genuine triumph of this play lies in its frighteningly sure grasp of the new order that David ushers in. For this is the world in which we ourselves live, a world where ultimate power is awarded to those who possess the most consummate skill in the manipulation of those around them. It is significant that David, in that telling final scene in which he consolidates his power over the crowd ("March 2"), has no need to maintain brute force but can afford the luxury of discarding his whip, for he amply possesses the verbal ingenuity to sustain his rule. The cruel and naked power that Saul's henchmen exercise in the episode "Inquiry" (a scene that in its parablelike simplicity might easily have come out of one of Brecht's didactic plays of the early 1930s) is totally unnecessary to a David. Indeed, the persuasive techniques he exercises in this culminating scene are precisely those he had earlier used ostensibly to heal the sick king and then, as Saul came to exercise his tyranny against him, to save himself through the litheness and shiftiness of his verbal talents. All those traditional ideals that David expresses—his concern for his ailing monarch and for the peaceful and orderly development of his newly acquired commonwealth—these constitute nothing less than a reification of what were once taken to be sacred human values and which he now voices to serve his own material interests and his thirst for power. And is this not precisely the way we are all manipulated and overpowered by those who seek to achieve and maintain power in our late-capitalist world? Except for an occasional reminder of force (like the whip that David cracks on the ground and then throws out), there is no need for those in power to keep their guns pointed at us in order to keep their economic system going. As long as they command sufficiently sophisticated means of manipulation (which they subject to constant testing procedures to make sure they will continue to work), they can sell their products to us as these emerge from the assembly line, convince us we need to continue using these products, and, as a result, keep their system running while refusing to relieve us sufficiently from our anxieties as consumers to reflect upon the tyranny they have so subtly inflicted upon us. The overt benignness with which material objects are utilized to impose order upon us represents a form of reification such as Marx and Engels, themselves accustomed to bruter forms of power, could never have imagined. The religious experiences that they saw as the opiate of the masses at an earlier stage of capitalism have now been replaced by the manipulative skills that the figure of David so splendidly represents.

And what of that other master of manipulation, Saul's Daughter, who, quite unlike David, must perish with the outgoing order? It is significant that Hennessy-García has eliminated Jonathan and instead centered upon Jonathan's sister Michal, who plays a considerably smaller role in the Bible than she does in the play. Through Saul's Daughter the author has told us something about the fate of a strong-willed and intelligent woman in our late-capitalist world. From her longer speeches—her persuasion of David's father to allow his son to heal the mad king ("Healing 1"), her

dissuasion of her own father from his suicide attempts ("Intermezzo")—
she displays manipulative skills fully the equal of David's. Yet in the
feminine role forced upon her, she must adopt a constant deviousness and
subservience of manner that distinguish her mode of manipulation from
David's. Once her father is defeated and she is able to show her true colors,
she launches into that fierce and uncontrollable rage ("Execration")
characteristic of those countless women whose energies have been repressed
too long by a system unable to use their talents in a humane way.

In his quiet isolation Hennessy-García has doubtless looked more
penetratingly into our present world than those more fashionable writers
who, even if he shares their elitism and, to some degree, their narcissistic
manner of expression, are so inextricably tied to our socioeconomic system
that they are unable to see it for what it is. Being a recluse (and by means
of private funds that were doubtless accumulated at an earlier, more
barbarous stage of capitalism) has perhaps proved an advantage that is
awkward and painful for a Marxist to admit. Yet the isolation that the
sweat of obscure and long-forgotten laborers has made possible for
Hennessy-García has also, by one of those ironies of history that Marx
could easily have appreciated, granted him a unique and powerful angle
of vision upon our world. One only wishes he had used his considerable
leisure time to immerse himself less then he obviously has in modernist
art and, instead, to contemplate new modes of expression more appropriate
to the admirable social critique that is the chief burden of his play.

A MEDITATION ON THE HENNESSEAN TEXT

Jay Grossberger

*Jay Grossberger of Harvard is by general acknowledgment the foremost
representative of French critical thought outside the French-speaking
domain. Although I make no pretense myself of being adept in this most
complex area of knowledge, I recognize the immense influence it is exert-
ing on philosophical and literary discourse these days and can testify that
on the few occasions I have found sufficient time to make my way through
a text by Professor Grossberger or his confrères abroad, the intellectual
rewards have considerably outweighed the pains one must dedicate oneself
to endure in order to experience their texts in the spirit in which they were
intended. It is a tribute to Orlando Hennessy-García that Professor Grossberger has been willing to lavish a most detailed commentary upon his
work. Since it is essential to the critical method practiced by Professor
Grossberger that a large selection of any particular author's work be examined, I sent him not only a copy of Saul's Fall, but all of H-G's other manuscript materials (together with the "Table of Analogues" I compiled) that*

comprise the present volume. My efforts, I am convinced, have not been in vain, for Professor Grossberger (he is so identified with the French cultural scene, incidentally, that it is customary, despite his Jewish-American background, to pronounce his name in the French manner, with the final syllable accented and, in fact, homophonic with his first name) has built up a following in this country to an extent that no literary critic since Lionel Trilling has been able to do. It is said that immediately after an essay of his has been pulled off his typewriter (and months before it can possibly appear in print) photocopies are circulating among advanced students of literature throughout the English-speaking world. (The copying is done not by Professor Grossberger, who is himself the most diffident of men, but by a local disciple who sends them to disciples at Yale and Cornell, where, somewhat in the manner of relay runners, additional disciples promptly provide copies for disciples at three or four other universities until, within a week or two, all but the most provincial centers of learning have had an opportunity to share in his most recent thinking.) I myself saw several photocopies of the present essay in the hands of Stanford graduate students (and even among some of our more earnest seniors). Since this was before the Drama Department's workshop production, there was no way that they could have been familiar with the play, so I asked one of them how she expected to comprehend a difficult essay about a difficult play she had neither seen nor read. In a tone that I can only describe as snippy in the extreme, she replied that it scarcely matters what texts Professor Grossberger chooses for examination, that in fact he uses these texts principally to work out his own quite formidable system of thought, whose magnitude and centrality neither she nor I had the least inclination to dispute.

1. In the beginning was the father—

but of course there was no Father, only fathers.

The primary fact governing the Hennessean text is the absence of the father. As the Growth Paper makes clear, the biological father was never seen, rarely talked about, and then only in a language too foreign to be properly apprehended. The Hennessean father assumes his grandest, most mythical proportions when he is least known, that is in the folktale Hero's Death in the Spanish Civil War, concocted in the mind of the thirteen year old from multiple scraps of children's tales, for of course he had no knowledge at the time of how precisely the "real" father had died. In this, the least selfconscious of subtexts within the total Hennessean text, the father superhumanly climbing the Gothic turret to rescue the desecrated flag can be allowed the most lavishly mythical of gestures. Such indulgences are never possible again (even if we recognize that in its early heroic manifestation, we are given nothing more than an epic apostrophe to a father long since lost both in his physical presence and in whatever traces of memory may have collected around him). Equally absent is the father of the episode Prophecy 1, for Samuel too is long since dead and must be called up from the underworld against his will. Yet nothing heroic inheres in him, only a few vestiges of authority that he voices with the cruelty and absurdity of the also absent Old Testament Father whose representative he claims to be. With the Spanish Civil War father one feels at least that the boy, had he witnessed him in battle, might himself have ascended the castle wall and received what blessings there were to disburse even in this most adverse of situations. With Samuel, instead of blessings there are only reproaches and a refusal, in fact, to address the son in anything but the coldly distant third-person pronoun. Indeed, the ritual of rejection to which Samuel subjects Saul in this episode is itself the most visible sign we can receive of the impossibility of recovering even what is at best a father substitute. Yet what of the occasional invocations of deity (very occasional indeed for a text drawn from Biblical sources) that we hear here and there? For the Daughter in her Execration episode it is simply "Powers that be" who are invoked to hear her rage. The plural and the vagueness of "Powers" hint that the invocation is nothing more than a matter of form, a rhetorical gesture toward an outward object—any object?—to make possible the rage which is that whole episode's reason for being. With the monologue Prayer, however, we find ourselves in something considerably more than a rhetorical situation. When Saul invokes his "You up there, wherever you are," he is overtly establishing what connections he can with a deity from whom he now knows himself estranged. Indeed, we are never to know whether the "you" Saul invokes is within himself, or without, or all-pervasive: such speculations are avoided so assiduously that their very absence suggests an uncertainty which in itself renders the Father's existence questionable in the extreme. Yet as Saul describes the history of the estrangement, it is evident that the relationship which he claims once existed was what he calls an "unselfconscious" one, and which by his current reckoning came temporally prior to the estrangement. As throughout the history of Western man, the fact of estrangement must be accounted for by the projection of some earlier relationship with a diety, presence, or whatever name one finds it convenient to pronounce. Yet the reality of this relationship is never rendered for us (though other texts before the Hennessean text have attempted to in one way or another). The only reality we come to know is that belated one of estrangement which the Hennessean text repeatedly portrays with the blunt fierceness of the "I defy you!" leveled at the lost Father in Prayer and in the blasphemous curses hurled at the capitalized *One* in the opening and closing poems of Lyric Suite 1. Yet the Father reveals his distant and equivocal presence by the most perverse displacement imaginable, namely, through the powerful women who people the Hennessean universe. The Witch of Endor, as gatekeeper and summoner of dead spirits, initiates the actions of Prophecy 1 to a degree that the supposed father, Samuel, cannot hope to emulate. In each of those episodes in which Saul's Amazonian Daughter appears together with her father—March 1, Healing 1, Intermezzo, and Prophecy 2—she conducts herself not in a filial but in a most overbearingly parental role. Her analogue, the mother in the autobiographical fictions, scolds her small son with all the capricious and cruel authority traditionally attributed to the Old Testament deity, though when the grown son undertakes his Three Projects to awaken her out of her madness to her natural parental role, he flees at the very moment that she threatens to reassume this role. Both in her madness and in her writing ambitions the mother carries no authority of her own, but exists only as an imitation of her beloved model, Virginia Woolf. Similarly, the son's madness (if that be the import of that mysterious passage Four Poses) and the role of writer that he wields so powerfully over us gain their authority through imitation of the mother, whose analogous actions were derivative in the first place. Whatever Father may ultimately be imagined presiding here "exists" (to use a word from a shopworn metaphysics) at too many removes to be worth anyone's while tracking down.

2. In the beginning was the scene—

but there were many scenes, and the priority of any one to the others is infinitely debatable.

Within each scene (or episode, to use the preferred word within the Hennessean text) we are invariably made to feel we have been there before. As we watch the messengers rushing in and out of Battle 1 (some twenty in all—and in a scene that would doubtless exhaust itself in eight minutes playing time), we remain aware of the messengers of those scenes in *Antony and Cleopatra* whose harried and hurried messengers outdo the heroine in the capriciousness with which they announce new and sudden shifts in the political winds. And behind all these there stand those messengers who mark, announce, in a sense even create the single great turning point within Greek tragedy in which that tender construct we call plot turns upon, into, and out of itself. For those who still insist on the primacy of temporal development, the single peripety effected by the Greek messenger must surely stand as a sample precedent against which the complex and multiple peripeties of Shakespearean and later dramatic texts must be measured and apprehended. From this point of view, Battle 1 exploits the possibility of peripety to what would seem its ultimate form ("later" texts will of course display new ultimates). One cannot of course speak of twenty peripeties in this episode, but rather of a series of attitudes toward the very idea of peripety. Except for the final messengers who accompany the head-bearing David, none of the messengers presides over a full, conclusive, or unambiguous peripety (anybody with a classificatory bent could pin a multitude of names upon them—the frustrated peripety [Messenger 4], the displaced peripety [Messenger 13], the premature peripety [Messenger 16], the aborted peripety [Messenger 19] *ad nauseum*). But temporal development, as we know all too well in our time, is only a single one of many possible modes with which to set up relationships among diverse texts. With the experience of the Hennessean text firmly embedded in our consciousness, no messenger scene, no peripety will ever again exert its power upon us in the direct (simplistic even) way we once thought inherent in the earlier forms of drama. The Oedipal messenger, the Medean messenger, the Hippolitan messenger—all become tainted as it were by the knowledge we carry within us how what might once have seemed a simple turning point in a simply narrated action is actually fraught with unsuspected complexities, that this turning point may contain within itself the danger of sudden truncation, deferral, disfigurement. The temporal order in which particular texts were set down in writing does not in itself confer any special authority on some text that happens to precede another in time. Within the totality of the Hennessean text, each subtext exists in analogous relationship with other subtexts and without reference to those diachronic criteria so dear to the heart of the nineteenth century. When we move from the episode Conspiracy, composed at around age forty, to the fourteen year old's Fairy Tale, we recognize the structural identity between the two, and if we move backward in time from the forty year old's disquisition On Relationship, we automatically note the ideological identity between this "later" composition and that of the adolescent. The Table of Analogues accompanying the Hennessean text is itself an analogue to the history of textuality—or should one perhaps say to the recognition that textuality has no "history" in the nineteenth-century sense, but rather that texts, whether remote or recent, do not exist within an inviolate temporal order, that through a network of analogies they play with, through, into, and out of one another? The Table of Analogues records an interplay not only within the Hennessean text itself, but an interplay between this text and a myriad of texts—scenes from "earlier" plays and operas, prefaces, treatises, and the like—no one of which can claim, enjoy, or exercise any special authority. There are doubtless some who would hope for such authority not among literary or philosophical analogues but in the so-called Holy Scriptures to which the Hennessean dramatic episodes bear obvious reference. Those who longingly seek a prototext that would record the voice of divinity booming oracularly through the universe are doomed to the usual disappointments suffered by those who experience, explain, expostulate through recourse to some ultimate origin, who, with boundless intrepidity, extrapolate "original" enactments that are themselves reenactments of previously extrapolated texts. Let these seekers read the varying accounts of Saul's death in 1 Samuel 31 and 1 Chronicles 10 to note the absence of that single authoritative voice, to recognize that all we have, in fact, is these Scriptures themselves, which, with their overt reference to writing—and in the plural form at that!— provide as scandalous an instance of intertextuality as anything one can locate within the so-called secular domain.

3. In the beginning was the word—

but which word among all that babble?

Throughout the Hennessean text there exists a covert recognition that words have no substantiality of their own, that they are nothing more than signs, that in fact the best we can hope for is that these signs may maintain some sort of relationship, tenuous though it may be, with their supposed referents. "Give me a sign," Saul calls out desperately to his unnamed deity in Prayer only to find there are no more signs for him, that in fact the alienation he experiences can be defined as essentially verbal in nature. To the extent that Saul is not receiving signs or is unable to interpret the signs that come his way ("You all have me hopelessly confused," he tells the messengers in Battle 1), the prevailing tone of the play is one of bitter nostalgia for a condition in which signs were inextricably, unambiguously tied to their referents. To a greater extent than any other episode, Prophecy 2 dramatizes the autonomy (and also, inevitably, the unintelligibility) of the sign, with the chorus constantly shifting the emphases (and hence meanings) of the words within the phrase "Saul must fall" while the two principal actors outvie one another with their conflicting interpretations of these words and their changes. The tragedy of the Spanish whorehouse (A Night Out with Cousin Paco) is at once the tragedy of the irreconcilability between word and thing, word and action; and it is symptomatic of this irreconcilability that the narrative illusion here is constantly broken by commentaries that are themselves candidly concerned with the inadequacy of the verbal resources available to narrative in our time. The passage Four Poses, together with those passages in the two novel manuscripts on the mother's madness, represents a rebellion against an order that seeks to impose a mode of relationship between words and things which has come to seem intolerable. Yet despite this crisis that so pervades the Hennessean text, words retain at least a functional (though in no sense substantive) value rare within contemporary writing. Particularly in Saul's Fall, and above all in the long set speeches of the Daughter and David, we witness an enormous deployment of verbal techniques to effect actions of the most diverse sort. One notes the Daughter's extended pleas (Healing 1) to Jesse to allow his son to try his healing arts, her attempt (Intermezzo) to keep Saul from wielding the knife against himself, or David's quieting of the unruly crowd (March 2), or, to cite one of the early narratives, the so-called Scoldings of the Week—in each instance a desperate (though also artfully contrived) barrage of words to persuade others to do (or not do!) something of urgent necessity at the moment. Though admittedly without substance or even without a stable set of referents, words become coins frantically tossed into slots to keep the machine running. If one traces the Hennessean text in its chronological development, it is clear that it maintains a constant awareness of this crisis in the relationship (or lack of it!) between words and external reality. The first of the uncompleted longer fictions, A Prelude to Nothing, attempts to demonstrate that the external world can be rendered verbally through the immediacy of an introspective first-person narrative. The shift to the third person in the second of the longer fictions, Cold Clay, is a tacit admission of failure, though still an attempt to apprehend this outer world by what would seem an antithetical method. In the early entries of Mendocino Diary the constant reminders to portray everyday doings without reading meanings into them display an honest facing up to the gulf that separates language from external things and actions, while the momentous final entries, which generate the play he is about to write out of a series of sound patterns, take this separation to what would seem its ultimate reach. The multitude of styles and generic forms that constitute the play and its paralipomena testify to the total arbitrariness between verbal forms and whatever outer world they purport to imitate, attack, influence, transcend. It is as though the Hennessean text has come full circle, as though the forty year old has rediscovered what the adolescent in his folktale on a Hero's Death and his Fairy Tale about a remote king already knew—namely, that words and things each go their own chaotic way despite the most heroic efforts to mediate between them.

4. In the beginning was the sound—

but of course there are no beginnings.

In its self-reflectiveness, the present text, like the Hennessean text itself, must acknowledge its posttextuality not only as a comment upon its own being, but as the characteristic condition of our time, perhaps (through our recognition of the atemporality of the writing act) as the characteristic human condition at all times. For much too long now (since at least the time of Plato) we have lived by, on, and for a most seductive myth—that our writing (we have of course no adequate word in English for the more encompassing French word *écriture*) is able to recapture, record, reenact

some authentic voice, be it that of the even-tempered Homeric muse or of
the capricious Jehovah, either of whom we see as a pre-text that, once we
have recognized the futility of achieving such authenticity, becomes simply
a pretext for endowing our writing with an authority that it never even
deserved in the first place. As soon as this recognition has taken place, any
text comes to have the status of posttext, at best an approximation, actually
a dissimulation of a reality that, in our unreflective, more passionate
moments, we long to see as prior, primary, primordial. The Hennessean
text, above all in its later stages, fully comprehends its own posttextual
status—especially from that moment recorded in the 29 May Mendocino
Diary entry where the text recognizes the total fortuitousness with which
the subject of Saul's fall suggested itself: by means, that is, of a simple
rhyme! (The omission of the year in the diary dates is itself a part of this
recognition, for the text's deliberate silence here serves as a tacit pledge
that temporal matters will no longer retain a privileged place.) By that
simple accident of rhyme the text is able to evoke a subject, a hero, an era,
a literary tradition, and indeed the whole closed universe of analogues
with which it then sets earnestly out to play. Note the parenthetical
comment accompanying the discovery that *fall* contains *Saul* among its
many possible rhymes—"Read up on him right away"—for the subject
was not even known in any detail before it was chosen. With its posttextual
skepticism toward the efficacy and the mimetic potency of words, the text
now comes to rely on sounds alone. Not that sounds are unable to make
pretenses of their own of expressing meaning or rendering some reality
other than themselves, yet by their very nature they foreground their
ambiguousness, their misinterpretability, to a more extreme degree than
words. Saul's offstage howls that continually punctuate the complex verbal
structures of the second episode (Healing 1) assert their primacy over all
the varieties of talk we witness in the course of the scene: the quibbles
over flower arranging, the stiflingly stiff stichomythic exchange between
Jesse and Michal, the latter's elaborate and interminable rhetorical pleas—
all these manifestations of writing must bow, demean themselves, assume
an embarrassed subservience to those howls for which we have no ready-
made meanings at hand: are we to suffer empathetically with that offstage
being from whom they emanate, are we to see them as manipulative in the
effects they intend upon the onstage characters as well as upon us, or
simply absurd through their juxtaposition with the elaborate verbal goings-
on, or (through the explicit reference to the Oedipal howl in one of the
stage directions) as a multiple display of pathos analogous to the multiple
peripeties of the episode (Battle 1) that will immediately follow? In its
recourse to musical accompaniments throughout the play, as well as to the
musical analogies delineated in the preface, the Hennessean text advertises
at once its refusal to depend on words alone and its consequent reliance

on sounds to remind us of the text's essentially nonmimetic, nonsymbolic nature. If these episodes are to tell us "about" anything, it is certainly not about what, at an earlier stage of textuality, was so confidently, blithely, and movingly referred to as human experience. If such a mode of experience "exists" (to once more apply this long-since exhausted word), we cannot know of it in textual terms—though many will go on blissfully, vainly seeking to "record" it until they have finally strangled whatever life they have claimed to find, sated us with a banquet of tidbits whose vaunted significance and relevance aroused our skepticism from the start. The Hennessean text, with its posttextual wisdom on such matters, is content to leave us with little more than a succession of sounds, all of which, in the Epilogue, come together once more in a piercing cacophony to remind us that even our desire for an orderly succession (which the play seemed at least tentatively to give us as Saul's fall gradually unfolded before us) must be frustrated once and for all. So we have nothing left but sounds without either order or meaning, though with a titillating touch of fury here and there. And then of course (and to our utter relief) silence.

Note: On disagreements among literary critics

Readers have doubtless noticed how often the contributors to this section disagree with one another as to the quality, meaning, and ultimate importance of the text under consideration. To the extent that these disagreements are of a genuinely intellectual nature, I heartily applaud them, for they add to the health and vigor of contemporary cultural life. But it is no use hiding the fact that many of my contributors—and these include some of the most talented minds within the American literary scene—do not much care for one another. It is sad for me to acknowledge this, for I consider all of them (except for our local newspaper critic, whom I have never met) my very good friends, and like all gregarious people I sorely want my friends to like each other. Nothing would please me more—in case they were ever in the Bay Area at the same time—than to have them all to my house for a party, but it is clearly evident they would not care to socialize in the same room. So instead I concocted another sort of party in which they could all participate, and that party is this book.

CONCLUSION

The Editor to the Author

By long-standing convention an edition of this sort should end with a bibliography that lists the various editions of the author's works, evaluates them in relation to one another (with whatever snide comments one might care to make about the incompetence of previous editors), and concludes with a selection of the best books and articles about the author and, in particular, that work of his to whose proper understanding the whole project has been devoted. Obviously that is not possible here, Orlando, for this is the first (though I trust it won't be the last) edition of your play, and the only secondary material that's been done on it consists of the essays I myself commissioned and which all those reading these words are holding in their hands this moment. Since the table of contents is all the bibliography you're entitled to at this point, I decided this was the appropriate place to include another bibliography that, as it turns out, is far more revealing than a conventional one would be; namely, a listing of what the suitcase you left in front of my office contained. I shall divide it into two distinct parts, your literary work and your memorabilia, and I can do so without having to go through my usual classifying agony, for that's precisely the way you yourself divided things up.

1. LITERARY MATERIALS

Note: I have provided a checkmark (√) before each item that has been included in this volume; those included only by means of excerpts have a cross-mark (✕) going through the check.

A. *Juvenilia*

√ 1. "A Hero's Death in the Spanish Civil War," *The Scroll* 5 (Winter, 1949): 11–14.

√ 2. "Fairy Tale," two pages of typescript.

   3. "Edmund and Ella," five pages of typescript that, like "Fairy Tale," was accompanied with a letter of rejection from the editors of *The*

Scroll. [*Since this story contains no discernible analogues to Saul's Fall, I was unable to include it in this volume. I very much regret having to omit it (despite its obvious immaturity), for it is distinctly a pastoral—one of the few literary modes that must remain unrepresented here. The plot concerns two foster siblings who, all the while they are growing up together on a Canadian farm, are unable to express their feelings to each other because of incestuous fears.*]

B. *Papers prepared for assignments at Bard College*

1. "John Donne's 'The Flea,'" six pages of typescript. [*An analysis in the New Critical mode prevalent at the time. I should have awarded it a B+ instead of the A it received. You've so outgrown it, Orlando, that I'm sure you won't take this criticism of mine to heart.*]

2. "Plant Imagery in *The Winter's Tale*," twelve pages of typescript. [*A typical New Critical image study, but this one fully deserved its A. What a shame the assignment was not on one of the plays you used for Saul's Fall, for instance Richard II or Macbeth, for that might well have justified the inclusion of a Shakespearean study of yours as an analogue within this book.*]

3. "Nietzsche *vs.* Schopenhauer," sixteen pages of typescript. [*The instructor refused to grade this one, but instead offered pungent refutations against your own quite passionate argument defending Schopenhauer's pessimism against Nietzsche's rage.*]

4. "Thoreau the Unthorough Solitary," twenty-five pages of typescript. [*An ill-tempered attack on Thoreau, whom you viewed as essentially "misleading in the pretensions he made to being a solitary." Your instructor awarded the paper an A for the quality of its argument, but he expressed strong disagreement with your point of view.*]

√ 5. "Growth Paper," sixteen pages of typescript. [*Although the "Table of Analogues" ties this paper to the "Prologue" and four episodes from the play, the analogues consist primarily of characteristic phrases such as "go my own way," "this is not possible," and "there are no bonds," which you were to continue using in your subsequent writing. Although these phrases technically justify the inclusion of the "Growth Paper" in this edition, the real justification lies in the fact that the biographical information in this paper constitutes the most we know about you, Orlando, and above all it provides key analogues to the passages from your autobiographical fiction, which themselves serve as analogues to episodes from Saul's Fall.*]

C. *Writings with mature literary pretensions*

✗ 1. A *Prelude to Nothing*, 423 pages of typescript without chapter divisions and broken off in the middle of a sentence.

✓ 2. "An Epistolary Exchange," two pages of typescript and five pages of handwritten manuscript described in more detail earlier in this volume.

✗ 3. *Cold Clay*, 580 pages of typescript divided into ninety-four sections, each with a title and ranging from less than a page to as much as twenty pages per section.

✓ 4. "Mendocino Diary," twenty-five pages of handwritten manuscript in a spiral notebook.

✓ 5. *Saul's Fall*, 156 pages of handwritten manuscript filling three spiral notebooks as well as the final 10 pages of the notebook containing the "Mendocino Diary." The scenes are in the following order, which, in the absence of any contradictory evidence, leads me to believe this is the order in which they were written (double bars between scenes indicate the start of a new notebook):

1. Healing 3	11. Healing 1
2. Conspiracy	12. Endings
———	13. March 2
3. Prayer	14. Battle 2
4. Prophecy 2	———
5. Healing 2	15. Council
6. Prologue	16. Intermezzo
7. March 1	17. Preface
8. Inquiry	18. Proclamation
9. Battle 1	19. Execration
———	20. Epilogue
10. Prophecy 1	

[Although you made a number of changes in each scene between the notebook manuscript and the typescript that you sent me through the mail, the surprising thing is how minor these changes were. I should have welcomed the chance to prepare a textual apparatus analyzing your revisions word by word, but I shall leave that till I've had a chance to run a seminar on your manuscripts, after which I'll put out a critical critical edition to supplant the present one. Still, I'm amazed to what an extent you knew what you wanted as soon as you started writing—except of course for the "Fragment from an Unfinished Verse Drama" which you included in "Lyric Suite 1" and some words of which are echoed in "Healing

Off the start to reassure their spectators that their
somebody like themselves up here.
(Ritornello)
At an earlier I should have been able to say I am here
to please you, but that is not possible now. Or I might
have sought to pour terror into your breasts but that
is not possible now. Yet please rest assured I shall
not scold you in hopes of reaching contact through
whatever anger ~~rage~~ anger I am able to awaken
in you
(Ritornello)
It is it's only fair to say from the start that I'm
not a tragedy, or a comedy, or a history play or even
one of those pieces to which they attached the word
absurd when none of the other terms seemed to
apply. The shape in which I come to you may
jar you at times, for instead of moving steadfastly
toward some clearly foreseen end, I keep saying
the same thing ~~again and again~~ over and over again,
though in a ^astonishing variety of ways.
(Ritornello) ~~to~~ ^to help
To help you to ~~take~~ your expectations, I should let
you give me any of these labels: a Story without
plot ... a history without plot reliability ...
an opera without song ... a ceremonial without
joy ... a riddle without solution ... a game
without fun ... a ~~logic~~ philosophy without
reason ... a revolution without authority. If
this ~~is~~ is not enough enlightenment, I can
only add: ATTEND ME!

End of "Prologue" from early draft in H-G's spiral
notebook; probable tea stain at top.

2." Did you really intend to write the whole play in blank verse, Orlando? (That's the sort of thing aspiring old lady dramatists do.) Let me know what it was you intended with that verse fragment. And what about the order in which you wrote the scenes? Except for saving the epilogue for last, the order has virtually nothing to do with the actual order either of the play's events or their final arrangement. One could imagine a fascinating speculative essay on the order of composition, and I'll surely assign it to a student in my textual seminar, though I'd much rather hear what you yourself have to say on the matter. Are you listening to me, Orlando?]

√ 6. "Saul's Fall Overflow," 167 pages of handwritten manuscript in three spiral notebooks. [I have reproduced the items in this manuscript in the section of this volume entitled Paralipomena exactly in the order in which you wrote them out. You must have composed the poems elsewhere before transcribing them here, Orlando, for there are scarcely any corrections in your manuscript, while the prose passages contain innumerable crossings out, which leads me to think they are essentially early drafts. Am I right? Let me know as soon as you read this. And why don't you send the early drafts of the poems? Analyzing the stages of composition would be a first-rate exercise for a class.]

√ 7. Snapshot of a statue of Saul with the words "Saul in his slump" in your own handwriting on the back. [Identifying this one proved a difficult exercise, and I admit it all came about by accident (that's the way some of the best scholarly discoveries are made) when Luella, obviously impatient with me about my unremitting absorption in this volume, talked me into taking her into San Francisco for the day. We stopped at the De Young Museum, where the statue you had snapped was standing near the main lobby next to one of Delilah and both of them sculpted by William Wetmore Story, whose work had inspired both Hawthorne and Henry James (what fine company you are placing yourself in, Orlando!). My first hunch when I recognized the statue (though this had not occurred to me when I first noticed the snapshot) was that it had been the inspiration for your play—all of which would make the generation of the play by means of an accidental rhyme, as you described it so forcefully in the "Mendocino Diary," seem specious in the extreme. I had all but lost my trust in you when I realized I had never before noticed the statue in the museum, so I asked a guard if it had been sitting in this place during all the years I had been in the Bay Area. He replied that all the statues behind the entrance had been locked in a storeroom until late in 1977, when they were brought out in connection with the museum's new display of American art. To my

"Saul in His Slump," title inscribed by H-G for the statue
King Saul by William Wetmore Story, with the same
sculptor's *Delilah* in the background.
(Snapshot by Orlando Hennessy-García)

great relief I realized that your 29 May diary entry (whatever the
year) recording the discovery of your subject must have been made
before you could have seen the statue. Once I regained my composure I allowed myself to speculate about what you must have
thought of the Delilah statue next to the Saul. Now that you've
doubtless read Dr. Goldblatt's essay in this volume, have you perhaps become aware of the sexual implications you so thoroughly
repressed in the writing of your play? Do let me know, Orlando.]

2. MEMORABILIA

A. *Items relating to H-G's relatives and foster families*

1. An ancient Christmas card full of affectionate jabs from one of your
   Canadian foster mothers who is wishing you well with the new
   family that has taken you in.

2. A snapshot of what must be your Spanish relatives, or at least fifteen of them ranging from infancy to senility and all with the same impersonal pose (wish I could figure out which one is Cousin Paco!) and with a note on the back reading "Esperando con mucha illusión verte aquí con nosotros—tu familia española—16 marzo 1955," which I translate as "Very much looking forward to seeing you here with us—your Spanish family—16 March 1955."

B. *Items relating to Beatrice Hennessy-García*

1. Scrapbook of newspaper and magazine clippings from the 1930s having to do with Virginia Woolf.
2. A large rock, mainly granite, weighing nine and three-quarter pounds, with a wire tightly surrounding it and a tag attached to the wire with these words in your handwriting, "Found in coat pocket of Beatrice Hennessy-García when she was recovered alive from the Carmans River, Long Island, N.Y., 23 October 1954."

C. *Items relating to H-G himself*

1. The 1954 edition of *The Arrow*, yearbook of The Morris School in Connecticut. [*I looked desperately for your photo, Orlando, but found you listed among the three graduating seniors who failed to show up for the picture-taking.*]
2. U.S. naturalization certificate, issued in New York City on 8 September 1954. [*Here again you've managed to elude me, for you carefully clipped out your photo before placing the certificate in the suitcase. Outdated though it may be, I should gladly have reproduced it in this book. Much as I'd like to have used it, there's a more important consideration here, for why would you leave so vital a document with me? Don't you realize that you need this certificate to prove you're a citizen, that you might in fact get into all sorts of difficulties if you fail to keep it in your possession? What if you need a new passport or have to apply for social security some day? Something tells me, Orlando, that you're trying to give me a signal with this one, but I'm not about to follow up on the implications—so on with your memorabilia, which I'm listing in chronological order.*]
3. U.S. draft card in your name, dated 13 November 1954, and classifying you as 4-F. [*No reason given, but I suspect it was what they so sweepingly called "psychoneurotic" in those days.*]
4. U.S. passport in your name, dated 17 May 1955, and long since expired, with stamps showing entry to United Kingdom (21 June 1955); France (25 July 1955); Spain (28 July 1955); United States

(7 August 1955). [*Needless to say, the photo's been clipped out, but not quite as neatly as it was in the naturalization certificate.*]

5. The Margo paper, described in detail earlier in this volume in the section entitled "The Margo Experience."

6. A To-Whom-It-May-Concern letter, dated 9 October 1960, from a New York City specialist in internal medicine, Dr. Hector Bellona, vouching for the fact you are "of sound mind and body." [*Now how do you expect me to interpret this one without any context? You're teasing me, Orlando. Together with the "Four Poses" section of Cold Clay, this is the only evidence you have supplied of what I call that "lost" decade of yours between your departure from Bard College and your settlement in Mendocino. And the worst of it is that when I tried to contact Dr. Bellona himself for information, I found he'd been dead since 1963. Well, that's hardly your fault, Orlando.*]

But now that I've finished cataloging your suitcase I must say frankly that I wonder just what sort of game you've been playing with me. It's been eight months since I had my last contact with you (and that was when you arranged for the suitcase to arrive in such a way that your absence would seem as conspicuous as possible). Yet all this while you've kept me totally involved with you as I went about compiling my analogues, commissioning essays, arranging a production, negotiating with publishers, fending off my students and my family to the point where anybody else would have felt forced into a full-scale breakdown from all the pressure—but there wasn't even time for that! There have been days I got to my office hour as much as thirty minutes late, sometimes not at all. And then every time Luella suggested a trip or even a night at the movies I had to come up with some excuse until she finally blew up and said, "Do you realize for a whole year now [it's actually been only two-thirds of a year, but people exaggerate under stress] I've been sharing you with a man I've never so much as met and whom you claim you've spent a grand total of twenty minutes with!" (That particular outburst set off the trip to San Francisco during which I was lucky enough to locate your Saul statue.) Actually I've had trips to Mendocino twice with her during this period, but she won't count these as vacations since she knew I was after your traces, which, as you can see, I gave her ample opportunity to record with her new instamatic, yet once I discovered your house was rented to somebody else, she noticed I didn't even suggest going to Mendocino anymore.
(*Pause.*)

Don't get me wrong, Orlando, I'm not complaining, and the last thing I ask is that you feel responsible for what's gone wrong with me. I still

Mendocino house that presumably served as the scene of
writing for *Saul's Fall.*
(Snapshot by Luella McGillicuddy Wolfson)

Probable tidepool area where H-G fingered an anenome
at foot of Heeser Drive, as recorded in 23 May entry of
"Mendocino Diary."
(Snapshot by Luella McGillicuddy Wolfson)

have faith in this book of ours, and I'm hoping, wherever you are right
now, you're feeling pleased at the context I've created for the writings you
entrusted to me. In fact, all I'm asking is just a sign from you—not necessarily that you're pleased (if it's hard for you, as I suspect, to articulate
such things, you needn't feel in the least constrained to do so), but just a
word to let me know you're all right. You needn't mention if you're writing
—I don't care in the least if you're blocked for a while, since I know that's
the most natural thing in the world once you've finished a project as

ambitious as this one. You needn't even tell me where you are if you're
nervous I might follow you—as far as I'm concerned you can arrange to
have a note posted thousands of miles from where you actually are and
you can be sure I won't play sleuth on you. All I'm asking (and you can be
as curt with me as you want) is a sign of your existence. You don't have
to say you liked (or disliked) the way I put this volume together, and,
except for addressing the note to me (I don't expect any more than that)
you don't even have to acknowledge the fact we've met or had any relationship whatever.

(*Pause, with a bassoon squibble.*)

Of course if the spirit should move you, you can add a word or two, tell
me you're at it writing again (you don't need to describe what it is, since
I know how difficult it is even for people like me to explain what they're
writing until they're well into it—done, in fact). Or if you're not too far
away (I can imagine you've found yourself another nest on the coast—
and one that's not yet the tourist town Mendocino turned into during the
years you spent there), you might want to pass through here quietly,
or suggest some inconspicuous place we might meet. I leave it to you. You
set the conditions and I'll abide in any way that suits you. You must know
by now you can count on me. And in case you feel like opening up a bit,
I won't do anything to scare you away. I'll be sensitive to any hints you
give. If you think you could use any advice or help, there's no need to feel
the least bit reticent. I'll gladly be your middle-man even if you don't want
to spell things out directly. As you can see from his essay in this book, Dr.
Goldblatt is already very much interested in you, but don't let my mention of him scare you away unnecessarily. I'm simply trying to say that in
case you should like to chat with him, it can all be arranged quite easily,
and if it's any encouragement at all I might add that his office is set up so
there's never anyone facing you in the waiting room and when you're done
you go out a back stairway where nobody can possibly see you. What Professor Grossberger in his essay calls the "tragedy of the Spanish whorehouse" was nothing more than what (if you'll permit me to use an everyday clinical term) we call premature ejaculation. It's no big deal, Orlando,
and Dr. Goldblatt claims it's one of the most common and easily remedied
ailments among males, with a success rate these days of 97.8 percent. (I
know what you're about to say—that you're sure to be one of the unlucky
2.2 percent.) The point is, Orlando, you've made a big and horrendous
issue of something that can be solved with a minimum of fuss. As far as
sex is concerned, it's really so easy, Orlando, easy as pie—the hard thing is
to keep from doing it. You've probably never even admitted to yourself
you have natural good looks—much better than mine, I might add, but
you've seen to it nobody's going to remember anything about you except

for that hang-dog look (that's the way one of the students who saw you in
my office put it). As far as looks are concerned, I have no illusions that,
compared to you, I've had nature against me all the way. There's nothing
in the world I can do to hide the fact I'm pudgy, short, balding and carry
around that shady look that no amount of shaving can ever hope to
remove. As you can see, I've got to where I am in spite of all sorts of
things, and it's not just a matter of looks, for people who come from back-
grounds like mine don't have the luxury of a hyphenated name (even if
yours was concocted along the way). But don't get me wrong, Orlando, I'm
not complaining, in fact I'm simply trying to say that in spite of all this
I have something I'm sure very few people (at least among the more
reflective ones in our world) have, and that's a sense of self: I know where
I'm at, and how I got here, and I also think I know where I'm headed.
And that's precisely why I hope I can get some sign from you, since if
you can just get over a hurdle or two (they're much more minor than
you've ever imagined), you'll be able to do things with your writing that'll
make even *Saul's Fall* (and I'd be the last person in the world to disparage
your play) seem like small stuff. Not only that, but wait till you see what
sorts of things can open up for you once you've shattered that protective
shell that's kept you so utterly removed from us all. Now don't get the
idea that I'm trying to "reach out to you" (to cite the words you yourself
used in your "Growth Paper" to ward off those you feared might hover
patronizingly over you). I leave the initiative completely to you and I
want you to feel you can choose your own time, place, and manner to give
me a sign (or, if it suits you better, not to give me any sign at all). But if
you choose to, there are all sorts of projects we could start thinking about
(again, the initiative will be yours, not mine, and we won't commit ourselves irrevocably to anything in advance). I don't mean simply repeating
a project like this book of ours. I'm frankly a bit weary of playing the
kind of editor who exists merely to give star billing to troubled persons
such as Clarissa, Julie, Werther (who even remembers those editors'
names?). Of course, I don't mean that I want you in any subordinate role
—far from it, for what I want is some sort of collaboration between the
two of us that will allow us to interact as genuine human beings. I'm even
willing to play Sancho Panza to your Quijote—we can take off for the
Sierras, or even the Coast Range if you feel the need to be in screaming
distance of the ocean—and every time you try to tell me the forests we're
passing through are hordes of people imposing themselves on you I'll
promptly bring you down to earth and remind you where we are.
(*Pause, with a short bassoon squibble.*)
   But I see I've gone too far, for I can feel you shying away into your Saul
role before I've even had a chance to explain what I mean. That's your

trouble, Orlando, you always expect to play Saul to other people's Davids, and though you succeeded in drawing me into that game for a while, I may as well warn you I see through it now. Though I'll admit there's a Saul principle and a David principle, I recognize these as pure principles neither of which is going to make any real sense out of either of us. Don't fool yourself, Orlando, you have your own David side, try as you will to hide it from the world. But it was the David in you that made you send me your play and that later left that suitcase on my doorstep—all of this with full knowledge that I was greedy to make a project out of you. You're as cunning and conniving as anyone I know, even if it's the Saul principle with which you hypocritically choose to display yourself before the world. And don't get the idea I'm all David principle myself. H-G is a mixture of both the Saul and the David principles, and the same can be said of MJW, much as he'd prefer to have the world see only his David side.
(*Pause, with bassoon squibbles that continue while he speaks.*)

In fact, after eight months of being absorbed in you, it occurred to me that I (of all people!) was deep in my own Saul-like slump. If you think *you*'ve suffered in your solitude, you have no idea what goes on from day to day in ordinary people's lives. First it's a sly hint from some senior colleague that I've not measured up to expectations (or that's at least the way I think he wanted me to interpret it), next it's a pregnancy scare at home (two centuries after the Industrial Revolution there's still no fully satisfying form of birth control, Orlando), then it's an article of mine that gets rejected not because of anything wrong with it but just because the editor happened to have an epileptic seizure while he was leafing through it, then it's an intestinal virus that makes its way through all five of us (and with such cruel timing it has three of us down and writhing at once), and sometimes for no reason at all I come home exhausted thinking dinner's on the table and what do I find but Luella flat on the floor in a frump! I tell you, Orlando, bourgeois life is hard. But then how could you possibly understand any of this from that solitary eminence in which you've so arrogantly placed yourself? If I admit I've begun to withdraw from people at departmental parties, or I've found myself driving surreptitiously to the ocean when I'm scheduled to be at a university committee meeting, perhaps that will ring a bell with you. But then why should I even have to bother courting your sympathy this way, Orlando? After eight months of letting your invisible presence hover over me, I've come to see there's something sinister in what you do to people (not to speak of yourself). I've been so careful trying to keep from scaring you off (that's how you've maintained your hold on me after all), I haven't dared say or even think what's really on my mind. But now that I've gone this far I realize I'm coming to feel free of you, to see with a sudden, almost blinding clarity what malevolence you spread wherever you go. I am speaking my mind without the slightest fear of you, Orlando. That's right, and as far as I'm concerned, you've cast a frightful pall over the universe. Lights burn more dimly than before. Lovers' passions cool. Children turn droopy at play, spirits in general sag. If I cared a jot about my fellow man, I'd stamp you out of existence.

(*Pause, no more bassoon squibbles.*)

But that's hardly necessary: I got your sign all right, even if I tried to hide it from myself as I looked at that naturalization certificate. The only question is how you went about doing it. I can imagine you looking for the most scenic cliff off State Route One and driving your car straight into the ocean (but then of course you don't drive). Or maybe you decided to continue the family tradition another (though also last) generation by seeking out an appropriate stream, but I can assure you I won't preserve any rocks in your memory like the museum exhibit you left in that suitcase. Or perhaps you did it as inconspicuously as possible (that's really most like you) by finding some impenetrable ravine deep in the Sierras, where you can take whatever pills you got hold of in virtual certainty you won't be found until you've been weathered down to that grim skeletal grin with which you've longed to confront the world all along. Do what you will, Orlando, for as you can see, I'm done with you.

(*Long pause.*)

That was easily said, and I admit it didn't feel bad at all. But I know it has nothing intrinsically to do with you or this book, that it is simply a testimonial to the infectious hold that I allowed you to have over me. Everything that's happened between us was in *my* mind, not yours. I was fool enough to hope my own star might draw what light it could from yours, when I should have known all the while you were determined to go your own way.

Note: On Closure

That was no note to end a book on. Many modern books have opted to end this way, which means they don't really have an ending, or what people used to call an ending. Now that I see what I have done, I recognize that both my courting and my diatribe were not my own, but H-G's peculiar way of bringing things to an end. Yet I for one am determined to stage a real finale. H-G would interject that this is no longer possible —or at least the Saul principle inside him would. I've reached the point where I won't have any more of that at all, and if anything's going to prevail inside me it's the David principle, and I'll stage my finale with all the bravura at my command, which means I'll do it in each of the three major arts. So here goes:

Away with self-pity, humility, guilt,
The hate, fear, and panic that ravaged old Saul,
It's time to wipe up all the blood that's been spilt,
And adjust our perspective to *After Saul's Fall*:

Said David, triumphant, "Orlando and Milt,
Plus all of you reading, please heed to my call
To gather yourselves in this palace I've built
And rowdily cheer as we drink to us all!"

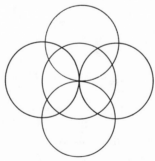

The Johns Hopkins University Press

This book was composed in Linotype Electra text and
foundry Garamond display type by the Maryland Linotype
Composition Co., Inc., from a design by Susan Bishop. It
was printed on 50-lb. MV Smooth Cream paper and bound
in Joanna Arrestox cloth by The Maple Press Company.

Library of Congress Cataloging in Publication Data

Lindenberger, Herbert Samuel 1929–
   Saul's fall.

   1.   Authorship—Miscellanea.   2.   Criticism—Miscellanea.   I.   Title.
PN165.L5   818'.5'407   78–22003
ISBN 0–8018–2176–2